I0826830

ANDREW G.
NELSON

DEDICATION

During the course of my writing career, I have often drawn inspiration from the people I worked with during my NYPD career. While some were foils, others served to highlight the camaraderie that comes when you work side by side with someone who you would happily go through a door with. Lt. Buddy Speicher was that kind of cop. A man with a heart of gold, a delightful sense of humor, and the epitome of a Cop's Cop. He might have been taken from us too soon, but he will live forever within these pages.

Fidelis Ad Mortem

In Loving Memory of

Lieutenant Henry 'Buddy' Speicher, NYPD (Ret.)

1961 - 2020

These things I have spoken unto you, that in me ye might have peace. In the world ye shall have tribulation: but be of good cheer; I have overcome the world. - John 16:33

Other Titles by Andrew G. Nelson

JAMES MAGUIRE SERIES

PERFECT PAWN

QUEEN'S GAMBIT

BISHOP'S GATE

KNIGHT FALL

GLASS CASTLE

SHADOW STRIKE

EXPOSED KING

ALEX TAYLOR SERIES

SMALL TOWN SECRETS

LITTLE BOY LOST

BROOKLYN BOUNCE

NYPD COLD CASE SERIES

THE KATHERINE WHITE MURDER

THE ROASRY BEAD MURDERS

NON FICTION

UNCOMMON VALOR – Insignia of the NYPD ESU

UNCOMMON VALOR II – Challenge Coins of the NYPD ESU

WHERE WAS GOD? An NYPD first responder's search for answers following the terror attack of Sept 11th, 2001

ACKNOWLEDGMENTS

The James Maguire series would not exist without the constant encouragement of my wife, Nancy. From the beginning she was my biggest fan, and without her the tales of James Maguire, and his many friends and foes, would have remained an *idea* locked away in my brain.

And I would be remiss not to acknowledge God, through whom all things are possible. Before I had the idea to write, he directed my life in ways that I now realize gave me the tools and experience necessary to draw from.

Romans 8:28

"A true king cannot lurk in the shadows but must court danger with calculated wisdom, for only through exposure is victory seized." — Anonymous

CHAPTER ONE

Brooklyn Night Court, N.Y.

Friday, May 1st, 2015 - 8:08 p.m.

The packed courtroom was filled with a dank, musty scent from the group of defendants waiting for their bail hearing to be called before the Honorable Judge Mordecai 'Bruce' Schiff.

"The People vs. Darnell Watkins," the clerk barked as she handed the judge the next folder from the stack positioned precariously on the edge of her desk.

"Please proceed, Mr. Sampson," Schiff said.

Assistant District Attorney Henry Sampson flipped the paperwork on the desk in front of him, examining the arrest information. "Your honor, the defendant is charged with assault in the second degree. The victim contends that Mr. Watkins assaulted him over a drug dispute. Considering his extensive criminal record, the people request that the defendant be held or bail be set at seventy-five hundred dollars."

"A violent drug user attacked my client, Your Honor," Reginald Brown, the legal aid attorney, replied. "Mr. Watkins was simply defending himself."

"As I previously stated," Sampson continued. "Mr. Watkins has an extensive criminal history, which includes felony drug sales, and the victim has been admitted to Kings County with a shattered jaw."

"Is the defendant considered a flight risk?" Schiff asked.

"Your Honor, Mr. Watkins—"

"It's a simple yes or no question, Mr. Sampson," Schiff snapped as he tossed his glasses onto the bench. "If he has a lengthy arrest record, has he ever fled?"

Sampson swallowed hard, knowing exactly where this was going. Schiff was a surly curmudgeon of a man who'd been on the bench longer than most of the people in the courtroom had been alive. He was one of the most liberal judges in Brooklyn and was overwhelmingly despised by the other ADA's in the office. Not that he was a great legal scholar who demanded excellence in his courtroom, but that he often took on the role of an activist judge who did most of the work for the defense. It was not a shock that he was consistently praised by those spearheading defendant rights.

"With all due respect, Your Honor, the defendant has previously been arrested on a warrant," Sampson replied, already knowing he was fighting an uphill battle.

"A simple mistake, Judge Schiff," Brown interjected. "My client was under the misguided belief that his presence in court on the date in question was unnecessary because counsel was appearing on his behalf."

"What's the defendant's financial situation?" Schiff asked.

"Mr. Watkins recently lost his job, Your Honor, and is currently seeking gainful employment, but it's proving difficult in these economic times. He also has a girlfriend and three children he is trying to support and is using what little money he—"

"There's no need for a soliloquy, counsel. The defendant is released on his own recognizance. Preliminary hearing is set for June 30th at 9 am," Schiff said as he brought his gavel down. "Court will take a thirty-minute recess."

"All rise," a court officer called out as the judge left the bench and entered his chambers.

"You're my man, dawg," Watkins said, slapping Brown on the back.

"Just make your next court date and stay out of trouble," Brown shot back. "Even Judge Schiff has his limits."

"If you need me, I'll be in church," Watkins said, as he brought his hands together as if he were praying, before breaking out into laughter.

Watkins turned and made his way up the aisle toward the rear door, pausing as he came up to Police Officer Bobby Hearn. "Yo, better luck next time, G. Run along and finish up your paperwork. I've gotta visit a sick friend."

Watkins continued out of the courtroom, Hearn following close behind. "You think this is a fucking joke, asshole?"

Watkins spun around, fists clenched. "Man, I know you ain't talking to me, bitch."

"You're exactly who I'm talking to, punk," Hearn replied, eyes narrowing menacingly as he got into the man's face. "Go ahead and swing, tough guy."

"Yo, you'd better fucking step off," Watkins sneered.

"Back up, back up," Sampson said, pushing in between the two men. "Counselor, do you want to have a word with your client?"

Brown grabbed Watkins's arm and led him away, while Sampson steered Hearn back down the corridor.

"You know where to find me," Watkins called out.

"Jesus Christ, what the fuck was that about?" Sampson asked.

"That motherfucker just threatened the witness," Hearn snapped.

"What did he say?"

"He said he was going to visit a sick friend."

"You know it won't hold up," Sampson replied.

"This is bullshit, Hank," Hearn fumed. "The whole fucking clown show in there was a joke. That little fucker has a rap sheet longer than my cock, and he just gets to waltz out of court while my vic gets to have reconstructive surgery just so he can eat again?"

"I'm not disagreeing with you, Brian, but it is what it is. Schiff lives in a different world. This shit doesn't affect him, and these new bail laws are providing him with ample opportunity to do what he wants."

"Schiff needs to be tossed out on his ass," Hearn said.

"Look, I agree with you, but the truth is that this is out of our hands. I just had a guy walk out of court on a murder charge. Did you hear me? A fucking murder charge, Brian. This guy has a rap sheet that goes back to the 80s. Robbery, drugs, assault, you name it. He confessed to the murder, yet they still let him walk. Watkins is a flea on this guy's ass, so you can't expect too much."

Hearn frowned as he stared at Sampson. "So what's the point of all this if assholes like Schiff are just going to let these mutts walk?"

"I don't know, Brian. I'm still searching for the answer to that question. Between you and me, I've been here four years and I'm about to hang it up. I just need to find myself a relaxing spot in the private sector doing real estate law."

"Yeah, well, being a cop is all I've got, so I guess I'm fucked."

"Forget Watkins," Sampson replied. "We'll deal with him at trial."

"Good fucking luck, Hank. I'll give you ten-to-one odds your boy never shows up."

"Best advice I can give you is to go grab a cold one and catch what's left of the Mets' game."

"What do I do when it's August and they are in last place?"

"Like George Carlin said, it's unnecessary for you to suffer and feel crappy because your team sucks, so I'd recommend becoming a Yankee fan."

"Fuck you, Hank."

"You're adorable, but you're not my type, Brian," Sampson laughed.

"Honestly, I think this is our year. Between Syndergaard and deGrom, I can see us going all the way."

"Keep talking like that and the job might put you out on a psych disability."

"You've gotta believe," Hearn laughed.

"What I believe is that I'll see you back in June, maybe sooner if Watkins does something stupid."

"That boy is so stupid that he once took an IQ test and the results came back negative," Hearn scoffed. "So, my bet is on the latter."

"We call that job security, my friend. Now go enjoy the Mets while you still have something to cheer about."

CHAPTER TWO

Brooklyn Night Court, N.Y.

Friday, May 1st, 2015 - 8:48 p.m.

Watkins stepped outside and looked around until he spotted Antwone Reed leaning against the black BMW and waving to him.

"I told you I'd be right out," Watkins laughed, as he clasped the man's hand and bumped against his chest. "Let's ride."

"You've got to lie low, D," Reed said, as he wedged his 6'6" frame behind the wheel, wheezing slightly as he shut the door. "You done fucked up Marley really bad. That bitch is gonna be sucking his food up through a straw for a long time."

"That nigga is lucky I didn't yeet his punk ass out the crib window," Watkins fumed as he lit up a blunt. "Just drive the fucking car."

"So whatcha want to do?"

"I want my motherfucking dead presidents," Watkins said.

"You think that's smart?" Antwone asked as he pulled the car onto Atlantic Ave and headed east.

"Let me drop some science on you. You either run the streets or the streets run you. From bottom to top, there is no half-stepping in my crew. Once you start letting these bitch-ass little niggas hold back on you, that's when you lose control. They can't ever be happy with what they've got. First they take an inch, and then they want a mile. Give em a fucking rope and suddenly they all think they're cowboys. You know I've got nothing but love for my people, but if you try to take a piece from me, I'll take a pound from you, and right now Marley still owes me."

"He's gonna be in the hospital for a while. You're going to have to wait to get your money."

"I'm done with that bitch," Watkins said. "Take me over to his crib; I'm going to have a chat with his old lady. That fine ass of hers will make a nice down payment on his outstanding debt."

"Man, we don't need that kind of heatwave coming down on us."

"Ant, you're my boy, but just do the driving and let me do the thinking."

Reed nodded as Watkins turned on the radio, putting an end to the conversation.

A few blocks later, he nudged Antwone's arm. "Hit up Tino's over on Washington. I need a drink to loosen up."

Reed made a right turn off Atlantic Avenue and headed toward the bodega.

"Man, I hate these cracker motherfuckers," the man hissed as he drove past specialty stores and restaurants, eyeing the diners casually eating outside suspiciously. "I miss the days when these were our streets. Niggas can't even afford the rent here anymore."

"You miss the violence, Ant," Watkins laughed. "That's why you are driving and not sitting in the passenger seat. You're looking at it the wrong way."

"How's that?" Reed asked.

"Man, I don't give a rat's ass if some nigga can't pay the rent. They ain't paying my bills, so why do I give a fuck about them? You look out and see a problem; I look out and see an opportunity. These motherfuckers have cash. They work all week, and come Friday, they want to party, and I'm here to help them. It's a simple matter of supply and demand, G. Stop looking at them as the enemy and start looking at them as potential customers. I ain't saying I want to hang with them, I'm saying I want to hang with their Benjamins."

A scowl grew on Reed's face, but he stayed quiet. He knew Watkins was reminding him how stupid he was, but he also knew the man was right, and that's what bothered him. Reed was Watkins' driver and muscle. He'd known Watkins since they were kids and running the streets outside the Fort Greene Houses. He once believed that he could escape Brooklyn through football, but a patellar tendon tear in his senior year ruined that chance. Only Watkins had stood by him, offering him more than just a future as a fry cook in some fast-food joint. Loyalty begot loyalty in his book.

Watkins was an OG, *original gangsta*, but he was also incredibly smart. Those two worlds occasionally clashed, like they did the other night with Marley Banks, and the results were rarely pretty, but when Watkins had control of his temper, he made the money rain down.

"You ain't never gonna live in their world, Dawg," Watkins said. "So you've only got two options. You either live in the world they give you or you make your own world. I ain't taking any motherfucker's leftovers. You with me, Ant?"

Reed bumped fists with the man. "Do or die."

Reed swung the BMW to the curb by a hydrant — one of the few spots always available in this gentrified mess. At this time of night, traffic enforcement agents were gone, and most cops didn't give a shit about parking on a hydrant if they saw the car was running.

"Whatchu want?"

"Get me an OE80," Watkins said, handing him a twenty, "and grab something for yourself. It might be a long night."

Watkins turned up the music and reclined the seat; listening to Jay-Z's Holy Grail coming out of the speakers. He'd always admired the man and how he had lifted himself off the streets to become one of the most influential people in hip hop. They were from the same world, growing up just about a mile from each other; a world ruled by drugs and violence, but Jay had made it out and so would he. He knew he couldn't compete with Jay's musical talent, but he didn't need to; he had a plan. All these niggas running out here with him were shortsighted; they blew their money on booze and hoes. He was different, and that difference would see him escape.

A smile grew on his face as he thought about the future he had planned for himself.

He moved his money, taking the dirty cash and making it clean through a series of laundromats and car washes that were quietly making him rich. After a few more years, and with choosing the right people to run his operation, he would say goodbye to the streets.

The smile faded as the interior of the car was lit up by alternating red and blue strobe lights.

"What the fuck," he thought, as he raised the seat up to get a better look. "Man, these little fucking bitches don't quit."

He reached over and turned up the volume, the car's windows thumping as the song changed to a more aggressive hip hop song. A moment later, a hand rapped loudly against the window.

Watkins hit the button, lowering the window, but did not turn down the volume.

"Are you Darnell Watkins?"

"Man, you know who the fuck I am," he said smugly, continuing to stare straight ahead. "Why do you motherfuckers gotta break my balls? Ain't enough real fucking crime to handle, or are you too scared?"

Inside the bodega, Reed stood impatiently in line as the elderly woman in front of him fumbled through her purse for the correct change to pay for her items. "Yo, Grandma, do you mind moving those hands a little quicker? I'd like to get out of here before the expiration date on my shit."

The old woman looked back and glared at him.

"You're probably getting close to your expiration date too, ain't you?" Reed asked.

The woman paid for her items and left quickly, as Reed set the drinks on the counter. The rear plate-glass window was shaking with the heavy bass sound coming from the car.

"Is that you making all the noise out there?" the Indian man behind the counter asked as he rang up the order.

"Man, cut the fucking chit-chat and just give me my shit," Reed said with annoyance. "I've wasted enough time.

"$16.53," the man replied.

Reed slid the twenty across the counter. "Keep the change for all your hard work."

He grabbed the bag and headed out the door. A moment later, he slid back into the car.

"They didn't have your OE, so I picked you up a Natty Daddy," he shouted as he reached into the bag and withdrew the beer can.

A spine-chilling scream briefly overpowered the music as Reed tumbled from the car and scrambled to get away. Inside, Watkins' lifeless body was slumped over in the seat, blood pouring out from the bullet wound in his head.

CHAPTER THREE

1 Police Plaza, Manhattan, N.Y.

Monday, May 4th, 2015 - 7:12 a.m.

"Good morning, got a minute?"

Maguire looked up from the report he was reading to see Sandy Barnes, his First Deputy Commissioner, standing in the doorway to his office.

"Pull up a chair," Maguire said. "Misery loves company."

"That doesn't sound very promising," she said, taking a seat across from him and putting her coffee mug on the side table. "How was your weekend?"

"I want to go back on patrol," he laughed.

"As a white shield?"

"They were much simpler times, weren't they?" Maguire asked.

"Indeed, they were," she agreed. "At least back then I knew I was done when my tour ended. All this seems very worky."

"You won't get any argument from me, but that doesn't sound inspirational coming from the Policewomen's Endowment Association, Woman of the Year recipient."

"It was a lovely gesture, but realistically it's just another plaque my kids will toss in the trash after I'm dead and gone," Barnes replied.

"That's very cynical of you."

"I'm always cynical before I've had my eighth cup of coffee," she replied, raising her glass in a toast. "This is only number five."

"Well, at least the city didn't burn down over the weekend, so you should still be able to get that eighth cup in before things get out of control."

"Summer hasn't even begun, so have this conversation with me at the end of June."

"Anything I need to know about?" he asked.

"Crime is spiking across the board, while retirements and resignations are killing us. We're losing our best and brightest, James, and I can't say that I blame them. They've lost faith in the system, and most are worried they are one viral video away from an indictment. Hell, we lost a captain last week to Suffolk County; a fucking captain."

"And to make matters worse, I got this in my briefing this morning," Maguire said as he slid a sheet of paper across the desk.

Barnes put on her reading glasses and read the document. "You're fucking kidding me? A five percent budget decrease?"

"Cuts are coming citywide," Maguire replied. "Every agency has been told to tighten its belt. The non-public safety agencies are being told to cut ten."

"That's still a quarter of a million dollars. It means we can kiss the next academy class goodbye, and we don't have enough people as it is. The average response time in the city is now over twelve minutes for serious calls; twenty-eight minutes on non-emergency ones. People get annoyed when their trash doesn't get picked up on time; they become absolutely apoplectic when they are being robbed and shot at and no one shows up."

"The problem is that those folks forget they are the ones who elected the clowns running this circus," Maguire replied.

"The unions will go bat-shit crazy. They'll turn City Hall Park into an encampment."

"Won't matter," Maguire replied. "Barone is so terrified of Nydia Flores that he won't call her out on her bullshit. He's so worried about political attacks that he's placating her and the City Council's every whim."

"They are either going to pay salaries or they are going to pay overtime," Barnes said. "I can't help it if they live in a fantasy world devoid of the truth."

"My old partner, Alex Taylor, would call this a *fucktastrophe*," Maguire smiled.

"She's not wrong."

"She rarely is; her problem is that she has a horrible bedside manner."

"A healthy dose of reality can be a hard pill to swallow," Barnes replied. "What are you going to do?"

"Well, my usual go-to options are pretty much illegal in this situation," Maguire said. "Right now I feel like the captain of the Titanic, and my shoes are getting wet."

"No, you're not," she replied. "That schmuck in City Hall is the captain. You're the one who tried to warn him what was happening, and he ignored you."

"That's what politicians do. Besides, it doesn't make much difference when the entire ship is slipping beneath the waves."

"They're not the ones standing in the breach trying to hold back the enemy, as our ranks dwindle. What is your plan?"

"What I have to do is going to be grossly unpopular," he replied.

"Will it work?"

"That's the million-dollar question."

"Well, you might as well just rip the Band-Aid off and tell me what you need."

"I want a breakdown of index crime by command, along with personnel levels Department wide. Not just at the bureau level. I need all the subunit levels as well, so I can reallocate cops from where it will hurt the least to where it can help the most."

"Dear God, I didn't know you were talking *about grossly* unpopular things."

"Do you have a better idea, Sandy?" he asked. "Because if you do, I'm all ears. I know that there are a lot of folks who managed to land cushy desk jobs who won't be happy, but we're cops, not a Fortune 500 company. No one forced us to take the job. We swore an oath, and that means something—even when it's inconvenient. This is like a marriage; you have to deal with the good and the bad."

"I think you just might push a few into looking for a divorce attorney," she replied. "Especially among those here at headquarters."

"Maybe, but to be honest, I'm more concerned about the ones in the street that are defending the breach than I am about those hiding out inside the castle. This is going to hurt, but I'll be damned if I am going to ask the street cops to do more without asking the ones sitting behind a desk to do something."

"I'll make it happen," she replied.

CHAPTER FOUR

Bayside. Queens, N.Y.

Monday, May 4th, 2015 - 9:23 a.m.

Charles Boyd lay in bed watching the curtains flutter against the crisp morning breeze; the morning sun lighting up the second-floor bedroom of his childhood home.

He'd spent the weekend locked away, struggling to come to terms with the bleak future that awaited him. One mistake had sealed his fate, and he knew that nothing he did could ever change that.

"I didn't even do anything," he mumbled. "It was just a stupid conversation."

Yeah, a stupid conversation with a cop, he reminded himself.

His memories were drawn back to the courtroom; listening to that district attorney bitch reading the transcript to the jury. He knew what was going to happen; he could see it in their eyes. The utter contempt they felt even though none of them even knew him. Judging his life by one stupid chat he had with a fourteen-year-old girl.

The fools sitting there in the jury box judging him, the so-called jury of his peers, were a joke. They weren't his peers, and they had no clue as to what his life had been like growing up. They could never understand what it had been like to be abused, both mentally and physically, and what that abuse had done to him. His psychologist had tried to help by explaining how those events had influenced the rest of his life, but it had only made him angrier to see his life, his most cherished feelings, made to be shameful.

Who are they to condemn me? he thought.

He knew what real abuse was, how deeply it had scarred him, and he would never do that to another human being. If you loved someone, you loved them; you couldn't just turn off feelings like that.

He remembered the picture she had shared with him of the innocent-looking blonde-haired girl curled up seductively on the bed holding a teddy bear. A shiver coursed through his body at the memory. Even now, even though he knew it was a lie, a photo used to entrap him by some fucking detective, he felt himself becoming aroused.

Why was it okay for a forty-year-old woman to marry a man half her age, but a thirty-year-old man couldn't do the same? he wondered. *Why did society get to set the age requirements for everyone else? Who made them the sole arbiters of right and wrong?*

History was rife with examples of underage marriage. The legal age in some European countries used to be twelve, and even Colonial America had followed this standard. Even today, there were still countries that allowed a minor to get married with consent. Some places were even trying to reduce the stigma, pushing for rights for *minor attracted persons*, but it felt like it was an uphill battle and most people just didn't give a fuck because it didn't affect them.

They don't care; no one cares. They just fuck you over and label you for life.

He pulled back the covers and swung his legs over the edge of the bed, staring down at the ankle monitoring device that kept him a prisoner in his own home.

"They just don't understand," he muttered. "No one understands."

Well, that's not entirely true, he thought.

He had a friend who shared his dilemma. They'd met previously in a chatroom, before all of this had happened, and she had stayed by his side through all of it, at least till they revoked his internet access, offering her support and encouragement. Michelle was a high school teacher in rural Georgia, and she'd had a series of relationships with some of her students. Like him, she found that youth had a certain emotional appeal that she couldn't shake; it was an innocence that was pure and sweet, in a world filled with jaded adults.

After his conviction, he had fallen into a state of depression. He knew it could have been worse. Jail time, even a brief one, would have been a death sentence for him. Fortunately, the judge understood and showed him leniency, but locked away in his home, with no access to the outside world, was an even slower kind of death.

One day, Michelle had surprised him with a visit and had slipped him a prepaid cellphone he could use if he ever needed to get in contact with her. Even his mother had taken a liking to her. After Michelle had left, his mom had talked about her for days, asking why he couldn't just meet a nice girl like her and settle down and have a normal life. He knew she wasn't being mean, but he still harbored deep resentment toward her. She was, after all, the woman who had allowed her abusive boyfriend to move in.

In her defense, his mother had always been a bit of an airhead when it came to the obvious things in life, like the freeloader she opened her door to. What she failed to see was the change in her son, the bruises; the emotional trauma that should have been evident. She chalked that up to little Charlie just being clumsy. While she was at work, paying to support that beer-swilling prick, he was home getting drunk and showing little Charlie all manner of perversions. That's what had changed him; that's what had made him into who he was. He'd lost his innocence, and he just wanted to find it again in the arms of someone life hadn't corrupted. If he could find that, he knew in his heart that he could keep that love pure.

He got out of bed and showered, letting the hot water ease the tension in him. He knew what he needed to do, and it thrilled and terrified him. Deciding had been incredibly hard, but he realized that if he didn't, he would never have a life again.

When he was done, he headed back to the bedroom and stood in front of the dresser. This was the first step he had to take; the commitment to change his life began here.

He opened the dresser and removed a neatly folded pastel blue polo shirt, along with a pair of socks and underwear. After putting them on, he went to the closet and selected a crisp pair of khaki pants. One thing his mother excelled at was always making sure his clothes were impeccable. As if his outward appearance was a direct reflection of her success as a parent. He then slipped on a pair of brown loafers and headed down to breakfast.

Anna Boyd was in the kitchen, singing softly, as she prepared his customary breakfast of scrambled eggs, bacon and buttered English muffins. He walked up behind her and kissed her on the cheek.

"Good morning, Momma," he said.

"Good morning, Charlie. Did you sleep well?"

"I did; how about you?" he asked as he sat down at the kitchen table.

"Enough," she replied. "I'll take a nap later."

"You should ask the doctor to give you something to help you sleep better."

"Oh, you know I don't like taking things," she replied, as she plated his food and set it down in front of him. "Besides, what if you needed me at night?"

"I'm a big boy, Momma. I can fend for myself," he said as he stabbed at the eggs with his fork.

"Well, maybe I don't want you to grow up. I like taking care of you."

"I know you do," he smiled. "Did I tell you that I spoke to my parole officer the other day?"

A frown appeared on Anna's face as she braced herself for bad news. "No, what did he have to say?"

"I can leave the house," he replied. "Well, at least for an hour every day."

"Are you serious? How? Why?"

"I am," he replied. "Apparently, they passed a new law in Albany that says total home confinement is tantamount to cruel and unusual punishment. There has to be a one-hour break within every twenty-four hours. I just have to call when I leave and call when I return."

"That is fantastic news. I'm sure it will be good for your mental health to get out of the house, even for an hour. Why didn't you tell me sooner?"

"I think I was still trying to process it all," he replied. "To be honest, it feels a bit terrifying."

"Why?"

"I haven't left the house in almost a year. I mean, yes, I have gone out into the backyard, and to get the mail, but it always felt like those were walls I couldn't cross. Now I get to leave, and I'm not sure what to do, if that makes sense."

"Why don't you just walk down to the park? I could go with you if that would help ease your mind."

He smiled. "No, I don't need a babysitter. I just need to adjust to it and take those first steps."

"Just don't abuse it, Charlie. Even if you get a full hour, be back before that. Don't give them any reason to take it away or worse."

"I won't, Momma," he said, pushing the plate away. "And you're right, I think I'll just head down to the park and come back. Baby steps."

"Good boy," she said as she picked up the plate and kissed his forehead.

He glanced down at his watch and noted the time. If he left now, he needed to be back no later than 11:30. That would give him about fifteen minutes to sit and relax. He placed the call to his parole officer's office and set the timer on his watch.

"Okay, here goes nothing," he said as he got up from the table. "I'll be back in forty-five minutes.

"Have fun, Charlie."

Walking past the white picket fence felt surreal. For a moment, it felt like a movie, and he half expected a cop car to pull up and take him to jail, but with every unmolested step he took, he felt a sense of euphoria that had been missing from his life.

As he walked along the street, he began to see things in a whole new light. It was like a blind man who had gotten his eyesight restored. The freedom that he had once taken for granted was now a gift he could truly appreciate.

A few blocks later, he took a right, heading in the park's direction. Technically, he hadn't lied to his mother. He was going to the park, but there were two, and the one he had chosen sat across from an elementary school. He wouldn't stay long; perhaps a minute or two. Just enough time to satiate the desire he had been repressing for months.

He tapped his pant leg, feeling the cellphone in the pocket. He would call Michelle on his way home so he could share the moment. She'd probably be at work, but he'd leave her a message. They'd talked about him moving down there, to start anew, and this taste of freedom made him realize he needed to get far away from here if he wanted to enjoy his life.

As he drew closer, he could hear the raucous noise emanating from the schoolyard. A blur of figures ran around, accompanied by the high-pitched sound of female laughter, as they played their games. He took a seat on a nearby bench and watched.

In his head, he calculated how long before school was out. By the end of June, they would move out of the confined schoolyard and into the park. Some of the high school kids might even join them. He loved summer, because it gave them a chance to show off their nubile bodies in the least amount of clothes. Most of their parents worked, so no one was around to see what they were wearing during summer vacation, and a few of them always took advantage. Tight shirts and skimpy shorts proudly highlighted their changing bodies.

Boyd felt himself becoming aroused at the thought, as his eyes kept watch on a young blonde-haired girl dashing around the yard in an orange shirt, doing her best to avoid being the latest victim of a dodgeball game. He glanced down at his watch, knowing he needed to get moving soon.

"Excuse me, aren't you Anna Boyd's son?"

The voice startled him, and he looked up to see a middle-aged man wearing a New York Yankees jersey.

“I am,” he replied. “Do I know you?”

“Nah,” the man smiled as he reached under the jersey and withdrew a silenced pistol and fired, “but I know you, you sick pedo fuck.”

Boyd slumped over, blood draining onto the wooden slats of the bench before pooling onto the concrete below.

A shrill scream sounded from the schoolyard as the bright red ball claimed the blonde-haired girl as its latest victim.

CHAPTER FIVE

City Hall, Manhattan, N.Y.

Tuesday, May 5th, 2015 - 10:35 a.m.

"James, I understand what you are saying, and I appreciate your concerns, but we have to make these cuts," Jack Barone said.

"You say this like it is the first time you are asking, Mr. Mayor, but we haven't recovered from the last round of budget cuts. There comes a tipping point when the damage is going to be irreparable."

"I just think we need to explore more constructive ways of utilizing personnel."

"Constructive? With all due respect, I don't think you fully appreciate the situation I am facing. We are a long way past constructive."

"What do you mean?" Barone asked.

"Crime is up on almost every index. I've had to add additional staffing to the Pension Section because of the increase in retirements and resignations, and I just had to tell the academy to postpone the next class until January at the earliest. Right now we are down to minimum manning in almost sixty percent of the precincts. I have had to order all non-patrol commands to reduce their personnel by ten percent just to fill seats in the commands with the highest crime stats. If you think retirements are bad now, wait till you see the wave that is coming."

Barone frowned as he leaned back in his seat. "We're all struggling, James."

"Is the City Council struggling?" Maguire asked. "Cause the twenty percent pay raise they just gave themselves seems excessive for the *quality* work they have been doing."

"I'll admit that was rather piss-poor timing on their part."

"You think? So where would you suggest I make these cuts?"

Barone leaned over and began rifling through the stack of papers on the desk. "What about overtime? It shows here that it has skyrocketed this fiscal year."

"Either I have enough people to do the job, or I have to pay overtime to get that job done. The reason overtime is up is because staffing levels are down. Anyone with half a brain, and under ten years on the job, has seen the writing on the wall and they are getting out."

"What do you mean?" Barone asked.

"Nassau, Suffolk, Port Authority," Maguire said. "You name an agency and our people are flocking to it."

"Why?"

"Are you being serious? For starters, they are getting paid a lot more money to deal with far less nonsense. If I cut out overtime, I can promise you that you will not have enough cops on the street when summer hits."

Barone stood up and walked over to the window and stared out, watching as people walked through City Hall Park, completely unaware of the drama unfolding within the building's marble and limestone walls.

I envy their ignorance, he thought. *I wish I could embrace it; to just walk outside and get away from all of this.*

The irony wasn't lost on him.

As a politician, this was the job he had always wanted, what he had aspired to, but wanting something and having it felt like two different worlds to him now. He had thought it was providence that had brought him to the mayoralty, after his predecessor, Alan McMasters, had taken a cabinet position with the Cook administration, but now he wasn't sure whether it was a reward or a punishment.

Running for office was always easy. Campaign promises were a dime a dozen, and blaming your opponent, or even better, blaming an incumbent, was Politics 101, but that all changed when you were the one in charge. Like Harry Truman had said, 'The buck stops here.'

His biggest dilemma was that he was a lame-duck mayor. The voters had not elected him, he had just been installed by virtue of his position in the line of succession. He would have to run on his record if he wanted to be elected, but that would most likely pit him against Nydia Flores, the powerful speaker of the city council. So far, Flores had been noncommittal regarding a potential mayoral run, and he had been doing his utmost to play nice with her, but the threat overshadowed every decision he made. He had hoped that a successful working relationship would remove any potential pitfalls, but Flores was a skilled politician. She knew she was a political threat, and she took every opportunity to get her way. He had caved to the whims of the City Council, even the most ludicrous ones, and now it was coming back to bite him in the political ass.

"I don't know what to do," he replied.

Maguire didn't know whether the comment was directed at him or if Barone was just admitting that he was in over his head.

"You have to pick your fights, Mr. Mayor," Maguire replied.

Barone turned around. "What does that even mean?"

"You're trying to appease the City Council when you need to worry about winning over the voters. People will put up with a lot of things, but the quickest way to alienate them is to remove the services they expect. Police, fire, sanitation, and once those slip away, the City Council will be the least of your concerns."

"What do you suggest?"

Maguire wrung his hands, doing his best to remain stoic even as the anger inside threatened to overtake him. In many ways, this reminded him of the old days, when the Naval Academy *ring-knockers* would screw things up so badly and then arrogantly demand those beneath them to fix it.

I highly recommend that you pull your head out of your ass and do your fucking job, *you little pussy*, he thought, before taking a deep breath.

"You're asking me for a solution to a problem I didn't create."

Barone sat back down in the chair, his shoulders slumped and the pained look of a man who had hit the proverbial wall. "I'm not asking you to fix the problem; I'm asking for your recommendations."

"Mr. Mayor, you don't want to hear my recommendations."

"We may disagree on things, but I don't believe your heart's in the wrong place," Barone replied. "Even if I don't act on it, I would prefer to hear what you have to say."

"The folks on the City Council aren't your friends, regardless of their party affiliation. In fact, those on the other side of the aisle might actually have more in common with you. You're trying to play nice, thinking they will do the same, when in reality they're just going to eat you last. The one thing I will say about them is that they are consistent. They told everyone what they were going to do when they got elected, but back then it was all theoretical. They pandered for votes, telling people what they wanted to hear. Once they had people believing they were the victim, it was easy to paint us as the jack-booted, heavy-handed enemy. They won their elections easily and doubled-down on the rhetoric. Now crime is skyrocketing, and their answer is that they need to defund the Department so they can pay to implement necessary change; change that comes in the form of mental health advisors, social workers, community violence ambassadors. Do you know what that is going to do to address the real problem?"

"No," Barone said somberly.

"Nothing," Maguire replied. "Absolutely nothing. Those idiots have no idea what is going on in the streets. They are insulated from the death and carnage we deal with daily. Take a ride with me to the Seven-Three, or, better yet, the Four-Four, and tell me what these programs are going to accomplish."

"I don't need a ride-along to tell me what's going on," Barone snapped. "I know my city, damn it."

"No, sir, you don't," Maguire corrected him. "You think you do, but you have no idea. Just like those folks on the City Council. I'm not blaming you; I'm just saying it is all theoretical to you. You have no idea what it's like to be a sixteen-year-old kid navigating his way home from school and wondering if he's going to get caught up in a drive-by shooting, or a seventy-year-old woman worried about getting mugged coming home from the grocery store, but these are the people you need to worry about. Right now, the politicians are focused on the wrong people."

"You don't think I know that?"

"What I know is that if you don't put a stop to this madness, the headlines here are going to sound a lot like those in Chicago."

Barone sighed as he rubbed his forehead.

"Look, I can cut back in some areas, streamline some units, and try to get as many cops back on the street as I can, but at some point it won't be enough. If the perpetrators are back out on the street before my cops even finish the paperwork, then we have hit the point of no return."

"I'm the executive," Barone argued. "I don't control the legislature. This is their mess, and they need to fix it."

"This might come as a shock to you, but half the people in this city don't even know what the legislative branch does, and the other half doesn't even know who their legislator is. When the news does stories about the chaos plaguing this city, they are going to be knocking on the door at City Hall, not the City Council. People are going to want to know what the man behind the mayor's desk is doing to fix things."

"And I want to know what you are doing," Barone argued. "You are the police commissioner; you work for me."

"I'm rearranging deck chairs on the goddamn Titanic and asking the band to play one more song in the hopes we get rescued," Maguire shot back.

A knock at the door cut off Barone's reply.

"Come in," he fumed.

Peggy Connolly, his secretary, peeked in. "I'm sorry to interrupt, but your eleven o'clock meeting is here, Mr. Mayor."

"Thank you, Peggy, please show him in."

Maguire stood up. A silent acknowledgment that Barone had effectively dismissed him.

He knew Barone would do nothing to help him. Maguire had always had lingering doubts about whether he was up to the task of being police commissioner, but any time he spent with Barone allayed those fears. Maguire at least knew how to be a cop; had spent time in uniform. Barone was the epitome of the modern politician; spineless, clueless, and loathed to take any action that might jeopardize his career.

Maguire was just about to walk through the doorway when another figure came into view.

"Commissioner Maguire," Reverend Archibald Jennings said, as he extended his hand. "It's so good to see you again."

Jennings was the city's self-appointed critic on racial inequality. If there was a problem anywhere in the city, you could count on the good Reverend Archie delivering a firebrand sermon while pouring gasoline over everything. Maguire had already had one run in with the man and Jennings was still paying the price.

"How's that tax audit working out for you, Archie?" Maguire asked, ignoring the man's hand.

Jennings opened his mouth to say something, but then quickly closed it with a frown.

Maguire shot a look back at Barone. "Let me guess, the Titanic just got a new social justice director?"

CHAPTER SIX

Rikers Island, Astoria, N.Y.

Friday, May 8th, 2015 - 11:42 a.m.

District 21 City Councilman Fernando Rodriguez approached the dais that had been set up in the park adjacent to the entrance of the Department of Correction Rikers Island facility. A medium-sized, raucous crowd had assembled to hear the man pledge to enact legislation that would lead to the closing of the city's largest correctional center.

Rodriguez was an up-and-coming star in his party. He was young, energetic and had a natural charisma that drew young people to him.

"For nearly one hundred years, Rikers Island has been a blight on this city," Rodriguez said, as he adjusted the microphone and then rolled up the sleeves on his neatly pressed linen dress shirt. "Severe overpopulation has led to inhumane conditions, and we must stand united to bring about necessary change. Prisoner rights are human rights, and we must never be afraid to fight back against the corrupt prison-industrial complex. Social remedies change people, not locking them away like animals. Prisons disproportionately affect young people of color. Since the start of the war on drugs, incarceration rates have tripled, and our young men have been victimized and criminalized. Instead of funding jails, we should be diverting that money back into our communities. We need to increase access to education and social programs that will give people good-paying jobs and break the cycle of government-sponsored incarceration."

The assembled crowd clapped enthusiastically.

"It is time city officials stood up and did something to help the most vulnerable in our society. Criminal justice reform is the pressing issue of our time, and that is why I am pleased to announce that I have drafted legislation that will finally see this facility shut down."

The crowd erupted in thunderous applause, and many of them began banging on drums and ringing bells.

Beyond the assemblage, rows of television news trucks lined the roadway as camera crews recorded the speeches and prepared for the planned march on the facility.

"With our combined voices, we can send a simple message to our leaders in Albany that we will no longer stand for the injustices being levied against our communities of color," Rodriguez continued. "We must double down on our efforts to elect representatives who will not buckle under the weight of the capitalist machine that drives a wedge between us. We demand that the people come first before profit. Now is the time to act. To permanently shut down Rikers Island and remove the stain that has plagued this city's rich history by being home to the world's largest penal colony."

Sadly, the irony was lost to most of those in attendancc that profit was the single overriding factor in the political push to shut down Rikers Island.

The original owner of the land, Dutch immigrant Abraham Rycken, had taken possession of the island in 1664, and it remained in his family until sold to New York City in 1884. Originally less than one hundred acres in size, the island was gradually increased using landfill until it eclipsed four hundred acres, and the jail began operation in 1932.

While the politicians had set their eyes on shuttering Rikers, it was not for the noble purpose they espoused to their constituents. The dirty little secret was that Rikers Island was prime real estate property, the epitome of a gated community, and something that the City was eager to monetize. Once its doors were shuttered, there would be a multitude of interests, both public and private, vying to get control over its future.

But that was all future speculation and something that Rodriguez knew would most likely not affect him in a way that would financially benefit from. No, he had been asked to set the stage for someone else's reward, but he was not about to squander it. His purpose in getting behind this political movement in its infancy was to get his face out there. He had aspirations that were far beyond the City Council. To him, his present role was simply to get his foot in the door. He needed access, and that was what his position as a councilman gave him. Now he needed to get out in front of the cameras on a major progressive battle.

The folks gathered with him today were a mix of die-hard social justice advocates and paid protestors, neither of which truly mattered to him; they simply served their respective roles. The advocates were the ones who would get in front of the cameras and eloquently preach the authentic message, while the paid ones would provide the rousing applause. Everything was a matter of theatrics these days. If he were successful, it would push the justice system to begin releasing prisoners from the overpopulated facility. He would accomplish this by leading a group march and attempting to cross the bridge and gain access to the island. He knew he wouldn't be able to, but that didn't matter to him, only the optics.

Word had already gotten back to him that the entrance to the facility was already blocked off. Correction's Emergency Service Unit had already secured the lone roadway into Rikers and the NYPD's Strategic Response Group was staged in the parking area. Notice had already been provided that anyone who attempted to gain access would be arrested; which was exactly what he wanted to happen. His plan called for a very vocal and visible arrest of himself and several other prominent activists that would all play out in front of the assembled cameras.

Rodriguez had an entire PR team waiting to parlay his arrest into speaking engagements with several prominent progressive organizations, along with a slew of news outlets lined up. If the stars aligned, he could whip up his base and leverage his new status to make a run for the congressional seat that was becoming available in the next election cycle.

"Now, with your help, the marginalized people of this city will know that they are not forgotten," Rodriguez said, "and those who have created this unjust system will know their time has come."

Rodriguez left the dais to rousing applause and proceeded over to where his contingent was assembling for their march.

"Excuse me, Councilman. Can I have a word with you?"

Rodriguez turned to see Emily Gutierrez, Channel Four's Community Events Reporter, approaching and flashed her a big smile.

"Emily, thank you so much for coming out," he said, giving her a hug.

Gutierrez was known as one of the kindred souls in the Rikers closure movement and had done a lot of coverage on the topic. She was one of the media personalities he needed in his corner. It also didn't hurt that she was extremely attractive, which would guarantee that the cameras would remain focused on him, as long as she was at his side.

"I wanted to thank you for taking a stand on this issue," she replied. "I just don't think people have a true understanding of the conditions here, and we need powerful voices like yours to bring awareness."

"We know that it's only the start of a long fight," he replied, "but at least we are taking the first steps."

"Would you mind if I walked with you? I'd like to get your insights into the matter," she asked. "I promise my cameraman won't get in the way."

"By all means," he replied. "Although I anticipate the police will act swiftly to shut us down, so please be careful when we get near the parking lot. I'm willing to take my chances, but I don't want to see you become a victim of the system's response."

The march took off at noon, a group of about a hundred people making their way east on 19th Avenue toward Hazen Street, flanked on either side by uniformed cops. Several in the crowd continued to bang on their drums, striking a beat for a bullhorn-wielding activist who led the others chanting, '*Hey, Ho, we all know, Rikers Island has got to go!*'

"Do you really think they will arrest you today?" she asked.

"Absolutely," he replied. "I have to do what is right by my constituents; what they elected me to do. If I don't go into the arena to fight for them, how can I expect them to support me? I made campaign promises, and I plan on delivering."

"That is so refreshing to hear," Gutierrez said. "So many politicians today pander to voters at election time and then forget them. I'd like to do a much more in-depth dive into the impact you are having on this issue. Would you consider giving me an exclusive interview back in the studio after your release?"

"It would be my pleasure," Rodriguez replied.

"I'd like to start out with the footage we get today," she said. "Set the stage to show just how far you were willing to go on the front lines of the closure project. I think it will resonate with my viewers. From there we can get into the particulars of what you are doing behind the scenes."

"I like the way you think. I can have my people call you when the processing is finishing up and maybe your camera crew can film the release."

"Please do that," she said.

As the crowd turned right onto Hazen Street, they met a wall of SRG officers in riot gear. Behind them, a large flatbed truck held a contingent of white-shirt supervisors, including Bernard Walker, the Department of Correction's Chief of Department. Walker raised his bullhorn and made an announcement.

"You are trespassing on Department of Correction property. At this time, you are being directed to disperse. If you attempt to gain access to this facility, you will be arrested and charged with trespass and obstructing governmental administration."

In response, the crowd began chanting louder and banging their drums harder.

"Well, I guess it's time to see who blinks in this showdown," he said, smiling at Gutierrez.

"We'll be covering it," Emily replied. "Good luck."

Rodriguez moved to the front of the protesters, grabbing a bullhorn from an assistant.

"What do we say?" he asked.

'Shut it down! Shut it down!' the crowd roared.

"These are the people who are intent on keeping the old ways," he shouted, as the noise of the crowd abated. "These are the protectors of criminal capitalism. It's time we showed them we won't stand for it anymore. That our voices are strong and our will is even stronger. I came here today to send a message, and if they don't want to hear that message, then they can arrest me."

The crowd roared, and the banging became so intense that it was deafening.

It's all coming together, he thought. *This is the moment they will all look back on and know that I seized my opportunity.*

Rodriguez smiled, raising his fist into the air and began pumping it.

He took a deep breath, ready to embrace his political watershed moment, when he felt his body slammed backward and he fell to the ground. At first, he thought the cops had moved in preemptively, snatching him up before he could do anything newsworthy, but then he realized the chanting had stopped and people were screaming.

All around him there was a flurry of activity. Some people were running, while others ducked, as the screams slowly faded. Then Emily was at his side. He looked up; expecting to see her smiling face, but it was contorted in terror, and her eyes were wide in shock.

Emily's lips were moving, but he couldn't make out the words she was saying. He tried to speak, to tell her he was fine, but he coughed instead, and it was at that moment he tasted the salty, metallic tang of blood on his lips. Panic gripped his chest as the edges of his vision began to darken, chasing away the activity swirling around him until all that was left was her face, and then that was taken away too.

CHAPTER SEVEN

1 Police Plaza, Manhattan, N.Y.

Friday, May 8th, 2015 - 11:44 a.m.

"Hey, Angel, how are things in Jerusalem going?" Maguire asked.

"Oh, you know," Melody Anderson replied. "It's a total shit-show."

"Well, you're only dealing with a couple of millennia of regional strife," he said. "You should be able to have this wrapped up quick."

"Oh yeah, totally easy peasy," she laughed. "If I can just convince the Knesset that Hamas is simply misunderstood, we should be able to close the book on this."

"I think it would be easier to convince Hamas that God will not allow their plans to come to fruition."

"If I'm being honest, I don't think this is ever going to be resolved," she sighed, "and it certainly won't be by me."

"Don't sell yourself short."

"No, I'm just being realistic," she replied. "It's kind of hard to have productive peace negotiations when one side is firing rockets and chanting death threats."

"Well, to be fair, Hamas is the end product, and trying to deal with them is probably as frustrating as it is counterproductive. They're just going to give you rehashed talking points. You have to go to the shot-callers if you want results."

"Iran?"

"If you're going up the ladder, then yeah, I guess," Maguire said, as he poured himself a cup of coffee, "but if that's the route you choose, you might as well just go pound your head against the wall. Everything with them is dressed in religion and once you get stuck in that quagmire, you're fucked. Even our friends in the region walk a very fine line. If you're asking what I would do, I'd be going up further on the ladder."

"So what do you suggest?"

"I'd shift my focus away from who Iran influences and look at who influences Iran."

"Russia and China," Melody said.

"Now you're over the target."

"The question is, can we afford to piss off those countries right now?"

"You're the diplomat," he replied. "I'm just a knuckle-dragger, but I don't think you have to piss them off to gain their cooperation. They need us."

"They need our money."

"That's even more reason to stand firm. Just threaten their pocketbooks and most will play ball, even if there is some reluctance. Remember what Theodore Roosevelt said, '*If you've got them by the balls, their hearts and minds will follow.*'"

"If that FBI slot falls through, I think I can make room for you over at State."

"Oh, that'll make you a lot of friends," he laughed.

"Speaking of friends, I met one of yours today."

"You did?" he asked. "Who?"

"General Shay Harel," she replied. "He said you two go way back, but told me it had been a while and to send you his warmest regards."

Maguire felt the air get sucked out of his chest. *Fuck!*

"He's quite charming," she added.

"It's all an act," Maguire laughed, doing his best to downplay his response. "Just keep him away from booze and broads."

"You military boys are all the same."

"Oh yeah, we're a riot," Maguire replied.

The shock he was feeling had already turned to anger and was threatening to move toward rage. General Shay Harel was many things, but friend was so far down the list that it didn't even make the paper. To Maguire, he was the father of Tzviya Harel and the man who was directly responsible for terminating their relationship.

"So when are you coming home?" he asked, changing the subject.

"I'm leaving for Brussels in the morning," she replied. "For yet another meeting with the European Union delegation that will be just as useless as all the other meetings have been."

"I'm convinced that EU delegates are the annoying people that no one likes in their home countries, so they promote them and ship them to Brussels and they have meetings just to have someone else annoying to talk to."

"You won't get any argument from me," she laughed. "I'm flying back to D.C. on Tuesday. Do you want to come down?"

"I've got a City Council meeting on Wednesday," he replied. "How about I come down Thursday and we can make it a long weekend?"

"That would be nice. It feels like we have had to fight tooth and nail for any time together."

"We do," he replied.

"I miss our old life," she said. "By the way, Henry says you haven't been at the house much in the last few weeks."

"Henry talks too much," Maguire laughed.

"He is my caretaker," she replied.

"I've been staying on the boat."

"Why?"

"Because when I'm at the house I feel like one of those attractions at the zoo," he replied. "A poor, pathetic caged animal who occasionally gets a visitor. You know I like Henry, but it only makes it worse knowing that his sole function is to be caretaker to me while I'm there. The boat feels more like my domain."

"I'm sorry."

"Me too."

"Have you given anymore thought to Cook's offer? It would give us more stability with you being down in D.C."

"I won't lie. It is attractive," he replied.

"I hear a *but* coming."

"But," he laughed. "I'd be nothing more than a hired suit."

"I hate to break the news to you, but you're a hired suit right now," she said.

"Yes, but this job I know. I could put my old uniform on right now and go back out in the street and know exactly what to do. There would be no learning curve for me."

"And you're afraid that you don't know what the Bureau does?" she asked.

"Not to be rude, but I don't know if the people who work at the Bureau know what they do," he replied. "Some of the people I worked with in the past didn't strike me as being the sharpest tacks in the pack. I mean, they were nice enough people, but, in terms of having investigatory skills or just that cop intuition, I was left thinking that some of them couldn't find smoke at a barbecue without some help."

Melody laughed. "God, you never cease to amaze me."

"Why is that?"

"Listen to yourself, James. Think about all your accomplishments. People would kill to have the career you have had, and yet you're worried about not being up to the task because you don't know the *ins* and *outs* of the Bureau. Randall Whitehead would get lost trying to find his way out of a paper bag, and yet they saw fit to appoint him to the spot, and that man is a complete schmuck."

"Schmuck," he laughed. "Wow, Israel has rubbed off on you."

"I'm serious. Maybe the problem is that no one has opened the windows at the Bureau and let some fresh air in."

"There's an argument to be made about allowing people to move up through the ranks. Institutional knowledge allows for a smoother transition."

"And as a cop, have you ever seen someone in the Department come up through the ranks that made you cringe?"

"You know the answer to that," he replied.

"Yes, I do. Every job has people who climb the promotional ladder because of the ass they kiss or latch on to. It has nothing to do with their abilities. Maybe what the Bureau needs is an outsider who can clean things up and make it easier for the actual workers to advance up the ladder for a change. I'm being serious when I say that you should consider the offer."

"I will, I prom—"

The door burst open, and Detective Amanda Massi barged into the room.

"Sorry, Boss, there's been a shooting at the Rikers' protest," she said as she turned on the television.

"Babe, I've got to go," Maguire replied, ending the call. "What happened, Amanda?"

"Still chaotic, and Operations is trying to get the particulars, but there is live footage of the incident being broadcast."

Maguire stared at the screen, which showed a visibly shaken reporter, her blouse stained with blood.

"Do we have any word on who the shooter is, Emily?" An off-screen reporter asked.

"There's no word at this time," Gutierrez responded, fighting to calm her voice.

This was her moment, the opportunity to be a witness to history, covered in the victim's blood in the national spotlight. She felt sorry for Rodriguez, but opportunities like this were rare and she was going to seize it and not allow anything, including her own emotional fragilities steal it from her. She swallowed hard and set her resolve.

"What I can tell you is that District Twenty-One Councilman, Fernando Rodriguez, had led a peaceful march to the entrance of Rikers Island when he was shot. I was standing just to his side when the shot rang out and did my best to comfort him while they administered first aid. The councilman was rushed to the hospital by EMS, but so far we do not have an update on his condition."

"Thank you, Emily, please keep us posted."

The image shifted back to a news anchor in the studio. "We will continue to monitor this developing situation at the Rikers Island Closure March. Sources are telling us that City Council Speaker Nydia Flores was originally scheduled to attend the event but could not due to a scheduling conflict. We are about to air footage from the event, but we want to warn our audience that it might be disturbing and viewer discretion is advised."

Maguire watched as Rodriguez broke away from the group of protestors and began addressing them through a bullhorn. Then the man's body was flung backward, a huge censor *blur* covering his chest and face, as he lay sprawled on the ground.

"What the hell is going on?"

Maguire looked up to see Sandy standing in the doorway.

"Boss," Amanda said, her hand holding her cellphone to her ear. "Rodriguez is on his way to Elmhurst General, but it's not looking good."

"All hell is about to break loose, Sandy," Maguire sighed, as he got up from his desk. "Amanda, where is Mike?"

"He's already down at the truck," she replied.

"Sandy, you have the ship," Maguire said as he grabbed his jacket from the coat rack just as Deputy Chief Liam Martin came into the office. "Liam, stay on top of Ops for me. I want to know whatever they know two seconds after they know it and notify the C.O. of Queens North that I'm on my way to the scene."

CHAPTER EIGHT

Rikers Island, Astoria, N.Y.

Friday, May 8th, 2015 - 12:57 p.m.

Maguire stood adjacent to where Rodriguez had fallen and scanned the area. The roadway was stained with blood and a drum lay abandoned near the curb. The entire area was shut down as a swarm of Homicide and Crime Scene Unit detectives conducted their investigation, while the warm air pulsed with the constant thumping of the rotor blades of the news helicopters circling above like vultures.

"Sorry, Commissioner," a voice called out from his left. "I just had to hurt some journalist's feelings."

He turned to see Assistant Chief Henry 'Buddy' Speicher approaching him.

"The media are going crazy, and they're not happy being penned up away from the crime scene. More news trucks are showing up by the minute, and they are harassing my cops."

"Deputy Commissioner Cleary is on the way, and he's bringing more of his people from Public Information to handle things," Maguire replied. "I don't need you tied up babysitting the press."

"Understood and appreciated," he replied.

"So what can you tell me, Chief?"

"Not much, unfortunately, sir," he said. "One shot and then all hell broke loose. Judging from where he was standing and line of sight, I'd say we're dealing with a long-range shot. According to the EMS folks, it went in and out, but I'm not optimistic about finding the bullet in this environment. I have the homicide guys and the local detectives canvassing the surrounding businesses and residential locations. ESU is up on the rooftops searching for evidence. Maybe we'll get lucky and find a spent shell casing, but it might not be until later this evening when we can gain access to some of the homes."

"I get the feeling that luck is going to be in short supply on this one, Chief," Maguire said.

"Sometimes that's all we've got," Speicher replied.

"And no one heard anything?" he asked. "Not even a potential direction that the shot might have come from?"

"You couldn't hear a goddamn thing with all those yahoos screaming and banging their drums. It was like a carnival."

Maguire frowned as he stared south down Hazen Street. The SEAL in him said it was the most likely area for the shot to have come from. He began to mentally tick off the number of rooftops and windows along with the approximate distance. None of them would have been a particular hard shot to make. All you needed was a decent rifle and a steady hand.

"Did the Intel folks have anything leading up to this event?"

"No," Speicher replied. "I got a briefing from them on Wednesday, and there was nothing of concern in their threat assessment. I even met with Rodriguez's team yesterday to lay out the ground rules and how any arrests would be processed, and no one seemed concerned with any potential violence. Most people seem to be in agreement with this whacko plan to shut down Rikers."

"Well, at least one person had a different opinion," Maguire said.

"That's a fair point."

A man in a dark blue polo shirt with the lettering DCPI on the breast walked over. "I'm sorry to bother you, Commissioner, but the press is asking if you can spare a minute and give them a statement."

"I'll be right over," Maguire replied. "If anything comes up, I want to know about it right away, Chief."

"Yes, sir," Speicher replied.

Maguire made his way over to the press area with Amanda Massi at his side, as the assembled reporters began shouting out questions.

He raised his hand, quieting the throng. "As you are all well aware, this incident is still in the very early stages of investigation, so there is not a lot that I am going to be able to tell you about."

"Commissioner, do we know who the shooter is?" a voice called out.

"No," Maguire replied.

"Did the Department receive any threats prior to the march?" a woman in the front asked.

"No, we were not aware of any threats directed toward the march or the participants."

"Do you think this was a right-wing attack?" she continued. "Perhaps an effort to silence Councilman Rodriguez's support for criminal justice reform?"

"What I think is that it is still much too early in this investigation to determine what the motive was or assign blame to any particular person or group," Maguire replied. "The Department does not have the luxury of speculating on crimes. We are charged with investigating them, and my people will do that to the best of their abilities."

"Councilman Rodriguez has been a very vocal opponent of the NYPD's practices and has called for cutting back its budget," another man said. "In light of that potential conflict, will you be asking for the FBI to assist you in this investigation?"

"Whatever opinions Councilman Rodriguez might have had about the Department, are his own," Maguire replied. "I can assure you that there is no conflict with us when it comes to investigating crimes, and we do so without fear or favor. There is a reason our detectives are known as the greatest in the world. So, in answer to your question, no, I will not be asking for anyone's assistance."

"Shouldn't you have expected something like this happening?" the reporter continued. "Councilman Rodriguez has been outspoken on what some would call highly controversial social issues. It is probably safe to assume that those positions made him a target."

"The population of this city is over eight million people, and the NYPD strives to provide a safe environment for these residents each and every day," Maguire replied. "That doesn't factor in the tens of millions that visit each year. With a uniformed force of just over thirty thousand, I will let you do the math, but suffice to say that we are doing the best we can, with what we have, to provide protection to everyone."

"Do you feel you are up to the task of handling the demands of this job?" another journalist asked.

"On most days," Maguire smiled. "Other days I wish I could just report on them."

Behind him, Massi reached out and whispered something to the DCPI representative.

"Thank you, Commissioner," the man interjected and brought the press conference to a close. "As soon as we have an update on the investigation, we will give you a fifteen-minute notice."

"You didn't have to save me," Maguire said, as he and Amanda walked away.

"I wasn't," she replied. "I was saving them. Besides, I just got an update. Rodriguez didn't make it out of surgery, and the mayor is on his way to the hospital."

"*Outfuckingstanding*," Maguire said, as they made their way toward the Suburban. "I guess it's time to go from the frying pan into the fire."

CHAPTER NINE

Jerusalem, Israel

Friday, May 8th, 2015 - 8:21 p.m.

"What's wrong?"

Melody turned away from the window she'd been staring out and saw her chief of staff, Genevieve Gordon, walking toward her. "Nothing, why?"

"Bullshit, Chicky," Gen laughed as she took the seat across from her friend. "The only time you stare out a window is when something is bothering you."

"Why did I hire you?" Melody asked.

"Because you need someone to keep things real," Gen replied. "You haven't been yourself all day. So what's wrong?"

"I guess I'm just feeling stressed," Melody lied.

Gen frowned, her eyebrow arching accusatorially. "You can lie to a lot of people, but I ain't one of them. So would you like to try again?"

"Shouldn't you be putting Wolfie to bed?" Melody deflected as she picked up her wineglass and took a sip.

"No, there's a soccer game on TV and Gregor is enjoying a little bonding time," Gen replied. "So there's no escape for you. Now tell me what is really going on."

"It's nothing. I'm just being silly."

"If it's nothing, then you should just tell me and stop making this like an exercise in pulling teeth."

Melody sighed. She knew there was no point in trying to protest. Gen was like a dog with a bone, and she would be unrelenting until she knew exactly what was going on.

"Remember the guy Avi introduced me to today?"

"The Mossad guy?"

"Yeah, that's him," Melody replied. "The conversation was going great until he mentioned something that kind of caught me off guard."

"What?"

"He mentioned he knew James," Melody said.

"So?"

"He also mentioned that his daughter had worked with James doing protection."

"I'm still not sure what you are getting at," Gen replied. "It's not a secret that James did protection. I'm sure he's worked with a lot of people over the years."

"No, you're right, but I mentioned that I'd spoken to him and James and commented about Harel being charming. He told me it was a disguise."

"Well, the man is with Mossad, so I can understand why James would want you to be cautious."

"I get that," Melody replied, "but it just felt strange. Like Harel was very congenial and made it sound like they knew each other well, but James was very dismissive and I got the feeling that he wasn't very fond of the man."

"Just because people have a working relationship doesn't mean that they like each other," Gen said.

"There was something else."

"What?"

"James never mentioned working with his daughter."

Gen leaned back in the chair, her mouth ajar and a quizzical look on her face. "Is that what this is about?"

"I'm just saying it was weird."

"Dear God, you're jealous."

"I'm not jealous."

"Really? Cause from here it looks like you're jealous."

"You see, this is why I didn't want to say anything," Melody scoffed.

"No, you didn't want to say anything because you knew I would call you on it," Gen replied. "It's been years since James did protection, Mel. Maybe it slipped his mind; maybe it wasn't important. Lord knows he has had a lot on his plate since becoming commissioner."

"I know, I know," Melody relented. "And you are probably a hundred percent right, and I'm reading into this way too much."

"But?" Gen asked.

"But what?"

"I know you too well, Chicky. I can see that *but* coming from a mile away."

"Maybe just do a little snooping around," Melody replied. "Lord knows you're good at that."

"You're so hurtful."

"Anyway," Melody continued. "See what you can come up with. I just want to know more about Harel and his daughter."

"I knew it!" Gen replied. "You are jealous."

"I'm the Secretary of State, Gen," Melody countered. "I'm not jealous, I'm territorial."

CHAPTER TEN

Southampton, Suffolk County, N.Y.

Friday, May 8th, 2015 - 10:09 p.m.

Maguire leaned back in his chair, watching the news coverage of the hospital press conference from earlier in the day. It still felt incredibly surreal to see himself on TV, surrounded by the mayor and other city leaders. It was a feeling that he was still uncomfortable with, even after a year and a half on the job.

Press conferences were rarely good, and this one was no exception. After beating up the politicians, the press pool soon turned its attention to him.

"Commissioner Maguire, Kate Leighton with the Brooklyn Chronicle. The city is experiencing a dramatic increase in crime. Do you think this played a role in the murder of Councilman Rodriguez, and if so, do you have an answer for those residents who live in fear?"

"It is too early in the investigation to make assumptions as to the motive behind Councilman Rodriguez's murder, but I can assure the citizens of this city that the men and women of the NYPD are doing everything in their power to keep them safe," Maguire replied. "The increase in crime we are facing is not the result of a lack of action by the Department, but a political sea change in the way crime is being prosecuted. That is something we cannot control, but that does not mean we will change the way we enforce the law."

"Commissioner, A.J. Springer with Channel 7 News. Would you care to elaborate on the Department's growing personnel shortage?"

"I won't get into the specifics, but we are facing a reduction in personnel levels," Maguire replied. "My executive staff is exploring options to put as many officers on the street as possible, without impeding the work of the non-patrol units."

"One follow-up question, if I may," Springer continued. "Some are expressing a feeling of no-confidence in your ability to lead the Department. What would you say to your detractors to convince them you are up to handling the job?"

"I wouldn't say anything," Maguire replied. "One of the great things about this country is that everyone is entitled to their opinion, and it isn't my place to say whether they are right or wrong. What I will say is that the Department is facing extraordinary times, and I am committed to doing everything I can to make the city safe for all its residents. So folks can criticize me from the sidelines all they want, but every day I am focused on doing what I can to find solutions to the problems and not vice versa."

Maguire picked up the remote and turned the TV off.

He knew exactly where the criticisms Springer referred to were emanating from. It infuriated him that the same people who had created the problem were trying to pin the blame on him, but he wouldn't take the bait. Nothing was ever resolved in a game of tit-for-tat. As hard as it was, he had to bite his tongue and keep a clear distinction between those who made the laws and those who enforced them.

He grabbed the cellphone off his desk and called Melody.

He listened as it rang several times and then a male voice answered. "Hello?"

"Who's this?" Maguire asked suspiciously.

"Thomas Barring," the man replied. "Who am I speaking to?"

"This is James Maguire. Can I speak to Secretary Anderson?"

"I'm sorry, she's not available right now," the man replied.

Maguire glanced down at his watch and did the mental calculation in his head. It was just after five a.m. local time. "When will she be available?"

"I don't know."

"Well, you're just full of useful information, aren't you?" Maguire snapped.

If the man had sensed any sarcasm, he didn't react to it. "Can I take a message?"

"No," Maguire replied and broke off the call.

He got up from the desk, with a mixture of annoyance and anger welling up inside him. Making his way to the kitchen, he refilled his glass with ice and Jameson before heading up to the upper deck.

Sitting down in one of the deck chairs, he closed his eyes and did his best to push the intrusive thoughts from his mind. There was a sense of peace in being alone, but at the same time the loneliness could be overwhelming.

Life was so much easier when I was just a door-kicker, he thought, as he took a sip of his drink.

That was one of the toughest hurdles for him professionally. Finding a way to navigate the line between who he had once been and who he was now. In many ways, his life as a SEAL, and later as a cop, had been pretty simple. Sure, the threat exposure was significantly greater, but in theory you did your job and, by the grace of God, you went home. You didn't get too concerned about the political bullshit, which was a job for the folks well above your paygrade; you just did your assignment and moved on to the next. Unfortunately, he could no longer take comfort in that luxury. Being the boss meant that there was no one above your paygrade, so you had to deal with the bullshit, whether you liked it.

Maguire glanced down at the cellphone and debated whether to call Melody again. He nixed the idea; clearly, she was busy. It wasn't that he was looking for empathy or solutions; he just needed someone to talk to.

The full moon cast brilliant streaks over the calm waters of the Shinnecock Bay. The cool, late spring air had a salty tang to it, and he felt a sense of tranquility.

He looked at the twinkling lights across the bay and then over at the house as he took a drink. It seemed surreal to him how much his life had changed in such a short time. The house was lit up, as it always was, and though he couldn't see them, he knew the grounds were being patrolled by the security team. There was a time he enjoyed being in the house, because she was there, but things had changed rapidly since Melody had taken the job of secretary of state. He didn't begrudge her; in fact, he had openly encouraged her to take it, just as she had encouraged him to accept the job Rich had offered him, but in retrospect he couldn't help but wonder if it had all been worth it.

Maguire felt a pang of guilt over feeling angry about the phone call. He knew the demands that he faced, and certainly her job was even more complex and time consuming, but he couldn't shake the feeling of being disconnected. He couldn't just sit around the house alone, waiting for her to pop back in for a visit. The isolation had begun to make him feel more like a possession, another piece of art that adorned her house, and that was something he detested.

These feelings were the reason he had never had a committed relationship while he was in the teams. It wasn't right to come and go out of someone's life on a regular basis; here for three weeks, gone for three months. Never knowing if or when the next return would be or if you'd come back to a Jody, military slang for someone who hooks up with lonely girlfriends or wives while their significant others are away serving their country, who's been keeping your bed warm.

Maguire laughed, the effect of the whiskey making it sound more comical than it actually was, as he raised his glass and began singing an old cadence.

"C-130 rollin' down the strip;

SEAL Team froggy gonna take a little trip.

Mission top secret, destination unknown;

I don't know if I'm comin' home."

I wonder what they call a Jody in political circles? he thought. *Probably a Thomas. Then again, everyone is fucking everyone else in politics, so I doubt they even care.*

It was because of all this that he found himself spending most of his time where he genuinely felt at home, which was on the houseboat docked on the other side of Meadow Lane. It had been drummed into him at BUD/S that you always made your way back to the water, and sitting here, staring out into the blackness of the bay, he felt at peace.

I wonder if any other police commissioners ever lived on a boat? he wondered. *Roosevelt would have, but I doubt any of the others would have.*

Maguire had a photo of Theodore Roosevelt hanging up in his office. Prior to ascending to the presidency of the United States, Roosevelt had been the president of the Board of New York City Police Commissioners. During his tenure, Roosevelt not only brought about radical changes within the Department, but he drew the ire of the powerful Tammany Hall political machine as well. Later, as governor of New York, he would sign an act that replaced the police commission with a single police commissioner.

Police Commissioner.

The title was still foreign to him, and it was a role that he was still trying to acclimate himself to since he was thrust into it after Rich's murder. It wasn't that he considered himself incapable of performing the job; it was just that it felt like an odd fit. He was a knuckle-dragger; the proverbial hammer that you brought in to fix a stubborn problem. Rich Stargold was a seasoned political operator; a former Secret Service agent who'd been around the political world long enough that he understood its machinations. When Rich had asked him to be his first deputy, he wasn't opposed to it, because he viewed that role as helping his friend navigate the internal waters of the job. Now that he was the P.C. he had to navigate both the internal and external politics, and it felt like he was sinking.

"I think it's fair to say that you suck at this," he grumbled, as he took a drink.

His reverie was cut short by the crackle of rubber on gravel. Maguire glanced over the port side just as the door of the black Land Rover opened.

"Well, fuck me blind," he muttered, setting his drink down on the table.

Maguire leaned back in the chair and closed his eyes and waited. A few moments later he heard footsteps coming up the stairs.

"It's been a long time since you've been here."

"I was in the neighborhood and thought I'd stop by," she said, as she ran her hand softly across his shoulder. "Permission to come aboard?"

"You're supposed to ask that *before* you board."

"I was always bad at following the rules," Tzviya Harel replied as she took the seat across from him.

"Unless they were your father's rules, Zee."

"Those were orders."

Maguire picked up his drink. "So, do you come here often?"

"Most of the time the lights are off," she said.

"Are you stalking me?"

"If I were, you wouldn't know about it."

"Don't kid yourself," Maguire laughed. "You want a drink?"

"That would be nice."

Maguire took his glass and retreated below, returning a few minutes later with two drinks. Zee was staring out over the water, and the way the moonlight reflected off her long black hair gave him pause, as forgotten feelings rose to the surface. She turned to face him slowly, and for a moment they just stared at one another. They didn't have to say anything; their eyes conveyed what they were thinking.

He swallowed hard, pushing down the emotions he was feeling.

"So what brings you here?" he asked, handing her the glass, as he took his seat.

"I had a meeting with Yoni," she replied, taking a sip. "The prime minister is coming into town at the end of the month. He's meeting with your POTUS in D.C. and then coming to New York for a fundraiser."

"So, is this a business visit?"

Zee shook her head. "No, it's strictly personal."

"So why are you here?"

She looked away from him and back across Meadow Lane. "How come you're not in the house?"

"I didn't realize that my housing accommodations were such a hot topic issue."

"I was just asking a question," she replied.

"You know me; I like simple things."

"You're right, I do know you.

"So why are you here?" he asked.

"I like simple things too," she smiled.

"This is anything but simple, Zee."

"It's as simple or as hard as we make it."

"I have a fiancée," Maguire replied.

"That's not my problem."

"She's the secretary of state, and she has the luxury of being able to sit down and have a friendly chat with your prime minister. Trust me when I say it's a problem for both of us."

Zee set her drink down on the table and stared at him. "Tell me you don't think about me. Tell me that when you're sitting out here, all alone, that you don't remember what we shared."

"That's not fair."

"Fair?" Zee scoffed. "None of this has been fair, James. I didn't want to let you go, but your life meant more to me than my happiness. I tried with all my heart; tried to move on, tried to let go, but nothing could dull the pain I felt in my heart for you. My world almost ended the day you got shot, and I knew no matter what, I would love you until my last breath."

"Your father had a chat with Melody," Maguire said, trying to deflect the conversation.

Zee smirked. "I assume he was probing. Trying to find out just what the new secretary knows or doesn't know."

"Maybe she knows more about things than she says," Maguire replied.

Zee stared at him, her face impassive, like a player in a high-stakes poker game deciding whether to fold or go all in. She picked up her drink and took a sip as she chose her response. "No, I don't think she does."

"Why do you say that?" Maguire asked.

"Because if she did, you'd be happy, and I wouldn't be here."

"I don't follow."

"Sure you do, James. I'm not saying you don't love her; I'm just saying that Melody doesn't know about me because you've never told her. It's a part of you that you have kept hidden from her, because you have truly never let go of me; of us. If you had, you would have told me to move on."

Fucking spies, he thought, as he picked up his drink and stared silently at the water.

What troubled him most was that she wasn't wrong in her assessment. He knew she wasn't calling him out; she was just stating the obvious.

Zee leaned back in her seat, joining him in the silence, which only made the tension more palpable.

"You know you're infuriating, don't you?" he said after a couple of minutes had passed.

"I've been called worse."

"What if I told you that I was happy?"

Zee finished her drink, set the glass down on the table, and got up.

"You can tell yourself that you're happy," she said, as she straddled his legs and sat down in his lap, staring into his eyes. "You can say that you've moved on and do whatever it takes to make yourself feel better, but what you can't do is forget, James. Even you can't erase the memories; our memories."

"That's the problem, Zee," he replied, as his hand gently caressed her cheek. "They are memories. Memories of our past; of things that once were, but we don't live in that world anymore."

"It doesn't have to be that way," she replied, taking his hand into hers.

"Why are you doing this?" he asked, the tone of his voice making it more of a plea than a question.

"Because I told myself all the same lies, James," she said. "I told myself that I did it to protect you. That time would make it easier and that I would find someone new. My brain was saying all the right things, but every night I would lay in bed and my heart would die another death."

"We're not the same people, Zee," he whispered. "Our lives didn't stop and, whether we want to admit it, we have moved on."

"That's not you," she snapped, as she pivoted in his lap and extended her hand toward the house. "This is you settling because you think it's the only choice you have. You can pretend all you want, but if it was who you are now, if you really had moved on, you wouldn't be here alone. I don't know whether you are trying to convince me or yourself."

"When did you get your doctoral degree in psychology?"

"I'm still working on my bedside manner," Zee smirked.

"I bet you are."

"You forget I know the real you," she replied, her tone softening. "You might wear the suit of the police commissioner, James, but it is an ill-fitting one. It's like you are one of those caged animals in the zoo remembering better days. You play the role because you have to, because it's expected of you, but it's not what you want. You don't do desks well, and you're no damn politician."

"Maybe I've just realized that I can accomplish more this way."

"Ha!" she laughed. "Name me another person in your position who has gotten his hands dirty like you? You'll never shake that door-kicker mentality. God only knows how you would handle being the FBI director."

"Jesus Christ," Maguire laughed. "Is there anything you fuckers don't know?"

"There is one thing I don't know," she smiled.

"And what would that be?"

"Do you still love me?"

CHAPTER ELEVEN

Southampton, Suffolk County, N.Y.

Saturday, May 9th, 2015 - 10:09 p.m.

His mouth found hers before either of them could think, before hesitation had a chance to intervene. The kiss was fierce, crushing, and desperate. Denial and responsibility bled out in one reckless instant, as Maguire pressed her against the wall, his hands tangled in her hair, while her nails dug into his back trying to claw him even closer, deeper, into the very marrow of her soul.

This was their hunger.

This was starvation breaking its fast as they gave into their insatiable desire.

Clothes became obstacles, and neither of them cared how they came off. A button tore loose, fabric ripped. Zee gasped as his hands slid over her skin, pulling her tighter, and he devoured the sound with another kiss. It was raw, almost violent in its urgency, yet mixed with an undercurrent of passionate tenderness in the moments their lips lingered, reluctant to part.

They stumbled together toward the bed, their bodies' never breaking contact, collapsing onto it in a tangle of limbs. He rolled, she followed, neither willing to surrender control, both desperate to consume and be consumed; two warriors who had turned the bedroom into their battlefield.

The rhythm built like combat, thrust and counter-thrust, every motion a clash of raw passion and desire.

Their bodies became a tangle of thrusts and grips, sweat and heat. The sheets twisted around them like chains they were both intent on breaking.

Every motion was war.

Every kiss, a weapon.

Every gasp, a surrender.

Her legs wrapped around him, pulling him closer, locking him in place, as her body took him deep inside her; waves of pleasure crashing over her with every thrust.

His breath burned against her skin as his hands roamed, urgent, greedy, claiming her like a man who knew she was both salvation and destruction. When she pulled his head down and kissed him again, her lips trembled, not from hesitation, but from the sheer violence of her need.

The world outside the room didn't exist; only the storm that was their love.

The sheets twisted beneath them, sweat dampened their skin, and their breaths turned ragged. Her legs clamped him like a vise, pulling his hips into the hollow of her. He answered with long, hard strokes that bowed her back and made the headboard rattle.

The sounds of their passion, half-scream, half-moan, grew like a crescendo, as he found the small, secret places inside her that made her whole body arch and her fingers clench the linen beneath her into white knots.

Sweat slicked their bodies; the scent of sex and desire saturating the sheets. When she rode him, it was not softness but a fierce claim, each movement a punctuation mark declaring him hers.

Their climax built until it tore through them, shattering and binding in the same instant.

Maguire collapsed onto her and she wrapped her arms around him tightly. They clung to each other in the aftermath, their bodies' slick and their breaths uneven.

As the frenzy slowed, as the rhythm softened, tenderness rose from the ashes of their chaos. His hand cradled her cheek, his eyes searching hers, both of them trembling from more than exertion. In that gaze lived the truth neither had dared to speak.

Zee buried her head against his shoulder, her tears mingling with his sweat.

"I knew you still loved me, James," she whispered, her voice breaking on the edge of relief.

•••

Morning light spilled across the room, gentle and golden.

Zee stirred, a smile forming on her face as she reached out across the sheets, seeking his warmth, and ready to pull him close again, but her fingers touched only cool linen.

Her eyes snapped opened and her heart sank. The other half of the bed was empty.

She sat up slowly, the smile fading into something hollow. For a moment she didn't breathe as the truth slid into her chest like a blade.

It hadn't happened. Not now. Not last night.

What she had felt, every kiss, every touch, was nothing more than the cruel, reoccurring dream that tormented her sleep; the memory of their first night together, replayed by a heart that refused to let go.

She pressed her face into her hands, shuddering, as the room closed in with its silence. When she finally lowered them, her eyes glistened with unshed tears.

"I still love you," she whispered to the emptiness, though she knew the only person who would ever hear it was herself.

And then came another memory, but this one was even crueler.

The office.

The cold, white walls of the sterile room were devoid of anything even remotely warm; a perfect metaphor for the hardness of the man who stood in front of her.

Her father, Brigadier General Shay Harel, stood behind his desk in his meticulous uniform, his knuckles whitening as he pressed them into the desktop, as if to punctuate the argument he was making.

She had grown up under that hard, unflinching gaze. A man accustomed to getting what he wanted, both at home and in the field. She and her siblings had not grown up as children, but as future lions of Judah.

She'd been summoned to return home immediately to discuss an *urgent* matter. Another person might have wondered if it was personal or professional, but in the Harel family everything was business.

"I'm warning you, Tzviya," he declared, his voice stripped of even the slightest hint of paternal compassion. "If you don't end this, I will."

His eyes had held no doubt, no hesitation. The implication hung heavy in the air; a sucker punch that stole her breath: James would be *dealt with.*

The words were like a blade that was cutting her from the man she loved, while being wielded by the man that was supposed to love her.

Accusations flew about Maguire and his background. That he was only using her to obtain information on government activities that could be used against them by the Americans. It was all baseless, but that didn't matter. Her father was a firm believer in the old proverb that, '*An ounce of prevention is worth a pound of cure.*'

The pain she felt soon turned into a white-hot fury, searing past the uniform, past the title, past the rank. She wasn't a subordinate standing before a superior officer. She was a daughter staring down a father.

"If anything happens to him," she had hissed, her voice low and trembling with rage, "if you hurt one solitary hair on his head, I promise that you will see a side of me that you'll take to your grave. And no one, not you, not your army, not this entire damn country, will be able to stop me."

The silence in that office had been suffocating. His expression had never cracked, but she had seen the flicker in his eyes — the recognition that his daughter meant every word.

Now, years later, in the empty room with the cold sheets, Zee pressed her fists to her eyes and shook, the memory of that moment clawing into her chest.

Her father might have stolen James from her, but he could never stop her from loving him.

CHAPTER TWELVE

1 Police Plaza, Manhattan, N.Y.

Monday, May 11th, 2015 - 8:21 a.m.

Yes.

Maguire sat in the leather chair, staring somberly out the office window, as the word still reverberated in his mind days later.

It was an unflinching answer to a question he had struggled with since that fateful meeting on the cold, windswept tarmac at LaGuardia Airport. From the moment he saw her, he had been struggling with his emotions. They were like a long dormant volcano that had suddenly erupted, and he could no longer suppress the feelings that flowed out.

He had done everything in his power to deny it; even blamed it on the Jameson, but the question had barely left her lips when he'd answered.

You can't just turn off your feelings.

Zee was right; she usually was.

He'd spent years pretending that he had moved on when, in reality, all he had done was simply suppress his emotions. With no other viable option at his disposal, he was left with having to grudgingly accept the fact that the relationship was over and find a way to move forward. With the revelation that it was her father, and not Zee, who was behind the breakup, and that she had left him to spare his life, Maguire's world had been ripped apart and the anger and bitterness he once had was replaced with questions of what could have been. He loved Melody, but he also couldn't deny his feelings for Zee, and he knew he had to find a resolution to these relational problems sooner rather than later.

The two women were polar opposites. Melody was the type of woman who could walk into a black-tie event and capture the room with her presence. She could hold her own in a boardroom meeting or political event and charm even the most recalcitrant attendee. If Zee was at the same event, she'd prefer to be in the shadows instead of the limelight, and she'd have a plan in place to kill everyone in the room if need be. In a way, Maguire felt more comfortable in Zee's company. They were two warriors, and they shared a bond that others would never understand.

You're not at war anymore, he thought. *Maybe that's why you're not happy.*

As simplistic as the thought was, it held merit. Despite the dangers, Maguire's time in the Navy held the fondest memories for him. There was a level of camaraderie that couldn't be explained to a civilian. Yes, being on patrol was similar, the bond you created with other cops working in high-crime areas, but there was something different, something missing. When a cop finished his shift, he hung up his uniform and usually went home. In the military, there was no hanging up the uniform, and home was often a foreign place that you didn't see for long periods at a time. The same guys you ran operations with were the same ones you hung out with afterward. Often you were closer to them than you were with any other family or friends, just by the same dangers you faced together.

He had a protective instinct with Melody, but Zee he could go into battle with, and it felt like his heart and mind were being torn between the two.

"Knock, knock."

Maguire looked up to see Billy Walsh, the chief of detectives, standing in the doorway.

"I can come back if this isn't a good time."

"No, it's fine. I could use a break from the mental gymnastics going on in my head, Billy," Maguire replied. "Pull up a chair and bring me up to speed on what's going on."

Walsh frowned as he took the seat across from him. "I wish I were giving you good news, but it's mediocre at best."

"I take it you haven't identified the shooter?"

Walsh shook his head. "No, but we know where the shot came from. The One-Fourteen got a call about a past burglary Sunday afternoon. When the sector arrived, the homeowners advised them that the backdoor had been forced open, but that there didn't seem to be anything missing. The location was about a block and a half away from the shooting scene, so they called the precinct detectives, who responded to the scene and determined that one of the second-floor bedrooms had a direct line of sight. Crime Scene went out and did some analysis. Based on the location where Rodriguez was standing at the time of the shooting, they are confident it's a match."

"And they didn't find evidence left behind, did they?" Maguire asked.

"Nothing," Walsh replied. "Whoever did this was a pro. No fingerprints, policed the brass, and was in and out before anyone was the wiser."

"What was the delay in reporting it?"

"Homeowners both work in Manhattan and went out of town," Walsh explained. "They attended a concert down in Atlantic City on Saturday and didn't come home till Sunday."

"Did you verify their story?"

"Yeah, I had a couple of our guys go over to their jobs, and both were working at the time of the shooting. They also ran their names, and neither of them has any record, not even a damn parking ticket."

"And we still don't have any witnesses?" Maguire asked.

"Nada," Walsh replied. "Most people were at work, and those who were around noticed nothing odd until after the shot was fired. By the time people realized what had happened, the scene was swarming with cops, and it was too chaotic. If we're talking about one person, he or she could have slipped away unnoticed."

"What about security cameras?"

"There are a couple of commercial places with them, but most of them are focused on the businesses themselves, front doors, back doors, that kind of thing, and none had a line of sight toward the subject location."

Maguire frowned. "We can't catch a break, can we?"

“We’re still investigating, so there is hope.”

“I already know the answer, but did Rodriguez have any haters?”

“My people have been talking to his staff about any threats he might have received, which were quite a bit. We’ve been running names and interviewing those we can identify. We also have a subpoena out to the phone company for any calls coming into his office and should have that later today.”

“Any you consider viable threats?”

“No,” Walsh replied. “At least not among those we’ve identified. Most of them are just disgruntled single-issue people who didn’t like where Rodriguez stood on things.”

“Anyone who was pissed off about the proposed Rikers closure?”

“Some, but so far they appear to just be angry ranters and not the trigger-pulling types. We’ll know more once we get the phone numbers back, but my gut tells me that whoever did this was too calculating to leave an evidence trail behind.”

“That’s my fear,” Maguire replied, “along with the potential for a copycat.”

“You think this might be the start of something?” Walsh asked.

“People are pissed, Billy, and crime is surging. It takes only one person to lay the foundation for others to follow. We both know this city has more than its fair share of nut-jobs.”

“That it does,” Walsh replied, “and you’re going to have every council member beating down your door to demand protection.”

“There has already been a few calls,” Maguire said.

“I can’t say that I blame them.”

“I don’t blame them either,” Maguire replied. “The problem is that I don’t know where I’m going to find a couple of hundred extra cops to play babysitter until we catch whoever is responsible, when I can’t even fill radio cars for patrol.”

“I wish I could help you, Boss.”

"Remember you said that when I come knocking on your door for personnel."

"Speaking of personnel," Walsh said. "I just got word Chief Acevedo put in his papers, so we no longer have a C.O. for Staten Island Detectives."

"When?"

"I got the call this morning from the Pension Section. Claimed he just couldn't take the commute anymore and had family issues that required his full-time attention."

"I'm kind of shocked he lasted as long as he did," Maguire replied, "but I'm skeptical about his reasons."

"I'm sure you had your reasons, but *demotion-promotions* tend to sour people."

Maguire nodded.

To the outside world, being named commanding officer of Detective Borough Staten Island was a significant accomplishment, but to those familiar with the inner workings of the Department, Deputy Chief Miguel Acevedo had actually been demoted; going from his position as executive officer of the Detective Bureau, where he was the number two person in charge of all detectives city-wide, to a significantly smaller subordinate command, after it was discovered that he had been leaking information. Although this latter part had been kept silent and was known only to a handful of people.

Under any other circumstance Acevedo would have been investigated and terminated, but his close connection to Nydia Flores, the person to whom he had leaked the information, made that choice extremely difficult.

So, rather than terminate Acevedo, Maguire had *promoted* him, giving him his own command, as well as a significantly longer commute; something commonly referred to in the NYPD as *highway therapy*, where an officer has additional time added to their daily drive to and from work to reflect on their transgressions.

Maguire had thought Acevedo would fold quickly, but he lasted six months as commanding officer, allowing him the opportunity to embrace his new role long enough to save face, before pulling the pin.

"Needs of the Department always trump personal career paths," Maguire replied. "It's the nature of the beast."

He trusted Walsh implicitly, which is the reason he had promoted him to Chief of Detectives, after making Sandy Barnes his First Deputy Commissioner, but some information had to remain on a need to know basis.

"I guess that's one way of explaining how two Brooklyn North guys find themselves sitting on the fourteenth floor," Walsh laughed.

"Well, you earned your spot, Billy. I was just parachuted in."

"Bullshit," Walsh replied. "Regardless of how you ended up in that chair doesn't negate what you did over the course of your career. We both could write up a laundry list of ass-kissers that rose up through the ranks without ever doing an iota of what you accomplished."

"I appreciate that," Maguire smiled, "but I still might have to steal some of your people."

"Needs of the Department," Walsh laughed, as he rapped his knuckles on the arm of the chair. "Speaking of which, I need to get my nose back to the grindstone if we are going to solve this case."

"Keep me posted," Maguire replied, as Walsh headed out of the office.

"10-4."

Maguire waited until the man was gone, then got up and walked out of his office and motioned for Detective Angelo Antonucci to come in.

"What's up, Boss?"

"I just got word that Acevedo put in his papers this morning for family reasons, Ang."

"I take it you don't believe him?"

"A part of me would love nothing more than to think he's going to be sitting around his pool all summer, sipping on Coronas and living his best life, but…"

"Nuff said," Antonucci replied. "I'll look into it and see what turns up."

"Thank you," Maguire replied. "And this stays between you and me. We have enough going on, and I don't want to make a mountain out of a molehill only to find out that he's spending his days bouncing his grandkid on his knee while they watch cartoons."

"Understood."

CHAPTER THIRTEEN

Brooklyn Heights, Brooklyn, N.Y.

Monday, May 11th, 2015 - 12:47 p.m.

Mordecai Schiff shuffled into the kitchen, the shower he had just taken doing nothing to alleviate the aches and pains coursing through his body. He filled his coffee cup and grabbed the newspaper from the kitchen island before making his way out to the sunroom.

He'd taken a rare day off from work to spend the morning playing racquetball and then having brunch with a childhood friend, who had flown up from Florida to attend a funeral.

At sixty-nine, he was fully aware that funerals were becoming all too common an occurrence in his circle.

Times like these were a constant reminder of the fragility of life and the inexorable journey he was on that led to a destination no one wanted to arrive at.

This is the shit they never prepare you for when you are young, he thought, as he sat down in one of the patio chairs.

He had buried his wife, Ethel, last July, and now he was facing a future alone and being forced to retire from the job he had loved and held for nearly four decades.

Retire to what? he thought. *This? A mausoleum of loneliness and tragedy?*

Forty years ago, life was so much different; so much more alive. Back then, Schiff was a charismatic young defense attorney, known for his oratory skills that routinely swayed jurors to return not guilty verdicts. His legal prowess had led the local Democratic party to push him to run for election, which he easily won, but his legal abilities did not make him any friends, because he held other attorneys to the same benchmark he'd set for himself. It wasn't his fault that they were ill-prepared for his courtroom.

He knew that the day of his retirement would be filled with false congratulations and empty platitudes from people eager to see him walk out the door.

He took a sip of coffee and stared at the vacant chair next to him. Almost a year later and he still had not come to terms with her passing.

His legal career had always taken precedence in his life, but Ethel had stood unselfishly by his side. Even through two miscarriages, she continued to support his dreams and aspirations. Now he was left alone, with no idea what to do with the freedom that his retirement was supposedly going to provide.

On days like this, they would walk along the promenade across the street from their brownstone. Ethel loved to sit and admire the Manhattan skyline and the tulips that bloomed in the spring. It had always been a chore for him to engage in these activities, especially with all the work he had, but now, in her absence, he realized that he had sacrificed far too much for all the wrong things.

He was alone now. No wife, no children, no real friends, and for the first time in his life he truly understood what that word meant.

The chirping of the cellphone drew him out of his thoughts, and he reached down to pick it up.

"Hello?" he asked, fighting to control the subtle tremble in his voice.

"Hi, is this Judge Schiff?"

"Who's asking?"

"Sir, my name is Alan Greenberg. I'm a writer for the Northeast Legal Gazette, and I was wondering if you would be interested in talking to me on the topic of criminal justice and bail reform?"

Schiff was well-acquainted with the NLG, and actually had a subscription to their magazine, albeit under his wife's name. The NGL was known for its liberal stance on criminal justice, many of which were in line with Schiff's personal views. Greenberg was a familiar name to him, and he'd enjoyed the way the man wrote and framed his arguments for the reader.

"Well, those are two topics that I am passionate about," Schiff replied.

"That's wonderful to hear, Judge," Greenberg replied.

"Please call me Bruce. I'm near the end of my career, and I don't stand on formality in social dealings."

"That's very kind of you, Judg... I mean, Bruce," Greenberg said. "Looking forward, the NGL wants to shed light on the need for judicial reforms in light of the social issues we face, to include the negative impact of bail constraints that disproportionately affect the at-risk communities on the lower end of the socio-economic ladder."

"Well, I would love to have that discussion, but as a sitting judge, I have to tread carefully. While I share many of the same views, and there is a growing awareness of the disparities within our system, we must realize that there is also a strong political opposition to change, so I must do my utmost to maintain the air of impartiality in my waning days on the bench."

"I understand," Greenberg continued. "What I'm looking to do is present a series of continuing articles that explore the changing legal world we find ourselves in. To start, I'd like to do a *who's who*, highlighting the careers and accomplishments of distinguished jurists, such as you, who have witnessed firsthand the ramifications of legal practices that have brought us here and to discuss potential solutions to alleviate the problems we are facing. Obviously, we respect the position you are in and the need to separate your private views from the ones you maintain professionally. In that regard, we would be more than happy to provide you with an outline of the questions first so you can decide which you are comfortable expounding on."

"That would be outstanding," Schiff replied, as the conversation was interrupted by a series of shrill beeps. "Can you hold on for a moment? I have another call coming in."

"Sure," Greenberg replied.

Schiff placed the call on hold and answered the other. "Hello?"

Silence filled the phone's speaker.

"Hello? Is anyone there?" Schiff asked.

A moment later, the silence was replaced by a dial tone.

"Asshole," Schiff muttered as he reconnected to the other call. "Alan, are you there?"

"I am, sir," Greenberg replied.

"Would this be an in-person interview or over the phone?"

"Personally, I prefer doing in-person, but I will let you decide what works best for you."

"Well, I can give you my clerk's email address, and you can send the questions to her for my review," Schiff replied. "Once everything has been vetted, she can make arrangements with you to set up a time for a meeting."

"That sounds perfect," Greenberg replied. "I'm ready to take down her email whenever you are."

"Okay, it's abhirsch@—"

The doorbell chime cut Schiff off.

"Alan, can you hold on a minute? I'm expecting documents for my signature, and I think they just arrived."

"Sure," Greenberg replied.

Schiff got up, making his way back into the house, laying the cellphone on the island as he made his way to the door. He looked through the peephole and saw a court officer standing outside, his back to the door, taking in the view over the East River toward Manhattan.

He opened the door, and the man turned around.

"Judge Schiff?"

"Yes, do you have the paperwork for me?"

"Yes, sir," he replied, holding up a worn, brown leather pouch. "Everything is inside."

As Schiff reached for the pouch, the man took a step forward and rammed it into Schiff's midsection, hard enough that it caused him to stumble backward and lose his footing, and he collapsed onto the marble entryway floor.

Shock turned to rage, and Schiff exploded. “How dare you! Don’t you know who I am?”

“I do,” the man said dispassionately as he stepped into the foyer and stood over Schiff. He withdrew a silenced 9mm pistol from the pouch. “And you’ve been found guilty and sentenced to death.”

Schiff’s eyes bulged in fear as the man pulled the trigger, the three 147-grain subsonic bullets striking him twice in the chest and once in the head, ending his life.

The man then stepped back, replacing the pistol into the pouch, and shut the front door with a gloved hand as he left.

Inside the kitchen, Alan Greenberg’s voice could be heard on the phone. “Judge Schiff? Are you there? Hello? I don’t know. He said someone was at the door, and I heard some muffled sounds and now nothing.”

CHAPTER FOURTEEN

Brooklyn Heights, Brooklyn, N.Y.

Monday, May 11th, 2015 - 2:11 p.m.

Maguire watched as a uniformed officer raised up the yellow crime scene tape, allowing Mike Torres to pull the Suburban onto Columbia Heights. He opened the door as soon as the SUV came to a stop and hopped out before Amanda could even get out.

He didn't know why, but there was a heightened level of anxiety that had a vice-like grip on him.

"What do we have?" he asked as he approached a plainclothes officer with a lieutenant's shield clipped to his belt.

"Sector Adam responded to an anonymous complaint of a possible aided case at 1301 hours, Commissioner," Lieutenant Alex Ramos, of the Eight-Four Precinct Detective Squad, replied. "When they arrived, they found an elderly white male, later identified as Judge Schiff, lying face up and bleeding profusely from an apparent gunshot wound to the head, as well as a wound to the chest area. They called for a bus and checked for a pulse, but couldn't find one. When EMS arrived, they pronounced him DOA."

"Any witnesses?" Maguire asked.

"None so far," Ramos replied. "I've got my people canvassing the surrounding area right now, and I'm getting some folks from the borough to come over and help us out. He has one of those fancy doorbells that has a camera on it, so I've requested TARU come out and give us a hand."

"Do you have any reason to believe this was part of a robbery or burglary gone bad?" Maguire asked.

"Doesn't feel like it, sir," Ramos replied. "The victim was dressed down, so he was most likely in the house at the time. Detectives found his cellphone lying on the kitchen island. My guys are pulling the phone records right now to see who he was talking to. His wallet was on the hutch, next to his keys, with money still in it. It looks to me like this was a targeted hit."

Maguire nodded his head as his brain made the connection with the anxiety that he had been feeling.

"Excuse me for a minute, Lieutenant," he said, pulling his cell phone out and walking back to the SUV.

"Is everything okay, Boss?" Amanda asked as she opened the door.

"I don't think so," he said, as he got back in.

He selected a number, and the phone rang twice before he heard Antonucci answer. "What do you need, Boss?"

"I'm out in Brooklyn, Ang," Maguire said. "A judge named Mordecai Schiff was killed at his home."

"Bruce Schiff?" Antonucci asked.

"Yeah, do you know him?"

"I know of him," Antonucci replied. "Or at least I know of his reputation. Most cops weren't big fans of him and referred to him as 'Let 'em loose Bruce.'"

"That's the one," Maguire replied.

"What do you need from me?"

"I want you and Tonya to drop whatever you are doing and get up to speed on both the Rodriguez shooting and this one."

"You think they may be connected?"

"Let's just say that I want to make sure that they aren't," Maguire replied. "I want you to get into the weeds and see if there is anything that links these two killings; whether they knew each other personally or professionally, any mutual contacts, events they might have attended, anything tangible."

"We can do it," Antonucci replied, "but it's going to take a lot of time."

"If you've got anything important going on, just give it to Chief Martin and tell him I said to reassign it. I need you focused on just this."

"You think someone targeted these two?"

"My gut is telling me not to bet against it, Ang."

"Okay, Tonya and I will get right on it. When do you need the information by?"

"Last Friday," Maguire said.

"10-4."

Maguire ended the call and placed another.

"Yeah, Boss?" Billy Walsh answered.

"I'm out in Brooklyn, Billy. Someone killed Judge Schiff."

"I got the call," Walsh replied. "I'm on my way down from the Bronx."

"Listen, I want you to head this one up personally."

"No problem," Walsh replied. "I'm already getting updates about it."

"I also wanted to let you know that I gave a heads-up to Antonucci and I'm having him do a little legwork on it as well, so make sure that your people are aware that he's working on my behalf."

"Uhm, sure," Walsh said. "Is everything all right?"

Maguire could hear the concern in the man's voice. "It's all good, Billy, and trust me, I'm not looking to step on any toes, and I have the utmost confidence in you and your people. I don't want to read too much into this one, but I've got a bad feeling about it, and Ang has a knack for connecting the most nebulous of dots."

"Well, I'm not going to say no to an extra set of eyes. I'll make sure they give him everything he needs."

"Thank you," Maguire replied. "I'm heading over to City Hall to update the mayor on what is going on. Let me know if anything comes up."

Walsh didn't necessarily like the idea, but it wasn't exactly wise to say no to his boss. At least it wasn't if you wanted to keep your day job. He had no doubts as to the capabilities of Antonucci; he was, after all, a detective, but he wasn't *his* detective. He'd ensure that Antonucci would get the access he needed, but he'd also make sure that *his* people were on their A-game. If a break came in the case, he wanted it to come from within the Detective Bureau.

"Will do," Walsh replied.

Maguire ended the call and stared out the passenger window toward Manhattan. The bright morning sun had given way to angry clouds, and the thick gray pall that hung over the skyline was like the smoke of a smoldering fire just waiting to erupt.

"I guess it's time to enter the lion's den, Mike."

Torres dropped the SUV into drive and pulled away.

CHAPTER FIFTEEN

Southampton, Suffolk County, N.Y.

Monday, May 11th, 2015 - 9:11 p.m.

"Are we all right?" Melody asked.

The question caught Maguire off-guard. "Yeah, why?" he asked cautiously.

"You don't seem okay. Thomas told me you called, and I tried calling you back yesterday, but it just went to voicemail, and I never heard back."

Maguire took a deep breath as he searched for the right words. He didn't want to get into it with her; he didn't want to try navigating feelings while thousands of miles apart, but he knew Melody, and she was not the type of person to be placated easily.

"Honestly, I'm feeling more than a bit overwhelmed," he said, which wasn't a lie.

"What's wrong?"

"I've got a nagging feeling that I have a potential shitstorm brewing and at the same time I find myself having to contend with the crown prince of the clowns running City Hall."

"Oh, James," she said. "I wish I could be there for you."

"This isn't your fight," he replied. "Besides, you have enough on your own plate right now."

"What's going on with Barone?"

"He's trying to push more budget cuts on me so they can dump more money into these bullshit social programs," Maguire replied. "I'm bleeding cops and this fucktard thinks everything is all rainbows and unicorns."

"Can't you just explain to him that you have no room to cut?" she asked.

"They just don't get it," he replied. "It's like trying to teach calculus to third graders. They get fixated on the bottom-line number and don't consider all the line items that money is spent on. All they see is five billion dollars and think, 'Well surely you can cut some of that.' They bitch about overtime, but then blow up my phone when crime rises in their district. Do they just expect them to work for free? I've gone so far as to cut out a hundred and fifty million from capital expenditures, but that's still not enough. They sit in their fancy offices and don't give a shit that my cops are working in buildings that, if they were privately owned, would be condemned by the city."

"I don't know what to say," Melody replied.

"It's not your problem, Angel, I'm just venting. That's the problem with being the boss; you don't have anyone to complain to, and you know that I don't do well playing these stupid games."

"Oh, I get it," she replied. "I at least have Gen to go off on. It doesn't fix the problem, but it at least helps to get it out of my system. Hey, if it's any consolation, I could add the Department in as an NGO and send you some State Department funding. I bet you could use it a lot more than Kyrgyzstan."

"If only it were that easy," Maguire laughed. "Added to all of that, I have a pair of homicides I'm dealing with that could get ugly fast."

"What happened?"

"A sniper took out a city council member from Queens on Friday, and I just had a judge killed at his home today."

"You think they are isolated incidents?" Melody asked.

"Maybe," Maguire replied.

"You don't sound very convincing."

"I don't know. I could just be reading too much into it."

"What do your SEAL spidey-senses tell you?"

"That's the problem," Maguire replied. "They're not telling me anything. It just feels like everything is normal, but I'm getting these random warning lights that are flashing red, and it doesn't make any sense to me. I don't even know how to respond to them."

"Remember, 'Absence of evidence is not evidence of absence,'" Melody replied. "Just because you can't see the problem now does not mean it doesn't exist. Long before you can see the smoke and flames of a house fire, there is usually a hidden defect that went undetected. Trust your instincts, Cowboy. You'll figure it out."

"Unfortunately, without anything to go on, I'm just going to have to wait until something else happens."

"Or maybe these were just disparate acts and it won't even be an issue."

"I hope you're right," Maguire replied. "By the way, who is Thomas?"

"What?"

"Thomas, the guy who answered your phone the other morning."

"Oh, no one really, just a new member of my advance team," Melody said. "Why?"

"It just caught me off guard that a guy was answering your phone at 5 a.m."

"James Patrick Maguire, are you serious?"

"I was just curious, Angel," he protested.

"Well, if you have to know, I gave him my phone because I was on a private call with Cook finalizing a few things before I headed out to Belgium, but if you feel the need to verify—"

"No, I don't need to verify anything," he interjected. "I'm sorry, I'm just stressed. You usually give your phone to Gen when you're not available."

"She went ahead to Brussels to make sure everything was running smoothly before I arrived. I can't get into it right now, but I'll just say that there's been an uptick in thunder in the east."

"Doesn't shock me," Maguire replied.

Even with Cook's reputation, foreign actors always rattled their sabers with a new U.S. presidential administration. Often it was just an exercise in chest-puffing, but sometimes they did it to gauge the response and see how far they might push things. Melody's reference to the *east* meant that it was most likely coming from a surrogate of Russia. If the response was tepid, they'd begin moving some assets toward their western borders, or engage in joint military exercises with their allies, to see how NATO would respond. One thing Maguire knew, Cook would hasten to put them on notice that if any of them wanted to *fuck around*, she would be more than happy to help them *find out*.

"Have you ever thought that you just need to get away for a few days and clear your head?" Melody asked.

"Right now that would feel like the captain of the Titanic taking off in a rowboat after hitting the iceberg."

"Yeah, well, don't forget, the captain of the Titanic went down with the ship," she replied. "Listen, I'm going to be flying back in a few days. Why don't you come down and we can spend some quality alone time together?"

"Why not come here?" he asked.

"Under normal circumstances I would," Melody replied, "but with what is going on in the Middle East, I think it's wise to stay local for now."

"Are we ever going to have a time when we aren't dealing with everyone else's troubles and just focus on us?"

"I guess we both have to learn not to encourage each other to do dumb things."

"Or at least do it one at a time," he laughed. "Okay, as long as the City doesn't implode, I'll head down to you on Friday."

"I can't wait."

Maguire heard the sharp beep of an incoming call. He looked down and saw Billy Walsh's name. "Hey, not to cut you short, but I've got a call coming in."

"Okay, I'll call you tomorrow after I get done with my meetings. I love you, James."

"I love you too, Mel," he said.

He ended the call and switched to the other. "Billy, what do you have for me?"

"Well, my guys say that they have identified a link in the Watkins case. Turns out that he had appeared in Schiff's court the night he was killed, and Schiff had released him."

"Well that's interesting."

"Unfortunately, beyond that connection, it's just a bunch of dead ends for the moment. I wish I had better news."

"Fuck," Maguire muttered. "Alright, anything new with Schiff?"

"Yeah, it turns out that he was on a phone call prior to the shooting. We tracked down the number and spoke with the guy he was talking to. He's a journalist for a legal publication and was talking to Schiff when the doorbell rang. He could hear what sounded like muted voices and a noise, and then Schiff never came back on the phone. When he tried calling back, there was no answer, so he just assumed something came up and made a note to do a follow-up call."

"Witnessed a murder, and it went completely over his head," Maguire scoffed.

"We both know that people are oblivious most of the time," Walsh replied.

"Is this guy legit?" Maguire asked.

"Yeah, he works for one of those bleeding-heart liberal magazines. Also, TARU was able to pull the doorbell footage from the program history on the Judge's laptop. The video was fairly clear and disturbing."

"Why?"

"At face value, it appears that Schiff was shot by someone impersonating a court officer," Walsh replied.

"Are you fucking kidding me?"

"We got a decent screenshot of the shield, and it was reported stolen back in 2012."

"Are we sure?"

"Court officer reported it to the Nassau County Police right after it happened. The report says he had gone to the gym and stopped off at a deli to get lunch. Someone broke the car's window and snatched his gym bag with the shield inside. Responding cops found glass outside the car, so it looks legit. Could be the same shield, could be a duplicate. I'm having my guys follow-up with some places that make dupes and see if anyone had one done recently with that number."

"What about our shooter?" Maguire asked.

"He pulled a gun from a leather bag, fired three times, and casually walked away. Hard to confirm, but the feeling is that he was using a disguise. We caught a video of a car leaving an adjoining street that coincided with the time of the shooting, but the plate comes back to a different vehicle. We tracked down the registered owner, Elizabeth Brighton, who lives in Westchester County, and paid her a visit. Her husband, John Brighton, advised that she was in Seattle for a business conference and had driven herself to the airport on Friday. They found the car in the parking lot, and the plates were missing. So we have a lot of information, but all of it is useless."

"That's just great," Maguire griped. "We can't even buy a break, can we?"

"We'll keep beating the bushes," Walsh replied. "This isn't a race; it's a marathon."

"I wish I had your positive outlook," Maguire replied, "but the Mayor, City Council, and the media all seem to think that we should be able to solve crimes within hours of them happening."

"I'll tell my people to beat the bushes harder and faster."

"I have every ounce of trust that your people won't leave any stone unturned, Billy. Call me if you hear anything else."

"Will do."

CHAPTER SIXTEEN

Southampton, Suffolk County, N.Y.

Tuesday, May 12th, 2015 - 4:23 a.m.

Maguire finished knotting his tie and grabbed his suit coat before making his way to the kitchen.

Despite everything going on, he'd slept amazingly well and had a good run this morning.

Maybe she's right; maybe I do need to take a few days off and get away from this circus, he thought as he poured coffee into the stainless steel travel mug sitting on the counter.

The issue he struggled with was that he was the head of the Department. Yes, he had surrounded himself with the best people, all of whom could easily fill in for him, but when a tragedy hit, they expected him to be front and center. The unpredictability of tragedy was the thorn in every commissioner's side.

One of his predecessors, Lee P. Brown, was given the title of the *Father of Community Policing*, but this notoriety was also a sword of Damocles in many ways. His constant speaking trips regarding this style of law enforcement had led to a new title: *Out-of-Town Brown*, which was not as flattering.

As police commissioner, the public expected you to be available when anything newsworthy occurred and, if you weren't, the politicians and the media would ensure that they knew about it.

Still, he knew the pressure would eventually take its toll and he would either take time off or be carried out of 1PP on a stretcher.

I'm sure there would be a lot of folks happy about the latter, he thought, as he slipped on the suit coat, grabbed his coffee and headed for the door.

There was a cool breeze coming off the Shinnecock as he made his way toward the waiting SUV.

“Good morning, Amanda,” he said, as she opened the door for him.

“Not for long, Boss,” she said gloomily.

He looked at her and could see that her jaw was clenched. “What’s wrong?”

“This got printed in the morning edition of the Post,” she replied, as she handed him the folded paper. “Operations notified us as we were on our way, and I picked up a copy.”

Maguire scanned the first few sentences. “Jesus H. Christ.”

“It’s going to be a very long day, Boss.”

CHAPTER SEVENTEEN

NY Post - Letter to the Editor

May 12th, 2015 - Morning Edition

Greetings and Salutations:

The purpose of this letter is to address the recent killings in the city and to provide some clarification for the citizens of this great city. This letter serves as notice that these were not accidental or random, but were carried out by a new system of judicial authority that bears no relationship to the fetid one that currently rewards criminality, while subjugating the law-abiding citizens of this once great state to live in fear. Some will label us as vigilantes, so be it, but if we were to take an honest look at the old system, we would discover that it has abandoned its sacred oath to the Constitution and abdicated its sworn responsibility. Those entrusted with this oath have become corrupt, both politically and morally, and have forsaken the citizenry they were charged with protecting. In the absence of true justice, anarchy will thrive, and that is something we cannot, and will not, allow to happen.

This new system is being carried out by a select group of jurists, attorneys, and law enforcement officials, who have sworn an oath to uphold the principles on which this great nation was founded. A new system that is grounded in the Constitution and that believes justice is blind, but certainly not ignorant, and that the law should be applied equally and without favor. We are composed of men and women of the legal system, from all walks of life and political affiliations, who have well over a century of experience and have emerged from the shadows to cry, Enough!

Politicians have seized on the opportunity to marginalize the majority of peace-loving residents, while at the same time catering to a fringe, albeit very vocal, minority. They have inexcusably locked the masses in their homes, forcing them to live in constant fear, while putting out the welcome mat for violent, depraved individuals whose bloodlust for the destruction of civil society knows no bounds. These politicians are no longer austere statesmen and women, whose service to their constituents is their reward, but hollow shills, drunk with their own power, whose political goodwill is purchasable by the highest bidder.

We have judges who have surrendered the title of 'scholarly jurists' for the unseemly mantle of activist ones; who judge, not on the sound merits of the law, but on the fickle winds of political feelings. These men and women, who were entrusted with meting out justice, have done more harm to the citizens than all the egregious laws ever written. They have struck down faith in the law, conspired to destroy the underpinnings of our legal system based on their own wicked beliefs, subverting the Rule of Law for the Rule of Man, and in doing so they have cheapened the robes they wear. Criminals now walk freely, unencumbered by laws they do not feel obliged to follow and who are openly hostile toward the men and women of law enforcement whom we task with protecting us. We must remember that a judge is nothing more than a politically connected attorney whose only allegiance is to those who can further his or her career.

This letter serves to announce that those days are officially over.

To the Legislative Branch: Creating fallacious laws that negate, and often reward, criminality will no longer be tolerated. As in the days of King George III, your actions have become grievous and contrary to the right of the citizens to live with dignity and respect. You are no longer safe from the folly of your actions. If you choose to align yourself with the radical mob, then equally radical action will be taken against you.

To the Executive Branch: You are hereby served notice that any attempt on your part that furthers this plague of abetting criminality, while oppressing the people, will be met with action. You will know no peace, even within your most well-guarded places. Even when you are among friends, you will wonder who can be trusted, until the fear that is gripping our streets takes a stranglehold on your hearts.

To the Judicial Branch: You were to serve as a check and balance to the above, but when you acquiesce, when you opt to uphold a politically expedient, but unjust, law, then you have become an anathema to the Constitution. Your robes will no longer protect you from the fallout of your judicial folly; your authority will be quickly stripped away so that when the citizens suffer, so will you.

To the Criminals: Your way of life is coming to an end. No longer will you walk the streets with impunity. You might flee from the police, but you will not escape our justice. Actions have consequences. When you choose to make war against the innocent, when you flood our streets with drugs, when you delight in causing harm to the weakest, know that your end draws nigh. The shadows will no longer be your ally; fear will no longer be your strength. Now you will learn the meaning of: The hunter has become the hunted.

To the Citizens: This letter is not to alarm you, but to offer you comfort. We are advising you of all this so that you understand why we have been forced to take this action. Your government has become dissolute. Your judicial system has itself become contemptible. As a result, your police have been vilified and rendered ineffectual by the leaders who have corrupted their oaths. We have heard your cries for justice, seen the tears shed over your departed loved ones, and we have responded. The streets will be yours again. No longer will you have to hide in your homes behind bars; to sit breathlessly wondering if your child will return home from school. The day has come when the predators who roam our streets will no longer feel safe.

Let the following information serve as our bona fides. These individuals were chosen to ensure that our message resonated with the people, so that you know we are focused on the entirety of the problem.

Darnell Watkins (23) was a convicted drug dealer with sixteen prior arrests and plea deals that allowed him to remain free and continue to peddle his poison to our children. His last arrest was on a charge of attempted murder of another man who had not paid him for his illicit drugs. The old system allowed him to walk free, but we overturned that decision for this prolific purveyor of poison. Charged, Convicted, and Sentenced.

Charles Boyd (31) was a former teacher who was arrested for attempting to groom a fourteen-year-old girl for sex and possession of child pornography. The system allowed him to plead to a sexual misconduct charge that kept him on the streets where he continued to present a threat to our most precious and vulnerable members of society. The judicial system forgot about him; we didn't. Charged, Convicted, and Sentenced.

NYC Council Member Fernando Rodriguez (44) was elected by the people on the promise that he would work for them, and once elected, he immediately partnered with radical elements hiding beneath the banner of so-called criminal justice reform. But his support for these causes was not without a price, and that came in the form of substantial campaign contributions. While you suffered, he was receiving a handsome payout to enact legislation that turned our courts into a revolving-door justice system and our streets safer for criminals, all while labeling opponents of these evil machinations as racists. Of late he had been spearheading the closure of Rikers Island, but what he failed to disclose in his bombastic rhetoric was that he was secretly being paid-off by a firm seeking to gain access to the Island's lucrative real estate. His actions jeopardized the very constituents he was sworn to protect, all for his own political and financial gain. Charged, Convicted, and Sentenced.

Judge Bruce Schiff (69) was selected to be a fair and impartial arbiter of the law. Instead, he used his position to garner favor with a select community that ensured the security of his position over the oath he swore to uphold. Justice must be administered without fear or favor, and it is because of this that we find his actions are so egregious. If the justice system cannot be trusted, then the rule of law becomes its victim. Behind closed doors, Judge Schiff tacitly lent his voice and support to a number of issues that now plague this city. Judges who cannot or will not be impartial do not deserve to occupy a place in the hallowed halls of justice. A thorough examination of Judge Schiff's record highlighted his callous disregard for our sacred laws in favor of his own misguided interpretations. He frequently leaned upon his own biases and beliefs in rendering decisions that made a mockery of jurisprudence; a trend that is on the rise within many of the city's court rooms. Charged, Convicted, and Sentenced.

This letter serves as an official warning. We know who you are, we know where you are, and we will be ruthless in our endeavors to purge every evil element from our civil society.

To the citizens of this great city: Your cries have been heard and, unlike those currently in power, we will not fail you. We remain anonymous in our actions in order to prove that we seek no prize, nor praise, for our efforts. We do so of our own volition, of our own sacrifice, and accept the inherent risks just as our forefathers once did when they fought against a tyrannical monarchy.

This is not the beginning. It is merely the verdict.

CHAPTER EIGHTEEN

1 Police Plaza, Manhattan, N.Y.

Tuesday, May 12th, 2015 - 9:37 a.m.

The auditorium in 1PP had been hastily set up to house the throng of angry politicians and various agency representatives who had descended on it for the briefing. Three dozen tables had been arranged in a horseshoe formation for the principal players, while the rows of chairs behind them were filled with aides furiously scribbling notes.

Maguire and Barone sat at the center of the main table, flanked on either side by their respective police bureau chiefs and deputy mayors. Members of the City Council, replete with black mourning bands on their arms, were seated on the right side, while Judge Samuel Moses, Deputy Chief Administrative Judge for the New York City Courts, along with various judicial representatives, district attorneys, and members representing the bar, were seated on the right.

Any sense of decorum had been lost as the room devolved into chaos; a cacophony of voices, each striving to drown out the others, were demanding immediate protection from the threat that had been delivered by the morning paper.

The press had been barred from the meeting and was assembled on the plaza outside. The official reason was the sensitivity of security information that could potentially be revealed, but the truth was that the attendees wanted to protect their public image and prevent the cameras from capturing their collective meltdown.

Maguire had never understood his old partner's penchant for smoking and drinking, but as he sat there watching the scene unfold before him, he realized that a cigarette and a tumbler of Jameson would be the perfect prop for the ringmaster of the political circus that was playing out.

"What are you going to do, Commissioner?"

"Why haven't there been any arrests?"

"We cannot live in a world where politicians have to fear for their lives when they leave their homes. This is a direct threat to democracy!"

"The courts have no intention of buckling under this pressure, and we are demanding increased security."

Trying to respond to the shouted questions was pointless. If this had been his meeting, he would have shut it down by now and had anyone who interrupted removed, but Barone was theoretically in charge and, to be fair, he found it more than a bit amusing to watch his impotent boss flounder so magnificently.

It took every ounce of energy not to get up and walk out of the auditorium. The irony was not lost on him that if he did it, it would probably shock the room into silence. Once again, he couldn't help but think that Rich was the one who was better equipped to handle these types of things. He had the political savvy to navigate a crisis like this.

Maguire knew he wasn't cut out to coddle people's feelings. He looked around the room and all he saw was a group of fools, men and women who had created their own problems and now begged to be rescued from the consequences, even while demanding that said rescue be done according to their rules.

His thoughts were interrupted by a loud bang, as Barone angrily brought his fist down on the table.

"Enough!" Barone declared. "This bickering has got to stop."

For several more minutes, the man did his best to rein in the chaos, but his pleas fell on deaf ears, as the assembled group shouted over each other as they continued to press for their demands.

Sandy Barnes leaned over and whispered into Maguire's ear. "They're coming for blood, you know that, right?"

Maguire shrugged.

"This is unacceptable," Nydia Flores said. "You're the mayor of this city, and you're allowing a criminal element to hold us hostage. How are we supposed to represent our constituents when we are faced with this threat of violence? The world is watching, and all you can do is sit there and tell us to calm down. Every year I get the same demands from the police department for more money, and yet when this city needs them, they are as ineffectual as Keystone Cops."

Barone looked over at Maguire. "For God's sake, James, can you please handle this? You are the police commissioner after all."

Maguire gritted his jaw as his eyes burned into Barone's until the man sheepishly looked away.

He stood up and took a moment to scan the room.

There were over a hundred people assembled; many of whom were well accustomed to the trappings of power and prestige; people who basked in the spotlight of the camera, but who were now cowering in fear behind locked doors and all he could muster was contempt for them.

"All animals are equal, but some animals are more equal than others," Maguire said.

A collective look of confusion fell over the group.

"I think it's pretty safe to say that many of you have never read Orwell nor learned the lessons he was trying to impart," he continued. "You came here to make demands, but you are oblivious to the fact that your own actions are the reason you are sitting here today."

Flores shot up from her chair. "Commissioner Maguire—"

"You had your time to talk, Madam Speaker," Maguire snapped. "You are in my house now, so if you want answers, you're going to have to sit back down and listen."

Flores' face flushed, and if looks could kill, he knew he would have been dead before he hit the floor.

Maguire waited patiently until she sat back down. He had already made the decision that if he was going to go down; he was going down in flames.

"All of us read the morning paper, but I don't think all of us got the same message," he said. "Ignoring the crimes for a moment, the substance of that letter should have resonated with all of you, but clearly it did not. I would like to take this moment to remind you that we work for *all* the people, not a select special class. If nine out of ten people are against something, we don't acquiesce to the one, just because they are more vocal. Yet, that is precisely what you have been doing, and until today you were all fine with that. You're right, Madam Speaker, I am the police commissioner and I have been sounding the alarm about crime. I would say that those warnings have been falling on deaf ears, but we all know the truth. You have all heard what I and many others have been saying, but it is antithetical to your beliefs. You have ignored the masses because, for the most part, they are docile until they are not. Let's be candid for a moment, shall we? The majority of you are not afraid of the criminal element. No, what terrifies you is the criminal element that you don't control."

Maguire paused, watching as most of them squirmed in their seats as the accusation sank in.

"Reading that letter should be a clarion call for you, but instead of it being a wake-up call, you're circling the wagons trying to maintain the status quo; feudal lords from the fifteenth century who are locking themselves away in the castle because they fear a peasant revolt. Frankly, the collective lack of self-awareness in this room is truly breathtaking. Do you know what terrifies me? The fact that I have cops on the front lines who go into harm's way every day with a target on their back. They are the ones who have to deal with the ramifications of your folly, and God forbid they make one mistake, because the wrath of the political establishment will come crashing down on them like Thor's hammer. I fear the phone call that notifies me that we have lost another brave cop who died protecting the citizens of this city from someone you released. And now that your practices have finally caught up with you, you show up here and demand protection because you think you're special and your position demands it, but how many of you have thought about what the average citizen faces? Do you ever wonder how the laws you pass affect the bodega owner who worries about getting robbed daily? Do you consider the life of a child who gets shot on the playground because of a gang dispute? What about the average citizen who lives in fear behind deadbolts and barred windows? No, no you don't. Because you've never had to live that kind of life, and now that you are faced with it, your natural instinct is to scream for help, but only if you can dictate the rules of that help. So now that I have addressed the issues we face, I will close this meeting and get back to my job of running this investigation. Thank you for coming to my TED talk."

Maguire picked up the leather portfolio from the table, pivoted and headed out of the quiet auditorium with Sandy on his heels.

"That went well," she said as they walked out.

"Fuck him and fuck them," Maguire growled. "You were right when you said they were coming for blood, so I decided to shoot first."

"Han Solo would be proud."

"Get out of my way!"

Maguire pivoted to see a wild-eyed Barone pushing past uniformed cops as he made his way toward him.

"Are you out of your fucking mind?" he demanded. "What the hell was that all about?"

"The meeting," Maguire asked, "or my response?"

"Both!"

"The meeting was a joke. No one back there gives a rat's ass about what is going on. All they are interested in is saving their own asses, and I'm not going to hand them free life preservers because they demand it."

"Who do you think you are? You work for me!"

"Yes, I do, but we all work for the people, and that goes for those morons in there. They are the ones who poured gasoline over everything and lit the match."

"I'd like to remind you that those morons are the duly elected representatives of the people," Barone replied.

"Spare me the bullshit," Maguire scoffed. "You're asking me to cut my budget, which is going to adversely affect my ability to protect the public. So how do you think that is going to play out with voters when they learn that we are now providing full-time protection details to the people that have made their lives less safe? I'm going to go out on a limb and say that's not going to go over very well. I know the press loves to bash the Department at every opportunity, so what do you think I should say when they ask me why I did it? You have to admit, it kind of reeks of the whole *'Rules for thee, not for me'* thing, doesn't it?"

Barone glared at him, but Maguire just stared back impassively, waiting for him to respond. He knew that he'd painted himself into a corner and, more importantly, Maguire knew it as well.

"I should fire you for insubordination."

Maguire reached into his pocket and removed the leather case containing his commissioner's shield.

He knew that doing this meant career suicide. National headlines and a black mark on a storied career that would never fade, but he also knew this wasn't a moment to blink. He jabbed it into the Barone's chest.

"You want it? Take it."

Barone stared at it for a moment and then looked at Maguire. He wanted to speak, but his brain wasn't processing things fast enough to formulate a response.

"I've spent my entire adult life in service to both this country and this city," Maguire said. "That means I wrote a blank check for an amount up to and including my life, and God knows I have the scars to show for it. I've faced death numerous times in foreign shit-holes with names you couldn't even pronounce, so don't think for one moment you're going to get in my face and threaten me. If you feel so inclined, take it and then find your balls and walk your sorry ass outside and tell the media that you just fired the police commissioner. I'll be home sitting on my couch with a drink in my hand watching as the press eviscerates you out on the plaza in front of the cameras."

The color drained from Barone's face.

"While you're at it, you can have mine too."

The two men turned to see Barnes holding out her shield as the rest of the bureau chiefs quietly closed ranks around Maguire.

Barone swallowed hard. Try as he might, he could not come up with a single scenario that didn't end in his political suicide. He wasn't necessarily afraid of the people back in the room; they could be reasoned with politically, but the press didn't care about political niceties.

'If it bleeds, it leads' was an old saying in journalism, which implied if violence, conflict, or death was involved, then a story would get top billing, and right now this situation had all three. Firing Maguire would be the drop of blood that would send the media sharks into a frenzy.

"You have till the end of the month," Barone said. "If you can't resolve it by then, I won't be able to protect you."

"I'll sleep easy knowing you have my back," Maguire replied.

Barone stormed off to the auditorium in silence to try to put out the political fires that Maguire's speech had ignited.

"Thank you," Maguire said, as he looked around at his people, "but please allow me to add to the record that you're all insane."

"It's your ship, sir," Chief of Department Tony Ameche chimed in, "but all of us are out in the ocean with you. If you go down, we all go down."

"Well then," Maguire replied. "I suggest we all keep rowing while we still have time."

CHAPTER NINETEEN

1 Police Plaza, Manhattan, N.Y.

Tuesday, May 12th, 2015 - 7:41 p.m.

"Boss, do you have a minute?"

Maguire glanced up from the report he was reading to see Antonucci standing in the doorway with Tonya Jeffries.

"Yeah, come in and close the door," he replied. "I hope you have some good news for me."

"Well, I have news," Ang said, as they each took a seat. "Whether it's good or not is your call."

"That's not exactly encouraging," Maguire replied as he got up and refilled his coffee mug.

"Unfortunately, we're no closer to finding out who is behind this," Ang replied, "but we think we might have some new leads to pursue."

"Things are still very much fluid, but in light of the letter we expanded the investigation," Tonya said. "We have no reason to doubt the writer's claims for the deaths of Watkins, Boyd and Schiff, but we think these may only be the most recent ones."

"Why is that?" Maguire asked.

"We think the ones they listed are the ones they fine-tuned," Ang explained, "but we believe there may have been more; practice runs for lack of a better term."

"How many?"

"Three potential ones dating back to March that might have flown under the radar," Ang said. "One was a guy named Darius Brown up in the Bronx who put his ex-girlfriend in a coma. She died in the hospital two weeks later."

"Why the hell was he out?" Maguire asked.

"She was alive when he was arrested, and he got bail," Ang replied. "A week after she died, someone popped him in the back of the head when he was getting off work. He had a pretty extensive rap sheet, including robbery, drugs, and burglary charges, and the precinct detective squad's theory is that he double-crossed someone and got what he deserved."

"I'm sure it was hard for them to sleep at night knowing his killer was on the loose," Maguire said.

"I'd say it was super easy, barely an inconvenience," Ang replied.

"The next up was Rigoberto 'Crazy Jay' Colon," Tonya said. "He was the head of Los Hermanos, an up-and-coming gang operating in Queens North with loose ties to Tren de Aragua. He got picked up on a narcotics raid, and there was an ICE detainer on file for him, but somehow the paperwork got lost, and he posted bond before the mistake was caught."

"Mistake," Maguire scoffed. "You ever notice how the mistakes never seem to go in our favor?"

"You're starting to sound like a conspiracy theorist," Tonya laughed. "Unfortunately for Crazy Jay, he ended up in the trunk of a Monte Carlo in Brooklyn with three rounds to the back of the head. They chalked it up to an ongoing feud with a rival gang from El Salvador."

"That's convenient," Maguire replied.

"The last one we have is a bit sensitive, Boss," Ang said, "but it feels right for this."

"Why is it sensitive?" Maguire asked.

"Because it involves Tom Donohue, who was a senior staffer for District 32 Councilwoman Melissa Van Kirk."

"I remember hearing about that," Maguire replied, "but wasn't he the victim?"

"Yes, at least theoretically," Ang continued. "His death was investigated as a robbery attempt gone south, but the detective I spoke to in the One Hundredth Precinct gave me the name of another detective in Special Victims who said they had been looking into allegations that Donohue may have been involved with underage minors."

"I'm guessing there is a lot more to this story," Maguire said.

"Donohue was gay and, besides his work with Van Kirk, he was also a promoter of drag queen events. It was all fun and games until allegations surfaced that he was getting a bit too familiar with some of the younger contestants. SVD was looking into him when he ended up face-planting in front of a train at the Broad Channel station."

"Could it have been a suicide?" Maguire asked. "Maybe he knew he was being investigated and decided to off himself."

"Engineer told the detectives that he saw Donohue running toward the train, like he was trying to get away from someone, and it appeared to him that he stumbled and fell onto the tracks. That's why they were looking into it as a potential robbery and he died trying to get away from the perp, but what if that assumption was wrong? What is it was an early attempt at a hit?"

"I can see why you think it would fit, but do you have any evidence that links them?"

"Nothing tangible," Tonya said, "but what if that's the thing that actually links them?"

"War game this for me," Maguire said. "I want your gut feelings about what we are dealing with."

"I think we have to take the letter at face value and accept that we are dealing with a modern-day, extrajudicial Star Chamber," Ang replied.

Maguire hung his head as he contemplated the full implications of what he was facing.

The origins of the first Star Chamber could be traced to 15th century England and was a separate judicial arm of the King's Council. Its name evolved from the ceiling of the room where it met, in the Palace of Westminster, which was adorned with golden stars. The court's primary focus was the impartial enforcement of the law when the parties involved were considered either too socially or politically prominent and whose status might overly influence a lesser court, resulting in a failure to convict them of their crimes.

While the Star Chamber was regarded as one of the most just and efficient courts of the Tudor era, at least initially, over time it became weaponized and was often used as a tool to punish those deemed to be a threat to the monarchy. It developed a penchant for handing down excessive physical punishment and ruinous fines and, on occasion, it even jailed juries for rendering verdicts the Star Chamber disagreed with. In the 17th century, the Long Parliament, and the introduction of the Habeas Corpus Act of 1640, abolished the Star Chamber.

On a professional level, it appalled him that a group of people had decided to take matters into their own hands and stand as an alternative to the legal system, but on a personal level he understood how it could happen.

You didn't have to be a political science major to realize that there had been a fundamental change. The black and white notion of right and wrong had morphed into shades of gray. It was deeply unsettling to most, not because this change had come at a grassroots level, but because it had all the hallmarks of being a manufactured change.

Politicians and so-called community organizations were selling a lie, funded by wealthy benefactors, and aided by a complicit media. Criminals were portrayed as victims of an inherently biased system, and their crimes were excused because of socio-economic conditions beyond their control. Maguire could never fully understand what economics had to do with raping someone or pushing an elderly man in front of a train, but clearly a segment of society believed it did.

Most of the city's eight million residents just wanted to live in peace; to go to work and come home and be able to spend time outside with their families without fear of being killed or becoming a crime victim. If you had the audacity to say as much, then you were labeled as intolerant and part of the societal problem harming the less fortunate.

"So how do you propose we connect the dots on these killings?" Maguire asked.

"To be blunt, it feels like the victims are inconsequential at this moment," Tonya replied. "The only thing that matters about them is what the letter said. They were charged, convicted, and sentenced."

Maguire got up, grabbing his coffee cup, and walked over to the window. The sun was just setting, causing the narrow streets below him to darken, while the headlights of the cars crossing the Brooklyn Bridge made their mass exodus from the city.

It was easy to focus on the cars — the noise, the movement, the blur of destination — but the bridge was what held them together, he thought. *Structure beneath chaos; order beneath collapse. If that snapped, everything went with it and plunged into the murky abyss below.*

He understood the weight of being the bridge.

Maguire turned to look at them. "If this is a Star Chamber as you propose, Ang, then the natural assumption is that there has to be a judge that presides over it. Maybe that is where we should start looking."

Ang and Tonya shared an uneasy glance.

"Do you disagree?" Maguire asked.

"I don't," Ang replied, "but my fear is that if we start poking that bear without justification, we might end up in a far worse place than we are now."

"The ultimate question is who can we trust, Boss," Tonya added. "Yes, the letter does imply that part of what we are dealing with are individuals aligned with the judicial system, so looking into that seems prudent, but who? At this point, we have to question everything and everyone. If we try getting a subpoena, do we risk exposing our hand? Is the judge we ask involved? Who do we trust?"

"I don't want to say it, but can we even trust our own Legal Bureau?" Ang asked. "We don't know if this is a local issue or if we are dealing with people at the state level. Hell, for all we know, it might even involve the feds."

"I understand your concerns, but we can't just sit on our hands waiting to respond to the next murder," Maguire replied.

"Right now the media is having a field day dissecting that letter, but eventually they will turn their wrath on us and the public will rightfully be up in arms."

"I don't necessarily want to bring this up, but there is something about the letter I think we need to discuss," Ang said.

"What's that?" Maguire asked.

"Who are the enforcers?" Ang replied. "As much as I love action movies, I'm having a hard time wrapping my head around the image of some overweight judge secretly running around the city as some modern Jason Bourne. That means someone else is carrying out the sentences, and my first inclination is to believe that we are dealing with either active or retired cops. Personally, I don't trust anyone who isn't in this room."

"I don't disagree with you," Maguire replied, "and I've had the same thoughts."

"So what do you suggest we do?" Tonya asked.

"I still believe we have to focus on the most likely common denominator," Maguire replied. "I want you to compile an open-source list of any active or retired judges who have sat on the bench in the last ten years. There shouldn't be all that many."

"You want us to focus on the law and order folks first?" Ang asked.

"No, I want them all," Maguire replied. "Criminal, civil, you name it. We have no idea what the genesis of this is. For all we know, we could be dealing with some Surrogate Court judge who had an ideological epiphany and ran with it."

"Then what?" Tonya asked.

"You just get the list together and give it to me," Maguire said. "It's my dumb idea, so it's my ass to risk."

CHAPTER TWENTY

Southampton, Suffolk County, N.Y.

Wednesday, May 13th, 2015 - 9:06 p.m.

"You're up late," Alex Taylor said. "I was expecting to get your voicemail."

"I have a couple of things on my mind right now," Maguire laughed as he swirled the ice around in his glass. "A part of me would like to say this is an unexpected call, but I've been waiting for it. If you're planning on gloating, I'm going to need to get a refill."

"You cut me real deep," Alex laughed. "No, I was calling to congratulate you."

"About what?"

"On taking the title of policing's biggest fucking black cloud."

"There it is," Maguire replied. "I knew you couldn't be nice."

"Seriously, what an absolute clusterfuck you have going on."

"And you don't even know the half of it," Maguire said.

"Kind of makes me happy that I didn't take you up on that *deputy commissioner of some sort of bullshit* you offered me."

"I'm glad that I can entertain you, but shouldn't you be out removing raccoons from trash cans?"

"Nah, I'm good, but seriously, what the fuck is going on?" Alex asked.

"Someone finally had enough of the criminals and coddlers and decided to do something about it. Oh, and I effectively called the mayor a pussy to his face, so there's that."

"Damn, what did I tell you about going scorched Earth?"

"You didn't tell me shit," Maguire laughed.

"Eh, it probably skipped my mind between gun runs," Alex replied. "Still, Barone is a pussy, so there is that."

"Easy to say when it's not your neck everyone and their brother is breathing down."

"It sucks to be you. Besides, I told you that you could come up here and be my X.O. The pay is shitty, but you would get to enjoy my cheerful disposition every day."

"In all the years we worked together in the Seven-Three, I don't recall you ever having a cheerful fucking disposition," Maguire replied.

"That's because you were a lot of work back then, Rookie. You're seasoned now, so I can finally relax."

"Kiss my ass."

"So what's the real problem down there?"

"Oh, you know, politicians and judges have screwed the pooch, and now that someone is out gunning for them, they are screaming for protection at the same time they are trying to slash my budget."

"Well, at least you have a gazillion detectives you can assign to the case."

"I'm not gonna lie, Alex, whoever is behind this is good. There are no ballistic matches, targets that have no apparent connection to each other, but I know there is a foundational link; I just need to uncover it."

"Sounds like the body count is going to continue to climb until you catch a break," Alex replied.

"Catch one or make one."

"What does that mean?"

"Let's just say I'm toying with an idea," Maguire said.

"Jesus, don't be such a dick," Alex replied. "Remember who you're talking to. What's going through that brain of yours?"

"It means I'm thinking of calling in a favor; the legality of which might be a bit gray."

"Well, fuck, now you're talking my language," Alex laughed. "So what is your quandary?"

"You mean besides the legally gray part?"

"Oh, for fuck's sake, James, you've got bodies stacking up in the morgue and you're on the fence about whether you should ask 'Mother, may I?'"

"I'm on the fence about becoming the thing I'm supposed to be fighting against," he snapped.

"You know, watching you thread the needle between trying to navigate the niceties of the civilian world and yearning to lay waste to everything in front of you has always brought me so much joy," she replied.

"I'm glad you find this funny."

"Hush, Rook, I'm about to drop some knowledge on you."

"I'm all ears," Maguire replied.

"Long before I was assigned to babysit your sorry ass, I worked with a guy named Tony Moretti," Alex continued. "If you thought I was tough, Moretti was me on steroids. He was an old-school cop and built like a fireplug. The fucker had five years on the job before I was even born, and before that, he was kicking ass in Vietnam. Along the way, he managed to rack up the Medal for Valor and three Combat Crosses. Lord only knows how many bodies he stacked in the war."

"Those old-timers were a different breed, weren't they?" Maguire mused.

"That they were," Alex replied. "Anyway, we got detailed to go to some big Italian festival in Bensonhurt. I was happier than a pig in shit, because it was a day out of the Seven-Three for me. We're there for a few hours, and it's one big happy party. There is a ton of food, music, and everyone's having a blast, but I look over at Tony and I realize he's staring down these three *goombahs* across the street who were standing in front of the social club that was organizing the event. I mean he's eye-fucking them real bad. So I tap his arm and tell him to be happy and have some fun. He frowns at me, pops a Lucky Strike cigarette, and says, 'What the fuck am I supposed to be happy about, Alex?' I felt like I'd gotten smacked across the face. He takes a drag, and he says, 'All these fucking people are idiots. They're out here having a good time on the dime of those criminal scumbags over there. The sad thing is that they don't even realize that if they said the wrong thing to one of those mutts, looked at them the wrong way, they'd wind up at the bottom of Jamaica Bay with fifty pounds of concrete wrapped around their feet,' and that is what you're dealing with right now. Yes, the people might not have a problem with whoever is doing this, but that's because it doesn't directly affect them. If someone takes out a really bad asshole, it's no sweat off their balls, but what happens when they run out of the really bad assholes? Do they go for the kind of bad assholes or maybe just the people they dislike? Like that commie douche said, 'Show me the man and I'll find you the crime.' Or what happens when there is collateral damage and some poor schmuck gets caught in the crossfire?"

"You're very motivational," Maguire said somberly.

"Yeah, I'm the fucking Hallmark card of policing," she laughed. "At the end of the day, if you have to bend a rule here or there to put a stop to this, so be it. But the longer you wait, the closer you get to a collateral damage event. If you think the press is bad now, wait until that day comes. You'll be so radioactive I couldn't even hire you. Hell, you'll be lucky if you can find a job scraping penguin shit off of rocks in Antarctica."

"Thanks for outlining my options."

"You're a good man, James, but you're no altar boy either," she replied. "The system has its merits, but it also has its flaws. As long as you're not planting evidence, sometimes you need to consider creative alternatives to overcome those flaws."

"Thanks for the pep talk."

"Anytime, partner."

"Not to change the subject, but how are things going with you?" he asked.

"It's going," she laughed. "I haven't had a body drop in a while, so the board has got nothing to bitch about. My cops are happy, my dog loves me."

"And what about the good doctor?" Maguire asked.

"Peter is Peter," she replied.

"Oh? I thought things were going well between the two of you."

"They are, but you know how I am."

"Yeah, you're a pain in the ass," Maguire laughed.

"Exactly, but it's who I am. He wants the house, the picket fence, the wife. I want my home, my dog, and quiet. Compromise has never been my strong suit."

"We all have to grow up eventually," Maguire replied.

"Don't lecture me about growing up. You're talking to me from a houseboat, Popeye."

"How do you know where I am?"

"I can hear the water lapping, and I'm pretty sure you don't have a pet seagull."

"Smart ass."

"Trouble in paradise?" she poked. "Did Madam Secretary kick you out?"

"No, it's all good. Just reducing my carbon footprint and I like my bathroom to be closer to the bed as I get older."

"And you call me a smart ass," she laughed. "Are you and Melody spending any time together?"

"Barely. It feels like life conspires at every opportunity. We were going to try to get together this weekend, but I had to cancel."

"I'm sure that went over well."

"Like a lead balloon," he laughed, "but she understands. On top of everything else going on here Cook called to let me know she was coming into town tomorrow. So my little getaway has been pushed back to God only knows when."

"Things were a whole lot simpler back in our Brooklyn North days."

"You mean like when the only number I had in my phone contacts was the PBA delegate and not the President of the United States?"

"Something like that," Alex replied.

"We should get together soon," Maguire said. "We can jump in a radio car and go hit the Seven-Three for old time's sake."

"Fuck that shit," she replied. "Go solve your case and we can celebrate at Elaine's."

"You're dating yourself, sweetheart. Elaine's shut down four years ago."

"Well, we still have Patsy's. If it's good enough for Sinatra, it's good enough for me."

"Deal," Maguire replied. "You keep your ass out of trouble and I'll do my best to solve this case without getting indicted. I'll be in touch."

"I love ya, partner."

"Love you too, Alex."

Maguire stared into his drink and wondered when the fight for justice had started to feel like a war for his soul.

CHAPTER TWENTY-ONE

Undisclosed Location, N.Y.

Thursday, May 14th, 2015 - 8:21 p.m.

"*I pledge allegiance to the Flag of the United States of America, and to the Republic for which it stands, one Nation under God, indivisible, with liberty and justice for all.*"

The five men assembled in the small, windowless room represented well over a century of legal experience, both as attorneys and judges. Outside their courtroom, they were friends, but within this room, they took their roles seriously and addressed one another by their appropriate titles. This was done solely for the purpose of reminding them of the solemnity of their duties.

Three of the men sat as judges, one of whom was designated as the chief judge, while the other two represented the prosecution and the defense. Once the case was heard, the judges would deliberate and return a verdict, and all guilty verdicts were required to be unanimous.

They took their seats around the conference table, the judges on one side and attorneys on the other, and began their hearing.

"You may proceed with your case, counselor."

"Your Honors, I appear before you this day to argue the case of Robert Conti," the prosecutor said as he stood up. "Mr. Conti is assigned to the Queens District Attorney's Office and serves in the capacity of an assistant district attorney. A position he has held for four and a half years. Despite handling over five hundred cases, Mr. Conti has a dismal conviction rating and is known for continually downgrading cases for plea agreements. In January 2014, he was assigned to the case of Randolph Hollerman. Mr. Hollerman was charged with the attempted murder of his girlfriend, Denisha Young. Ms. Young was two months pregnant at the time and suffered serious injuries in the attack that required hospitalization. She subsequently lost the baby. Mr. Conti downgraded the charge to second-degree assault, arguing that Ms. Young's prior drug use could have been seen as a contributing factor in the death of the unborn child. The charges were downgraded, and Mr. Hollerman pled guilty to second-degree assault and was released with time served and probation. In February of this year, Mr. Hollerman was arrested for the murder of Denisha Young. This is but one case; however, Mr. Conti's prosecutorial record shows that he has a severe indifference to the plight of crime victims. A review of said record over the last eighteen months indicates that on at least fifteen occasions he has downgraded charges that allowed career violent criminals to walk free, and most those same criminals were rearrested within months. It should also be noted that in March 2013, he gave a plea deal to Antonio Salazar, an illegal immigrant from El Salvador who was charged with criminal possession of a firearm and criminal possession of a controlled substance. After his release, Mr. Salazar was arrested for the murders of Luis Alonso and Yolanda Perez, who had been acting as confidential informants for the police department."

"Your Honors," defense counsel replied, "to be fair to Mr. Conti, the Queens DA has implemented the practice of expediting cases. He has instructed his staff to aggressively pursue these deals to alleviate the caseload in their office."

"Yes, and it can certainly be argued that plea deals are an appropriate tool in non-violent crimes," the prosecutor argued. "However, Mr. Conti makes no distinction between the violent and non-violent individuals. He once said, and I quote, 'This city is a fucking zoo and I don't care if they are killing each other. Today's victim is just tomorrow's perp. If they off each other, it just makes my life easier,' end quote. "

"Objection, Your Honors," defense counsel replied. "This is hearsay, and the prosecution knows that. It should be stricken from the record."

The chief judge, the oldest of the three, cleared his throat, his voice clipped. "Counsel, you know the rules."

"Your Honors, if it may please the court," the prosecutor replied. "I was in the room when Mr. Conti made the statement; I was the one he said it to."

The defense attorney flipped his pen onto the desk, leaning back in frustration.

"Closing arguments."

"Your Honors," the prosecutor said. "Robert Conti was appointed to be the attorney for the people of the county of Queens and seek justice for the victims. Instead, he has abdicated that responsibility. He has repeatedly provided sweetheart deals, aid and comfort, I would argue, to recidivist criminals who are waging war on the good citizens he swore an oath to protect. Aristotle once said, 'At his best, man is the noblest of all animals; separated from law and justice he is the worst.' Absent the law, what do we have? The justice system is supposed to provide redress to the people, but those like Robert Conti are apathetic to their needs. He no longer feels the need to properly represent the people, but rather his own goals and aspirations and, while he is only one cancer, in a body riddled by disease, his failure to uphold his oath has led directly to the deaths of innocent people and, as such, he should receive the same sentence they received. I know we are all versed on the founding fathers, but I would like to close by reminding you of the words of Benjamin Franklin, 'Justice will not be served until those who are unaffected are as outraged as those who are.' Until now, Robert Conti has been unaffected by his actions and I ask the court to return a verdict that will correct this injustice. Thank you."

"Your Honors," the defense said, rising from their chair. "The prosecutor has done a formidable job of painting the defendant as a heartless monster; someone immune to society's plight, but please allow me to paint a different picture. All of us here have been in the defendant's shoes at one time or another, facing a daunting challenge of seeking justice, while navigating the bureaucratic morass of the criminal justice system. In a different time, we might find ourselves in the docket facing accusations of malfeasance. Since my esteemed colleague is so fond of quotes, allow me to add one more, 'There but for the grace of God go I.' Yes, Mr. Conti's failure to secure higher charges might have led to unintended consequences, but does he bear this burden alone or does the system, and those who legislate, bear some culpability? Dare I ask whether some of the victims themselves bear guilt because of the unfortunate choices they made? I would argue that Mr. Conti is no different from a soldier sent to the front lines to defend against a blitzkrieg-style attack with inadequate resources, all while generals critique his performance from the safety of half a world away. Yes, there have been failures, some have died, but is he alone responsible for the failures in the system? I ask the court to consider that someone in this position would inevitably develop a level of cynicism; a dark humor to shield themselves from the tragedies of their environment. The sad fact is that Mr. Conti is working within a system that has itself failed to protect the ordinary citizen, and an employee is no better or worse than the system he works for. Let us not cast guilt upon the soldier for the rules foisted upon them by their leaders."

"Thank you, gentlemen," the chief judge said, as the prosecutor took his seat. "We will now take this matter under advisement, and a ruling will be issued forthwith. Now, in the case of the previously heard People versus Michael DiMarco, does either the prosecution or defense wish to enter into the record any exculpatory evidence that might have surfaced since this case was first heard or have any objection to a judgment being made?"

Neither attorney spoke up.

"Let the record reflect that there is no additional evidence or objection. Therefore, this court finds the defendant, Michael DiMarco, guilty as charged. The defendant, having been found guilty by unanimous agreement, is hereby sentenced to death."

No one flinched. The gavel didn't fall, but the verdict hit like a guillotine.

"The prosecution is charged with notifying the marshal of the court's verdict and ensuring that the sentence ordered is carried out as expeditiously as possible."

“I will notify him this evening, Your Honor,” the prosecutor replied.

“Thank you, gentlemen. This court is now adjourned.”

CHAPTER TWENTY-TWO

JFK Airport, Queens, N.Y.

Friday, May 15th, 2015 - 4:59 p.m.

Maguire watched as the Boeing VC-25 slowly taxied toward the waiting motorcade. Once it had come to a stop, the crew moved the airstair into place and a moment later the door opened and President Eliza Cook appeared.

There were a handful of people waiting to greet her, and she spent several moments speaking with the group before making her way toward the waiting limo. Just as she was about to enter the *Beast,* she spotted him and waved him over.

"Ride with me, James," Cook said, as she got inside.

Maguire signaled to Amanda and walked over to where a Secret Service agent held the door for him.

"I don't want to intrude, Madam President," he said as he entered the limo.

"Oh, please," she replied. "I could use the company. What's going on?"

"About?" he asked.

"Has anyone ever told you that you are wildly infuriating?"

"Frequently," he replied, as the motorcade began to move.

"Good, I'm glad that you're getting the recognition that you deserve," Cook laughed. "I feel like I have to pry everything out of you."

"You're the President. I'm pretty sure that you have more things to worry about than what is going on with me."

"That is true, but I am the President of the United States, which also includes New York City, and I like to keep abreast of things going on here, especially the bad news. So what's going on with these murders?"

"Someone, although it's more likely several people, has set themselves up as judge, jury, and executioner," Maguire replied.

"Are you making any progress?"

"I wish I could say that we are, but it is like trying to find a needle in a haystack, and that haystack is in a field of haystacks, located in a state that produces nothing but haystacks."

"I'll take that as a resounding no," she replied. "What's going on with the investigation?"

"Well, we know now that whoever is doing this is targeting the system," Maguire said. "They're going after criminals, the politicians pushing this agenda, and at least one judge who had a history of extreme leniency. So far, the killings have been random, and there has been no evidence to link any of them. We have some leads we are trying to follow, but if I am being honest, they are tenuous at best. The issue is that crime is up, arrests are down due to manpower, and even the ones that are being arrested are usually back on the street before my people are even done with the paperwork. Right now we are in a guessing game as to who might be the next potential target out of the ten thousand arrests we make each month, not to mention the politicians and court personnel."

"Jesus Christ," Cook fumed. "You know, I tried to warn them; these idiots who stoked the fire for political points without ever once thinking about the potential ramifications of what they were doing. I honestly don't know where this new breed comes from. I miss the old days of politics. Sure, you disagreed on principles, but it was collegial. You didn't go and burn your house down to make the other person homeless."

"Well, there's at least one politician who learned the hard way that actions have consequences," Maguire said.

"Rodriguez?" Cook asked.

"Yes."

"It's just too bad that the others won't learn from that lesson."

"No, in fact some of them are doubling down on the blame game," Maguire replied.

"I've seen some quotes. 'From Hero to Zero.'"

"Yes, it's very catchy," Maguire said.

"Here's a political lesson for you, James. Never pay attention to the opinions of spectators."

"I don't," Maguire replied, "but the Mayor does."

"Word on the street is that he wants to replace you."

"Bad news does travel fast."

"It's only bad news if you're desperate for the job," Cook replied, "and you have never struck me as the desperate kind."

"Well, a few months in the Bahamas doesn't sound like a bad idea," Maguire laughed.

"I was thinking more like D.C. in the fall."

"Fired police commissioners aren't exactly in high demand."

"So don't get yourself fired," Cook laughed.

"It's not just Barone," Maguire replied. "I doubt I'm on the City Council Speaker's Christmas card list, and we already know the media's gunning for me."

"How can I help?" she asked.

"Do you have any crystal balls you want to lend me?"

Cook slapped his leg. "I've seen your folder, James. You don't need any balls other than the ones you already have. You've already proven that you are very resourceful in handling unforeseen adversity. So, I have every confidence in your capabilities to deal with this investigation."

"I appreciate that," Maguire replied.

"Still, if you need anything, all you have to do is ask. FBI, Marshals Service, hell, I can even send you a busload of IRS agents if it will make your life easier. All you have to do is let me know, and I'll make the call."

"Thank you. I'll let my Chief of Detectives know he has access to those options if the need arises."

"That being said, let's get to the real reason I wanted you to ride with me," Cook said. "Have you given any thought to my offer?"

Maguire shifted in his seat, staring out the limo's window as the motorcade crossed the Robert F. Kennedy Bridge as it made its way from Queens into Manhattan. "I have."

"You're being infuriating again, James."

Maguire turned to face Cook. "It seems you're not the only one who has taken an interest in me."

"Oh really? Care to fill me in?"

"This isn't an open-air kind of conversation," he replied, nodding at the two men sitting in the front seats.

"We need some alone time. Thomas," Cook said to her Secret Service agent as she pressed a button that raised a partition.

"Yes, ma'am," the man replied before the passenger cabin was closed.

"Okay, so what is this all about?" she asked.

"I got a phone call from an old friend," Maguire replied. "He told me that Secretary Alan McMasters was doing some digging on me."

"Why would the Secretary of Defense be asking about you?"

"That's the same question my friend had. McMasters gave him an excuse, claiming that he just wanted to know more about me."

"You certainly are popular," Cook replied, "but I get the feeling you think there is more to this than simple curiosity."

"I'm trying not to be paranoid, but I learned a long time ago that it's best to trust your gut. What worries me is that McMasters brought up an operation I was involved in twenty years ago; something that ended up having a bit more baggage than what we'd been told."

"I wasn't made aware of anything in the initial vetting process," Cook replied.

"This was a Special Access Program," Maguire replied. "One of your predecessors sanctioned it. The key players were the CIA and the Department of Defense."

"Okay, give me the details," Cook scowled.

"Do you remember back in 1990 we lost a DEA agent in Mexico?" Maguire asked.

"Yeah, it was a cartel hit."

"Well, in response, then-President Calvin McManus authorized Operation High Sierra. He felt the Mexican government was dragging its heels with the drug cartels, but the Mexican president was considered pro-American and they didn't want to upset the apple cart. So the CIA was tasked ID'ing the person responsible for Agent Pedro Montoya's murder, and we were sent in to take him out."

"I can see where an op like that on foreign soil would best be clandestine," Cook replied.

"Agreed," Maguire said. "The op was supposed to be a quick in and out, just me and my swim buddy, Anthony Kowalczyk, to take out the target and extract, except it didn't go as planned. The CIA intel was that it would be a small group with the target, no more than a dozen, but the reality turned out to be a lot more, and they came loaded for bear. It was a setup. We engaged in a protracted gun battle in which my teammate was killed. I made it to the secondary extraction zone only to realize they were waiting there. Obviously, someone had fed them inside information. After the hit, we were supposed to be taken out to tie up loose ends. There'd be no response, because no one would dare risk having to explain why we were doing wet work in a friendly foreign country."

"How'd you get out?" Cook asked.

"I didn't," Maguire replied, "at least not initially. I made it my mission to track down those responsible, starting with the men who were waiting at the secondary site and working my way up. What I learned made it all a lot worse. The target of our op was an undercover working for the DEA, and the cartel learned about it from one of ours."

"Who?" Cook asked.

"Kenneth Samuelson," Maguire replied. "He was a career CIA agent assigned to the Mexico City station, and he was hooked up with Gilberto Torres, who was the number two guy in the Mexican Intelligence Service. Both of them had their hands in the Sonora Cartel."

"If memory serves me correctly, Samuelson went missing in Mexico," Cook replied.

Maguire remained silent.

"Jesus Christ," she replied. "Does the CIA know?"

"Know? No. Suspect? Maybe, but the dead don't talk," Maguire replied. "That being said, Samuelson was on the DEA's radar, so maybe the CIA decided to take the win and just let everyone rest in peace and move on."

"Can McMasters find anything if he tries to dig?"

"There are only five people who know the entire story, including you and me, and one of them passed away," he replied.

"And you have no concerns about those two?"

"I'm one hundred percent confident that they will take it to their graves."

Cook nodded. "You know what the problem is with the vetting process, James? It only tells you so much about a person, but it doesn't tell you what is in their heart."

"I understand," Maguire replied. "Still, I want to tell you that it was an honor to even be considered for the FBI director position."

"Dear Lord," Cook laughed. "I wasn't talking about you. The problem with politics is often that the people who should have the job rarely want it and the ones who do shouldn't have it. McMasters was a good pick on paper. He has the qualifications, but you really don't know how a person will react to power until they have."

"I can't argue with that," Maguire replied.

"I've always seen you as the reluctant warrior. Doing what is asked of you, not because you cherish the accolades, but because you have a profound sense of duty and honor. Don't worry about Mexico and let me worry about McMasters."

"Yes, ma'am."

The limo came to a stop outside the Waldorf Astoria.

"So, to my previous question, have you given any thought to my offer?"

"I have," Maguire replied, "and if the offer still stands, it would be an honor to serve as the director of the FBI, although I get the feeling you already knew what my answer was going to be."

"I was about ninety-five percent sure, but you have always had a penchant for holding a wild card or two up your sleeve."

"Can you call off your pit bull now?" he asked.

"Melody is a rather tenacious diplomat, isn't she?"

"She's something."

"I'll get the ball rolling as soon as I get back to D.C.," Cook said, "but we will keep things quiet until you reach a resolution here. No need to add anything more to your plate."

"And if I don't reach a resolution? What if there's no way to resolve this within the framework of the law?"

Cook stared silently for a moment, choosing her words carefully. "You know, throughout my political life, I have always tried to play within the rules. I did not set them, but I felt a certain obligation to adhere to them. Someone would disagree, but those are usually the ones I bested. However, during that time, I also encountered a number of adversaries who attempted to gain leverage on me by changing the rules to their advantage. Once that happened, I no longer felt the need to play nice. I think that's a trait you and I both share. It seems to me that you are faced with an adversary who has revised the rules to the opposite extreme. If I were you, I'd shove the rule book up their ass and do whatever you need."

"Yes, ma'am."

"Now, if you'll excuse me, as much as I prefer spending time with you, I have my own collection of asses to be shaken up waiting for me inside." Cook said, signaling the agent waiting outside that they could open the door. "Good luck, James."

"You too, Madam President."

Cook beamed a big smile at him. “Oh, I’m not the one who needs luck tonight.”

Maguire waited until his door opened and stepped out. He walked over to the SUV where Amanda was waiting.

“Everything okay, Boss?”

“It is now,” he said, retrieving his cellphone as he got into the back.

A moment later, he heard a familiar voice on the other end. “I need your help.”

CHAPTER TWENTY-THREE

Waldorf Astoria, Manhattan, N.Y.

Friday, May 15th, 2015 - 5:57 p.m.

Jack Barone sat on a couch in the Presidential Suite, nervously awaiting the arrival of the President under the unflinching gaze of a Secret Service agent. He'd thought about opening one of the water bottles on the coffee table, but didn't want to run the risk of needing to use the bathroom.

"The President is on her way up," the agent announced.

"Thank you," Barone replied, his hands subconsciously smoothing out his jacket.

He'd met her before, but the experience of meeting the leader of the free world was one you never grew fully accustomed to.

A moment later, the door opened, and Eliza Cook entered the room.

"Madam President," Barone said as he stood up. "It's a pleasure—"

"Spare me, Jack, I'm in no mood," she barked, as she walked over to the mini-bar and poured herself a drink. "That'll be all, Michael. Please tell Emerson to give me fifteen minutes."

"Yes, ma'am," the agent replied, as he slipped out and shut the door behind him.

Cook walked over and sat down on the couch across from Barone.

"I'm sorry," Barone said, forcing himself to remain calm, as he sat back down on the couch. "Did you have a bad flight?"

Cook took a sip of her drink and set the glass on the coffee table. "I can't express what a stunning job you have done in just six short months, Jack."

"Thank you, Madam President."

"Oh, that wasn't a compliment," she said tersely.

Barone felt the heat on his face as his cheeks flushed. "Excuse me?"

"This is New York City, the flagship of this great nation, and my absolute favorite city, and you are turning it into a goddamn crime-ridden cesspool."

"Madam—"

"Shut up, Jack. I'm here because you are fucking up so badly that if I don't get things back on course, I fear you will make it impossible for me to un-fuck-up your mess."

"I'm... I'm... Sorry," Barone stammered.

"You're clearly out of your depth, Jack, but I will not allow that lack of ability to cause me to lose this city to that bitch, Flores," Cook said, as she picked up her glass and took another drink, cradling it in her hand. "Not that she's more capable than you, but because her incompetence comes with a wholly undeserved superior attitude."

Barone squirmed in his seat like a fourth-grade Catholic school student being berated by the Mother Superior.

"You're trying to match wits with a woman who doesn't give a rat's ass about you or any concessions you are willing to make. She's a political shark, and she smells blood in the water, and you're on the menu."

"I'm doing the best I can," he protested. "I'm just the mayor—"

"Quiet!" Cook glared. "I'm not asking what you are going to do, Jack. I'm telling you what you will do!"

Barone swallowed hard. He was angry, but lashing out at the President, deservedly or not, was political suicide, and he was already holding onto his career by a thread.

"This city is at a tipping point," she continued. "If you try to appease Flores and her ilk, you will go down as the worst mayor in New York City history, surpassing even John Lindsay."

"What do I do?" Barone asked.

"You're going to become the law and order mayor," she replied. "Pull out all the stops to restore safety in this city."

"We're grappling with some financial issues," he protested. "We're losing businesses, and revenue from tourism is down."

"No shit, Sherlock. The folks visiting from Des Moines tend to frown on getting shot in Times Square, and businesses tend to rethink investing in cities that allow their stores to get pillaged. The short-term financial issues will be resolved, but I expect you to address the issues on the street."

"But the laws—"

"I don't care," Cook interrupted. "Lock them up."

"They just get released."

"Then lock them up again and then lock them up again. Keep locking them up until they either give up or move out of town or the system collapses from the sheer volume of paperwork."

"Madam President, I don't think you fully understand the complexity of the—"

Barone stopped mid-sentence, seeing the malevolent look in Cook's eyes.

"China is complex, Jack. North Korea is complex. Iran is complex, but do you know why they don't fuck with me?"

"No, ma'am," he replied.

Cook stared at him, her face softening a bit, as if she'd had a sudden epiphany. She scrutinized the man sitting across from her, the way a scientist would examine a lab experiment.

"No, I don't think you do," she replied, her tone warming. "And therein lies the problem. You were a helicopter pilot, weren't you?"

"Yes, ma'am," he replied. "Coast Guard Air Station North Bend."

"How many were in your crew?" Cook asked.

"Typically four: pilot, co-pilot, flight engineer and rescue swimmer."

"Would you have allowed anyone else to pilot?"

"I guess the co-pilot if anything happened to me," he replied.

"But not the engineer?"

"No, ma'am."

"What would happen to the engineer if they tried to take over?"

"They would be subdued and subject to a UCMJ hearing."

"So why are you allowing this city to be run differently?

"I beg your pardon?"

"You are in charge, but you are allowing others to run amok without taking any steps to correct it."

"I don't control the City Council," he argued.

"And they don't control you, but you are allowing them to dictate how you respond. In effect, the engineer has taken over, and instead of taking back control, you're trying to give them flying lessons."

"I'm just trying to run the city."

"You're good intentions are about to crash the proverbial helicopter and kill the entire crew."

"What do you suggest I do?

"You're a good man, Jack, but you need to find your balls and put them to good use. Instead of trying to play nice with everyone, recognize the threat, go on the offensive. Get out in front of the cameras and shine a light on what is going on. Have your police commissioner arrest violators and show that bitch you are in command."

"I think there needs to be a change in the police department," Barone replied.

"Why?" Cook asked.

"Let's just say that Maguire and I don't see eye to eye," Barone explained. "He served the Department and the City well, but I think a change would help to move forward."

"He stays," Cook replied.

"What? Why?"

"Why?" Cook asked. "Because he's my choice, Jack."

"But Madam President, I'm the mayor; this is my city. I should be able to appoint whomever I want."

"Are you fucking serious? Maguire could have single-handedly destroyed your political career, your family. He could have handed your seat over to Flores tied in a goddamn bow, and he didn't. He has more courage and conviction than all of you put together, and he stays. Is that understood?"

"Yes, ma'am."

"Don't try me on this, Jack. If I hear that you are trying to sabotage him, I will turn off the financial spigot, and you can watch your career wither up and die."

Barone nodded glumly.

"Unlike you, Maguire knows what he is doing and what needs to be done. You'll extend your hand to him and give him whatever he needs to right this ship. Understood?"

"Yes, ma'am."

There was a knock at the door, and Emerson Lee popped her head inside. "It's time, Madam President."

"Thank you, Em," Cook said, as she stood up. "Do you have any questions, Jack?"

"No, ma'am," he said dejectedly as he stood up.

"Well then, you have your marching orders."

CHAPTER TWENTY-FOUR

Southampton, Suffolk County, N.Y.

Saturday, May 16th, 2015 - 5:21 a.m.

It was just before dawn as Maguire made his way east along the shoreline. A thin ribbon of gold split the dark horizon, creating a bright purple skyline that gradually chased off the remnants of night with each passing second. Off to his right, a thunderous roar reverberated through him as angry waves pummeled the deserted shoreline. He glanced down at the Luminox watch on his wrist and quickened his pace.

Maguire felt her presence long before he saw her. It felt like they shared a transcendent bond, as if his thoughts and hers were connected through some unidentifiable link.

"You're late," he muttered, as she drew abreast of him, keeping an even pace as they made their way through the sand.

"I had to warm up," Zee said effortlessly.

"You must be getting older," he laughed. "I don't remember you ever having to warm up before."

"That's because you usually had me warmed up by the time we started our runs together."

"Touché," he replied.

"So why am I here?"

"Your cousin still keeping the kids in line at 8200?" he asked, referencing the Israeli Intelligence Unit responsible for clandestine cyber operations, such as signal intelligence, code decryption, and other aspects of cyber-related warfare.

"That depends."

"On?"

"On exactly what you're about to tell me," she replied.

Maguire slowed his pace as they reached a desolate area, coming to a halt as Zee continued on. He took a deep breath as he stared. Her lithe form clad in black spandex running pants and sports bra, her long brown hair pulled through the back of the baseball cap she was wearing.

She ran another thirty feet before coming to a stop and turning back to face him. "You used to have more stamina."

"Maybe I just wanted to enjoy the view," he replied.

She walked back to him until mere inches separated the two; her green eyes boring deep into his soul. "You could enjoy more than just a view if you could just get over your hang-ups."

"Zee—"

Tzviya poked her finger hard into his chest. "Ante up or fold, James. I'm in no mood to play games."

"That's a cute finger," he replied, holding her gaze. "You want to keep it?"

"Is that your idea of foreplay?"

"I can't even begin to articulate how badly I want you right now."

"Then why are you fighting it?" she yelled in frustration. "Look around you; there is no one here to see you. It's just us."

"You think I'm afraid of being seen?" Maguire asked.

"I don't know. Are you?"

Maguire grabbed her and pulled her close, his lips pressing against hers as they kissed; the frustration, anger, and emotions boiling over into a passionate kiss that conveyed more feeling than any words ever could. He wrapped his arms around her tightly, feeling her arms return the embrace as the two former lovers gave in to their desire, the rekindled spark burning with white-hot intensity.

"James," Tzviya said breathlessly.

"I love you, Zee," Maguire said. "I always have, I always will, you gigantic pain in the ass. Do you think I wouldn't take you here in a heartbeat? Just to feel the passion we have for each other one more time?"

"Then do it," she begged. "Take me — here, now, make it make sense, because I don't know why you are fighting it."

“Because I love you, Zee,” he said.

“I don’t understand.”

“I won’t ask you to share me; to hide in the shadows.”

“What about me?” She asked. “Do I get a say in any of this? I don’t care who you are with. I don’t care if it breaks the rules.”

Maguire turned away, facing toward the ocean, the dark, churning waters matching his feelings.

“What’s wrong?” she asked.

“I agreed to accept the FBI director position,” he said somberly.

The words resonated within the deepest recesses of her soul. They could hide their relationship here, but there would be no chance of that once he accepted the job. She wrapped her arms around him tightly, her face buried against his back.

“Fuck,” she whispered.

For Maguire, it felt like his world was crumbling for a second time, but this time it was a decision he was making and not one being forced on them, and it made the pain even worse.

Tzviya wiped an errant tear from her cheek and fought to suppress the tumultuous feelings raging inside her. He had asked for her help, and it was time to find out why. “So why am I here?”

“You know what’s going on in the city,” he replied. “I’ve hit a roadblock, and if I don’t act outside the box, more people are going to die.”

“From what I’ve read, society isn’t losing out on much.”

“Society always loses once the law fails and vigilantism takes hold,” he replied. “Maybe not at first, but eventually everything collapses.”

“So what do you need from me?”

Maguire turned around and handed her a USB drive. “There’s a list of numbers here. I need to know if there have been any repeat customers they have been talking to. Names. Connections. Patterns. Anything that repeats. If I can’t find a nexus, I’m screwed.”

"Surely you have people who can do this. Why do you need me?"

"I'm grasping at the only straw I have available, and I can't get a warrant for this type of information without the potential for tipping off those involved. Plus, the three-letter folks aren't big on warrantless spying of Americans."

"That's a load of bullshit, and you know it," Tzivya laughed. "There's nothing they don't like spying on."

"Maybe I just don't want to give them a reason to know."

"Or maybe you just don't want to give them a marker to hold over the new FBI director's head."

"Would you?" he asked.

"But you're okay with me holding that marker?"

Maguire took her hand in his and stared into her eyes. "You've never needed a marker with me."

"That's because you know I would never call it in," she replied.

"You're the only one I can trust, Zee."

"I'll see what I can do," Tzivya replied, as she pocketed the USB.

"Thank you."

"Promise me one thing, would you?"

"If I can," Maguire replied.

"Please be careful for me," she said.

Something in the way she said it, an unexpected softness in her voice, made it sound almost like a plea, and it sent a shiver through him.

"I'm always careful," he smiled.

"No, you're not, but you need to start," she replied. "Yoni got a psychological assessment of who might be behind these killings so we would know if there was any potential risk to our protectees."

"What did it say?" Maguire asked.

"Their opinion was that it was an internal threat, but that it would most likely escalate."

"How so?"

"They feel that the goal in the killings is to get the average citizen to connect them, their organization, with removing the bad actors; criminals or those who would outwardly undermine the system and pose a threat to safety. Once that goal is accomplished, and the people support them, they will begin to direct their attacks toward those whom they view as political opponents of their worldview."

"Good thing I'm not a politician," Maguire laughed.

"There is nothing funny about this, James," she said, her expression impassive. "In case you didn't know it, you represent the armed wing of the political machine."

"I'm the police commissioner," he replied, as he moved in close and kissed her forehead. "Not the Chairman of the Committee for State Security, but I promise you that I will be careful.

She began to walk away in frustration, but stopped and looked back at Maguire. "I don't care what title you have, James, and I don't care how long I have to wait. I won't give up on us. Not now, not ever. I love you."

"I know," he replied.

"Once I hear something I'll let you know."

Maguire watched as she jogged away, and he was filled with the same sense of dread that it might be the last time. The feelings harkened back to Mexico and the bitter lesson he had learned about just how fragile and fleeting life could be.

CHAPTER TWENTY-FIVE

Prospect Park, Brooklyn, N.Y.

Monday, May 18th, 2015 - 6:01 a.m.

The man sat on one of the park benches that dotted the perimeter of Prospect Park, drinking his coffee and reading the morning newspaper. He had on a pair of jogging shorts and a zipped-up tracksuit jacket. To the casual passer-by, he would be otherwise unremarkable; just another fitness idiot they would see and then just as quickly forget.

He glanced over the top of his paper and spied her jogging in place as she waited to cross from 14th Street.

"Just like clockwork," he muttered.

A moment later the light turned, and she crossed the street and began heading north.

The tall brunette was wearing a pair of dark gray spandex jogging pants and a black sports bra that was struggling to contain her substantial breasts. The headphones she was wearing might have helped keep her in the zone, but they also provided just enough of a distraction that she was unaware of the danger she was in.

"Goddamn," he muttered, as his eyes locked onto her ass.

He waited for her to get about a block away before discarding the paper and coffee cup into a nearby trash receptacle and jogging after her.

The woman was a creature of habit, never straying more than fifteen minutes off her schedule. He remembered the first time he had seen her several weeks ago; that incredible rush of desire, as he mentally undressed and had his way with her. She became an all-consuming obsession, and over several weeks he had meticulously mapped out her weekday running schedule. It often amazed him just how comfortable people got in their routines. They were so focused on the task at hand that they ignored all the potential warning signs in their surroundings.

He knew the exact path she would take. He had followed her so many times that he could run the route blindfolded. She would go north through the park on West Drive, past the Picnic House. Then she would make the loop between Meadowport Arch and the Endale Arch, before heading back south on East Drive. Once she made her way to the Battle Pass Marker, she would head off into the Ravine, where she would zigzag her way back to the starting point.

As she passed the Picnic House, he veered off, heading east toward an area in the Ravine that he'd previously selected. It was a desolate part of the park this time of the morning, with a series of stone stairs that led down from one path to another. She would have to slow down to navigate them, and that was when he would grab her. Immediately off the steps was a densely wooded gully that would shield them from view, even if another wayward jogger should pass. He didn't worry about her screaming; they never screamed when they saw the knife. Their fear of dying far exceeded their fear of being raped.

Even now, as he lay in wait for his prey, he could feel his arousal growing; a primal urge that he could never fully satiate. This morning it was even worse, a mix of anticipation that had been building for days, coupled with the image of the outfit she was wearing. He rubbed himself through the shorts, feeling his aching manhood, as he began fantasizing. Feeling the rush as he imagined throwing her to the ground, clutching the knife he would use to threaten her into silence before cutting off her clothes. His body trembled at the thought of her naked body before him; a vanquished victim awaiting her inevitable fate.

A wave of anger rushed over him as it always did in the moments before an attack. He knew he wouldn't last long; betrayed by his own lust and desire. Thirty seconds, a minute if he were lucky, and then he would be done.

Maybe I need to rethink the next one, he thought. *If I kidnap them, I could take them someplace where I could actually enjoy them longer.*

He knew that would require a lot more work, extensive planning, but the payoff would certainly be worth it. Opportunities like this relieved the pressure for a while, but they did little in the long term. Finding a place, maybe up north, where he could take his victims and use them over a longer period might help to achieve the satisfaction he desperately desired. He wished it could be her, but he couldn't walk away now and wait. If he didn't do something to satisfy his needs he would go crazy. He knew from his past that it was when he got like this that he made mistakes, and he wouldn't let that happen again.

He was so caught up in his thoughts that he almost missed the telltale sound of footsteps on the stone pathway. Taking a deep breath, he readied himself and waited for her to come into view.

He sprang from his hiding spot, grabbing her arm and jerking her violently into the woods, coming to rest on top of her.

"You fucking scream and I'll cut your goddamn head off, bitch," he hissed, pressing the knife just under her jawline. "You understand?"

"Please… please… don't hurt me," she pled.

"Shut the fuck up."

The woman's eyes were wide and filled with panic, and she nodded her head meekly.

He drove the tip of the knife under the bra and cut through the fabric in one clean stroke, watching as her firm breasts came into view; his eyes locked on her large pink areolas.

He reached down, and tore through the spandex leggings and ripped her panties to the side, as he pulled his swollen shaft from his shorts and pressed it against her lips.

"Oh, we're going to have so much fun, baby," he growled.

Her mind raced in the chaos—all those self-defense classes she'd taken the hours practicing strikes and escapes flew out the window in a blur of terror. *Breathe, fight, run,* the instructor's voice echoed faintly, but her body froze, every lesson drowned in the knife's icy edge. Survival instincts kicked in raw and unfiltered:

play dead, buy time, wait for the opening. Her eyes were wide and filled with panic, but she forced the submission to mask the storm building inside.

The woman began whimpering, tears welling up in her eyes, just as the 124-grain Hydra-Shok round tore through the base of the man's neck, severing the spinal cord and causing him to topple forward onto the woman. She let out a bloodcurdling scream as she clawed and pushed the man off of her before scrambling to her knees and running away. The gunman emerged from the woods and approached the would-be assailant.

The paralyzed man could do nothing but lie there and wait for what was about to come.

"Michael DiMarco, you have been found guilty and sentenced to death," the man standing above him declared, before firing the kill shot into the man's head.

The man retreated back into thc woods, satisfied that he'd removed another violent predator from the streets.

CHAPTER TWENTY-SIX

Prospect Park, Brooklyn, N.Y.

Monday, May 18th, 2015 - 7:42 a.m.

Maguire stared down at the body on the ground, the man's lifeless eyes staring up at the sky, glassy and vacant like a discarded doll. A neat entry wound dimpled the forehead, but the exit in the neck, just above the man's clavicle, was a ragged mess of shredded flesh and congealing blood.

"So what do we know?" he asked.

"Attempted rape that ended in the death of the perpetrator, Commissioner," Deputy Chief Hugh Edelmann, Commanding Officer of Brooklyn South Detectives, replied. "Passersby encountered our victim, Emily Wright, by the zoo screaming hysterically. Seven-Eight Sector Boy responded, called for a bus and did a canvas of the area and found the perp deceased."

"They get a statement from the victim?" Maguire asked.

"She was in shock," Edelmann said, "but the basic gist was that she was jogging through the park when he attacked her. Cut off her sports bra and was about to rape her when he was shot by an unknown gunman."

Maguire looks around at the scene, taking in the details of the secluded wooded area and stone staircase. It was completely obscured from all but the closest observation. "This wasn't a 'stars aligned' moment where the victim, perp, and our shooter all converged at the same time."

"I agree," Edelmann replied. "Most likely, our perp had become so fixated on hunting his target that he didn't realize that he had become the hunted."

"Were we able to get a description of the shooter?"

Edelmann shook his head. "Victim said it happened too fast, and she got away as soon as she could. To be fair, I doubt she would help us anyway. Who in their right mind is going to rat out the person who saved their life?"

"Can't say as I blame her," Maguire replied.

"What's up, Boss?"

Maguire turned to see Antonucci and Jeffries looking down from the stone staircase. "It looks like we have another name to add to the list."

"Excuse me, Commissioner, I need to call Operations and give them an update," Edelmann said, before heading back up the stairs.

"The deceased was in the middle of committing a rape when someone showed up and ruined the rest of his life."

"Damn, he got fucked up," Antonucci said as he examined the man's wounds.

"Certainly wasn't the happy ending he was expecting," Tonya replied.

"You know, this would make an outstanding book."

"Yeah, well, when you figure out the part about *whodunit,* can you let me know?" Maguire replied. "It would be nice if you could do it before the sequel comes out."

"We're working on it," Antonucci replied.

"Grab what you can from the responding officers; they should be over by the zoo, and then check in with the squad later to see if they could come up with a name for our DOA and then dig into their criminal history. From the looks of this, I don't think this was our mope's first rodeo."

"Will do, Boss."

Ang and Tonya made their way back up to the roadway and headed toward the line zoo.

"Yo, Nucci!"

Ang turned around to see a man walking toward him, a gold detective shield pinned to his suit jacket.

"Holy fucking shit," Ang exclaimed. "They let you out on the street, Chrissy?"

"Step aside for homicide, baby," the man laughed, as they hugged each other.

"Tonya, this is Chris Vandenberg," Ang said. "Chrissy here is a legend in his own mind. We went through the academy and field training together."

"What brings you to this part of town, Ang?" Vandenberg asked.

"We work for the P.C.," Ang replied.

"No shit, I'm impressed."

"Eh, it's more like an over-glorified clerical spot," Ang replied. "I get to bullet point the key details for the brass, but at least I don't have to do any of the heavy lifting."

"I bet that's been keeping you busy with all the shit that has been happening," Vandenberg replied. "Things are returning to the bad old days."

"Just a bit," Ang replied, "but I guess we knew the good run would not last forever, especially not with the nitwits they keep fucking electing to run things."

"*Oofah*," Vandenberg replied, "don't get me started. I've gotta listen to my old man every Sunday bitching about them. I swear he's going to talk himself into a heart attack. He spent sixteen years on the City Council, and the only people who knew him were the ones who lived in Dyker Heights. Now you can't turn on the TV or pick up a paper without seeing one of these jabronis bitching about diversity or equity bullshit. It makes me sick."

"How is the old man doing?" Ang asked.

"Oh, you know, good days, bad days," Vandenberg replied. "Mom died three years ago, so he's lost.

"Sorry about your mother," Ang said. "She was a real sweetheart."

"Thanks, she always liked you. I go over for dinner on Sundays to keep him company. We watch sports, and I listen to his tales of the old days."

"I guess we're all headed in that direction someday," Ang said.

"What's the story here?" Vandenberg asked.

"Looks like a would-be rapist got his check cashed," Tonya said.

"Not gonna lie, it's nice to see some of the trash being taken out."

"No argument from me," Ang said. "The way the system has been going, it was bound to happen."

"You can never tell what will happen when folks get pushed too far," Vandenberg replied. "What was the movie Bronson did? The one about the vigilante?"

"Deathwish?" Ang asked.

"Yeah, that was it. Maybe someone woke up one day, and they decided they'd had enough."

"The way the city is slipping into the shitter, they're gonna be more overworked than you," Ang said.

"Job security, baby," Vandenberg laughed. "How's the boss handling it?"

"He's getting beaten up," Tonya said. "Everyone from the mayor to the press is breathing down his neck. He handles it better than most would."

"Lucky for him, he's got detective blood running in his veins." Vandenberg replied. "I guess getting paid the big bucks isn't all it's cracked up to be."

"I'd rather just have the overtime," Ang laughed.

"Well, fuck, duty calls," Vandenberg said, as he saw the Chief waving him over. "It was good catching up with you."

"Likewise," Ang replied. "You stay safe, Chrissy."

Vandenberg pulled a business card from his pocket and wrote down a number. "That's my personal cell phone. Call me when you're free and we can get together and compare war stories."

"Sounds good, and I will."

"It was nice meeting you, Tonya," Vandenberg said. "Keep this guy out of trouble, will you?"

"I will," Tonya replied, "and it was nice meeting you too."

Ang and Tonya watched as the man walked away.

"He's quite a character," she said.

"Chrissy's a great cop," Ang said. "He comes from a family of cops. His dad was on the job and ended up being put out on a three-quarters medical disability from an RMP accident while responding to a 10-13. He'd already been elected to the City Council when we came on the job and made some phone calls to get us assigned to Field Training Unit 10. Whenever we got in a car, we'd head over to his house for meals. Times were a lot simpler back then."

"Okay, Methuselah," Tonya laughed. "That's enough reminiscing about the good old days. We've got work to do."

"That's enough yapping out of you, Rook."

CHAPTER TWENTY-SEVEN

1 Police Plaza, Manhattan, N.Y.

Monday, May 18th, 2015 - 6:02 p.m.

"An attempted rape in Prospect Park has the city on edge tonight, and Channel Seven's Kristine Kaiser is on the scene live," TV anchor John Schaeffer said. "Kristine, what can you tell us?"

"John, police are advising us that the man who attempted to rape a woman this morning was himself killed by a person who remains at large," the reporter said. "Police aren't providing many details at this time due to the ongoing nature of the investigation, but the residents of this area had plenty to say."

The screen changed to the reporter conducting interviews in the park.

"He's a hero," a Hispanic woman said. "I walk this park every night with my dog, and I rarely see the police out here. I'm glad someone is watching out for us. We need more people like that who are willing to step up. I think they should give him a medal."

The screenshot transitioned to a male being interviewed. "Personally, I'm sick and tired of living like this. No one cares about us. All the politicians are to blame. The only time we ever see them is when they want our votes. They're all bums. My car has been broken into three times this year. I call the cops, and they tell me there's nothing they can do. They tell me not to keep valuables inside. Seriously? That's your answer? What the hell am I paying taxes for?"

A live shot of the reporter came back on the screen. "John, residents in this area are clearly angry, and they are demanding the mayor and police do more to fix the surging crime problem. One woman I spoke to said she used to jog in the park but bought herself a treadmill for home because she feared becoming a victim herself. She said that the park has become a haven for criminals and that she feels like a prisoner in her own home."

"Clearly there are issues that need to be addressed," Schaeffer replied, as the camera returned to him. "We spoke to the NYPD's Public Information Officer, who told us that, while recruitment remains down, the Department is working hard to provide coverage throughout the city."

"It's easy to understand why people are upset, John," Co-Anchor Marissa Gomez replied. "According to the NYPD, five of the seven index crime categories are up double digits year to date, with the largest increases occurring in rape, felony assaults, and robbery. NYPD officials who spoke on condition of anonymity said that recidivism rates are at an all-time high and they blamed a revolving-door justice system has the criminals they lock up back on the streets, often within hours."

"Unfortunately for the police, they are the ones who are going to bear the brunt of the residents' anger," Schaeffer said. "It makes you wonder if Commissioner Maguire can survive their fury?"

"Channel Seven has looked into the claims," Gomez added, "and it appears that prosecutions of criminal charges are down almost fifty-four percent on average throughout the five boroughs."

"Welcome back to the eighties, folks," Schaeffer said.

"Coming up next," Gomez said. "The City Council will be holding hearings this week on how to move forward with plans to close Rikers Island."

"Jesus Christ," Sandy Barnes muttered, as Maguire turned off the TV. "They're going to eat us alive."

"I don't blame them," Maguire replied, swirling the Jameson around in his glass. "The people have a right to be upset."

"It's not us," Barnes scoffed. "There's not a single cop out there who is happy about what is going on."

"That doesn't matter. We're the face of their frustration. They see us every day; not the courts, not the politicians."

"Maybe they should, maybe we should parade them around and let the people have a word with them."

"We have one dead politician," Maguire replied. "We don't need any more."

"I'm not sure if we have a say in that," Barnes said. "Someone's going around this city lighting matches and one of them is going to burn it all down."

Maguire looked up as he heard the knock at the door and saw Billy Walsh standing there.

"Is this a private party or can anyone join?" Walsh asked.

Maguire waved him in and set another glass on the desk.

"The enemies are inside the gate, Billy," Barnes said, hoisting her glass. "We're getting ready to make our last stand."

"Well, I guess we had a good run," Walsh said as he poured himself a drink and sat down.

"Any updates on the Prospect Park shooting?" Maguire asked.

"We've just identified our DOA as Michael DiMarco," Walsh replied. "His rap sheet dates back to 1998. They're mostly sexual abuse charges. Ended up with probation on a rape charge in 2010 that was downgraded. DiMarco got arrested again for rape in 2012 and was supposed to do three years, but got cut loose after eighteen months. The Seven-Two Squad had him on their radar. They were looking at him as a potential suspect in an assault case. In that case, someone matching DiMarco's description followed a woman into an alleyway and grabbed her, but got scared away by a guy taking out his trash before he could do anything."

"The press is going to have a field day with this," Barnes said.

"We had almost a hundred and twenty-five thousand arrests last year," Maguire replied. "Even if you just focus on the violent felony arrests, that's still a massive potential pool to draw from. What do they want us to do? Babysit every criminal in this city?"

"Oh, there is another thing," Walsh said. "It might not mean anything, but I figured you'd still want to know. A burned-out vehicle that matches the one from the Schiff shooting turned up just off the Belt Parkway by McGuire Fields."

“How ironic,” Maguire scoffed.

“Think someone might be trying to send you a message?” Barnes asked.

“I gave up believing in coincidence a long time ago,” Maguire replied. “Who found it?”

“A crew from JFK Airport was checking on one of their radar beacons when they spotted the fire and called it in. Six-Three responded and ran the VIN. It was stolen from Woodmere in Nassau County last month.”

“I’m assuming we didn’t get any evidence,” Maguire asked.

“No, by the time FD got there, it was burned down to the rims,” Walsh replied. “Fire hoses finished the job.”

“Sounds like all we can do is sit around and wait,” Barnes said.

“One or two more of these, and we are all going to be sitting around at the unemployment office,” Maguire replied.

“Hey, Boss,” Maguire looked up to see Detective Luke Jackson standing in the doorway. “I’m sorry to interrupt, but the mayor is on line two.”

CHAPTER TWENTY-EIGHT

City Hall, Blue Room, Manhattan, N.Y.

Tuesday, May 19th, 2015 - 9:13 a.m.

Jack Barone stood at the lectern, speaking to members of the press corps with Maguire at his side.

"Mr. Mayor, what do you say to the people living in fear?" Veronica Hamill, a reporter for the Times, asked.

"The city will not be held hostage," Barone said, "nor are we going to be politically blackmailed because some people disagree with the way things are done."

"But there is growing unrest with residents who feel that this is a self-inflicted wound," the reporter followed-up.

"Veronica, I understand the need of the press to sensationalize events like this, but the reality is that this is New York City, and it doesn't matter if we like it or not, there is always going to be a certain level of crime that we cannot prevent."

"With all due respect, Mr. Mayor, a vigilante group operating in the city is profoundly different from a random shooting," Hamill protested. "People are asking whether the police commissioner is up to this task, and I think that is a question that deserves to be answered."

"Commissioner Maguire has a proven track record," Barone snapped, "and he has my complete trust to lead the Department."

"No one is questioning his qualifications or casting aspersions on his service, but we are questioning what he is doing to remedy these threats."

Barone looked over at Maguire, who stepped up to the microphone.

"I understand your line of questioning, Ms. Hamill," Maguire said, "and I appreciate the concerns that the residents have. I have the same ones, and there have been a lot of sleepless nights since this first came to light. The people of this city need to understand that we are working tirelessly to identify those responsible and bring them to justice. That being said, we have to work with the tools that are available to us. This is the real world and not some episode of a detective show where we can materialize evidence out of thin air."

"Commissioner Maguire, can you reassure residents you have the resources and the right people handling this investigation?" Jason Pritchard from the Post asked.

"There is a reason that our detectives are called the 'Greatest in the World,'" Maguire replied. "These are the same men and women who found the VIN plate at the World Trade Center bombing in 1993. They are the same ones who work tirelessly day after day to bring criminals to justice. What I can tell the people of this city is that they will leave no stone unturned in their pursuit of those behind these heinous murders."

"Commissioner, can you offer any advice to the people?" Hamill asked.

"At this time, we are not aware of any credible threats to the people," Maguire said. "However, we are advising anyone who might be at risk, given the criteria set out in the published letter, to exercise extreme caution at this time."

"Will you be providing increased protection to those at risk?" Pritchard asked.

"Because of the sensitive nature of the investigation, I won't be getting into the specifics of how we are responding to this threat," Maguire replied.

"Thank you all for coming today," the Mayor's Press Secretary said. "This will conclude the press conference."

Maguire and Barone watched as staff began escorting the reporters out of the room.

"That went okay," Barone said, as the last of them left.

"For now," Maguire replied, "but they'll be back."

"Listen, James, I know things have been tense between us lately," Barone said. "A lot of that has been on me, and I wanted to apologize."

"No need, sir," Maguire replied. "We're both doing the best we can under the circumstances."

"We all like to believe that we will rise to the occasion when things go south, but sometimes you don't know how you will react until it happens," Barone said. "I came down on you because I didn't have the answers, but I know you are doing the best you can. I also wanted to tell you that I am rescinding the budget cut for the Department. We can cut from other places and revisit this after this issue is resolved."

"I appreciate that. Let's hope that it is sooner rather than later."

"Are you making any progress?"

"Whoever is behind this is good," Maguire replied. "They know the system and how to game it. The problem is that we are limited in what we can do. At this point, we are reactive instead of being proactive."

"What's stopping you?" Barone asked.

"I'd say mostly the Fourth Amendment. We have suspicions that the people behind this might be involved in the legal system, but that is all they are, suspicions. If this involves, judges, attorneys, or even cops, we have to make sure everything we do is ironclad. Absent probable cause we are screwed. There is a link somewhere, but at this point it feels like we won't know unless they fuck up, and I'm not sure if they will."

"What about the letter?" Barone asked.

"Clean," Maguire replied. "No fingerprints or DNA. Like I said, whoever is behind this knows exactly what they are doing."

"Is there anything new in the Schiff shooting?" Barone asked.

"They found what could be the car that was used, but it was burned out. I hate to say it, but we might be stuck waiting for them to get complacent."

"And how many bodies will that equate to?"

"I don't know, but it won't be zero," Maguire replied.

"Okay, keep me posted and let's pray for the best."

CHAPTER TWENTY-NINE

NY Post - Letter to the Editor

Thursday, May 21st, 2015 - Morning Edition

Greetings:

"Mankind are more disposed to suffer, while evils are sufferable, than to right themselves by abolishing the Forms to which they are accustomed. But when a long train of Abuses and Usurpations, pursuing invariably the same Object, evinces a Design to reduce them under absolute Despotism, it is their Right, it is their Duty to throw off such Government and to provide new Guards for their future Security."

These solemn words from the Declaration of Independence were true in 1776, and they are equally true today.

Over the course of decades, the system we live under has become corrupt; rotted from within by those who seek to better themselves on the backs of others. Politicians and their sycophants have flourished, enjoying a life crafted through deceit and cunning, while the people have languished; victims of the policies that do not apply to their lawmakers. With each unmet promise, the citizens have sunk deeper into a malaise to where they are no longer able to break free from the shackles imposed on them, but break free they must.

Just as in 1776, the time has come for a few to stand up for the many. Where they lack the will, we do not. It is our desire, our sworn duty, to open their eyes and show them that for necessary change to occur, they have to become the change they seek. Those who would seek to subjugate and cause the law-abiding citizen to live in fear must be shown that their actions have consequences. The ballot box is no longer a remedy for us, so we have now turned to the cartridge box.

While we respect the hard work and tenacity of New York's Finest, the average police officer has been reduced to nothing more than an ineffectual lap dog, castigated to the point that they are impotent by bureaucrats, who have abandoned their own oaths to the ever-changing whims of their political overlords. If the criminal does not fear the police, then it is time that he learns to fear the fury of a patient man.

This letter serves as a warning to those who lust to break the law: Make peace with your lives, because your days are numbered.

The shadows you once moved safely in will no longer protect you from our all-seeing eyes. We know who you are, we know where you live, and we will hunt you down in the places you once felt safest in. The fear you once stirred in the hearts of this city's residents will soon grip your own until you are the ones hiding behind closed doors. You will know no peace, and you will question the loyalties of everyone around you. It will be safer for you to be in jail, to beg prosecutor and judge alike to throw the book at you, than to be caught on the streets.

This once great city has devolved into a state of anarcho-tyranny, whereby the government willfully fails to enforce the law, while simultaneously oppressing its own citizens. One by one, those who engage in this type of petty dictatorship will see their lives quickly cut short. The broken system that has protected the lawless will soon be brought down and its corrupt underbelly exposed.

No sane man wishes for this moment, but when he is finally pushed to take action he must be so committed, so severe in his response, that the memory of what he does will echo throughout the future and serve as a stark warning to those who might one day try again to subjugate the innocent.

We are that man, and we are coming for you.

CHAPTER THIRTY

1 Police Plaza, Manhattan, N.Y.

Friday, May 22nd, 2015 - 9:53 a.m.

The uniformed chiefs sitting in the conference room stood as Maguire and Barnes walked in.

"Sit down," Maguire said as he took his seat. "We've got too much to do to stand on ceremony. I'm sure you all read the latest diatribe to hit the paper."

Everyone nodded.

"I think we have to take them at their word," Maguire said. "So there is a very strong likelihood that we'll be dealing with another victim soon. If there is a silver lining to this black cloud, the Mayor has informed me that we are off the chopping block in terms of budget cuts. I'm not sure how long it will last, but at least it won't be an impediment for the foreseeable future. Carlos, what's going on with patrol?"

"This morning, the Six-Eight responded to a report of shots fired at the office of Councilwoman Miranda Nussbaum," Chief of Patrol Carlos Hernandez replied. "The glass window was shot at overnight, but the preliminary investigation determined that the damage was consistent with a pellet gun. Obviously Nussbaum's staff are making more of it than it warrants, but I directed the sector to pay special attention to the location."

"I think that is one of my fears," Maguire said. "That these letters are going to serve as motivation for the fringe elements to start acting up. I doubt they rise to the same level, but we don't need to waste resources running down this bullshit either."

"I've sent out a bulletin to all commands detailing proactive measures," Hernandez replied. "We're starting to see pop-up protests at some council offices, but so far they have been peaceful; just a bunch of folks carrying signs. I've notified all commanding officers to identify any locations in their commands that have a political affiliation and, where possible, assign foot posts to cover them during hours of operation. If they can't, then the sectors will make hourly visits."

"Have your guys looked into the Nussbaum incident, Billy?"

"I had the Six-Eight Squad go over and talk to them," Walsh replied. "They weren't too happy about being told it was probably just some kids. With the way the staff was acting, you would have thought it was an anti-Semitic machine gun attack. Honestly, more than likely you are going to get a call from Nussbaum about it."

"Well, they do like to be dramatic," Maguire replied. "I'll call Nussbaum and ask her to lower the heat in her office. I know everyone is on edge, but I don't think they realize that it is physically impossible for thirty thousand officers to provide individual protection for eight million people."

"Yes, but they're special," Barnes chimed in.

"Yeah, special needs," Maguire replied.

"I hate to break the news to you, Boss, but that train pulled out of the station already," Chief of Intelligence Daniel Shea said. "My phone has been blowing up with calls from council members demanding full-time protection details. I even got a call from the mayor's chief of staff asking if we had any plans for providing assistance."

"What did you tell them, Danny?" Maguire asked.

"I told them the truth," Shea said. "We do not have the manpower or resources to provide protection for fifty-one members."

"We already have one dead politician, so it's not an idle threat," Maguire replied. "Have your people done a risk assessment?"

"Yes, thirty-eight council members actively backed Fernandez's calls to shut down Rikers, so theoretically they could all be at risk. Fortunately, not all of them have been as vocal, so I think they might be low on the list, but they still could end up being targeted."

“I know you don’t want to, but at some point you’re going to need to consider providing protection to some of the more at-risk folks,” Barnes added.

“I know,” Maguire replied. “The problem is that once one person gets it, they are all going to want it and, like every new perk, once they get it, they will never let go.”

“I hate to add to the mix, but I’m already receiving calls from the Secret Service and Diplomatic Security Service regarding coverage for the United Nations General Assembly,” she said. “They’re asking what our plans are in the event that this case isn’t resolved before then so they know if they are going to have to bring in more people. I’m going to have a hard enough time covering UNGA details as it is, and if Billy can’t supply his people because they are tied up on this investigation, there is no way I can take on covering the City Council.”

“Can I make a suggestion?” Chief of Counterterrorism Jessica Hawley asked.

“Please,” Maguire replied.

“I can talk to the C.O. of Special Operations,” Hawley said. “Between his Strategic Response Group and my Critical Response Teams, we should be able to provide additional coverage and free up patrol. If Danny’s people can do a basic dignitary protection course, I can get some of my people trained up and be on standby if the need arises. It’s not a perfect solution, but it’s an option if we need to move fast.”

“Well, to paraphrase General Patton, ‘A good plan now is better than a great plan later,’” Maguire replied. “Sandy, I want you to take the reins on this and coordinate all the moving parts.”

“Will do,” Barnes replied.

“I don’t want this turning into a media circus, so the quieter we can keep it, the better off we will be,” Maguire said. “Where do we stand with the courts?”

“I spoke to the chief of public safety this morning,” Barnes replied. “While they have not identified any threats at the courthouses, he has increased court security officer patrols of judge and district attorney parking areas. He also told me that they have been looking at any judges or any assistant district attorneys who might be considered soft on crime, and they are going to provide us with a list. Of course, it is all *unofficial,* and I promised that we would keep it under wraps."

"Why do I get the feeling it is going to be a long list?" Maguire sighed.

"Probably, but the good news is that he's willing to work with us," Barnes replied. "Since things seem localized, at least for now, he's going to bring in his people from the surrounding counties to beef up security for anyone deemed at risk. He thinks they can handle it for now."

"That's one silver lining," Maguire said.

"Gotta take the wins where we can," Barnes replied.

"Okay, you all know what you have to do," Maguire said. "If anything comes up, let me know right away."

CHAPTER THIRTY-ONE

1 Police Plaza, Manhattan, N.Y.

Friday, May 22nd, 2015 - 4:41 p.m.

"You wanted to see me, Boss?"

Maguire looked up to see Antonucci in the doorway.

"Yeah, come in and close the door, Ang," Maguire replied.

Antonucci walked in and took a seat.

"Where's Tonya?" Maguire asked.

"Range day," Antonucci replied.

"Why didn't she just use the HQ range?"

"Her girlfriend is a firearms instructor up at Rodman's Neck," Antonucci explained. "They don't get to see each other that often, so she likes to go up there. They are making it a girl's weekend of it."

"Well, aren't you lucky?" Maguire laughed.

"Excuse me, but the way you just said that leads me to believe that it isn't the 'I just hit the lotto' type of lucky."

"I guess that all depends," Maguire said.

"On?"

"On the fact that I'm counting on you to be the luck," Maguire replied.

He held up a USB drive, his gaze lingering on it as if he were allowing himself a moment longer to wrestle with the moral dilemma that was raging inside. He took a deep breath and made his choice, tossing it to Ang.

"What's this?"

"Maybe a clue," Maguire replied. "I'm hoping you can use that luck of yours to search through the data and find out who is behind these killings."

"This is based on the numbers I gave you?" Antonucci asked.

Maguire nodded. "It should show all the interactions for those numbers and with whom they had repeated contacts. If I'm right, the evidence we need is contained somewhere on that drive."

"Do I want to know where—"

"No," Maguire said, "you don't, and I wouldn't tell you anyway."

Antonucci's eyebrow arched. "I guess it's a good thing I love a nice mystery."

"Right now I need you to focus on solving the mystery on that drive."

"I think it's safe to say that this is going to be a hell of a lot of work."

"Good thing you have the weekend free," Maguire said with a grin.

"Not to sound ungrateful, but the Mets have a three-game series this weekend that I was looking forward to watching."

"I'll save you some time," Maguire replied. "They're probably going to lose."

"That's mean, Boss. I expect that from Commissioner Barnes, but not from you."

"Truth hurts, Ang," Maguire replied, "but in all seriousness, I'm counting on you. This is our best shot at a quick resolution. If you can't find any correlation to the numbers leading up to and after the shootings, we're going to be walking around with our thumbs up our ass as the body count climbs."

"No pressure," Antonucci said.

"I just need one loose thread I can pull to unravel this, Ang, and I need you to find it. Whatever you need is yours for the asking."

"I'll do my best, Boss."

"Get me some actionable intelligence and you'll be watching Mets games from a suite at Citi Field, Ang."

"That would certainly take the sting out of losing," Antonucci laughed.

“Call me as soon as you know something,” Maguire replied. “I don’t care what time it is.”

“Will do.”

CHAPTER THIRTY-TWO

Midtown Manhattan, N.Y.

Sunday, May 24th, 2015 - 8:11 a.m.

"Good morning and welcome to Wake Up, New York, the show that tackles the tough issues facing city residents. I'm your host, Madison Greer, and on today's show we will be talking to John Connolly, a professor of economics at NYU who recently announced his candidacy for New York City mayor," the reporter said, as the camera pulled back from the young, blonde journalist to reveal her guest.

"Thank you, Madison; it is a pleasure to be with you," Connolly replied.

John Connolly had the academic locked in. A trim man in his early fifties, with salt and pepper hair and beard, he wore jeans coupled with a button-down shirt and tie under a gray tweed sport coat and a pair of wire-rimmed glasses. Factually, he had all the right arguments to present, but he knew that he also had to tap into the plight of the everyday resident. He needed to present a strong, cogent economic argument for his campaign, but he also had to strike at the moral dilemma the city was facing.

"Professor Connolly, even before you announced your candidacy, you were an outspoken critic of this administration. Can you tell our viewers why you think Mayor Barone is doing a terrible job?"

"To be fair, Madison, I have been a critic of the last several administrations and their failed fiscal policies," Connolly replied. "There is a fine line between responsibility and folly, and unfortunately the last several mayors have chosen the latter. That being said, I also find that the City Council bears its fair share of culpability in all this. Between the two of them, we have the makings of the perfect storm."

"Can you elaborate a bit on the causes that have led us to this point?"

"Well, for starters, those in power seem hell-bent and determined to make it economically unviable for businesses and residents to remain here. I'm sure that anyone watching can attest to the fact that the living conditions have plummeted while taxes have skyrocketed; whether its property taxes, sales taxes, income taxes, or business taxes, residents and business owners are paying the price for the political machines inability to see the writing on the wall."

"And what does that writing say to you?" Greer asked.

"You're too young to remember, but some of your viewers might recall a headline in one of the local papers in the 70s that read, 'Ford to City: Drop Dead.' Then-President Ford refused to bail out the city on the eve of potential bankruptcy. It was a dark day, but the reality was that the city was a victim of its own poor policies. Back then we were four hundred and fifty-three million in debt. Now we are over a hundred billion. It doesn't take an economics degree to understand that the path we are on is unsustainable."

"What do you think the leading causes are?"

"Sadly, many of the conditions we face today are the same we faced back then," Connolly replied. "You have soaring crime, an exodus of businesses and middle-income families, along with a surge in government jobs and wasteful spending."

"It does sound like a recipe for disaster," Greer replied.

"It might be considered heresy in political circles, but I believe that if we are to fix this problem, we need to tighten our economic belts. That might mean cutting some social programs that for too long have been considered sacred cows. That might seem heartless to some, but it is a destination we are going to arrive at sooner or later. The time to focus on fixing things is before it gets too bad, not when you've maxed out every credit card."

"Some have called your position xenophobic because you have spoken out about cutting the number of programs that help migrants."

"Ah, yes, the perennial argument of the elites," Connolly smiled. "When they can't argue the merits, they turn to spurious name-calling. Let me be crystal clear to your audience. Like many New Yorkers, I am the product of immigration. I am a third-generation American, and both of my paternal grandparents were immigrants who came to America from Ireland. Legal immigration built this city. I'm living proof. But what we can't do is bankrupt ourselves in the name of compassion."

"Staying with the topic of compassion for a moment," Greer said. "Some would argue that it is a humanitarian problem driving this issue and that they have no other option than to flee their home countries and come here just to survive."

"Just a few blocks from this studio is the United Nations, a body that was founded on the principle of protecting human rights and preventing wars," Connolly replied. "Can someone explain to me what they are doing? Why are they not being more proactive in fixing issues so that people don't feel the need to flee their homelands? Their ineffectiveness should not be our burden."

"So would you end our status as a sanctuary city?" Greer asked.

"On day one," Connolly replied. "Let me be clear. I have always been a firm believer in helping out others who are less fortunate, but I won't take food off my children's plates to feed them."

"What other policies would you explore if you were elected?"

"To start with, I think we need to cull the bloated bureaucracy. Everywhere I go, I hear the same complaints. People's taxes are too high, and they are not seeing any substantive return on that money. In fact, many are complaining of a significant decrease in services, despite paying more."

"So what would you do differently?"

"Well, first and foremost is to restore law and order," Connolly replied. "No city can survive if it can't protect its residents. If people are afraid, then they have no reason to live here or start businesses. We also have to restore tourism, which is a huge revenue source and something that has been on the decline in recent years. No one wants to be a crime victim while they are on vacation. So, my first goal would be to increase our police presence and restore safety to our streets."

"Wouldn't that just create more of a burden on the city's finances?" Greer asked.

"It would if we did nothing else," Connolly replied, "but one of my first actions would be to implement a two percent budget cut across all non-emergency agencies. It's unfair during these tough economic times to ask our constituents to do more with less when we refuse to apply that same standard to government."

"That won't make you very popular," Greer said. "In fact, some say that your plan would disproportionately hurt the poor, especially if those cuts affect social programs. What do you say to critics who call that cruel?"

"I can appreciate that no one likes to see their budgets cut," Connolly replied, "but would be cruel, and I'd argue grossly irresponsible, is to pretend that those cuts are not coming, one way or the other. We're living like a household that maxed out every credit card and hopes payday comes before the lights get turned off. We need to get into the mindset of saving for the future and not kicking the can down the road. My plan would allow for changes to be made gradually with the least potential impact on people and services. If we do nothing, then there will have to be even more drastic cuts in the future, and that is something no one wants to admit. Years ago, the city endured the pain of layoffs, and this deeply affected me because my father was a firefighter and one of those who got laid off. The goal is to take the necessary steps so that we can once again become America's safest big city. Once we reach that point, the revenue from business and tourism will return."

"One of the hot-button topics is the plan to close Rikers Island," Greer said. "Is that something you support?"

"Not at all," Connolly replied. "In my book, it's a non-starter."

"Why do you say that?"

"Because it's fiscally irresponsible," he replied. "I've listened to all the arguments, and what I hear is a lot of promises, but very few facts. Selling off something with the promise of a future windfall, even if true, negates the present time. I've asked the closure proponents where they intend to house prisoners, and what I have been told is that we will build new facilities in each of the boroughs. That's the plan. Spend more money we don't have in the hopes of maybe getting it back at a later date. Maybe when we have a budget surplus, we can revisit this conversation, but until then my answer is a resounding no."

"I'd be remiss if I didn't ask you, but what are your thoughts about the recent letters being published?"

"I'd like to say I'm shocked, but I'm not. Don't get me wrong, I do not agree with the premise they claim to be operating under, but I understand the underlying sentiment. Rising crime affects everyone, whether you live in Forest Hills, Brownsville, or the Upper West Side. Sadly, we have become a city ruled by unaffected elitists who scold us for having the audacity to plead for our safety. Where is the outcry when DAs release rapists and predators back into society? When will judges wake up and realize that someone with a multiple-page rap sheet is a menace to society? I have yet to hear one cogent response from the mayor addressing these issues. The vacuum created by the absence of strong leadership will inevitably be filled. The best way to prevent this type of activity is to be aggressive in doing the job you were elected to do."

"It sounds like you blame the mayor," Greer said.

"I believe that Mayor Barone is a genuinely nice person who was wholly unprepared for the difficulties of the job he found himself thrust into," Connolly replied. "The public advocate, a role he previously held, is something of an aberration. It's supposed to serve as a watchdog for the electorate, but that hasn't really worked out well now, has it? The office was created in 1993, when the City Council renamed the position of President of the City Council, but then later created the position of Speaker of the City Council. The truth is, we didn't elect Barone; we got stuck with him because of the line of succession. Instead of being an effective chief executive, he is trying to appease everyone, but failing to fix the actual problems."

"You're a registered independent," Greer said. "Do you think that's a political liability?"

"I think it was," Connolly replied, "but times have changed. I think more people are becoming aware that their parties have left them behind ideologically. They're only important every four years when politicians come around looking for a vote and offering promises that never seem to come to fruition. My candidacy provides them with an alternative choice, one that gives the power back to the people. My question to the residents of this city is simple. Is your life better now than it was? If the answer is no, then when you get in the voting booth, cast your ballot for someone who is willing to make the changes that will benefit your lives and not those of the political class and their donors."

"It seems like there is a great divide between the mayor and city council," Greer said. "How will it be different with you?"

"I am a firm believer in working with anyone willing to get the job done, but I also believe in transparency. As mayor, I will be committed to informing the citizens about the functionality of government. If the City Council chooses to work against the wishes of the people, then I will expose that and allow the voters to decide."

"Well, I want to thank you for joining me today and sharing your vision for the future," Greer said. "You certainly have your work cut out for you, but it sounds like you're ready for the fight."

"Thank you for having me on, Madison, and I implore all New Yorkers to get out and vote for change come the next election."

CHAPTER THIRTY-THREE

Plainedge, N.Y.

Sunday, May 24th, 2015 - 2:41 p.m.

"Jesus H. Christ!" Antonucci roared, as he watched a hard line drive scream by the second baseman, allowing the Dodgers' runner on third to score easily. "This is going to be another long fucking season."

He tossed the paper he'd been reading onto the coffee table and headed to the kitchen for another beer.

"One season," he snapped, as he removed the cap and took a swig. "Can we just get one fucking season over five hundred? That's not asking for much, is it?"

There was little joy in being a Mets fan in New York City, not when you had the Yankees as your crosstown rivals. Sure, the Yankees had some lean years, but they also had a gajillion post-season appearances to go along with their twenty-seven World Series wins. As a fan, it felt like the Mets organization was being used as a tax write-off at times. Sometimes they'd get lucky and sign a dominant player only to have them get injured or fall into a slump, and the losing cycle would continue.

"Maybe I should go over to the dark side," he laughed, as he sat back down on the couch. "Barnes would laugh her ass off if I walked in wearing a Jeter jersey."

Two innings and five runs later, he turned off the television and returned to the task at hand, begrudgingly accepting the inevitable Dodgers series sweep.

The living room of the small apartment looked like an episode of some crime thriller show. The coffee table was covered with papers and a laptop, and situated across from him were four whiteboards with copious notes concerning the details of each of the murders.

He picked up the laptop and began reexamining the data. Each of the phone numbers was presented along the lines of a class diagram. The subject number first and a series of numbers that had interacted with it. The vast majority of numbers were one-offs, with a few having just one or two interactions. These were the ones he had focused on first in order to rule them out. On the remaining ones, where there were multiple calls between the target number and frequent recipients, it listed times and dates of each call. If those recipients called anyone else, it indicated those connections and the pertinent details.

He had thought that he'd been given an impossible task, considering the number of phone numbers they had collected, and that it would be a tedious task trying to collate the data, but he'd been amazed to find that the vast majority of the legwork had already been done.

He scrolled through the pages, shaking his head at the level of detail the diagrams contained. Listed on the pages were the private phone numbers of some of the city's most influential people: politicians, celebrities, the movers and shakers in the financial industry. It was all there in black and white.

"Jesus Christ," he muttered.

He had no idea who was behind the treasure trove of information that Maguire had gotten, but one thing he knew was that it wasn't something locally produced. The Department certainly didn't have this level of sophistication. The feds did, but considering the legal ramifications of something like this, he had his reservations that they would help in a regional situation like this.

"Stop worrying about the who and begin focusing on the where," he chided himself. "You have a job to do."

As the clock on the wall kept its steady march, Antonucci scoured through the data in silence, feeling his frustration grow as each lead withered and died before him.

"It's here, dammit. I know it is."

He leaned back and rubbed his eyes, wishing Tonya had been there to help him. She had a keen sense for picking out things that didn't belong. He'd lost track of the hours he'd logged in this weekend, but was fully aware of the mental toll it had taken. Sleep beckoned him, and he was losing the fight.

"Five minutes," he muttered as he closed his eyes and submitted.

"Hey, *stunad*, what the hell are you doing?"

Antonucci opened his eyes abruptly, but instead of being in his living room, he found himself sitting at a desk in a dingy squad room. Across from him sat the imposing figure of his father, Vincent Antonucci, in his NYPD uniform, his dark, wavy hair slicked back and a scowl on his face.

"Dad?"

"What the hell are you doing, Angie?" the elder Antonucci asked.

Vincent Antonucci was the only one who ever called him Angie. He'd hated it as a child, but now the familiar nickname brought a sense of comfort he'd long forgotten. His father had been killed in the line of duty when Ang was just a young boy, and his memories had grown fleeting over the decades that had passed. Now, sitting across the desk from him, it all came flooding back.

"Is it really you?" Ang asked.

"Of course it's me, Angie, but you haven't answered my question."

"I'm investigating a string of murders," Ang replied, "but I'm stuck."

"That's because you're trying to find a needle in a haystack when you should be trying to find the haystack that goes with the needle."

"I don't know what you mean," Ang replied.

He watched as his father got up from his chair, listening to the gentle creaking of the leather jacket he wore coupled with the jingle of keys on his gun belt.

"That fancy gold shield of yours has detective written on it," his father replied as he poured a cup of black coffee. "So why aren't you detecting?"

"I know the connection is there; I just can't find it, and I'm running out of time."

"Time is the only thing you need, Angie," his father said, as he sat back down.

"Right now I would be happy with a little luck," Ang replied.

"I had an instructor at the academy who told us that every cop starts their career with two bags. One is empty, and the other is filled with luck. The key is to fill the empty bag with experience before the other one runs out of luck. You're a great cop, and I'm proud of you, son, but you don't need luck to find a needle when you have the experience to know which haystack to search."

"Is it too much to ask for a sign?" Ang asked.

"Typical detective," his father laughed, "always wanting the patrol guys to handle the heavy lifting while they take the credit."

A crash jarred Ang awake, his eyes frantically scanning the room for the source of the noise until he spotted the clock lying on the carpet across the room.

"*Sonofabitch*," he exclaimed, as he got up and carefully examined the device. A shard of glass had wedged itself into the cardboard body, pinning the broken arms at 12:58.

He sat back down on the couch and grabbed his laptop and began searching. Then he picked up the stack of papers from the coffee table and rifled through them until he found the one he was looking for, circling one of the boxes with a red marker.

"You can't be serious," he muttered.

CHAPTER THIRTY-FOUR

Kew Gardens, Queens, N.Y.

Sunday, May 24th, 2015 - 3:56 p.m.

Robert Conti fumbled with the key, doing his best to unlock the door quickly, as the house phone on the other side rang incessantly.

"C'mon, c'mon," he said with annoyance, as the jiggling key engaged with the lock pins and he was able to open the door.

He laid the plastic grocery bags on the counter and snatched up the phone. "Hello?"

"Bobby?" a familiar voice asked. "Is that you?"

"Yes, Mom," he said, as he slammed the door shut. "What's wrong?"

"I've been trying to reach you all day!" Eleanor Conti exclaimed. "Where have you been?"

"Work," he replied, as he navigated the kitchen, putting away the groceries while tethered to the phone.

"On a Sunday?" she asked.

"It's easier for me to get work done when no one is around."

"What's wrong with your cell phone?"

"Nothing," he replied. "I just had the sound turned off so I could concentrate."

There was a brief silence followed by a loud sigh. "For the love of God, Bobby, I have been worried sick all day."

"I don't know what to say," he replied. "Sorry, I guess."

"You guess? That's your answer?"

"Mom, is there something specific you called me about?"

"Don't you dare get an attitude with me, Robert Michael," she snapped. "I'm your mother. I don't need a reason to call you."

"Okay, so why were you trying to call me all day?"

"God, you are such an insufferable ass at times."

Conti continued putting away items in the fridge as he waited for her to get to the point. For being a former attorney, his mother sometimes took a while to get to her conversational destination.

"What is going on down there?" she asked.

"It's New York City, Mother, can you be a little more specific?"

"These killings; the letters in the newspaper," she replied. "I had no idea what was going on until your Aunt Linda told me. Not that you would ever share with me."

"That's because there is nothing to share," he replied. "It's just some moron looking for his or her fifteen minutes of fame."

"I'd say murder is a bit more than someone looking for fifteen minutes of fame," she replied. "Have you read their letters?"

"I've heard about them, but I haven't had time to read up on it," he said, as he removed a Chinese food container from the fridge and sniffed it, recoiling in disgust before tossing the offending item into the trash. "Assistant district attorneys tend to be busy down here."

"They are targeting people within the criminal justice system, Robert. Are they taking any precautions at work? Are you?"

"Precautions for what?"

"I can't believe you're taking this so lightly. I don't know what's happening down there, but it's got me scared to death for you."

"Mom, I'm fine," Conti replied, sitting down at the kitchen island. "You don't need to worry about this. It's not like I'm wandering around dark alleys looking to get jumped. I go to work, I do my job, and I come home."

"Don't you dare brush me off like that, Robert. We both know it's not that cut and dry."

"We're not going to get into this again, are we?" he asked.

"Robert, they are targeting people who hold radical views like you."

"Radical?" he repeated. "I wouldn't call wanting the criminal justice system to be fair and impartial a radical view."

"You know what I mean," she replied. "Whether you want to believe it or not, your position on bail reform, talking about the police like they are the enemy, is not endearing to the average citizen."

"The average citizen has no clue about what is going on," he snapped. "You, of all people, should know that."

"You're right, I do," she replied. "Don't forget that your father and I practiced law a lot longer than you have. I know exactly how the system works and just how fast things can get ugly when people stop trusting it. I'm terrified that your outspokenness is going to put you in someone's crosshairs."

"Not to sound rude, Mom, but you and Dad were attorneys in Greenwich, for God's sake. You spent your days litigating tax evasion for hedge fund guys and estate disputes for old money. You don't have a clue what it's like to practice in a real city and deal with a justice system that has been grinding poor people into dust for decades. I'm not playing it safe up in Connecticut; I'm trying to fix something broken."

"It doesn't sound rude; it is rude, Robert. Your father and I worked hard, and we believed in the law, same as you. But if you are so hell-bent on these liberal crusades, bail reform and coddling defendants, why didn't you just become a defense attorney? That's where you should be fighting for the underdog, not in the prosecutor's office."

Conti sighed loudly; frustrated that they were having this conversation again. He'd grown up inspired by his parent's work in the legal profession, but there was a great divide between a child who was proud of his parents' work and an adult who saw the disparities in the application of the law. His parents had practiced in a world that was insulated from the ugliness that he dealt with.

"Because defense attorneys can only try to patch up the damage after it is done," he explained. "They are stuck reacting, doing their best to win cases one at a time while the system keeps churning out the same garbage. Genuine change, Mom, systemic change, has to come from within. Prosecutors have to take an active roil in deciding who gets prosecuted, who walks, what justice even looks like. If I don't take a stand, the entire system stays rigged."

"Bobby, you keep talking about how the system is rigged, but you ignore the fact that people are not being forced to commit crimes."

Conti laughed. "Are you serious, Mom? God, you need to get out of your little bubble and see how the average person lives. Yes, they are being forced to commit crimes."

"So you're telling me that the person holding a gun to someone's head has a gun being held to theirs?" she asked.

"In a manner of speaking," he replied. "There are a lot of factors, but we can't just ignore that income inequality, unemployment, lack of education, and unstable housing can create a sense of hopelessness that can push some toward illegal acts."

"But at the same time, you are conveniently ignoring that there are plenty of people who face tough conditions who don't commit crimes," she shot back. "And, as you like to point out, rich people commit crimes too, just different ones."

"That doesn't negate the fact that cops tend to overcharge, judges rubber stamping sentences, and poor people languish in Rikers because they can't afford the five hundred bucks to get out."

"And what about the people who shouldn't walk, Bobby?" she asked harshly. "You let someone out with no bail, and he goes right back to dealing drugs, or maybe he goes back to the girlfriend he beat and finishes the job. Despite what you want to believe, your father and I saw cases where the system worked. It kept dangerous people off the streets and gave innocent victims a chance to heal. Bail is not perfect, but it is a tool. If you throw it out, you are gambling with people's lives and not just your theories."

"It's not a tool; it's a weapon," he snapped. "Do you know what happens when you set bail at a grand for some kid who's barely even an adult? He sits in jail for months and loses everything. Meanwhile, a grand to some Wall Street jerk is a joke. He spends more than that on drinks with the boys at the Jersey Shore. The data backs me up, Mom. Most of those no-bail releases don't re-offend before trial. It's the cops and the tough-on-crime crowd that want you scared, not the facts. I'm not gambling with people's lives; I'm just leveling the playing field for everyone."

"Leveling the field? Tell that to the woman who gets stalked because her ex didn't need bail thanks to you."

"That's not fair," he replied. "I'm not releasing people who are dangerous."

"Okay, maybe you're not, but we know how these movements can take on a life of their own. You draw the line at someone who is dangerous, but what about the next prosecutor? Maybe they don't have the same moral compass as you. I'm not saying the system is flawless. I know that it can crush people who don't deserve it. Your father and I had clients who paid their way out of messes they caused, and it wasn't always fair, but there has to be a middle ground, Bobby. Do you think that the people who are responsible for these killings care about your data? No, to them you are nothing more than a bleeding-heart DA in a city that is falling apart."

"Mom, I get it. There are risks, and sometimes a bad guy slips through, and it keeps me up at night. But the bigger risk is to do nothing; to maintain the status quo. You and Dad never had to see it up close. The single mom crying because her son's locked up on some bullshit charge and the bail she can't pay is turning a mistake into a life sentence. I'm not naïve. I know that my positions are unpopular with a lot of people, but if I don't push back, who will? Prosecutors are in a unique position to stop this machine; to push back against its abuses and not just defend the wreckage it causes."

"And what happens if the people behind the killings push back harder?" she asked. "I don't need to know all the details to understand that my son's in danger. Your father is gone, Bobby;

the stress of this profession killed him, and I can't lose you to it as well. All I am asking is for you not to be as stubborn as he was."

"I'm not trying to scare you, Mom," he said in a soothing voice. "I'm not Dad and I have no plans on getting burned out over rich people's problems. What I'm doing matters and someone has to do it, but I'm also not naïve. They've increased security at my office and inside the courthouse. I'll be careful, I promise."

"I don't care how noble your fight is," she replied. "You're my son, and I want you safe."

"I won't give up the fight, but I promise that I'll tone things down a bit. Can we make a deal?"

"I think that's the best I can hope to get out of you," she replied, "but until this issue resolves itself, you better answer my calls on the first ring. Is that understood?"

"I can work with that," he replied. "Now, if you don't mind, this has been a brutal week and I need to unwind."

"Okay, but make sure you call me daily to let me know you're alright."

"I will, Mother."

"Don't *mother* me, Robert."

"Goodnight, *Mom*," he laughed. "I'll call you tomorrow."

CHAPTER THIRTY-FIVE

1 Police Plaza, Manhattan, N.Y.

Monday, May 25th, 2015 - 6:39 a.m.

"So, where in the world are you today?" Maguire asked, sitting in the back of the SUV as it headed south on the FDR Drive.

"Germany," Melody laughed. "I'm on my way to meet with the Foreign Minister. Cook wants me to convey her disappointment with their dismal funding habits for NATO."

"Good luck with that," Maguire replied. "The West seems to have all but forgotten the threat."

"Looking at the numbers, I can't disagree with you."

"You can always threaten to pull some of our troops out. I'm sure Poland or the other Eastern countries would be thrilled to have our military contributing to their economies."

"Going to try the carrot before the stick approach," Melody replied, "but, between you and me, Cook has already raised the issue of potential base realignments."

"There'll be pushback," Maguire warned.

"Isn't there always?"

"Yeah, but just remember, the Pentagon works under a different mindset. They'll do their best to delay, obfuscate, and deploy smoke, in the hopes of waiting you out. They seem to think that they always know best, which is to say they're always thinking about their wallets."

"It always comes down to the almighty dollar," Melody replied.

"That's because there are no consequences when you're spending other people's money."

"So how are things going there?"

"Not great," Maguire replied. "I'm just about to head into the lion's den and see what new hell awaits me."

"I take it there haven't been any recent developments?"

"No," Maguire replied. "It's like we are playing a game of cat and mouse with a solitary ghost that has free rein over the city."

"We both know that safety is an illusion," Melody said. "People believe in it because they don't want to admit to themselves that the police can't be everywhere at all times. It's a thankless job, because you never get the credit when things are going well, but you get all the blame when they're not. You'll figure this out, James, I know you will."

"Can you share that enthusiasm with the city council?" Maguire asked. "I don't think they have the same level of confidence."

"It's always easier to stand on the sidelines and complain about things. You know that."

"I do," Maguire replied, "but for once it would be nice if I only had to fight the enemy in front of me and not the ones behind my back holding knives."

"It's not personal; it's just politics," Melody replied. "Isn't that what you're always telling me?"

"Don't use my words against me," Maguire laughed.

"Oh, isn't that the pot calling the kettle black!"

"Not to cut this short, but I'm about to pull into the garage. Wish me luck."

"You don't need luck, just do your job," Melody said.

"I love you, Angel. I'll call you when I get free."

"Okay, Cowboy, have fun."

Maguire ended the call as the SUV pulled into the underground parking lot. Despite Melody's support, the weight on his shoulders was becoming unbearable. It was like Log PT during BUDS, but this time he was the only one holding up *Ole Misery*.

Melody was right, but that didn't negate the fact that he was still the one responsible for it all, and he knew the target he wore on his back would only continue to grow.

They rode the private elevator to the 14th floor in silence. Both Massi and Torres knew the stress he was under, but they were in no position to help, so they left him alone with his thoughts.

As he made his way into the office, Maguire scanned the office for Antonucci, but he wasn't at his usual desk.

"Tonya," he called out as he headed toward his office.

Maguire was hanging up his suit jacket when Jeffries appeared in the doorway. "You wanted to see me, Boss?"

Maguire waved her in as he sat down at his desk. "Where's Ang?"

"Oh, he took the day off," she replied.

Maguire looked at her quizzically. "He did what?"

"He took the day off," she repeated.

"You can't be serious. He was working on something for me, and I expected those results first thing this morning."

"I'm sorry, sir," she replied. "Ang just texted me last night and said he had something to do today. He didn't mention anything to me."

"Jesus Christ, can anyone do their job here without me babysitting them?" Maguire snapped, causing Tonya to recoil.

"I didn't know," she apologized.

"It's not your fault, Tonya. Track him down and tell him I need that information ASAP, or else."

"Yes, sir," she said. "I'll get right on it."

Tonya practically leaped out of the chair as she made her escape, nearly crashing into Amanda Massi, who was coming through the doorway.

"Boss, we have another murder," Massi said. "ADA in Queens was shot and killed."

"Are you fucking serious?" he asked.

"Want me to come?" Tonya asked.

"No, we'll handle this," Maguire replied as he grabbed his coat from the rack. "Just find your partner and tell him to get his head out of his ass and get me my information."

CHAPTER THIRTY-SIX

Kew Gardens, Queens, N.Y.

Monday, May 25th, 2015 - 7:32 a.m.

Maguire stood over the dead man, staring at what remained of his face. It was evident that he'd been shot just above the bridge of his nose and the resultant blood loss had turned the front of his white dress shirt a crimson color. The man was slumped against a retaining wall in the parking lot of the Long Island Railroad Station on Austin Street, within the confines of the 102nd Precinct.

"What do we know?" Maguire asked.

"Our victim's name is Robert Conti. He's an assistant district attorney here in Queens," Captain Paul Manicone replied. "A commuter found him this morning when he was pulling into the lot. It was still dark out, and he saw him slumped over against the wall, and thought he was a drunk who'd hit his head. So he called 911, and when the sector arrived, they realized he'd been shot."

"Could he have been a mark?" Maguire asked. "Maybe a robbery gone bad?"

"Not likely, Commissioner," Manicone replied. "He's still wearing a nice watch and had his wallet on him. The search revealed about two hundred bucks and a receipt from the bar down the street. It looks like he paid his tab just after midnight and was walking home when he got popped. He lives about two blocks down on 82nd Avenue."

"Any chance this was an altercation that started in the bar and went south?"

"One of my guys pulled the precinct business card file for the bar and spoke to the owner," Manicone said. "He was working last night and said that it was pretty quiet, just our vic and a half dozen others. Guy is a regular patron, and he has never had a problem. Doesn't overdo it and gets along with everyone."

"What do we know about him?" Maguire asked.

"Officially or unofficially?"

"At this point, both," Maguire replied.

"To be blunt, he's a prick, sir," Manicone said. "It's like having a public defender in the DA's office. You could catch someone standing over a body holding a smoking gun in one hand and a written confession in the other, and this clown would plea bargain it down to a disorderly conduct."

"Sounds like a real winner," Maguire replied.

"I can't tell you how many times my Integrity Control Officer had to have a chat with him about downgrading charges. He even tried to talk to the DA about it, but he's just as useless. Basically, the DA told my ICO that it wasn't his place to tell his staff how to do their jobs and implied we were the ones who were creating the problem by overcharging perps. Not gonna lie, Commissioner. There won't be too many cops losing sleep over this one."

"Understood, but I still expect it to be investigated as if this guy were a saint," Maguire replied. "Is that understood?"

"Loud and clear, but it might be a very long list of potential suspects with this one."

"What about witnesses?" Maguire asked as he looked up at the apartment windows overlooking the lot.

"The squad already canvassed all the apartments that face the lot, but no one heard anything. Guessing the shooter used a silencer. They're hitting the nearby houses right now."

"Are there any cameras that might have caught it?"

"One," Manicone replied, pointing toward several nearby stores. "The pharmacy has one that looks into the parking lot, but the Apollo moon landing was less grainy. You can see shapes walking around, but it's not even clear enough to establish if it was our vic or someone else. The parking garage for the apartment next door has one, but the shooting took place just outside its field of view."

"Okay, canvas the entire area and when you're done, re-canvas and see if you might have jarred any memories," Maguire replied. "We need a break."

"I've got three detectives working today," Manicone replied. "I can have the squad C.O. call in the four to twelve, but that will only give us four more bodies."

Maguire nodded. "I'll call the Chief of D and have him send reinforcements. If you get any information, I want you to call me right away."

"Yes, sir," Manicone replied.

CHAPTER THIRTY-SEVEN

1 Police Plaza, Manhattan, N.Y.

Tuesday, May 26th, 2015 - 8:04 a.m.

Mike and Amanda stood next to the closed door, sharing concerned looks with each other, as the otherwise busy office came to a stop. Even Chief Martin had stepped out of his office to see what was happening.

Inside Maguire's office, the muffled sounds of an argument could be heard. Depending on the moment, they could make out parts of the strained conversation.

"I don't work for you; you work for me, goddamnit. What part of that do you have a problem understanding?"

"This is my job, not my life! Where does it say I can't take time off?"

The arguing continued for several more minutes until a sudden disquieting silence set in.

Without warning, the door flew open and Antonucci stormed out of the office.

Amanda was the first to look in, checking to see if Maguire was alright. "Boss?"

"It's fine, Amanda, send Chief Martin in," Maguire said.

His tone, coupled with the scowl on his face, told her that things were in fact not fine. "Yes, sir."

Tonya rushed after Ang and caught him in the hallway. "What the hell was that about?"

"Not now," Ang said brusquely, tugging his arm from her grasp.

"Angelo!"

"I said not now," as he turned and headed toward the elevators.

"Please tell me what's going on," she begged, but Antonucci continued walking until he disappeared around a corner.

Back inside, Liam Martin made his way into Maguire's Office.

"Is everything okay, Commissioner?"

"Shut the door, Liam," Maguire said, as he continued to look down at the paper he was writing on.

Martin closed the door and walked over to the desk, continuing to stand.

"Effective 0001 hours, Detective Antonucci is transferred to the Seven-Eight Detective Squad," Maguire said, sliding the paper across the desk. "Please notify the Chief of Personnel immediately."

Martin picked up the paper, reading the confirmation of what Maguire had just told him. "Sir?"

"Detective Antonucci doesn't work here anymore, Liam."

"If you don't mind my asking, was there a problem?" Martin asked.

"Yes, there was a problem, Liam," Maguire replied. "When I ask for something to be done, I expect it to be done when I ask and not when someone decides to do it. Is that clear enough?"

"Crystal, sir," Martin said, swallowing hard. "I'll make the notification."

"Thank you. That will be all."

CHAPTER THIRTY-EIGHT

Seven-Eight Precinct, Brooklyn, N.Y.

Wednesday, May 27th, 2015 - 3:37 p.m.

Antonucci got out of his car and headed into the five-story building, located at 6th Ave and Bergen Street, that once served as the police headquarters for Brooklyn. The precinct's construction harkened back to the days when they were built to exude strength and a sense of safety, but a century of use had put the once grand building's best days behind it.

He appeared before the desk officer and showed his shield and was directed to the detective squad office. He made his way up the stairs and, a few moments later, got the first look at his new workplace.

The C.O.'s door was open, and Antonucci looked inside, spotting a middle-aged man in an ill-fitting suit pouring over several case folders spread across his desk. "Excuse me, sir, I'm Detective Angelo Antonucci. I was just assigned here."

The man looked up from the paperwork and waved him in.

"I'm Lieutenant Roger Steinberg," the man replied as he stood up and shook Antonucci's hand. "Grab a seat, Detective. Would you like some coffee?"

"No, I'm good, sir."

The man poured himself a mug from the coffeemaker atop a nearby filing cabinet and returned to his desk.

"Welcome to the wonderful world of Brooklyn," Steinberg said as he sat back down. "You go by Angelo?"

"Most people call me Ang," Antonucci replied.

"Okay, Ang, let me start off by saying I don't know what happened that got you jettisoned here, and personally I don't care. I live by the philosophy that shit happens, but if it's not my shit, then I don't get involved."

"I give you my word that I'm not a problem child," Antonucci said.

"Don't worry, I already know that," Steinberg replied. "When I got the notification, I did some digging and reached out to my buddy, Mitch Robinson, over in Cold Case. He spoke very highly of you and said you were one of the best detectives he ever had."

"Lieutenant Robinson is a good man," Antonucci said.

"I'll take the word of Mitch over any suit in 1PP, even if the person wearing the suit happens to be the police commissioner. As far as I am concerned, whatever happened in 1PP stays there. You work for me now, and Lord knows I can use all the help I can get."

"I appreciate that, sir."

"Mitch told me your dad was killed in the line of duty, and I put two and two together," Steinberg said. "I cut my teeth as a rookie in the Seven-Five and saw his memorial plaque every shift. I'm sorry for your loss."

"Thank you," Antonucci said.

"Right now, our most pressing case is a homicide that's hard to get excited about," Steinberg said. "Victim's name was Michael DiMarco, and he got popped while trying to commit a rape in the park."

"I'm familiar with that one."

"Good, then it won't take you too long to get up to speed. The lead detective is Bobby Hayes. He's at the range today, so pull his case folder out of the cabinet and bring yourself up to speed. Maybe some of your Cold Case voodoo will show up and you can find a thread to pull on."

"I'll do my best."

"I know you will," Steinberg replied. "Here's the thing: we're doing God's work. Everyone here is an adult, and that's the way you'll be treated. I was a detective once myself, and I hated bosses who needed to be treated like fucking demigods. We all worked our way up from snot-nosed rookies, who struggled to do a 61, to who we are today. Just do your job and know that my door is always open. Hell, if you need to go on an interview, and no one else is around, just let me know. I don't need an excuse to get out of this paperwork hell. Just give me enough time to pop some Advil and wash it down with coffee and we'll be on our way."

"Duly noted," Antonucci laughed.

"There's an empty desk out in the squad room by the holding cage. Go make yourself at home and then go find my killer so I can stop getting daily calls from Chief Walsh's office."

"I'll get right on it, sir."

"Welcome aboard, Ang."

CHAPTER THIRTY-NINE

City Hall, Manhattan, N.Y.

Thursday, May 28th, 2015 - 10:32 a.m.

Jack Barone stared out the window at the plaza below him, which was lined with media trucks. They had become a regular fixture as the killings had escalated, and it felt like he had to run a gauntlet of salivating reporters every time he left, shouting questions he had no answers to. For him, City Hall had become a fortress under siege.

"They're like rabid fucking dogs out there," he fumed, as he turned and sat back down, "just waiting for the right moment to attack."

"It's the nature of the beast," Maguire replied.

"I'd love to have a goddamn job where I had no heavy-lifting to do and I got paid to question and criticize the work of everyone else."

Maguire remained silent. He knew what Barone was feeling; he felt it too. People always expected swift action and immediate results during a crisis. When that didn't occur, then the inevitable cries would begin for someone else. It was unrealistic, but not unexpected. Barone had requested regular updates on the investigation, but it was evident that he was unhappy with the lack of meaningful progress.

"James, I'm not trying to tell you how to do your job, but is there anything that can be done to speed this along? This ship is going down, and the sharks are circling."

"Mr. Mayor, I've flown in countless helicopters in my career, but I would never presume to tell the pilot how to fly based on my mere presence as a passenger," Maguire said. "With all due respect, you have never done a criminal investigation and you have no idea what goes into it. There is no crystal ball that we can turn to and make evidence magically appear in our laps. Yes, it would be nice if we could catch a break, but what you have to understand is that whoever is behind these murders is not some drugged-up idiot knocking over a 7-11 to feed his drug habit. Whoever is doing this is calculated and methodical."

"There has to be something we're missing," Barone fumed.

"Let me try to explain this to you simplistically," Maguire replied. "This city employs roughly three hundred thousand people. If I sent one of my cops out to steal an item from one of those employees in a random borough every few weeks, could you catch them?"

"No, of course not, but you already knew the answer."

"Yes, I did, and I'd like to remind you that city employees only make up about four percent of the total population. We have no witnesses and no substantive evidence. Whoever is behind this has the luxury of choosing their targets, studying the surroundings, scouting the best possible location, and executing their plan under optimal conditions. I can't fabricate evidence to lead me to the killer; I have to wait for them to give that evidence to me."

"I understand that, but the people are paying us to get a job done," Barone replied. "What am I supposed to say to people when they ask what their tax money is being used for? I'm being beaten up in the press daily, and it's going to be used as political fodder come election time."

"You tell them that there are seventy-seven precincts in this city and that I have an obligation to provide service to everyone," Maguire replied. "I could take every cop off the street and put them into this investigation and it wouldn't change a goddamn thing. There are detectives all over this city dedicated to finding the killer or killers, but so far we have yet to have any actionable evidence just fall into our laps."

"I'm sorry," Barone said. "You're not to blame. I'm just frustrated."

"Trust me, there is a lot of that going around," Maguire replied. "I guarantee you that every detective involved in this investigation is doing his or her absolute best to apprehend whoever is behind this."

“Speaking of detectives, I heard that there was one transferred out of your office.”

Maguire pursed his lips. “You heard correctly.”

“Any problems?” Barone asked. “I assume leaving such a coveted spot isn’t an ordinary occurrence.”

“It was a personal issue, and it was addressed.”

“That’s it?” Barone asked.

“That’s it.”

“Alright,” Barone said. “I guess you need to get back to work.”

“That I do,” Maguire replied, getting up from the chair. “I’ll let you know if anything turns up.”

“Thank you.”

Maguire waited until he was clear of the office to let the anger set in. It was one thing to be called out on the investigation, but another thing to be questioned about personnel issues. He was already hot by the time he reached the plaza out front, but had to suppress those emotions as the throng of reporters converged on him.

“Commissioner Maguire,” a female reporter asked, thrusting a microphone toward his face. “Is there any update on the investigation?”

“We are doing everything in our power to identify and arrest the individuals responsible for these murders,” Maguire said, as he kept his pace and made his way toward the SUV.

“What do you say to our viewers who are worried about their safety?”

“The Department is implementing plans to address the protective needs of those we have identified as being potentially at risk.”

“What about the ordinary residents and their safety?” she continued.

“We do not believe that there is a risk to the average resident,” Maguire replied, “but they can be assured that the NYPD is doing everything it can to ensure the safety of everyone that resides, works, or visits the city.”

"But if you have no leads," she asked, "how can you state with any specificity that they are safe?"

"Because we understand the motivation behind these killings," Maguire said tightly, as he pivoted to face her. "It would be nice if the media could report the actual news and not engage in an endless buffet of fear-mongering."

Amanda interjected herself between Maguire and the reporter, giving him clear access to the open door.

"Do you believe that you have the backing of Mayor Barone?" a male reporter asked as Maguire got into the Suburban.

"I would like to think so," Maguire replied. "He understands the complexity of this investigation, but I believe that's a question you'll have to ask him. Have a great day."

Amanda slammed the door shut and got into the passenger seat.

"Get me back to the office right now, Mike," Maguire barked as the truck sped out of the lot.

CHAPTER FORTY

East Harlem, Manhattan, N.Y.

Thursday, May 28th, 2015 - 11:39 a.m.

Enrique Herrera pulled the 2001 Toyota Camry to the curb at the corner of East 116th Street and 1st Avenue in front of Marissa's Bodega. He'd popped the car an hour early from the teacher's parking lot at the nearby school. So even if someone managed to get the plate number, it would most likely not be reported stolen until after school. He only needed to get a couple of blocks away before he'd hit the FDR Drive and then dump it.

The Bodega's original owner had sold it years ago to Prajeet Khan, but that was of no consequence to Herrera. He'd been watching the place for several weeks, learning the routine of the store's owner. It wasn't the outcome that he would have liked, but the fact was that the old man always made his weekly deposit to the bank around the corner on Thursday afternoons.

This was his initiation into AYD, *Asesinato y Dinero*, which stood for Murder & Money, a Venezuelan gang that was expanding their territory on the East Side. They gave him the target and a timeline, and he was not about to blow his opportunity.

Herrera reached under the seat and removed the Glock 17, checking to make sure there was one in the chamber and that the magazine was seated properly. He didn't expect the old man to put up a fight, but if it came to that, killing Khan wasn't an issue. As the gang name implied, murder and money were the only things that mattered to AYD, and if he didn't come back with one or the other, it would be his head that would take the bullet.

He'd made several visits to the location over the past weeks, and the man was usually safe behind a wall of bulletproof glass, but he'd figured out an exploit. He opened the door and slid a pair of crutches out of the back seat, and hobbled his way into the store.

"Yo, Ese! How's it going?"

Khan looked up and smiled. "It's good."

Herrera walked down an aisle and stopped in front of a refrigerator case. Resting the crutches on the door next to it, he held the open door as he balanced on one foot and reached up to grab a bottle from the top shelf before losing his balance.

"Fuck!" he exclaimed, as he fell to the ground.

The old man emerged from behind the counter as Herrera struggled to his knees. "Are you okay?"

"I'm good, I'm good," Herrera exclaimed before driving the Glock into the man's ribs as he stooped down to help him up. "Now you be good too, homie, or I'm going to scatter your guts all over this fucking floor."

The man nodded as Herrera led him back behind the counter. "Give me the money!"

Khan opened the register and removed a handful of bills.

"Stop playing old man, give me all the money, not that bullshit. Where's your deposit?"

"I… I don't… I don't know what else you want," Khan pleaded.

"The deposit, you little fucking bitch," Herrera roared, slapping the gun's frame across the side of the man's head, its front sight tearing a large gash in the skin. "Where's the fucking—"

Herrera screamed in agony as a large metal pole came crashing down, shattering the radius bone in his right arm and sending the gun clattering to the floor.

The adrenaline surge, coupled with tunnel vision, had caused him to miss the threat that appeared from the small office just off the counter where the man's son, Kabir, had been preparing to make the weekly deposit since his father had not been feeling well.

The younger Khan, who towered over Herrera, grabbed him in a fit of rage and flung him out through the security door, where he slid into a snack display that collapsed on him.

Realizing that things had gone horribly wrong, Herrera struggled to his feet, clutching his shattered arm, and made a valiant effort to get out of the store, but just as he pushed the door open, Kabir slammed into him from behind sending both men tumbling into the street.

"Get the fuck off me," Herrera screamed as Kabir began maneuvering to get him in a chokehold.

Several young men hanging out on a nearby stoop saw the commotion and ran over.

"He fucking broke my arm," Herrera screamed.

The men began trying to pull Herrera free, causing Kabir to strike out at them wildly as he fought to maintain control.

One man began punching Kabir, screaming for him to let go of Herrera.

"Help! Police! He's trying to rob us!" Kabir cried out as he tried to fend off the new attackers.

A few moments later, several construction workers who had been having lunch across the street joined the brawl and began viciously beating Kabir's attackers.

CHAPTER FORTY-ONE

1 Police Plaza, Manhattan, N.Y.

Thursday, May 28th, 2015 - 11:52 a.m.

"Liam, I want everyone in the conference in five minutes," Maguire barked from the doorway of Martin's office.

"Everyone, sir?" Martin asked quizzically.

The police commissioner's office was never quiet during workdays, with a continuous series of calls from various department units along with other agencies and officials. Shutting down the operations in the middle of the day never occurred without someone left behind to field calls.

"Is there a problem with my vocabulary, Chief?" Maguire snapped.

"No, sir, I just—"

"Then why, when I ask people to do a simple task, is there always a problem?"

"I'll have everyone in the conference room in five minutes, sir," Martin said.

"See how easy that was?"

Maguire walked into the packed conference room just before noon with Massi in tow. Once inside, Amanda started to close the door, but Maguire stopped her.

"No, leave it open," he said. "I'll keep this brief. If anyone has a problem following orders, I suggest you save us all a lot of trouble and leave now. I have a lot of hardworking commands who could use some help. I'm sure we can find one close to home for you."

Maguire waited for a moment to see if anyone took him up on the offer.

"The police department is a paramilitary organization," he continued. "A concept a lot of you might have forgotten. Just like in the military, there can only be one person who is ultimately in charge, and I am that person. As police commissioner, it is my responsibility alone to make the decisions and to deal with any ramifications. Working in my office should be considered a luxury and not a birthright. There are cops out there right now who are worried about making it home alive. Meanwhile, your biggest concerns are what to have for your meal and avoiding paper-cuts. If anyone has an issue with the way I run the Department or handle personnel issues, then it's best if you put in a transfer request before the end of your tour. Is that clear?"

The room remained quiet as, one by one, they nodded their heads.

"Let me put this as plainly as I can. If I ever go to another meeting with the mayor and get blindsided by a question because someone in this office ran their mouth, I will fill every empty midnight sector, in every A-house throughout the city, by 0001 hours. Understood?"

"Yes, sir," the group said collectively.

"Focus on your jobs and let me do mine. That's all. Dismissed."

Maguire turned and made his way to his office, slamming the door behind him.

A few minutes later he heard a knock.

"Come!"

The door slowly opened, and Liam Martin walked in. "Permission to speak, sir?"

"You don't need permission, Liam," Maguire said. "Have a seat and speak your mind."

Martin closed the door and took a seat. "You're the police commissioner, but I'm the commanding officer of this office. Is there a problem I missed; something that I should be aware of?"

Maguire leaned back in his chair and rubbed his face. "No, Liam, you're doing a great job, and I am sorry if you felt that I held anything back from you. To be honest, everything hit a bit faster than I could process."

"Was there a problem with Detective Antonucci's performance?" Martin asked. "You brought him aboard, so I didn't feel like it was my place to question his activities."

"Let's just say we had a philosophical difference in the way things needed to be handled," Maguire said. "He's a skilled detective, but it's not his ass on the hot seat. I need things to be done the way I want, and not when it is convenient for someone else's schedule."

"Understood, sir," Martin replied. "I know there is a lot of pressure on you, most of which is unjustified. People have been conditioned to believe that crime gets solved the way it does on television. They don't understand how unrealistic that is."

"Yeah, but they don't want to hear that," Maguire replied. "It doesn't help that every ex-cop is seizing their fifteen minutes of fame on the news shows and telling them how they would handle things better and painting me out to be some Keystone Cop who can't find his way out of a phone booth."

"You're dating yourself there, lad," Martin chuckled. "I don't believe we have phone booths anymore."

Maguire laughed. It was a much-needed moment of levity in what had become a never-ending procession of bad news.

"Can I be honest with you?" Martin asked.

Maguire viewed Martin as the quintessential Irish cop; the kind you saw in his old choker coat and twirling a nightstick while walking a foot-post, but behind the bright blue eyes and slight brogue, was an honest to God cop; someone who had served his time in the city's trenches and bore all the scars. He was the type of cop that you listened to in the streets when they were giving advice, because you couldn't buy their wealth of experience. Martin had never hidden behind his rank; he used it to lead the men and women under him and keep them safe.

"Please."

"I've been in this game a bit longer than you," Martin said. "I've seen a dozen police commissioners come and go. Some were good; some were merely seat holders who focused solely on the prestige but had no stomach for the work. I didn't know what to expect when Commissioner Stargold brought you in with him and I admit that a part of me was concerned about a retired detective being selected to be the first dep, but from the beginning you have handled yourself with a poise and devotion to duty that has far exceeded whatever the Department could have expected. I've seen you step into the role of police commissioner under the worst possible scenario, and lead it through its darkest days. The people on the television besmirching you are not worthy to sit in that chair, lad. They are political hacks, not unlike those across the street, or, dare I say, even in this building, who will do anything to elevate their position. The real metric is the cops on the street, and they know who you are and what you have done. Being the police commissioner is easy until it isn't. This isn't the first high-profile case, nor will it be the last. You're not a man who dresses the part; you're a cop. You'll solve this, and then the naysayers will be gone like yesterday's news."

"That's the problem, Liam," Maguire replied. "They'll be gone, but who undoes the damage they've done to the Department?"

"Worry about crossing that bridge when you get to it," Martin replied.

The office door swung open, interrupting their conversation, as Mike Torres stepped inside. "Sorry, sirs, but we've got a big problem brewing uptown."

CHAPTER FORTY-TWO

East Harlem, Manhattan, N.Y.

Thursday, May 28th, 2015 - 12:46 p.m.

A marked radio car backed up, allowing Maguire's SUV to pull onto East 116th Street. A line of uniformed cops wearing riot helmets and holding nightsticks held the line stretching from corner to corner, doing their best to maintain a fragile semblance of order, as a throng of angry people looked on and verbally assaulted them. On the western end of the block, a similar scene was being played out.

"This could get ugly fast, Boss," Amanda said.

"We're definitely going to have to wrap this up quick," Maguire replied

The Suburban stopped across from the bodega, and a uniformed captain approached as Maguire was getting out.

"Sorry to drag you up here, Commissioner," Captain Sonny Grosso, C.O. of the 25th Precinct, said.

"What the hell happened?"

"Perp's name is Enrique Herrera," Grosso said. "From what we've pieced together, he went armed with a Glock in to rip off the owner, Prajeet Khan. He must have thought the old man was alone until the son, Kabir, emerged from the back and began to administer a major league ass-whooping that spilled onto the street. Once it got outside, some local shitheads joined in and started stomping on Kabir and trying to pull Herrera away. Kabir was shouting that he was being robbed, and a couple of construction workers ran over and tuned up the teens. They held them here until my cops arrived. That's when things went south. People were pissed and trying to administer some street justice to the perps. Scuffles began to break out as they were trying to get the perps out of here."

"Injuries?" Maguire asked.

"Herrera is at Harlem Hospital with what looks to be a broken arm along with one of the teens," Grosso replied. "The victim is at Metropolitan with facial injuries and possible broken ribs. The other perps were removed to the precinct and being treated by EMS along with one of my guys who was hurt when a flowerpot came flying from above and shattered the windshield of the RMP."

"Where are we at with the investigation?"

"Crime scene is finishing up, and we're going to pull out as soon as they are done. Until then, I have Special Response Groups One and Four maintaining the perimeter and SRG Two is on standby in Queens if we need them, but I think things are stabilized for now."

"What happened to the construction workers?" Maguire asked.

"We took their information and let them go," Grosso explained. "I'm going to let the D.A. make the call on this one. If he wants to charge them, so be it, but if we tried to collar them now, I think the community would storm the station house."

"Good call," Maguire said. "We don't need to pour gasoline on this situation when we already have enough fires we're trying to put."

"Commissioner!"

Maguire turned to see a gaggle of reporters across the street waving toward him. "Well, this should be fun."

"Want me to come along?" Grosso asked.

"No, just wrap this up as quickly as you can so we can pull everyone out and let things simmer down."

"Yes, sir."

CHAPTER FORTY-THREE

Seven-Eight Precinct, Brooklyn, N.Y.

Friday, May 29th, 2015 - 3:51 p.m.

"Our reporter, Cynthia Delgado, had a chance to talk to one man who saved the life of an East Harlem shop owner who was being robbed yesterday," the nightly news anchor said. "Cynthia, what can you tell us about the incident?"

"Yes, John, in an Action News exclusive, I spoke with Salvatore Perazzoli, a construction worker who was at the scene yesterday, to ask him what happened. Here's my interview with the man many New Yorkers are calling a hero."

The image on the TV screen changed to an on-site interview with Delgado standing next to a burly man wearing a bright orange vest and construction helmet.

"Mr. Perazzoli, can you tell me what happened?" Delgado asked.

"Sure, my buddies and I were hanging out having our lunch when suddenly we hear this guy screaming that he's being robbed," the man replied. "So we ran over and this poor SOB was getting clobbered by these feral youths, so we stepped in and put a stop to that."

"That had to be scary," the reporter said.

"Nah, it was just four little punks beating up one poor guy," Perazzoli replied. "They were crying when we got done with them."

"What are your feelings about the recent letters in the paper? Did that motivate you to step in and help Mr. Khan?"

"You're damn right," Perazzoli said. "I've lived here all my life, and now I'm ashamed to say I'm from here. The mayor, the politicians, those bastards down at the courthouse who think this is a joke and let these skells walk. They are the ones who are destroying this city."

"Did the police say anything to you or thank you for what you and your co-workers did?" Delgado asked.

"C'mon, be serious," Perazzoli laughed. "They're like trash collectors now; they only come when the garbage is already bagged up. I don't blame them. What's the point of doing this job? Try to be a good cop and the perps will sue you and that clown D.A. will indict you."

Perazzoli turned as something caught his eye across the street.

"Hey, look who had the balls to show up," he shouted. "Don't worry, Commissioner, the people did your job for you. Go back to your fancy office and hide. We don't need you up here."

The camera panned over toward Maguire, who looked back and then turned away.

"Our fearless leader," Perazzoli said mockingly. "No wonder the cops do nothing."

The TV image changed back to the studio. "So, as you can see, John, tensions are running high in the city. We spoke to several others who shared Mr. Perazzoli's sentiment. They said they are afraid to go out to do what used to be normal tasks, and several said they only go out when they can do so in groups."

"Any comment from City Hall, Cynthia?"

"We spoke to a representative of Mayor Barone, who said crime is a nationwide problem, and he assured me that New York remains one of the safest major cities in the United States. They also wanted me to remind viewers that if they do see a crime occurring, do not try to take any action and instead call 911."

"Sounds like that representative doesn't get out of City Hall too often. Thank you for that reporting, Cynthia, and coming up next on Action News, your weekend weather outlook."

"Damn, your old boss is getting bitch-slapped," Bobby Hayes said as he swiveled around in his chair.

Antonucci looked up from the case folder he was reading. "Well, you know what they say: you reap what you sow. So he can just go fuck himself."

"Folks like that never get screwed over," Hayes replied. "Just the peons like you and me."

"It's not just a job; it's an adventure, right?" Antonucci laughed.

"It could have always been worse, I guess," Hayes said. "Could have shipped your ass to Staten Island and raped you for the toll every day while you slowly died of boredom."

"Well, there's the power of positive thinking."

"You know what's funny to me?" Hayes asked.

"What?"

"I've got a shitload of active cases that no one gives a shit about," Hayes replied. "Just ordinary schmucks working paycheck to paycheck and trying to live their lives in peace until some mope with a dozen priors comes crashing down on them like the fucking Kool-Aid man. One of my vics is a sixty-eight-year-old woman who was walking home from the grocery store and got mugged. Little prick wasn't content to just grab her purse; no, he shoved her down so hard she cracked her head open like a watermelon on the sidewalk. Meanwhile, a piece of shit gets offed trying to rape a woman and suddenly the world is coming to an end and we're expected to drop everything else and solve it. What about that old lady who nearly died for the last few dollars she had in her purse? Where is the outrage for her? The reporters lined up outside demanding answers? A phone call from the Chief of D looking for updates? Hell no, there's just fucking crickets."

Antonucci frowned and shrugged his shoulders.

"And don't get me started on the politicians," Hayes continued. "All this dog and pony show shit because that fucking pussy in City Hall is having a bad news day. They ever capture the killer, we should just give them a reward for saving the taxpayers some money."

"You're preaching to the choir, brother," Antonucci replied.

"Eh, I'm just frustrated," Hayes replied. "Puzzle Palace gets beaten up in the news, and it's 'All hands, drop everything.' Meanwhile, I get calls from victims asking what's going on with their case, and I gotta lie to them and say I'm still investigating it because I can't tell them the truth. What I want to say is, 'Oh, sorry, you're not a political priority.'"

"That's because no one gives a fuck, Bobby, you should know that by now," Antonucci replied. "The mayor, the city council, the PC — none of them give a shit unless it personally affects them. All they care about is how they look in front of the camera. I used to think he was different because he had been one of us, but I learned my lesson the hard way."

Hayes nodded. "Lately it feels like there's no justice, just us."

"A-fucking-men," Antonucci replied.

Hayes looked down at his watch. "Well, I'd like to stay and chat, but fuck that."

"Are you working banker's hours?" Antonucci asked.

"I took lost time," Hayes replied. "I'm heading up to the Bronx to catch the Yankees game with some of the guys I worked with in the Four-One. Here's my personal cell number. Call me if you need anything."

"Enjoy the game," Antonucci said, as he took the piece of paper. "This isn't my first rodeo; I'll be fine."

"That's refreshing to hear," Hayes laughed. "Last guy that got assigned here, it took me three months to get him off the tit."

CHAPTER FORTY-FOUR

Southampton, Suffolk County, N.Y.

Saturday, May 30th, 2015 - 8:11 p.m.

"How's it hanging?" Alex asked.

"Lord knows I've had better days," Maguire replied, as he took a sip of his drink.

"You've had worse ones too, so suck it up."

"That's why I love talking to you," Maguire laughed. "I can always count on you to emphasize the positives."

"Well, you know me; I'm all about the sunshine and lollipops," she replied. "So what's going on? Are you making any progress on your big case?"

"Oh yeah, we went from vigilante killer to a people's uprising. In a couple more days, I expect to see them erecting guillotines outside 1PP."

"Jesus, you really know how to piss people off, don't you?"

"I guess all those years of riding with you rubbed off on me," Maguire laughed. "So cheer me up and tell me how things are going in the Great White North."

"Oh, you know, I'm dealing with the usual crime wave up here. Let's see, had to bust a notorious gang of skateboarders over at the high school. Oh, and there was this big burglary job I responded to that turned into a foot chase."

"Really?" Maguire asked curiously.

"Yeah, a trash panda climbed into old Mrs. Crandall's kitchen window and scoffed down half an apple pie she baked for the church potluck. Then we had to chase it around the house with a broom to get it out the door."

"That had to be quite traumatic," Maguire laughed. "Did it give you flashbacks to the Seven-Three?"

"I was pretty confident that he didn't have a gun, but you never know," Alex replied. "So what the fuck is going on with you?"

"Well, I have about half a dozen bodies that I know are linked, several others that might be linked, and now the people are revolting."

"What are they pissed about?"

"We had a bodega robbery up in East Harlem the other day," Maguire replied. "Couple of construction workers jumped in and tuned up the perp and some locals. We cut them loose, but the Manhattan D.A. bent the knee to the criminal justice reform clowns and announced that he is charging the construction workers with assault; the whole, 'No one is above the law' bullshit and that there is no place in this city for vigilantism."

"Talk about tone-deaf," Alex replied.

"Yeah, tell me about it. So now I have 100 Centre Street walled off with cops because the people are protesting and calling for the D.A.'s head. If I'm being honest, I can't say that I blame them. There's a lot of frustration out there right now with the revolving-door justice system we have going on."

"Yeah, but that's not your fault," Alex replied.

"You know that, and I know that, but they don't know that. Hell, I'd postulate that ninety-nine percent of the people living here have no clue as to what judges sit on the bench or what A.D.A. is making deals. Most will tell you they hate the political system, but those same people keep voting for their local politician. Me? They see me in the paper or on the TV, so, whether it's right or wrong, it's easy to put a face to the problem even if it is the wrong one."

"You're doing everything you can, James," Alex said. "This isn't goddamn CSI: New York. It took them over a year to catch David Berkowitz, that Son of Sam psycho, back in the 70s, and that was purely because of dumb luck. If he had never parked on a fire hydrant, the body count would have continued to rise. Sometimes you can do your absolute best, but you just keep getting the wrong cards dealt to you."

"Not according to the media," he laughed. "They are loving every minute of this, but I guess that's their job."

"No, it's not," Alex replied. "Their job has always been to tell the truth and let the chips fall where they may. They're not reporting the news; they are manipulating it to push whatever narrative is popular. You've got reporters running out screaming about how heavy-handed we are and need to be restrained, but in the next breath they're screaming that we are not doing anything and must be incompetent buffoons. They need to be called out on their bullshit."

"You never win a pissing match with a journalist," Maguire replied. "Besides, right now I'm the incompetent buffoon, which is fine as long as they leave my cops alone to do their job."

"No, you're not, and we both know that," she replied. "It's always been crazy to me how quickly you can go from hero to zero and vice versa. It's why I avoid the media like the plague. I don't have time for that bipolar shit."

"You'd make a great DCPI," Maguire laughed. "The press would hate you, but it would be hysterical to watch you eviscerate them."

"The answer is still no," she replied. "Besides, I'm getting used to all this no traffic and friendly people."

"Must be nice."

"So what are your plans?" Alex asked.

"Well, I'm thinking about doing the thing I don't want to do," Maguire replied.

"What's that?"

"As much as I hate it, I can't ignore the fact that the biggest target right now seems to be the politicians and legal," he replied. "We're going to have to start providing protection details based on risk assessment."

"The irony is thick," Alex said, "protecting those who created the problem from the consequences of their actions."

"Yeah, I know. I'm sure the media is going to have a field day with it if they find out. I'm running out of resources, and now I'm going to have to find more to cover the courts."

"Your OT is going to be lit," she laughed. "That'll piss off City Hall, but it sounds like you already have a target on your back, so you might as well go all out and put a spotlight on it."

"I'll let them know I want you to do my eulogy if anything happens."

"Why are you even doing this, James?" Alex asked.

"What do you mean?"

"You've shed more blood, sweat, and tears for the Department than anyone I know," she replied. "You don't need to prove anything, and Lord knows you don't need the aggravation. Pull the pin and tell them to go fuck themselves."

Maguire leaned back in his chair and took a sip of his drink. She wasn't wrong, and it was a question he'd already been asking himself. He'd been content in his retirement and had only come back to the job at Rich's request. Helping his friend out had seemed like the right thing to do, but now the weight of being the top dog was wearing on him.

"I'm not going to give them the satisfaction of thinking that they ran me out of town," Maguire replied, "and I can't leave while this is hanging over my head. If I step down with a black cloud over my head, all my people are at risk, and I can't let that happen. Too many good people have sacrificed too much to get jettisoned by some political flunky who'll eagerly kiss City Hall's ass."

"God, you're such a stubborn SOB," Alex replied.

"That's rich coming from you."

"So where do you go from here?" she asked, ignoring the jab.

"I wish I knew," Maguire replied. "Waiting for them to make a mistake doesn't seem like the greatest of plans, but right now it's the only card I have to play."

"Then let's hope they fuck up spectacularly."

"I just need something tangible to pursue, even if it's just a parking summons."

CHAPTER FORTY-FIVE

NY Post - Letter to the Editor

Tuesday, June 2nd, 2015 - Morning Edition

Greetings:

"For what shall it profit a man, if he shall gain the whole world, and lose his own soul?"

The time has come for new leadership within the New York City Police Department. Police Commissioner Maguire has shown where his priorities lie, and it is not with the people of this once great city, but with the political machine that subjugates and leaves them defenseless against the scourge of crime. If he were truly a man of conviction, he would step aside and speak out against this broken system, but he chooses to remain and silently condone the injustices being committed against the people. He has sacrificed his soul to hold on to the temporary strings of power.

Every day, the citizens of the five boroughs live in fear, wondering if they will make it through the day without falling prey to the lawlessness that has laid siege to our beleaguered streets. Instead of focusing his attention on the victims, Commissioner Maguire has sided with those who have created the problem; the elites, the failed politicians, judges and district attorneys who have made a mockery of their oath and pursue charges against the citizenry, while turning a blind eye toward the guilty. He is now utilizing scarce police resources to protect those who gleefully persecute the innocent.

Crime is the scourge of any civilization, and those who prey on the population are its enemies. It has become a war — good against evil. Some of our elected officials have betrayed their sacred oaths and have provided aid and comfort to the criminal element. They have failed to uphold the Constitution and have not faithfully discharged the duties to which they have been elected, appointed, or hired to execute.

Our leaders have failed us. They have turned their backs on the people who elected them and now embrace the vilest members of society. All we wanted was to be left alone, to exercise our inalienable rights to life, liberty, and the pursuit of happiness, but they have taken that from us, and now they will see that their actions have repercussions. They claim that no one is above the law, so we shall hold them to that same standard.

We had hoped they would have taken heed of our warnings, but alas they have chosen to ignore them. As a result, we have no other option but to declare that they have, in effect, committed treason.

In 1787, future-President Thomas Jefferson wrote: *'The tree of liberty must be refreshed from time to time with the blood of patriots & tyrants.'*

The time has come for those who would seek to prey on society, as well as their protectors, to know that the sheep now enjoy the protection of a good and honest shepherd.

Police Commissioner Maguire, when you accepted the job, you took an oath of office that called for you to uphold and defend the Constitution. Your actions of late indicate that those solemn words meant nothing to you. A man of true integrity would have chosen to stepdown, but you chose to lie down with the gluttonous pigs whose appetite for power is insatiable.

To this we say: May God have mercy on your soul.

CHAPTER FORTY-SIX

Seven-Eight Precinct, Brooklyn, N.Y.

Wednesday, June 3rd, 2015 - 4:47 p.m.

"Seven-Eight Squad, Lieutenant Steinberg," the man said as he answered the phone on his desk.

"Hey, LT, it's Sergeant Muniz. Two of my guys just brought in a perp, Jamal Hendricks, for criminal possession of a controlled substance and an outstanding warrant. I got a note here on the desk to notify you guys of all drug arrests."

"Thanks, Eddie, I'll send my guys down to have a chat with him," Steinberg replied.

He hung up the phone and headed out into the squad room. "Patrol just brought in Jamal Hendricks for CPCS and a warrant. Go down and find out if he'd like to be a productive member of society for a change and give up any information he might have on criminal activity."

"That little shit-bird was born with warrants, Boss. Can I just do a DD5 that says 'Go fuck yourself' or do I need a formal verbal declaration of the defendant's desire not to assist the police?"

"That's your problem, Bobby. Your jaded pessimism prevents you from believing that people can have a change of heart," Steinberg laughed.

"I'm just a realist, Boss," Hayes replied, as he grabbed a folder off his desk, "but maybe Ang will bring us some luck."

"That's the power of positive thinking," Steinberg said, returning to his office as Hayes and Antonucci secured their weapons before heading downstairs.

Jamal Hendricks looked up as the two men entered the interview. The look of annoyance on his face changed to one of contempt. "Yo, I don't have time for this. When am I getting out?"

"Relax, Jamal, they're still doing the paperwork; it's going to be a little while," Hayes said as they sat down across from him. "I just need to ask you a few questions."

"*Aight*," Hendricks laughed. "Go ahead and ask your questions so I can tell you to fuck off."

Hayes gave Antonucci a sideways 'I told you so' look before redirecting his attention back to Hendricks, who slid down in the chair and flashed him a toothy grin.

"Look, it's already been a long fucking day, so why don't you quit your bullshit and just listen to the man?" Antonucci fumed.

"Damn, what the fuck are you all uptight about?" Hendricks said as he glanced over at Antonucci as if he was sizing him up.

He knew most of the cops and detectives in the Seven-Eight, but he'd never seen this guy before. Something about the way the man stared at him was unsettling. Most cops here didn't give a fuck; they just showed up for the paycheck, but this guy felt off. He'd have to remember that if they ever crossed paths out on the street.

"Hey, Jamal, stay focused," Hayes snapped as he opened the folder and slid a photo across the desk. "Do you know anything about this guy? His name is Michael DiMarco."

Hendricks examined the photo and slid it back to Hayes. "Nah, what did he do? Steal someone's lunch money?"

"He tried to rape a woman in the park," Antonucci scowled.

"Fuck, I ain't down with that sick shit," Hendricks replied. "If had any knowledge about that, I would give it to you for free."

"What do you know about Darnell Watkins?" Hayes asked.

"Lil bitch got his ass capped," Hendricks replied, "but you already knew that."

"Anyone have a beef with him?"

"D had a beef with everyone who didn't kiss his ass," Hendricks said. "Motherfucker thought he was the Pablo Escobar of Brooklyn."

"Any rumors going around about who might have pulled the trigger?"

"I mean, I hear a lot of shit," Hendricks replied, "but what's in it for me?"

Ang bolted from his seat and jerked Hendricks out of the chair, pinning him to the wall, as the man's eyes went wide in fear. "You think this is some kind of joke? Stop fucking playing games!"

A second later, Hayes grabbed him, pulling Antonucci off the man.

"Jesus fucking Christ, enough," Hayes yelled as he pushed Antonucci back toward the door. "Go get some fucking coffee."

"Hope all your friends are just as helpful when someone pops your sorry ass," Antonucci said, as Hayes ushered him out of the room.

"Fuck you," Hendricks called out as the door shut.

Five minutes later, Hayes emerged from the room. "Let's go get some food."

"I'm okay," Antonucci replied.

"I wasn't asking," Hayes said, as they approached the desk. "He's all yours, Sarge."

Muniz looked up and nodded. "Did he give you anything?"

"Yeah, a headache," Hayes laughed.

The two men walked out of the precinct and got in the unmarked car.

Hayes pulled out his cellphone and called Steinberg. "Hey, Boss, that interview was a bust. Ang and I are going to grab a bite. You want anything?"

"No, I'm good," Steinberg replied. "See you in a bit."

Hayes ended the call and pulled away from the curb. "You want to tell me what the fuck that was all about?"

"Nothing," Antonucci replied, as he stared out the passenger side window. "I just lost my cool for a minute. I'm sorry."

"You don't have to apologize to me, partner," Hayes said. "I just want to make sure you are alright."

A brief silence ensued as they made their way north on Flatbush Avenue.

"No, I'm far from alright, Bobby," Ang replied.

"Still pissed off about getting transferred?"

Antonucci shook his head. "No, that shit doesn't bother me. I just got a letter from the parole board that the guy who killed my father is being considered for clemency."

"Are you fucking serious?"

"Like a heart attack," Antonucci replied. "I've been on the phone with the PBA for the past few days trying to light a fire under their asses while trying to convince my mother that it will all work out."

"Those fucking cocksuckers in Albany love shoving their knives deep in our backs."

"What is the point of arresting these scumbags when they just let them go, Bobby?" Antonucci asked. "You fucking murder a cop and get a life sentence and then some fucking snot-nosed douchebag with a bleeding-heart liberal degree gets to say 'Fuck it, your time is over,' and they just release them."

"It's the system, brother," Hayes replied.

"The system can go fuck itself," Antonucci replied. "The only thing working in this fucking city right now is some vigilante group, and now the system is pissed that someone is actually doing their job."

"Sometimes justice is just us," Hayes replied.

"They should be fucking pinning medals on them if you ask me."

"Look, I know you're pissed, Ang, and you have every right to be, but outside this car you need to tone it down. The last thing you need right now is some blue falcon, cock sucker dropping a dime on you to IAB."

"I know, Bobby. I'm just frustrated."

"The last thing you want to do is give that cocksucker in 1PP an excuse to fuck you even harder," Hayes replied. "You know, I thought he was going to be decent, being a former detective, but that didn't pan out."

Antonucci laughed. "Trust me, the stories I could tell you! People like that, those fourteenth-floor fuckers with their gold shields — they forget you are even around and you start to see the way they really are, hear the way they talk about each other, about you. Maguire doesn't give a rat's ass about anyone except himself. He wants a head on a platter with this whole thing, legally or otherwise, so he can get the heat off himself before..."

An uneasy silence filled the car.

"Before what?" Hayes probed.

"Never mind," Antonucci replied. "I just need to let it all go. He'll fuck himself without my help."

"Jesus, you need to get it off your chest, Ang. Whatever shit you're holding onto is eating away at you. If the LT ever catches you unloading on a perp, he's going to save his career, not yours. You'll be lucky if you end up as a white shield working midnights in the Bronx."

"I just need to bide my time and wait him out."

"You might be waiting a long time," Hayes said.

"I don't think so," Antonucci replied. "In a couple of months he'll be gone."

"What the fuck are you talking about?"

"Don't share this shit with anyone," Antonucci replied, "but he's leaving here. In a couple of months he'll be heading down to D.C. and he won't be my problem anymore."

"What is he going to be doing?" Hayes asked.

"Not sure," Ang replied, "but now you know why he's always kissing politician ass. He's lining himself up for a cushy fed job."

"Get the fuck outta here."

"Hand to God," Antonucci replied.

“I don’t even know why he’s doing this shit,” Hayes replied. “If I were banging the secretary of state, I’d be fucking living the dream, not out playing cops and robbers.”

“You should see his fucking house,” Antonucci laughed. “You need a goddamn road map and an overnight bag to use the frigging bathroom. The place has got closets bigger than my crappy apartment.”

“No wonder he’s protecting these piece-of-shit politicians,” Hayes said. “He wants to join their club.”

“The only thing he’s protecting is his own self interests,” Antonucci replied. “It’s all about CYA.”

“Speaking of covering asses, we better get our food and head back before Steinberg chews ours off.”

CHAPTER FORTY-SEVEN

1 Police Plaza, Manhattan, N.Y.

Wednesday, June 3rd, 2015 - 5:18 p.m.

"You're just out there winning friends and influencing people all over the place."

Maguire looked up to see Sandy Barnes standing in the doorway holding a newspaper. "More like the people's punching bag. Grab a seat."

Barnes shut the door and sat down.

"I guess it was inevitable," Maguire said. "This is not my first rodeo with a target on my back."

"Yeah, but I still wouldn't be taking any unnecessary risks," Barnes replied.

"I've already had this conversation with the head of my security detail."

"And?"

"And nothing," Maguire replied. "We talked, and the matter is over."

Barnes looked at him in amazement. "You're not worried?"

"Sandy, I'm sitting in this seat because some godforsaken psycho took out Rich with a rifle," Maguire replied. "What am I supposed to do? Lock myself away in this office? Have ESU escort me to the bathroom? I can see the headlines now: 'As murders go up, Maguire goes into hiding.' No, I'm not going to feed that fucking insatiable media machine."

Barnes sighed. "I need a drink to deal with you."

Maguire removed the bottle of Jameson from the desk drawer and poured two drinks.

"Thanks," she said, as she took the glass tumbler. "You know what I envision my role to be as your first dep?"

"Besides providing comic relief during difficult times?" Maguire asked.

"To tell you the shit no one else has the balls to say," Barnes replied.

"You're starting to sound a lot like my old partner."

"Well, someone around here has to be the voice of reason," Barnes said.

"I'm not worried, so you shouldn't be either," Maguire replied.

"Of course you're not," Barnes scoffed. "You were a Navy SEAL. Why should you be worried?"

"You know, people keep saying that like we're some mythical creature, but we're not. We bleed and die just like everyone else."

"And that's precisely my point, James. You've already taken one bullet for this job. The next time you might not be so lucky."

"The reason I'm not worried, Sandy, is not because I think I'm immortal, but because I know I have that target on my back. It's the whole forewarned is forearmed thing. My concern is for the ones who don't know it. It's not an exaggeration to say I have zero in common with the belief systems of most politicians in this city, but that still doesn't mean I want them dead. So if they want to come after me, so be it. That just means they're not coming after someone else. Plus, it's not like I'm an easy target."

Barnes shook her head. "Just remember, there is a reason that generals don't go into battle. It's not necessarily about you, but the next person to take that seat."

"So what you're telling me is that it would be bad for the Department if I were to get myself offed?"

"In a manner of speaking, yes," Barnes replied.

"That's a helluva pep talk," Maguire laughed.

"It sounded a lot more profound while I was practicing it in my head."

"I promise I'll do my best to remain on the top side of the grass so you won't have to redecorate my office."

"How about starting out small?" she replied. "Maybe wear a vest until we solve this case?"

"If I do, I think the smart play is to wear both panels in the back."

"Probably not a bad idea on the days you go over to City Hall," Barnes replied, as she got up. "Anyway, that's all the words of wisdom I have. Now I get to run home and play mommy. My daughter, Ashley, is graduating, and I need to listen to some school administrator drone on about what a momentous occasion this is. It's elementary school for crying out loud; it's not like she's graduating from Yale."

"And that is precisely why I will never have kids," Maguire laughed.

Barnes paused at the door. "Promise me that you'll consider what I said. These twisted fucks think they're on a mission from God."

"I will, I promise," Maguire replied.

"I'll see you tomorrow."

"Night, Sandy," Maguire said.

He was just about to finish up when he heard a knock and looked up to see Tanya standing in the doorway.

"Sorry to bother you, but do you have a minute to talk, sir?"

"Sure, come in."

Tonya closed the door and sat down.

"What's on your mind?" Maguire asked.

"Sir, I don't know what happened between you and Ang, and maybe it's not my place, but I wanted you to know that there is something wrong with him and maybe that's behind whatever happened."

A puzzled look came over him. "What are you talking about?"

"I've been trying to talk with him since all this happened, to get him to open up, but he has been very distant," Tonya said. "Like even the most basic conversations have been strained. Anyway, last night I showed up at his place to see what was going on with him, with us, and he started his shit, and I just unloaded on him. Well, something must have hit a nerve, because he broke down."

"What do you mean?" Maguire asked.

"He just started crying, and I kept asking him what was going on and…"

"What's wrong with him?" Maguire asked with genuine concern.

"He got a letter from the parole board, sir," Tonya said. "They want to release his father's killer."

"Holy shit, when did that happen?"

"I don't know when he got it, but it could be the reason that his head wasn't in the game."

"Jesus," Maguire said, as he got up and walked over to the window. "Why the hell didn't he say anything?"

"You know how he is, Boss. He just handles shit, but I guess this one was too much for him."

"Look, I'll make some phone calls," Maguire replied. "See if I can put some pressure on them to reconsider."

"I just don't want him to know I told you," Tonya said. "Things are still kind of tense between us right now, but I thought you needed to know."

"No, I understand. I'll do it quietly. He won't know."

"If you don't mind, sir, I do have something else on my mind."

"What is it?" Maguire asked.

"I just don't know where I fit in now."

"Meaning here?"

"Yes," Tonya replied.

"I know you were partners, but what happened was between me and Ang. I know that's easy for me to say, and in light of what you just told me, I wish it hadn't happened. That being said, I have no problem with your work, Tonya. I think you're an outstanding detective and I want you to stay, but if it comes down to it, and you need to leave, just let me know and I'll send you wherever you want to go."

"Thank you. Can I have a few days to think about it?"

"Absolutely," Maguire replied. "Does anyone else know about the parole board thing?"

"Not that I'm aware of," she replied. "Maybe his mom, but I'm not sure. I just felt I owed it to you to make you aware, if just to make sense of what went on with him."

"Okay, we'll keep this between us for now," Maguire replied, "and I'll make some calls."

"Thank you, sir," Tonya replied. "I know Ang would appreciate that."

CHAPTER FORTY-EIGHT

Southampton, Suffolk County, N.Y.

Thursday, June 4th, 2015 - 9:08 p.m.

Maguire set his drink down on the table and picked up the phone. "Maguire."

"This is Sergeant Ryan from Operations, sir," a man's voice said on the other end. "Sorry to bother you at home, Commissioner, but we have a homicide up in Fieldston in the Five-Oh."

"Do we have any details yet?" Maguire asked.

"Preliminary reports are that the deceased's name is Robert O'Rourke, and it looks like it might have been a carjacking that went south," Ryan replied. "O'Rourke is an exec at Deutsche Bank, and he was pronounced dead at the scene."

"Who's on the scene?"

"Bronx duty captain and the Five-Oh Squad C.O.," Ryan replied. "Bronx duty chief is in route and Chief Walsh has been notified."

"Okay, thank you, Sarge," Maguire replied and ended the call.

He selected Walsh's number and waited for him to answer.

"I guess you got the notification," Walsh said when he answered the call.

"Yeah, I just got off the phone with Ops," Maguire replied. "Are you heading over?"

"I'm just pulling out of my driveway. I spoke to the lieutenant in the squad. His opinion is that this isn't connected to the vigilante killings, but more likely a crime of opportunity. They've had an uptick of stolen cars in the area, and our victim might have just gotten unlucky."

"It won't matter," Maguire replied. "The news will try to spin it for ratings."

"If we get any news crews at the scene, I'll do my best to nip it in the bud," Walsh replied.

"Your people know their job, Billy, but make sure they take a dive into this guy's past and make sure he doesn't have any potential connections or activities that might have made him a target," Maguire replied.

His head shifted as he spotted the lights of a car turn off the road and into the parking area in front of the boat.

"My concern is that they might be changing tactics," Maguire continued, "trying to make it harder for us to connect any potential dots."

"I've thought about that as well," Walsh replied. "I'll make sure they keep an open mind in the investigation and don't get locked in on the carjacking theory."

"Let me know if I need to make an appearance."

"I will," Walsh replied. "If anything changes when I get there, I'll call you with an update."

"Thanks, Billy, be safe," Maguire said, ending the call as he heard footfalls coming up the ladder.

"You know, one day you're going to pop in unannounced and it's going to be awkward," Maguire said, as Zee sat down on the couch across from him, a drink cupped in her hand, and put her feet up on his lap.

"Awkward for whom?" she asked slyly.

Maguire laughed. "I have never known anyone with less fucks to give than you."

"It makes life less complicated that way," Zee smiled. "Besides, you act as if I don't know where she is every minute of the day."

"Be careful," he replied, taking a sip of his drink. "One day you're going to miscalculate."

"If she were here, they would have a checkpoint up, more aggressive countermeasures," Zee replied. "No, she's in D.C. and probably preparing for her meeting with representatives from AIPAC. Things are getting hot in the Middle East."

Maguire felt the pressure of her heel rubbing against his thigh. "You don't say?"

"I blame it on climate change," she laughed. "The heat makes us do crazy things."

"Why are you here?"

"We had a meeting," she replied. "With everything going on, Yoni wanted to start prepping early for the General Assembly. You're going to get a call about adding a counter-assault team to the motorcade."

"And that's why you stopped by?"

"No, I wanted to find out if the information I gave you was useful," Zee said. "And to see if there was anything more you wanted from me."

"You realize how hard you make this, don't you?"

"That's the whole point," she replied. "If you had moved on, you would have told me to leave at the beginning, but you didn't. I'm not trying to make your life hard; I'm just trying to remind you that you still have a choice."

"And what if I said yes, Zee? Then what?" Maguire asked. "We run away? Go hide somewhere in the mountains, always looking over our shoulders because you disobeyed your old man and didn't marry a nice Jewish boy?"

"My father doesn't run my life," she snapped. "I let him do it once; I'll never let it happen again."

"Don't you get it? It doesn't matter what you will allow, Zee; it's what he is willing to do. Shay Harel plays by his own set of rules. You understood that at one time, recognized the threat for what it was, otherwise you wouldn't have walked away from me. Just because you changed doesn't mean he has softened up in his old age."

Zee's jaw rippled in anger, but she knew also he wasn't wrong.

"Do you want to spend the rest of your life, the rest of our lives, gambling that he won't follow through on his threat?"

She got up and made her way toward the front of the deck. It wasn't out of any desire to have space to think, but to shield the tears from him.

Maguire got up and walked over, wrapping his arms around her.

"I hate this," she said. "I hate that I can't let you go, James. That you are the first thing on my mind when I wake up and the last thing I think about before I go to sleep; that my dreams have become nightmares because I lose you when I open my eyes. The truth is that I don't know how to move on because I don't want to."

Maguire slowly turned her around, a knot forming in the pit of his stomach as he saw the look of despair on her face, and gently wiped away her tears. He wrapped his arms around her and pulled her close to him, breathing in her familiar scent.

It was hard not to get lost in the ensuing flood of memories—the laughter, the love, the silliness, the passion. Something about the forbidden always made it more valuable and equally terrifying. In their hidden world they had found solace in each other's arms and they could be who they were and not what everyone expected them to be, but it was a love destined for the shadows; unseen, unspoken, and maybe that's what made this so different.

He wanted to tell her that it would all be okay, but he couldn't lie to her. Love could be a cruel thing at times, but it also couldn't be denied and would be far crueler not to have had it. A part of him wanted her to go, to make life easier for both of them, but deep down inside he knew it wouldn't. The bond between them was too strong, burned too brightly, to ever be fully extinguished.

Zee's arms wrap tightly around him as she buried her face into his chest. He wanted things the way they had been, when it was just the two of them, where they could hide away in anonymity, but that life was a fleeting dream that had passed them by long ago.

"I just want this again," she whispered.

He wasn't sure if she was saying it for his benefit or hers.

He gently kissed her head, and she pulled away, looking into his eyes. "After the last time, I swore I'd never kiss you again; that I wouldn't allow myself to cross that line."

"And?" he asked.

"And it's not as easy to lie to myself when you're standing here in front of me," she said, as she brought her lips up to meet his in a passionate kiss.

CHAPTER FORTY-NINE

Seven-Eight Precinct, Brooklyn, N.Y.

Friday, June 5th, 2015 - 3:11 p.m.

Antonucci walked out of the station house and rounded the corner, making his way east on Bergen Street to where his car was parked.

The street was alive with the sounds of summer as some of the local kids were getting in their last few buckets on the Dean Playground basketball court before the sun went down. The chest-thumping sound of a heavy bass hip-hop track emanated from somewhere within the park. Ang fished his keys out of his pocket and was just about to open the door when a voice from an adjacent car bellowed out.

"Jesus Christ, the rumors are true. You are working for a living."

Ang spun around to see Chrissy Vandenberg sitting in the unmarked black Impala next to him.

"Everyone's a fucking comedian these days," Ang replied as he leaned down on the door frame. "Did you come here to gloat?"

"Nah, I just needed to see it with my own eyes."

"Good news travels fast," Ang replied.

"Like they always say, 'No matter what assignment you have, you should always have a uniform in your locker that fits, just in case.'"

"Ain't that the fucking truth."

"Do you have any plans tonight?" Vandenberg asked.

"I'm just heading home to get some sleep so I can wake up tomorrow and live the dream all over again."

"Hop in and let's go grab a drink and catch up."

"I don't know," Ang replied. "It's been a long-ass day."

"C'mon, one drink," Vandenberg said. "You're not a headquarters pussy anymore."

"Okay, just one drink," Ang said, as he opened the door and got in, "but I don't want to hear any bullshit about your fucking Yankees."

"Not a word," Vandenberg replied. "Besides, I don't start gloating till late August."

"Nice to see that you have matured in your golden years," Ang laughed.

The two men caught up on old times as Vandenberg navigated the Chevy through the back streets of Brooklyn before getting on the Gowanus Expressway and heading south. Fifteen minutes later, they exited the expressway and made their way over to 4th Avenue.

"Jesus, this place has changed a bit," Ang said, as they drove past one of the foot posts they had walked back in their old FTU days.

"The whole fucking city has changed, Ang, and not all of it has been in a good way."

"The old timers called it job security."

"Something like that," Vandenberg scoffed as he pulled the car over. "At least some things haven't changed."

"Are you fucking shitting me?" Ang asked incredulously as he stared out the passenger window. "How the hell did they not close this place down?"

"That's a question I've asked myself a thousand times," Vandenberg laughed. "It's one of the last solid cop bars left in this city. I still stop by on the way home every once in a while just to walk down memory lane."

The two men got out of the car and walked inside.

For Ang it was a trip down memory lane, and it didn't disappoint. Gallagher and O'Brien's Tavern had been a staple of the Bay Ridge community for nearly a hundred years. Despite changing ownership several times, the interior remained unaffected. A long mahogany bar, with old brass footrests, ran almost the entire length of one side, while a pool table and several booths occupied space on the opposite side. The walls of the bar were filled with a variety of police regalia. While most items were readily apparent, such as hats, patches and uniform apparel, others were a bit more nuanced; memorabilia, either comedic or tragic, of which the true details were known only to the few who'd responded to the call.

Vandenberg waved to the old man behind the bar and held up two fingers as he led Ang over to one of the booths in the back.

"I remember the first time we came into this place after a four to twelve," Ang said. "It was like we were being initiated into a secret society."

"I guess in a way we were," Vandenberg replied. "I think it was the old timer's way of saying we were being accepted."

"How are you doing, Chrissy?" the bartender asked as he placed two beers onto the table.

"I'm doing well, Dutch," Vandenberg said. "How's the old lady feeling?"

"Better, now that I'm back to work," the man laughed. "I don't think she liked my being at home so much."

"You'd better stop chasing those female rookies around the bar. You're not as young as you once were."

"Chasing them is the simple part," the man said. "It's what to do with them after I catch them that is my problem."

"Hey, this is Angelo Antonucci," Vandenberg said. "He's an old FTU guy and works in the squad now. He used to come in here with me back in the day."

"Nice to meet you, sonny," Dutch replied. "I probably met you already, but the memory ain't what it used to be. Let me know when you boys need another round."

"Will do," Vandenberg said.

"Jesus, I can't believe Dutch is still alive," Ang said after the man had returned to the bar.

"Yeah, that tough old bastard has been beating the city out of a pension for over four decades now," Vandenberg replied.

"God bless him," Ang replied, "although it's probably only worth a couple of hundred bucks a month."

"Did you know he was in Korea before he came on the job?"

"No."

"Yeah, he served with the 1st Marine Regiment and fought at the Chosin Reservoir. He was awarded the Bronze Star and Purple Heart."

Ang looked over at the old man in a new light. He already respected him for his time on the job, but the men who fought at Chosin were a different breed. He remembered the famous quote by Lieutenant General Lewis 'Chesty' Puller, "*We've been looking for the enemy for some time now. We've finally found him. We're surrounded. That simplifies things.*" It could easily have been passed off as braggadocio, but Chesty was the most decorated Marine in United States history.

"They don't make them like his kind anymore," Ang said.

"That's the truth," Vandenberg replied. "Damn near lost him back in January."

"What happened?" Ang asked.

"He was closing up early during a snowstorm and took a header as he went to get in his car. Broke his hip and cracked his head open pretty badly. Lucky for him, a Six-Eight sector had stopped to get coffee next door, so they were able to render aid and get a bus here quick. They saved the old fucker's life."

"Getting old isn't for the weak," Ang said, as he lifted his beer in a toast and took a sip.

"Sometimes it isn't even the years, it's the wear and tear," Vandenberg said. "Speaking of which, how are you holding up?"

Ang frowned and shrugged his shoulder. "You know how it goes. I've had better days, and I've had worse."

"It sounds to me like you got a raw deal."

"You know how the job is, Chrissy. When shit rolls downhill, it comes at you fast. You either get out of the way or you get smacked."

"The fourteenth floor is a pretty big drop."

"Maybe I needed it," Ang replied. "I'm a detective. Sometimes you just need to get away from all the bullshit and get back to your roots."

"True, but it would be nice if we had some job satisfaction like we did when we first started coming to this joint," Vandenberg replied.

"We were full of piss and vinegar back then, weren't we?" Ang laughed.

"Back then we were cops, and we were allowed to do our jobs."

"I think it's safe to say those days are long gone," Ang replied. "I mean, what's the point of being proactive anymore? You go out and do your job, and for what? The politicians continue to make the laws more lenient. Even when you lock someone up, the DA either declines to prosecute or cuts them a sweetheart deal. Hell, if it even makes it to trial, you're the one that is scrutinized. At this point, I can't blame anyone who wants to skate into retirement."

"Change is coming."

"Sorry, brother, but I'm not as optimistic as you," Ang laughed. "I don't think anyone is going to ride in at the last minute, like some modern-day cavalry, and be able to change this in time."

"Sometimes we have to be the change," Vandenberg said.

"Yeah, I'm pretty sure that is frowned upon."

"Yes, but by whom?" Vandenberg asked. "The people in charge? The ones who created all the problems in the first place?"

"I can't disagree with you, Chrissy, but let's be realistic. How do you change things when the people keep electing them?"

"Well, that's not really true."

"It's not?" Ang asked. "You could have fooled me."

"How many people live in New York City?" Vandenberg asked.

"I don't know, about eight million, give or take," Ang replied.

"Correct, and how many are old enough to vote?"

"I didn't know there was going to be a test I needed to study for," Ang laughed.

"About eighty percent," Vandenberg replied. "Which is roughly six million people. Do you know when the last time was that we had more than a third of that actually vote?"

"No clue," Ang said.

"Nineteen fucking sixty-nine," Vandenberg fumed. "Hell, there have been elections where they only got a million votes between the two candidates. What does that tell you?"

"People don't like the candidates?"

"Exactly!" Vandenberg said. "They don't see a point in voting because the candidates suck. They've lived long enough to see a constant parade of politicians promise one thing and then fail to deliver, and they have become apathetic to it all. We don't have actual choices, only what the corrupt parties give us, and everyone knows it. So voters don't even bother to show up."

"I don't remember you being so philosophical back in the day. So what's your suggestion, Detective Plato?"

"Bottom line is that we can either talk about change or we can bring it about. Every man has to choose what side of the fight he wants to be on."

"I thought we already had when we took this job."

"I know you, Ang," Vandenberg replied. "You bleed blue, but let me ask you a question. Do you think everyone else in the Department feels the same way as you do?"

Antonucci took a sip of beer and frowned. "No, of course not."

"You're damn right. Do you think those shitheads in City Hall or the City Council give a rat's ass about us? They stab us in the back at every opportunity while we risk our lives to protect them. Then they have the audacity to come to a line-of-duty funeral and cry for the cameras, ignoring the fact that their actions are the very reason that led to that cop's death in the first place."

"I mean, you're not wrong, Chrissy, but two fucking disgruntled detectives crying over their beers aren't going to fix this city's problems."

"There is an old saying, '*Out of every one hundred men, ten shouldn't even be there, eighty are just targets, nine are the real fighters, and we are lucky to have them, for they make the battle. Ah, but the one, one is a warrior, and he will bring the others back.*' It kind of reminds me of the job. Out of a hundred cops, eighty are just there for the paycheck. They know the job doesn't give a fuck, so neither do they. They're just doing their time and waiting to make their twenty or get a better offer. Then you have the ten who shouldn't be there. It's not that they are incompetent, but that they're competent with malice. They don't give a fuck about anyone or anything, unless it benefits them. That leaves just the real street warriors, and you're one of them."

"And just how do you know that?" Ang asked.

"I've seen your folder, the arrests, the medals, all of it," Vandenberg said. "An *Honor Legion* man, discarded like yesterday's trash by one of the ten looking to protect his own legacy. If you're like me, it's got to make you bitter that you're out there fighting the good fight and getting shit on, while the bosses are fighting for themselves, and their best interests, while jumping in bed with the politicians and judicial douchebags."

"I won't lie," Ang said. "This has been a pretty hard pill for me to swallow."

"We became cops for a reason and those fuckers have stolen it from us to coddle these lowlifes who prey on the weak; scumbag career criminals who have fifty, seventy, a hundred collars on their rap sheets, but get released before the ink is dry on the latest arrest report. It's fucking demoralizing."

"So what do you suggest we do?"

Vandenberg rested his elbows on the tabletop and leaned in. "What if I told you there was a better way; a way in which you could make a difference? To not just be the warrior who fought the battles, but to be the one who won them."

"I'd say you sounded like one of those bullshit recruitment videos," Ang laughed.

"I'm being serious."

"You're talking about the shit that's going on out there."

"You've always been a smart guy, Nucci," Vandenberg said, "but before we get into that kind of conversation, you have a choice to make."

"Okay, I'll bite. What's the play?" Ang asked.

Vandenberg got up, drained the last of his beer from the mug and tossed a twenty onto the table. "I'm going to walk outside and get back into the car. When you join me, you can either tell me to take you back to the command, and we'll leave it at that, or you can choose to make a real difference and opt for what's behind door number two, but you need to understand that if you opt for the latter, it's an all-in decision. There's no do-overs, no second chances, or 'I changed my mind.' So whatever choice you make, you need to understand that it is life and death."

"Jesus, Chrissy, you make it sound like *La Cosa Nostra*," Antonucci said. "Do I have to prick my finger and swear an oath?"

"We're just two old cops having a hypothetical conversation, but that ends now," Vandenberg said. "I'll see you outside."

Antonucci watched as the man walked away, leaving him alone with his thoughts.

He picked up the beer and took a drink as he gazed around the room. The irony wasn't lost on him that this conversation had taken place in a bar.

Boston's Green Dragon Tavern had served as the planning location for the Boston Tea Party and Philadelphia's City Tavern played host to the Founding Father's as they worked on the Declaration of Independence and Constitution. Even New York's Fraunces Tavern played a prominent role in American history, serving as a meeting place for the Sons of Liberty as well as the location for the British-American Board of Inquiry at the end of the Revolutionary War.

Clearly insurrectionist activities went better with alcohol.

All of this didn't make sense, but yet, in some dark, primal way, it also made perfect sense. It was like watching a train wreck that didn't have to happen, but needed to. There was an inherent need for order in the world, and when that order was missing, something would fill its place.

Antonucci had a long-held belief that people were not good and, if left alone, they would inevitably choose what was wrong. He'd seen it firsthand, both personally and professionally, but this was something different.

For the first time in his life, he was actually seeing the system go rogue. Until now, things like this had been academic; lessons learned in a history book, but not something he'd ever thought he'd see happen in New York City. Yes, there had always been crime and, despite their best efforts, there always would be, but now the system was partnering with it in a perversion of the basic laws.

How can the system survive when it is being brought down from within? he wondered.

The answer was that it couldn't.

History was littered with examples of societies falling because of internal abuses; when the system became so corrupted that it looked to serve its own needs, its own desires, over the will of its people. That was the unfortunate period they now found themselves in.

Desperate times call for desperate measures, he thought.

It was a line in the sand that no one ever really knew how they would respond to until they arrived there. As bad as things got, you always prayed for a change; someone who was smart enough to pump the brakes, slow it down and make adjustments to get everything back on course, but it was different now. The system wasn't changing; he'd seen that. Even after the warnings written in the indictment of their actions, they held fast. They would never admit the error of their ways, at least not willingly. Theirs was a belief system built on a fallacy, and they were willing to burn it all to the ground before they would admit they were wrong.

"I guess Burke was right after all," Ang muttered as he drained the last of his beer and got up. "The only thing necessary for the triumph of evil is for good men to do nothing."

He walked out of the bar, waving goodbye to Dutch, before getting into Vandenberg's car.

The silence that filled it seemed appropriate given the seriousness of the situation. Antonucci assumed Vandenberg understood. The man had probably been in the same position once; had wrestled with the same life-altering decision?

"Well, what's it going to be?" Vandenberg asked, breaking the silence.

"How do I know this isn't a setup?" Ang asked.

"Like what?" Vandenberg asked. "I drive around the corner and the Rat Squad scoops you up?"

"I've been shit on a lot lately, Chrissy, so please excuse me if my trust level is kind of low."

"To answer your question, you don't know, but it isn't. I'm offering you an opportunity because we believe you have what it takes to be part of our organization."

"You're showing a lot of trust," Ang replied.

"Why do you say that?"

"Let's be honest, this would be quite the feather in my cap; a shot at career redemption if I chose."

"Like I said before, all of this has been a hypothetical discussion, Ang," Vandenberg laughed, "but, for the sake of playing devil's advocate, let's just say that you took the chance. The problem is that I'm just a nobody, Ang, and I know very little. It's called being insulated. I'm nothing more than a spoke on a wheel, but I'm not even on the same bicycle. So, it wouldn't be much of a feather in your cap. But the ones on the other bike—well, they know everything and long before you found them, they'd find you. So you'd want to enjoy that celebration while you could, because it would be pretty short-lived."

"Fair enough," Antonucci replied as he stared out the window. "Is it worth it, Chrissy? I mean, I understand the reasons behind it; any fool with half a brain can see where society is headed, but is it going to change things in the end?"

"You and I both know it's just a drop in the bucket, Ang," Vandenberg replied. "You're not going to make an impact taking out a bunch of shitheads on the street. They reproduce faster than we can keep up."

"So why do it? Why go through the trouble?" Antonucci asked.

"Do you know who Crispus Attucks is?" Vandenberg asked.

"The name sounds vaguely familiar, but I'd be lying if I said I remember the details of where I heard it."

"Attucks was a sailor of mixed African and Indigenous ancestry, and he was killed by the British Army along with four other men. Do you know when that happened?"

"The Revolutionary War I assume."

"Correct," Vandenberg replied. "Many consider it to be the opening salvo of the war. It was March 5th, 1770. England had accumulated a massive amount of debt due to its military campaigns, and the king needed to increase its national income. Colonists were upset at the taxation being imposed on them without representation in Parliament. For several years prior, hostilities escalated between colonists and the royal customs officials. To quell the violence, England deployed British soldiers to occupy Boston. Unfortunately, this only exacerbated the issue. Five years before the shots fired at Lexington and Concord, and six years before the Declaration of Independence was signed, British soldiers opened fire on colonists at the Boston Massacre and set in motion events that would lead to a revolution. The moral of the story is that change doesn't happen overnight, Ang, but it does happen when patriots finally say enough. So what's your answer going to be?"

"You know, I grew up in this city, Chrissy. I lost my dad to it and I watched too many of our brothers and sisters follow him into the grave. We've shed blood, sweat, and tears to help clean it up, only to watch some corrupt fucking politicians piss it all away. Well, I'm done doing it the right way. I can't keep showing up to do my job only to watch these fucking scumbags walk out the door grinning. I'm in; just tell me what I have to do."

Vandenberg didn't say anything; he just put the car in drive and pulled away.

CHAPTER FIFTY

Hoboken, New Jersey

Friday, June 5th, 2015 – 4:23 p.m.

"Mom?"

"What is it, Em?" Mary Stargold called out from the kitchen.

"Why is Uncle James sitting in the driveway?"

"What are you talking about?" Mary asked, as she wiped her hands on the kitchen towel and walked out into the living room.

"Look," Emily said, pointing out the window

Mary looked out from behind the blinds and saw him sitting behind the wheel of a black Chevy Tahoe.

"I don't know," she said, her voice a mix of curiosity and concern. "Wait here."

"Is everything alright?" Emily asked.

"Yes, I'm sure it is," she said, as she opened the front door and walked outside.

Maguire was staring out into space when she walked up and knocked lightly on the driver's side window, startling him.

"Jesus, Mary, I didn't know you were home," he said, as he rolled the window down.

"Sophie's done with school," she explained. "I came to pick her up and take her back with me to D.C. What's wrong?"

"Nothing," he replied. "I'm sorry, I didn't mean to—"

"James Patrick Maguire don't you even start to try to lie to me," Mary scolded him. "I know you too well, so don't put me in the position of having to beat my boss's fiancé."

"I seem to recall you being a lot more maternal," Maguire laughed.

"That was before I had a daughter in college and another who sees me as the world's village idiot."

"And this is why I will never have children," Maguire chuckled.

"You're deflecting," Mary replied. "If you make me burn dinner, you'll have to deal with the wrath of your goddaughter."

Maguire turned off the engine and got out. "Lead the way."

Once inside, the memories came flooding back, and he felt his knees buckle, as part of him waited for Rich to emerge from the back of the house while another part knew it would never happen.

Emily came over and hugged him. The little rambunctious girl with pigtails was quickly changing into a young woman. It felt like the world had moved on and left him trapped in a place that no longer existed.

"Hey, Em," he said, holding her tight and kissing the top of her head.

"I've missed you," she replied.

"I've missed you too."

"When are you coming to D.C.? Mom said you're getting a new job."

"A few more months," he said, as he let go of her.

"Cool," she said, sitting back on the couch and picking up her video game controller.

"I think you used up all her words for today," Mary interjected.

"Whatever, mother."

Maguire laughed as they continued back toward the kitchen. "When did she turn into Sophie?"

"Her new school is filled with pretentious little shits," Mary whispered. "Not gonna lie, it's tough doing this alone."

Maguire felt a knot in his stomach. "Want me to talk to her?"

Mary shook her head. "No, I'll deal with it, but I might call for backup once you get to D.C."

"I'll make sure to spend more time with her once I get settled down there."

"I know," Mary said, squeezing his hand. "Let's eat dinner and then you can explain to me why you were sitting in my driveway."

For the first time in a very long time Maguire felt almost normal. Rich's presence was certainly missing, but the four of them managed to catch-up and even share a few laughs. University life had matured Sophie. The sometimes obnoxious introvert had been replaced by a confident young woman that resembled a young Mary. She had even wrangled Emily after dinner and the two of them marched off to the kitchen to do dishes, giving Maguire and Mary time to escape to the back deck.

"So, what really brought you out to Hoboken, James?" Mary asked, as she took a sip of wine.

"I don't know," Maguire said, as he stared down at his drink searching for an answer. "I guess I was looking to reconnect with a better time."

"Did you find it?"

Maguire shook his head.

"He's gone, James, and things will never get better until you reconcile yourself with that and let it go."

Maguire looked at her. "Have you?"

Mary set the wine glass down and took his hand in hers. "Yes."

The word hit like a sledgehammer.

Rich and Mary had been his second family. They had been the benchmark for everything he considered good in the world; a couple who complimented and elevated each other. He loved Rich, but he knew that she loved him more, and yet here she was telling him that she had let go of the man she loved.

"How," he muttered, as his brain fought to process it.

"After Rich died, I was a zombie. I'd go through my day forcing myself to move from task to task. Wake up, brush my teeth, get dressed, etc. Routine things suddenly became monumental hurdles. I lived for the moment when I finally got Sophie and Em to bed so I could collapse. I'd grab a bottle of wine and sit on the balcony of the apartment in Battery Park and drink myself to sleep. With tears running down my cheeks I'd sit there and stare out across the Hudson River to where we are now and I'd curse him. Curse him for taking the job and curse you for convincing him to do it."

Maguire bit down hard, the muscles in his jaw rippling, as the words he dreaded most where finally given life.

He had convinced Rich to take the job, and he had put the target right on his back. Rich was dead, not by some random nut job, but because the girl he once thought he loved had turned into a psychotic killer.

Maguire squeezed his eyes tight, fighting to keep the tears back, as he saw Tricia's face come into focus.

No, not Tricia, Tatiana, he thought.

Tricia had been the first victim in all of this. The girl he once knew had died long before the bullet from his gun had torn into her after she had kidnapped Alex.

"*People die, James. That's just life. Sometimes they die for other people's amusement.*"

Her confession, and what he had done after, had haunted him.

"I'm… I'm sorr—"

"Stop!"

Maguire looked up to catch the flash of anger in her eyes, something he had never seen before.

He knew Mary was a strong woman, stronger than most, but he had never seen it.

"It took me a long time to realize that I was wrong, and it's a lesson you had better wrap your head around before it kills you," she said sternly. "Yes, Rich died, but he died doing what he loved. I sat on that balcony trying to kill myself, to drink away the pain as I struggled to find someone to pin the blame on. Hell, I even blamed myself. I kept asking why I didn't tell him no; didn't put my foot down and tell him to stay where he was, but you know what happened?"

Maguire shrugged his shoulders and nodded.

"I'd wake up," she said. "Sometimes I'd still be on the balcony, shivering, watching the sunlight glinting off the buildings on the shoreline. And every day I would wake up and I would realize it was a new day. No matter how much I questioned, how much I cursed and blamed, Rich was gone, but I was still here, and so were Sophie, and Em, and you, and all of us, and I imagined him looking down at me, at what I had allowed myself to become, with tears in his eyes. I wasn't honoring his memory and neither are you."

Maguire swallowed hard.

"Rich loved you, James, but more importantly, he respected you," she said. "I'd sit here and listen to him talk about something you said, something you did, and it was like he was in awe. He never doubted your capabilities. In fact, he believed that you were the most capable person he knew. He didn't ask you to become his first dep out of friendship or even charity, he asked out of need. He knew you had what it took. Out of everyone he knew, and Lord knows Rich knew a lot of people, you were the only one he trusted. Stop worrying about whether you are up to the job and start doing the job he knew you could do, the one I know you can do."

"Thank you," Maguire whispered.

"Look, I get it," she said, her tone softening. "When Melody asked me to be her counselor at the State Department, my first thought was, 'Here we go, pity job,' but she sat me down and said something I will never forget. She said that she didn't know if she could do the job of secretary of state, but that Cook believed she could and you don't say no to the president, even when you have self-doubts. But then she added that if she was going to have any chance of being successful, she had to surround herself with people who would increase her odds."

"Sounds like Mel," Maguire laughed. "She is very pragmatic."

"Yes, she is," Mary replied. "She explained that Gen was going to be her chief of staff, because she trusted her and that she was her *barometer outside the beltway*. But then she added that she needed someone she could trust that knew the inner workings. Melody recognized that a lot of the people that would be coming in could have their own agendas and she needed a counter-balance to that; someone who could pump the brakes and say, 'Let's think about this for a moment.' I realized that she wasn't offering me a job because she thought I needed it, Melody was asking me to take the job because she needed me and that's exactly why Rich asked you. James, you are not honoring his memory by being a prisoner to the past, you need to honor it by going out and building a future on it."

CHAPTER FIFTY-ONE

Long Island City, N.Y.

Friday, June 5th, 2015 - 5:21 p.m.

Vandenberg's car headed eastbound on Borden Avenue, the trip from Bay Ridge gripped by an uneasy quiet. Antonucci understood the reasons for his choice, but that didn't make what was about to happen any easier. Chrissy was right; change didn't happen overnight. In fact, change often occurred at a snail's pace, and the time between inspiration and achievement could often be measured in blood.

The system was utterly broken; anyone with half a brain could see that. The insanity was to think it could continue to go on this way without reprisal.

Whether it was for power or greed, or even some misguided belief they were doing something noble, the politicians and leaders had turned their collective backs on their constituents. What did they care? It didn't affect them; they were the protected class. The human carnage of their decisions did not affect them. No, it was the poor schmucks, who paid their taxes and just wanted to live their lives, who had to deal with the wreckage. They had long ago given up on trying to change the system and just accepted the greed and corruption as business as usual until they could take it no more.

That's what Solzhenitsyn meant, he thought. *That when the men who just wanted to be left alone were forced to fight, they would 'fight with raw hate, and a drive that those who are merely play-acting at politics and terror cannot fathom.'*

Society had arrived at the place everyone feared. Maybe not all of society, at least not yet, but a core group who were willing to do what was necessary to rip the blindfolds off the masses, and he was here for a front-row seat.

The car turned off the road and pulled into a construction site. For a brief moment, Antonucci saw the running lights on a white panel van flicker.

"This is it," Vandenberg said as he pulled alongside the van. "The end of the road, so to speak."

"That doesn't sound too encouraging," Antonucci replied.

"This is just where we part ways, Ang," Vandenberg said. "At least for the moment."

As Antonucci watched, the side door of the van opened and two men got out wearing black balaclavas and carrying M-4 rifles.

A feeling of dread gripped him, and he instinctively reached for his weapon.

Vandenberg reached across and grabbed him, holding his hand still and preventing him from drawing his gun. "Easy, Ang."

"What the fuck is going on, Chrissy?"

"It's nothing. Those are our brothers; you don't have anything to worry about," Vandenberg explained. "It's just a security precaution. They're going to take you on the next leg of your journey. Just do what they tell you to do."

"You're not fucking with me, are you? I'm not going to end up in the fucking landfill with my head blown off, am I?"

"If I wanted to kill you, I could have done that before the fucking beer," Vandenberg laughed. "No, I give you my word. If you do what they say it will all be fine. Just remember, you wanted in, and this is the process. We've all gone through the same thing. When you come out the other side, you are one of us. Until then, this is how it has to go down."

Antonucci nodded and got out of the car, watching as Vandenberg drove away.

"Empty your pockets and do it slowly," the man closest to him ordered. "Your gun, shield, wallet, keys, all of it; you'll get them back when you're done."

Antonucci complied, handing each item to the man.

"You got anything else on you?"

Antonucci shook his head. "No, that's it."

The other man patted him down. "He's good."

"Get in the truck and put this on," the other man said, handing Antonucci a black hood.

"That's a little theatrical, isn't it?" Antonucci asked as he got into the back of the van and sat down.

"Our game, our rules," the man replied, as he watched Antonucci put it on. "Be quiet and enjoy the ride. This won't take long."

The man rapped his knuckles on the partition wall, and the van quickly pulled away.

Antonucci had tried to pay attention, to get some idea of where they were taking him, but it soon proved pointless. The men were obviously good at their job and took great pains in making the process as opaque as possible.

He knew where they had started from, but the van had taken so many lefts and rights that it eventually became hard to judge whether they were still in Queens or if they had ventured into Brooklyn. Judging from the speed they were at now, they'd obviously gotten onto a highway, but he couldn't tell if they were on the Long Island Expressway, the Grand Central Parkway, or the Brooklyn-Queens Expressway. After a while, he gave up and settled in.

It was probably an hour into the drive when the van came to a stop and he heard the sharp metallic squeal of a commercial garage door opening. A few moments later, the van pulled forward and stopped, the wheels of the door squealing again as it closed.

Once it had slammed shut, the van door was opened.

"End of the line," the man said as they helped Antonucci out and removed his hood.

Ang's eyes slammed shut as the darkness he'd become accustomed to was replaced by the brilliant white light from the industrial-grade bulbs that lit the interior of the warehouse. As he slowly became acclimated, he could see a man sitting at a table in front of him wearing a mask.

"Detective Antonucci, please have a seat," the man said congenially. "It's a pleasure to meet you."

"I'd say likewise, but you have me at a bit of a disadvantage," Ang replied.

"Only for the moment," the man laughed. "I promise that all will be revealed in due time. Please have a seat."

Ang took the chair across from him and sat down.

"You're here because you chose to be," the man continued. "You made the choice to be part of something greater than yourself, but I am sure that you also have a million questions about who we are and why we have chosen this path."

Ang leaned forward, his elbows resting on the table and his hands balled together. "I think I understand your reasoning, although I must admit that it feels like a tall mountain to climb in the grand scheme."

"You're smart; I like that," the man replied, "and you're not wrong, but as the old Chinese proverb goes: 'A journey of a thousand miles begins with a single step.' This was not the journey we chose, but one that we were forced to undertake because the system made us. The men with me are known to you already. They are neither right nor left, but patriots who have come to the conclusion that our political parties have become a cancer that has taken over not only this city, but our great nation as well. In time, you will understand the grave personal risks we are all undertaking to reestablish the natural order. In many ways, it is not dissimilar to what our founding fathers went through.

"We often marvel at the extraordinary accomplishments of our founding fathers, but they were not as optimistic of what they had accomplished," the man continued. "In 1787, Benjamin Franklin was walking out of Independence Hall after the constitutional convention and someone shouted out, 'Doctor, what have got? A republic or a monarchy?' Franklin was quoted as replying, 'A republic, if you can keep it.' It was both a witty retort and an ominous warning. Two hundred plus years and who we are as a nation is a far cry from who we were then. Back then we shared some core foundational beliefs: a common language, a belief in the principles of common law and constitutionalism, religion, a shared revolutionary experience, and, perhaps most importantly, an economic environment which promised an independent sufficiency. Today, most of those beliefs lie in tatters.

"It is true that this nation has suffered through some evil days. There were periods in our collective history that are a stain on the moral fabric of our nation, but this is equally true for just about every other nation on this planet. Despite these national sins, no other country has had the prosperity that we have had. Those born here are gifted the American dream, while others try to capture it by any means necessary, but instead of being grateful to our creator for his blessings, we divide ourselves into increasingly smaller groups and argue over inconsequential things. In 1904, Theodore Roosevelt argued that there was no place in this country for hyphenated Americanism. In 1920, Woodrow Wilson went further and said a hyphen was like a dagger carried by a man ready to plunge into the guts of this nation whenever he was ready. Today, hyphenated ethnicity has been replaced with socio-hyphenism, and its threat to the Republic is even more pervasive. It has caused us to become a divided nation that argues against its best interests.

"The threat to our way of life is no longer a foreign adversary at our doorstep, but a familiar friend who is inside our home. Disparate voices, sometimes with the best of intentions, but often not, have undermined our national foundation. A minority will has been rammed down our throats with no consideration to the inherent damage it is causing. We are living in a time that George Washington warned us about in his farewell speech. A time where cunning, ambitious, and unprincipled men will subvert the power of the people in order to usurp the reins of government and then destroy the machine that lifted them up to unjust dominion."

"You're painting a rather bleak picture," Antonucci said.

"If we don't stand up to them now, our city, our Republic, will be lost and we will have no to blame but ourselves, but, we also have an obligation to ensure that our actions are aligned with the tenants of our founders. If not, we just become part of the greater problem."

"I'm not going to lie," Antonucci said. "I'm in, but it does feel to me like this is just a small drop in a very big bucket. Do you believe that in the end you can survive this?"

"Yes," the man said, "provided that our work is carried out properly and justly. There is a historical precedent for a moment such as ours. Are you familiar with the San Francisco vigilantes?"

Antonucci shook his head.

"Back in the mid-1800s, two groups sprung up to counter rampant crime and government corruption; the first in 1851 and the other in 1856. California's Gold Rush had transformed the small settlement of San Francisco into a major city, as thousands flocked there to make their fortunes. The town went from about eight hundred residents to over twenty-five thousand. As you can imagine, this sudden influx of people also brought with it the worst of society; murderers, swindlers, thieves, prostitutes, and carpetbagger politicians. When local government officials proved incapable or uninterested in maintaining order, the vigilantes stepped in. They went to great lengths to be just and fair; crafting a committee and drawing up bylaws before taking it upon themselves to enforce law and order. They acted quickly, lynching several men accused of murder. Word spread, and the crime rate declined rapidly. Their success spawned other groups who saw what they did as a way of restoring justice in their cities. When their mission was complete; they formally disbanded and returned law enforcement to the elected authorities.

"Unfortunately, their success was short-lived as a new threat emerged from the shadows, the scourge of political corruption, which soon became rampant throughout the city. From stuffing ballot boxes to bribing voters and intimidating those who couldn't be paid off, the politicians did everything at their disposal to remain in power. This included electing their own judges, who would then insulate them from any criminal liability while they looted the city coffers. In 1856, a politician named James Casey murdered James King, the editor of a newspaper known for exposing the misdeeds of corrupt political figures. Casey trusted that the political machine would take care of him, so he surrendered himself for protection from King's friends.

"Moved to action by King's murder, William Coleman, a member of the original committee, was approached by citizens who asked for help. Reluctant at first, Coleman was eventually persuaded to lead another group against the corrupt politicians. Drawing on experience, Coleman acted fast. A former soldier, Charles Doane, was given charge of the military details. The politicians were surprised by the quickness of the group's preparation and they tried to form up the police and hoodlums against them, but these quickly failed. They then sought help from the Governor as well as the federal government, but both declined their assistance. Coleman's group descended on the jail and took possession of Casey and another prisoner, who were tried and found guilty and executed. The group remained in power until they had rooted out corruption and then disbanded. So you can see that a justice organization can carry out its mission and not become a part of the entrenched system."

"And that's how you see this going?" Antonucci asked. "Rooting out the evils and then stepping down?"

"This is not something we wanted to do," the man rep "So to answer your question, yes; every member of this organization has sworn an oath to return control back to the people when the problem is resolved."

"And you are convinced that this is the only feasible way?"

"Are you asking me, or are you trying to convince yourself?"

"Maybe a bit of both," Antonucci replied. "I find that it helps if you believe in the cause you're fighting for."

"I'm sure you have heard the old saying, '*Nature abhors a vacuum*,'" the man said. "Well, in this case, the vacuum that has been created will either be filled by us or angry men. It is something we took into consideration when we first started out. The criminality that has been unleashed could only last for so long without being addressed. We knew that we had a brief window to act before someone else would. We explored what that could conceivably look like, and it wasn't pretty. Any group acting purely out of hatred for the system, and without a strong moral compass, would eventually succumb to pettiness. You cannot act out of anger, or your anger will ultimately control how you act. What good is standing up to the tyrant if you only end up being a tyrant by a different name?"

Antonucci nodded. "So where do I fit in with all this?"

"When we first came to an agreement, we understood that we would ultimately be judged on our actions and could not allow ourselves to succumb to the pitfalls of mob rule. So we set out to create a system that follows the original intent of the founders. There is a legislative branch, which weighs the rightness of the law. Then there is the judicial branch, which impartially deliberates the facts of the cases that are presented to it and decides whether an accused is guilty. Because of the severity of the punishment involved, in these matters all judgments must be unanimous. The last branch is the executive, of which I have the honor of heading. My role is to oversee those responsible for carrying out the execution of the judicial judgment, and you are here because you will be a member of the executive branch."

"Well, since everyone except Chrissy has been wearing masks, I assume the jury is still out on me."

"Yes," the man replied with a lighthearted laugh. "As you can imagine, the risk of our bringing you in is significant. Therefore, your allegiance must be proven to be absolute before trust can be conveyed."

"And how do I accomplish that?" Antonucci asked.

"The judiciary has issued a decree that needs to be carried out, and that will be your assignment."

"When?" Antonucci asked.

"Tonight," the man replied.

"You certainly do move fast."

"Alas, there is no secluded hotel for us to put you up in while we wait for you to prove your allegiance," the man smiled, although the veiled threat was clearly evident. "A day, a week, a month — it won't matter. You are either in or you are not.

"I assume that I don't have much of a choice at this point, do I?"

"No, you don't," the man replied. "Please understand that this is not personal. I believe you to be a man of fine moral character. That is one reason we invited you. Det. Vandenberg explained the rules; you made your choice, and now it's time to act upon that choice. If this is something you cannot do, then I am afraid we must do what is necessary to protect the organization and its work."

"I understand," Antonucci replied.

"If it is any consolation, the judgment decree will be enforced, either by you or someone else."

"I knew what I was getting into. I made the choice to join, and I am prepared to live by that choice," Antonucci replied. "Who's the target?"

The man opened a manila envelope and removed a photo and slid it across the desk.

Ang picked up the photo and frowned.

"Will this be a problem?"

"You boys aim high, don't you?" Antonucci asked.

"Acceptance into this organization comes at the highest professional price. It is the only way to ensure one's personal commitment to our cause. You have flexibility on how to accomplish this assignment, but you only have a forty-eight hour window to plan and execute. One of your new comrades will assist and accompany you on the assignment."

Antonucci nodded. "It might be a little conspicuous if I am getting chauffeured around by someone driving with a mask on?"

"No, there won't be a need for masks on this trip."

"Why's that?" Antonucci asked.

"Because you will either fulfill the assignment that you have been given, and come back as a full member of this organization, or you won't be coming back."

CHAPTER FIFTY-TWO

Southampton, Suffolk County, N.Y.

Sunday, June 7th, 2015 - 3:37 a.m.

Maguire put his coffee cup down and picked up the cellphone from the table. The caller ID showed Barnes' number.

"Sandy? Is everything alright?"

"I didn't want to wake you," she apologized.

"No worries, I was already up," Maguire replied. "What's going on?"

"Reid Delaney is dead," she replied.

"What?" Maguire asked incredulously. "Please tell me you're not serious."

"I wish I were," she replied. "I'm over in Hell's Kitchen with Billy. We're still trying to piece it together, but as of right now, it looks like he took three to the chest while sitting in his car. "

"Fuck!"

"We're trying to keep it under wraps until we figure out what's going on, but that's not gonna last very long," she replied. "Crime Scene is here doing their thing. Once they wrap things up, we'll have the car towed."

"What's your gut tell you?" Maguire asked as he headed into the kitchen to refill his coffee mug.

"Fuck if I know," Barnes replied. "Prior to all this bullshit, I might have had a read, but now your guess is as good as mine. The car was parked on West 52nd, next to DeWitt Clinton Park. Some club-goers thought he was drunk and called 911. Midtown North had a car sitting on a titty bar a block away, and they responded."

"The press is going to have a fucking field day with this one," Maguire fumed. "Right or wrong, they are going to try to link this to the vigilante killings."

"I know," Barnes replied. "The North Anti-Crime Sergeant should get a medal."

"Why's that?"

"He's the one who bought us some time," she said. "Patrol Sergeant was on meal, so he responded. Once he knew who it was, he scooped up the guy's wallet and worked some voodoo magic shit and convinced EMS that he felt a pulse and they transported as a John Doe."

"I'm sure they were happy about that," Maguire replied.

"Nothing a Hallmark card and a few boxes of donuts won't fix," she laughed. "It won't buy us a whole helluva lot of time, but maybe enough to figure things out before it's page one news."

"Okay, keep me updated," Maguire replied. "Reach out to Tom Cleary and make sure he knows to contact us if the press starts snooping around. Maybe we'll get lucky with it being the weekend and we can fly under the radar."

"Will do," Barnes replied.

"I won't reach out to Barone until you get back to me with an update, say ten o'clock? I don't trust him not to panic and do something stupid."

"That'll work," she said.

"Okay, call me as soon as you know something," Maguire said and ended the call.

He checked his phone messages one last time. His mind was already in gear before the call; now he had even more on his plate to contemplate.

He made his way to the back of the boat and sat on the deck, putting on his running shoes.

It was a predawn ritual that he once found enjoyment in; a quiet time to clear his mind before the rigors of the job took hold, but this morning it felt like one of those forced runs when he was in BUD/S.

Okay, maybe it's not as bad as heading down to Camp Swampy, he thought, as he grabbed a jacket off the hook and zipped it up. Then he returned to the bedroom and grabbed the holstered pistol from the dresser and clipped it to the belt on his shorts.

As someone who had spent his entire adult life carrying a gun, putting it on now seemed to carry much more emotional weight. He couldn't remember a time when he had to carry during something as mundane as a routine morning run, but nothing about these times was routine. Whether as a SEAL or a cop, he had always known there was a target on his back, but that was an occupational hazard that came with the job. He'd always viewed it as professional, but now it all felt very personal. He wasn't just some anonymous uniform in a precinct; he was the name and face of the Department. That meant that if someone wanted to take a shot at him, they would see him long before he saw them.

Maguire made his way up the dock and paused at the top to stretch. Taking a deep breath of salty air.

In his past life, before he'd been domesticated, he would have headed down Dune Road, enjoying the ruggedness of the desolate ocean-side terrain, but the Shinnecock Bay now stood in the way of his old stomping grounds and he had to make do with what he had available.

He walked out to the roadway and headed west on Meadow Lane, jogging at a controlled pace and doing his best to ignore the latest encroachment of multimillion-dollar construction that threatened to erode even more of the precious natural landscape. Try as he might, he couldn't seem to shake the feeling of dread that gripped him.

Reid Delaney's death would send shock waves reverberating through the city at a multitude of levels. He was a tech billionaire whose fingers clawed deep into every corner of society. He was considered a flamboyant rock star in the liberal social scene, but his outward flair played cover for the real Delaney, the one who was cool and calculating.

Delaney had grown up in a sprawling lakefront home on Mercer Island, an affluent suburb of Seattle, and embraced many of the causes supported by his parents. Privilege had given him a tremendous edge in life, part of which was to be shielded from the consequences of his beliefs. To Delaney, failure didn't mean his positions were wrong, just that the true implementation had been thwarted. This usually took the form of a counter-political belief that could be blamed for the failure without any actual evidence.

His success in the tech field had allowed him to work at changing that by giving significant amounts of money to social justice causes and political election campaigns that would crush any dissenting opinions. For Delaney, one-party rule was the easiest way to get his message out and ultimately bring about the change that would prove he was right. As a result, he bankrolled a lot of campaigns that ended up electing candidates who, although popular, were not the most capable for the job. The fact wasn't lost on Maguire that one of those candidates had been City Councilman Fernando Rodriguez.

Injecting truckloads of money in order to sway local elections had drawn the ire of those on the opposite side of the political spectrum, but none of those objections mattered to Delaney. Dubious political qualifications meant little to him, just their allegiance to his causes. He had learned long ago that the only thing that mattered to a politician after they had first been elected to office was keeping that office. If that meant voting favorably on an issue supported by a wealthy donor, then so be it.

Delaney's current *cause célèbre* was immigration policy, and he fought for the ending of all national borders through his philanthropic group: *Reimagine*. The group's goal was to end what they called man-made imaginary lines and create one global nation. Delaney's vision was built on a utopian belief that all the calamities plaguing civilization — wars, famine, racial strife — were predicated on the fallacious argument of *us* versus *them*. Delaney was also a firm believer in alien life and hinted at a deep understanding of the issue because he'd been *brought in* by those in the know.

He felt that humanity was being judged by advanced life forms and that our progress was held up because of our behavior toward one another. He argued that we could not become galactic citizens until we extinguished the things that separated us and became true citizens of Earth.

It was these esoteric thoughts that made him popular in lecture halls and media studios. Most mainstream voices gave little credence to the things he said, but few would openly call him out because of the immediate backlash from his army of sycophants and the well-funded attack machine that would quickly destroy all those who dared to question Delaney's positions.

The problem with change agents like Delaney was not that their ideas were necessarily bad, but that they were based on the misguided belief that all people were inherently good. He viewed the system as corrupt and the cause of all things that ailed the planet, and he thought it needed to be destroyed. Of course, there were sound arguments to be made against brutal governments that victimized, starved, and even killed their own people, but in order to prop up this false argument, Delaney had to ignore the fact that the governments were composed of the people. Whether those leaders were put in power through succession, election, fraud, or coup didn't really matter; they were still human beings that could be swayed to act in ways antithetical to being a good leader. For his part, Delaney failed to grasp the irony that he was engaging in the same pattern by electing only those politicians who would be swayed to act on his beliefs.

It was possible, even if highly unlikely, that Delaney had been the victim of a random crime, but even if his death was unrelated to the recent vigilante murders, the media would still float the idea just to capitalize off of it. Facts didn't matter when you were trying to be first. Salacious headlines made money, while the truth and corrections got buried.

Not that any of it matters, he thought, as his footfalls broke the early morning quiet. *They're still going to come for your head on a platter.*

"I hope you're having a good laugh, Rich," Maguire said, glancing up at the darkened sky, as he picked up his pace.

Up ahead, he could make out the small attendant booth at the entrance to the Shinnecock East County Park, while off in the distance the flickering lights of Hampton Bays twinkled on the horizon.

Maguire proceeded into the park and turned around at the speed limit sign. On another day he would have gone to the end of the island, but with the Delaney shooting he knew he didn't have that luxury. He cut his run in order to get a quick shower in before the storm of chaos descended on him.

He was just approaching the booth when his peripheral vision caught movement; a shadow emerging from the darkness. Instinctively, he went for his gun, clearing the holster as his brain attempted to identify the potential threat, but it was already too late. The morning darkness exploded in a brilliant flash of light, and a split-second later he felt the bullet impact his chest. Maguire had gotten one round off, but it had gone wild as he fell to the ground, the gun knocked from his hand as it struck the pavement.

He grabbed at his chest as his right hand patted the ground frantically, desperate to find the pistol as the figure drew near.

"Ang?" Maguire said as the man came into view.

Antonucci's face was devoid of expression, just cold eyes boring into Maguire's.

Maguire winced as he raised himself partially up, his hands behind his back and his feet pushing at the ground as he struggled in vain to get away.

Without saying a word, Antonucci raised the pistol and fired point blank and calmly walked away.

CHAPTER FIFTY-THREE

Forest Hills Gardens, Queens, N.Y.

Sunday, June 7th, 2015 - 7:19 a.m.

Antonucci sat in the corner of the oak-paneled study, cradling a cup of coffee, as he assessed those gathered in the home of New York State Supreme Court Justice Reginald Albright.

Crystal tumblers glinted under the room's recessed lights, and the air was thick with cigar smoke and secrecy.

Around a half-dozen people sat in high-backed leather chairs, their faces etched with the grim weight of the purpose for this meeting, while a few others stood in front of a massive library filled with law books that under the circumstances now seemed to be a bit archaic.

Each man's posture felt tense, save for one.

Vincent Marlowe, a sergeant in the Counterterrorism Bureau, who'd driven Antonucci to what he described as Angelo's *rendezvous with destiny*, leaned forward in his chair, his exuberant voice slicing through the room's anxious mood.

"Jesus Christ, you had to see it," he said. "This guy has a pair of titanium balls. He just walks up and pop, pop; drops him like it's just another day at the office. I'm telling you he has ice water in his veins."

Antonucci caught some appreciative nods, as Marlowe continued, describing in detail Maguire lying in the roadway in an expanding pool of blood.

The room was filled with a veritable who's-who of the City's elite. Besides Justice Albright, he'd been welcomed into the organization by Lynn Clark, the Staten Island District Attorney, as well as City Council Minority Whip Mitchell Dowling and State Senator Chris Reed. He'd also noted Karl Williamson standing next to Albright. Williamson was Deputy Mayor for Communications and most likely the person behind the letters sent to the newspaper.

"Welcome aboard, Angelo."

Antonucci looked up to see Chief Robert Barker, the head of the Housing Bureau, standing in front of him with his hand outstretched.

"Thank you, Chief," Antonucci replied, shaking the man's hand. "You were in the warehouse, weren't you?"

Barker smiled. "I was."

"I thought your voice sounded familiar."

"You can only be so cautious and the rest you must leave up to fate," Barker replied, as he sat down next to Antonucci, "and please, call me Bobby. Behind these doors, we are all equal men fighting for a common purpose."

Antonucci nodded, still hesitant to call a chief by his first name.

"Was it tough?" Barker asked.

"Yes and no," Antonucci replied. "I'd be lying if I said I didn't feel a pang of remorse going into this. Part of me wanted to hold on to what had been. I respected him, thought he'd be the leader the job needed; but I think I expected too much and in the end he turned out to be just another politician."

"I guess that's why they say you should never meet your heroes," Barker said. "Although, when it is all said and done, the history books will record what you did today as being heroic."

Antonucci glanced up and saw Albright motion him over.

"Excuse me, sir," Antonucci said, as he made his way over to the man.

Albright led them through a set of doors that opened onto a surprisingly large, well-manicured garden.

"So I guess I passed my initiation?"

Albright laughed. "To put it mildly."

Albright was a large, congenial man, whose disposition was that of a grandfatherly figure; at least in this unofficial setting.

Professionally, Albright had earned a reputation for being a by-the-book jurist, which had invoked the ire of some who claimed he was too harsh, but his judicial record was unblemished and there had never been a successful appeal of his decisions. Even his harshest detractors acknowledged that his sound jurisprudence provided little ammunition for them to argue against.

"I have to admit that you exceeded my expectations," he continued.

"How's that?" Antonucci asked as they walked along a crushed stone pathway.

"Until now, the actions we have undertaken have been to establish who we are. We focused on polarizing figures, people who had historically been associated with issues that the average resident was against; criminals, radical politicians, activist judges and lawyers. In doing so, it allowed us to garner support because people could understand what we stood for. We considered it a *kitchen-table* approach, where the forgotten individual could sit in his home and safely acknowledge that someone was fighting on his behalf. But these were just minor players, foot soldiers in a greater war, and we knew that we would eventually have to take the fight to the generals."

"You took out *the* general," Antonucci said.

"It had to be done," Albright conceded. "Maguire was our shot across the bow, so to speak, to warn those in high office that they were not immune from punishment for their actions. Criminals and two-bit elected officials send a message, but it is subtle. Maguire's death will serve notice as to how we handle things from now on, and it will send shock waves through the system. For those who carried out the initial judgments, it was simply professional, but I knew that things would escalate, and I realized that we would need someone we could trust; someone who would answer the call no matter who the judgment was leveled against."

"And you thought that was me?"

"I'd hoped it would be you, but hope will only get you so far," Albright replied. "When Chris Vandenberg recommended you, I had Bobby pull your folder. I'm not one to be easily impressed, but you are quite accomplished."

"I just tried to do my job," Antonucci replied.

Albright laughed, patting Antonucci on the shoulder. "You don't need to be humble, son. You already got the job."

"I'm not being humble; I'm just a realist. Accomplished detectives don't get dumped."

"No, they don't," Albright frowned, "but it wasn't your abilities that caused that. I've read through some of your cold case investigations. You are a man of great aptitude and intelligence, but you fell victim to an amoral system that preys upon the competent; using them until they are no longer needed and then casting them to the side. People like Maguire, and others we will soon be turning our attention toward, are nothing but parasites. They don't care whether something is good or bad; they just look for ways to benefit themselves. They are opportunists who subvert the system to enhance their own lives; their own ambitions."

"Oh, he certainly had ambition," Antonucci laughed.

"He did indeed," Albright smiled, "but they were unrealistic."

"What do you mean? I heard he was slated to be the next FBI director."

"I'm sure you have heard the old saying, '*You can indict a ham sandwich, but that doesn't mean you can convict it.*' Well, the same can be said for nominations, and I can assure you that he would never have been confirmed."

"Wow, and here I thought he was well liked."

"It doesn't matter who likes you, Angelo," Albright replied. "The only one that matters is the person who knows your secrets and doesn't like you. People like Maguire, Barone, and a lot of other politicians forget that they live in a world that isn't real, but just because they think that they got away with something doesn't mean that karma isn't patient. As it says in the Bible, '*For there is nothing hidden that will not be made manifest, nor anything secret that will not be known and come to light.*'"

Antonucci nodded.

"Maguire was the first domino to fall, and he was the most important, but he won't be the last. When Vincent called to say you had completed the task, it was like an enormous weight was off my shoulder. Your resourcefulness was quite astounding."

"Not really," Antonucci replied.

"Why do you say that?"

"You sent me out to kill one of the most protected people in the city, and that doesn't even factor in his military career or that he was once a cop himself," Antonucci replied. "Realistically, I only gave myself a ten percent chance of success."

"But you did succeed," Albright replied.

"Yes, but only because I had to think outside the box and strike when I thought I had the best opportunity. You don't go after someone that powerful when they are prepared for it. I knew I had to get him out in the open, when he was alone, but also on familiar ground so that his guard would be down, and I just hoped for the best possible outcome."

"And that is precisely why I believed you were the right person for this assignment. Not to disparage the others, but in my eyes they are just muscle, and that concerns me."

"Why is that?" Antonucci asked.

"The beginning of any movement has a tremendous amount of flexibility, but that window closes rather quickly," Albright said. "Tell me, Angelo, are you familiar with WWII history?"

"A little," Antonucci replied. "I had family who fought on both sides."

"Hitler's rise to power was aided by a group called the *Sturmabteilung* The SA, who were also referred to as Stormtroopers or brown-shirts, were a paramilitary organization that provided protection for Nazi rallies in the early days. They were also utilized to disrupt the rallies of other parties and waged battles against groups who held different ideologies. They were a necessary evil in Hitler's eyes, but he didn't necessarily trust them.

He formed another group called the *Schutzstaffel,* or SS, that initially served as his bodyguard element and would ultimately take down the hierarchy of the SA and leave it a shell of its former self."

"I see where you are going with this, although I think some might be a little squeamish at the thought of being compared to either group."

"Which is precisely why we need people like you," Albright replied. "This organization needs those who are committed to the cause, but who are clear-minded enough to see beyond the present moment and plan ahead; quiet professionals that can be leaders and properly train others to think before they act."

"And you don't think you have that now?" Antonucci asked.

"Let's say that until now things have been fairly unambiguous; good versus evil, but in the future the lines will become a bit more blurred and members of this organization must be prepared to stand resolute if we are to achieve great things. It's not enough to remove the most well-known threat; we are also going to have to take out those behind the scenes that are providing material support. For every politician and jurist who is vocal about his or her radical policies of coddling criminals and subverting the constitution, there are a dozen others, hiding in the shadows, who support them. A mix of old money and new that is funding them and promoting their causes on social media."

"I see now why you're worried," Antonucci replied. "People don't care about pedophiles getting popped, but they might get a bit upset at their favorite social influencer ending up dead."

"What we are facing is akin to a national cancer. If we only treat the visible signs, the cancer will spread until no amount of treatment can cure it. That will be a hard pill for many to swallow, but if we do nothing, our republic will die. I won't sit idly by and allow that to happen, which is why I need you to be the vanguard of that policy; the epitome of the saying, 'The ends justify the means.'"

"Oh, I'm sure that you will find that when I am given an assignment that I am absolutely ruthless in the pursuit of justice."

"That is what I am counting on," Albright replied. "Take a walk with me. I want to show you where things get done."

"In your backyard?"

"Not quite," Albright laughed as he led him down a meandering path that led to the entrance of an expansive garden atrium. The air was thick with the pleasant aromatic scent of diverse plants and colorful dwarf trees. A cobblestone path led to a large, ornate marble water feature in the center, which added a melodic sound to the room.

"Not exactly the kind of place I expected life and death decisions to be made," Antonucci said, as his eyes scanned the impressive room.

"Looks can be deceiving, young man," Albright replied. "This is my wife's sanctuary; her happy place away from the chaos of the real world. Mine is a little more subdued."

Albright walked over to a large cedar retaining wall and slid a key fob over one of the boards. A small edge piece popped open to reveal a hidden keypad. Albright entered a code, and a hidden door in the opposite wall opened.

"Impressive," Antonucci said.

"It gets better. Follow me."

Albright closed the door and led him down a steel staircase that came to a halt about a story and a half below ground. He punched another code on the second keypad and opened the door. A series of motion-activated lights lit up the cavernous room as they walked inside.

"Welcome to the heart of our little operation," Albright said.

Ang was suitably impressed as he looked around the room. It was tastefully appointed, with warm oak wood panels and artwork that offset the harsh black metal bunker design. A large mahogany conference table and a dozen leather chairs dominated the center of the room, while along the far side of the room a series of monitors hung on the wall providing a live feed of the entire property. An informal sitting area and small liqueur cart occupied one corner of the room, and he could see two other doors that led to additional rooms.

"This is pretty impressive."

"It should be," Albright smiled. "Considering how much it cost. It started its life as a doomsday bunker, and there are several other rooms with provisions, sleeping quarters, and sanitary accommodations along with other amenities. This area was originally the living room, but I repurposed it about a year ago to accommodate our needs."

"You don't strike me as one of those preppers."

"I'm not so much a prepper as I am a realist," Albright replied. "I had this built when I imagined the threats facing us were foreign, potential acts of terrorism, but, for the life of me, I never expected that it might one day have to protect me from domestic ones. It's pretty sad that we find ourselves living in a country where feral youth and political radicals pose a greater threat than violent extremists."

"You paint a grim picture," Antonucci said.

"I live by the motto that chance favors the prepared. I would strongly suggest that you embrace that as well as you embark on your new endeavor."

Antonucci nodded.

"This is where the actual work takes place," Albright said. "We can focus on the task at hand without fear of prying eyes or ears."

"I'm impressed by what you have been able to hide in plain sight."

"Admittedly, it was quite the talk of the street when we first undertook the project. A generation ago it would have been a concern for me, but the mobility of people these days makes it less impactful. Only one of the current neighbors was even around when we installed this, and they are quite elderly. I doubt they even remember it. Should the need arise, we could take refuge here and be secure while still maintaining operational control of our assets far beyond these walls."

"What's the endgame?" Antonucci asked. "All of this seems a bit overkill for what is happening here."

"You're a smart man, Angelo. What you have seen is just the tip. The reach of this organization extends far beyond the confines of New York City. We chose to expose the rotten core of the city first, so our reasons would be understood. The growing protests from the citizenry prove that our message is resonating. Even though time is against us, we must ensure that we do not act too hastily or we run the risk of a potential backlash. The ultimate goal is a country we no longer need to enforce; a nation where the morally bankrupt no longer run things and oppress the citizenry."

"You think you can do all of that from here?"

"The truth is that we are but one cog in a much larger machine. The scourge of political abuse and criminality that New York City is facing is no different from cities like Chicago or Los Angeles or Portland and even D.C., but New York City provided the right media environment to pave the way. What happens here reverberates out to the rest of the country like an echo. Our aim is to restore the values of our founding fathers."

"If I'm being honest, that sounds like a pretty tall order."

"I'm sure many thought the same thing back in 1775, and yet here we are today," Albright replied. "It's our belief that people are poised for a change. They were asleep politically, but they have awakened to the dangers before them. They want to live free, to live in safety, and will be willing to back anyone who offers that security to them."

"Are you sure about that?" Antonucci asked. "Some might argue that if you need the promise of government to live in safety, then you're not really free."

"Admittedly, it's a slippery slope, but we would be naïve to think we don't require some measure of government. The key is to appoint wise people who can navigate it justly. Associate Supreme Court Justice Robert Jackson said it best when he argued, 'The choice is not between order and liberty. It is between liberty with order and anarchy without either. There is danger that if the court does not temper its doctrinaire logic with a little practical wisdom, it will convert the constitutional Bill of Rights into a suicide pact.'"

"And you believe that you can enact this change beyond New York City?"

"We have cells from coast to coast that are just waiting for the signal to be given. They have all the groundwork laid out and are just waiting for the tide to turn here before they show other cities the change they so desperately crave. It will be a snowball effect that will sweep across the nation."

"Hmmm," Antonucci frowned.

"Do you question our commitment?"

"Oh, no, I didn't mean anything like that," Antonucci replied. "I just noticed that one of your screens went out."

Antonucci pointed at one of the monitors.

Albright pivoted, a quizzical look on his face.

"That's strange," he replied as he walked over to the desk and began tapping some keys.

"Have you ever had any issues with the system before?" Antonucci asked. "I have a cousin in the Bronx who installs high-end security systems for celebrities in Manhattan. I could have him give yours a checkup."

"No," Albright said tersely as his fingers tapped a keyboard. "This system was installed by a former member of the Technology Branch of the Secret Service. It has built-in redundancies that make it foolproof."

A second screen went dark, followed a moment later by a third.

"I'm no expert," Antonucci said, "but you might want to see about getting a refund."

Albright ignored him as he grabbed a walkie-talkie from its cradle. "Perimeter One, status report."

Static filled the air.

"Perimeter One, status report," Albright repeated. "Perimeter Two, are you on the air?"

A red light began flashing on a large board that showed the property, and a shrill alarm began sounding.

"Son of a—"

A fourth screen erupted in a brilliant flash of light and as the picture returned to normal, they could see the wrought-iron gate at the entrance to the property being ripped from its hinges and heavily armed members of the Emergency Service Unit pouring in through the opening.

"What the fuck do we do now?" Antonucci asked.

"Nothing," Albright replied, his voice calm, but clearly frustrated as he continued to watch uniformed cops storm the property. "There's nothing we can do, but we do have contingency plans for this."

He pushed a button on the console that killed the power to the doors, effectively sealing them inside.

"We're safe in here," Albright said. "If they somehow manage to find the entrance, they won't be able to get through quickly. If it comes to it, there is an emergency exit that leads to the sewer system that we can escape through."

"What about the others?"

"It's already too late for them," Albright said dejectedly.

"That's a lot of people who are going to be very willing to talk and make deals."

"They all knew the risks when they signed up," Albright replied. "We all did, but the reality is they won't be able to give up anything beyond what is already known. The only thing left to do is to send a message notifying the others that our cell has been compromised and let the system self-destruct so that it cannot be forensically analyzed."

Albright reached over to grab his phone, but the chair spun around quickly, his forearm slamming into the keyboard in front of him and sending it flying across the room. When the chair stopped, he was looking down the barrel of Antonucci's pistol.

"Touch that phone and you'll be dead before you hit the ground," Antonucci hissed.

"I don't… I don't understand…" Albright stammered. "You… you killed him. You're one of us!"

"I warned you," Antonucci smiled. "When I am given an assignment, I am ruthless in carrying it out."

CHAPTER FIFTY-FOUR

1 Police Plaza, Manhattan, N.Y.

Monday, June 8th, 2015 - 6:18 p.m.

"You know I should be pissed," Sandy Barnes said, as she sat in Maguire's office along with Ang and Tonya. "At both of you."

"I couldn't agree with you more, Commissioner," Tonya chimed in.

"I'm sorry, Sandy," Maguire replied, "You too, Tonya, but it had to be done this way."

"Because you know I would have had a fit if you did," Sandy said.

"No," Maguire replied, "because if we had to escalate this, I needed your reaction to be natural."

"You mean my natural reaction if I had gotten the notification that you were dead?"

"Basically," Maguire said sheepishly.

"Now that you're hearing it, do you realize how ludicrous all of this sounds?"

"Maybe this will help ease your pain, Sandy," Maguire said, as he opened the desk drawer and removed the bottle of Jameson. "Grab some glasses for me, Ang."

"Ah yes, the old 'let's get drunk and forget it all happened' ploy," Sandy laughed.

"More like 'let us celebrate our victory and not contemplate how we could have lost,'" Maguire said, as he filled the four glasses and passed them out.

"Now that the dust has settled, I'd love to know how the hell you figured it all out," Tonya asked.

"I second that," Sandy said.

"Just your old-fashioned detective work," Maguire lied.

It wasn't that Maguire distrusted Sandy or Tonya, but this case was too big to risk on an unfortunate slip. Ang had done the legwork on the phone records and found the lead to pursue, but only Maguire knew the source of where those records originated. The records allowed Ang to establish a direct link between Judge Albright, Chief Barker, and Detective Chris Vandenberg. He identified several calls that were placed before the first known murder, when they were most likely in the planning stages and before they clamped down on operational security.

Fortunately for them, Ang had sifted through the case folders until he was able to find a thread they could pull as their inspiration. It had just enough meat to be plausible, and that's all they needed to craft a simple tale of hard work and a lot of luck.

"The break came in the Schiff murder," Maguire said. "There was a call logged at 12:58 while he was on the phone. It lasted only a couple of seconds, but it turned out to be the four-leaf clover that unraveled the whole damn thing."

"How so?" Sandy asked.

Maguire nodded to Antonucci. "This was your baby, Ang."

"The number came back to a pay phone, so it ended up getting filed away as a dead-end," Antonucci explained, setting his drink on the corner of the desk and omitting the *broken clock* hint his father had given him, "but it made me a bit curious, so I wanted to see where the phone was located. Maybe there was something more to go on."

"Where was it?" Tonya asked.

"It was half a block away from the Seven-Eight," Ang replied. "I could see the station house from the phone. I knew it could be nothing more than a coincidence, but the investigation was at a standstill, and there wasn't anything else to go on, so I started snooping around. Our first vic was killed in the Seven-Seven, but the original crime was committed in the Seven-Eight. I looked through the case folder and saw that Bobby Hayes had been assigned the case. He was also the detective assigned to the Prospect Park rapist case. So I pulled the roll call, and he was doing a day tour when Schiff was murdered. What sealed the deal for me was when I pulled his personnel record. There was a copy of an order in there where he had been awarded a commendation. Chris Vandenberg was also listed for a commendation and was assigned to the same precinct. Turns out they were radio car partners. It was tenuous, but we had nothing else, and you know how much I hate coincidences."

"That's when we came up with the plan of bouncing Ang out in order to make him appear disgruntled," Maguire added.

"I don't understand," Sandy said. "What did Ang getting bounced have to do with anything?"

"I had an old colleague reach out to me and let me know that a psychological assessment indicated that the group would most likely start targeting those who were in political opposition to their goals," Maguire said.

"So you were trying to make yourself look like a target?" Tonya asked.

"We knew there was a leak here; we just didn't know if that played into anything, so we decided to go big and test it. If I were on any potential list, why not try to make me look even more appealing to them by placating the political class while ruthlessly disciplining a hardworking cop?"

"Jesus Christ," Sandy said. "I take it all back. I'm glad I didn't know."

"That still doesn't explain why you couldn't tell me, Ang," Tonya said. "I'm your partner."

"It wasn't his fault, Tonya," Maguire said. "I made the call not to tell you. We had to make it convincing. Your genuine response to Ang getting bounced was necessary in the event someone was watching. After the incident at the mayor's office, we didn't know who we could trust. It turned out that incident was unrelated, but it helped fuel the narrative of instability, and it allowed us to establish Ang as someone who was angry and had an ax to grind against me. Then we came up with the story about the parole board, which put him up against the system as well. We effectively made him the perfect bait."

"TARU was monitoring Hayes' number, and it didn't take long before there were several calls made to Vandenberg," Ang said. "That's when we knew things were in play."

"So what was your plan?" Tonya asked.

"There wasn't one really," Ang replied. "We were kind of winging it. Then last Friday, Vandenberg showed up and invited me out for a drink that was basically a fishing expedition to see if I was in line with their beliefs. Obviously, I was convincing enough because that's when I got the offer."

"What kind of offer?" Barnes asked.

"To kill me," Maguire interjected. "Turns out that my concession to increase security for the city council members and the courts didn't sit well with them, and it was enough to put a target on my back. They wanted to make a big splash in order to send the message that no one was off the table. They figured that taking out the top cop would be just what they needed in order to get everyone back on the straight and narrow. I played the cards I had and then we just relied on Ang sharing his inside knowledge and hoped that it would make its way back, and it did."

"Did you ever consider that they might use someone other than Ang to get the job done?" Sandy asked.

"It crossed my mind and, you'll be happy to know, I wore a vest everywhere I went just to be on the safe side," Maguire replied, "but knowing how much discipline they had in making sure they weren't caught, we knew we could mitigate things a bit. With my security detail, I was a hard target, and they were struggling with how to take me out. They'd telegraphed their move with the letter to the editor, so we knew they had to be scheming. Ang was now a very appealing candidate because getting him onboard, with his intimate inside knowledge, was seen as an invaluable addition to accomplishing their goal. When presented with his assignment, he convinced them that I was most vulnerable on my morning run, so that was the most opportune time to take me out. Early morning, isolated, no protection detail, no witnesses. They thought they'd hit the jackpot."

"What if you had said no?" Tonya asked.

"It would have been a one-way trip for me," Ang replied. "They were very clear that once I agreed to join there were no other options available to me."

"I could kill you myself," Tonya fumed.

"I wasn't the target, babe."

"Explain to me how you guys did this on the fly," Sandy said. "How did you know where he'd be?"

"TARU special," Antonucci said as he held up a small religious medallion. "Well, not this one, but a replica of it that they could put a tracker inside."

"We had surveillance vehicles on him twenty-four / seven," Maguire replied. "We had him on a very short leash. His life consisted of home and work, and he would call an undercover phone number whenever he left or arrived at either. So we had real-time tracking, physical surveillance and phone verification. When he left work without calling, and they saw him get into Vandenberg's car, we knew something was up. I would receive constant updates as to his location. Once we saw him heading east, and cross over into Suffolk County, I knew that it was going down."

"How did he warn you?" Tonya asked.

"He shot me in the chest and not in my head," Maguire laughed.

"What if you missed? Or the bullet penetrated the vest?" Barnes asked.

"Trust me, it wasn't something I was looking forward to," Ang replied. "It felt like an eternity as I lined up the sights to make sure I was hitting dead-center."

"This also wasn't a standard-issue vest," Maguire added. "It also had a special blood-packet modification so that when I got hit, it provided an effect that would serve as reasonable visual evidence to anyone who might have been observing."

"But if you were tracking him, why couldn't you have just arrested them when they made the offer?" Tonya asked.

"We couldn't take the risk, Tonya," Maguire replied. "We had no idea what was going on with Ang. All we knew was that his actions were out of the ordinary. It was a safe bet that something was in play because of the places he went, but we could only speculate. If we moved too fast, we could have ruined everything. We had to assume that these folks would have access to the best defense attorneys, so our case had to be ironclad."

"And having the job completed would make a stronger case," Sandy added.

"Exactly," Maguire replied. "The last thing we needed was to jump the gun only to find out that we were only at the feeler stage. We knew that this might be the only chance we got, and we didn't want to waste the opportunity."

"Is it just me, or does all of this feel a bit bittersweet?" Sandy asked.

"What do you mean?" Maguire asked.

"I mean, we won," she said. "You solved the case, arrests were made, but in a way it feels like the bad actors are the ones who benefited the most."

Maguire frowned as he took a sip of his drink. "You're not wrong, Sandy."

"I'd like to think that there would be a moment of introspection, at least for the politicians and the media, but I'm not naïve either," she replied. "We'll get hollow platitudes and good press for a couple of days and then it'll be business as usual."

"You're probably right," Maguire agreed. "It will be like how we went from heroes after 9/11 to being vilified once the dust settled. It's difficult as a cop to hear all the negative comments being directed at you. At times it feels as if we are kids caught up in the middle of two parents fighting, and we are being blamed for all their problems."

"What do you mean?" Tonya asked.

"Well, on one hand you have the people who elect their representatives. Then on the other you have those representatives who go on to enact laws. Then we get blamed by both when we are constitutionally obligated to enforce those laws. You can think of the media as the extended family who enjoys fanning the flames."

"Yeah, but hasn't it always been this way?" Tonya laughed. "We get blamed for everything. We either do too much or we don't do enough."

"You're right, but that's not the way it was supposed to be," Maguire replied. "Sir. Robert Peel, who is considered the founding father of law enforcement, and the man who started the London Metropolitan Police Force, asserted that the true measure of the effectiveness of police work was gauged by the absence of crime and disorder, rather than by direct evidence of action. But he also said that policing was a partnership with the public and that for policing to be successful the police needed to secure the willing cooperation of the public to follow the law. So the question becomes, 'What happens when the public no longer follows the law?' One of the most misunderstood truths in modern civic discourse is the misunderstanding between the public, lawmaking, and law enforcement. The public, frustrated by laws they view as unreasonable, see the police carrying them out and direct their anger at us, instead of at the creators of the law whom they elected."

"Add to that the fact that at every turn we are being systematically thwarted by politicians placating a minority agenda that borders on anarchy," Sandy added.

"Peel had a brilliant theory, but I doubt it will ever play out well in Brooklyn North," Ang said.

"I agree with you," Maguire replied. "I think you could look at any major city in the United States and make the same argument. It doesn't matter where it happens, if the criminals are treated as the victims, and the police are vilified for enforcing the law, things tend to unravel rather quickly."

"So do you think they were right?" Tonya asked.

Maguire pondered the question for a moment. "Not right in the way they went about it, but I can understand their sentiment.

The problem is as old as time in that the people choose their politicians, but they rarely choose the right ones. We've slowly inched away from equal protection under the law to where the system throws the book at those they don't approve of while treating others with kid gloves because their viewpoints happen to align. When that happens, all the people see is a two-tiered justice system and look for a scapegoat to pin the blame on instead of addressing the real problem. So we become the bad guys, even though we are just as bound to the system as they are. There's also another perspective that gets overlooked in all of this. It's not what any of us in this room think, but what does the average person believe? That's who gets lost in all of this. The poor schmuck who gets shot because he walked down the wrong street, or the guy that gets ripped out of his car and beaten in front of his family because he got caught in the middle of a violent protest. You can only push good people so far before they will rise up, and my fear is that if we don't move back from this political precipice we are at, what we just went through will look like a Sunday stroll in the park."

"Which we will get blamed for too," Ang added. "We're damned if we do and damned if we don't."

"Fuck 'em, you guys did a damn good job," Sandy said. "And I think that deserves another round."

"*When the righteous are in authority, the people rejoice, but when the wicked rule, the people mourn*," Maguire said, as he refilled the glasses.

"If you're quoting Proverbs, I know I need another drink," she laughed.

"I don't want to damper the party," Maguire said. "We did do good, but I guarantee you that we will face another problem soon enough. Like you said, bad actors thrive on chaos. It might be a week or a month, maybe longer, but they'll be back, and we will be forced to deal with them again with even fewer resources."

"Especially if the City Council continues to go after our budget," Sandy replied.

“Leave the City Council to me,” Maguire said.

“That’s all well and good,” Sandy said, “but what happens when you’re gone?”

A frown formed on Maguire’s face. He wasn’t sure how word had leaked that he was in the running for the FBI slot, but it had, and it covered the two hundred miles from D.C. to New York faster than a California wildfire being fueled by Santa Ana winds.

“No one stays in this chair forever, Sandy,” he said somberly, “but a lot of things can happen between nomination and confirmation. Until then, it’s still my job to battle those knuckleheads.”

“Fair enough,” Barnes replied.

“Look, just being considered for the job is an honor, but things aren’t the same politically as they were twenty or thirty years ago. Back then, presidents used to get the people they asked for, but things are so polarized now on Capitol Hill that nominations are never guaranteed. Melody has butted heads with a few people who could very easily hold a grudge and use it to send a message. So until the vote is held, let’s just assume I’m not going anywhere, unless, of course, I get fired first.”

“That nitwit won’t fire you,” Barnes laughed. “Barone knows no one is dumb enough to take your job.”

“And I was going to recommend you if I got the director’s slot.”

“Twenty seconds after you’re out the door, I’ll be down at the Pension Section,” Barnes replied. “I have zero desire to waste my breath dealing with Barone or Flores.”

“Uh, you know we’re still here, right?” Ang asked. “Could you at least lie to us and tell us everything is going to be okay?”

“It will be, Ang,” Maguire replied. “No matter what happens between now and then, you and Tonya will be fine.”

Ang nodded his head.

“Okay, let’s close the file on this one and get ready for the next case,” Maguire replied, rapping his knuckles on the desk and signaling the end of the conversation. “The one thing about this job that we can count on is that there will always be something waiting just around the corner."

Tonya laughed and raised her glass. "Let's hear it for job security."

CHAPTER FIFTY-FIVE

Kalorama Triangle, Washington, D.C.

Wednesday, June 10th, 2015 - 8:01 p.m.

"I'm done," Gen declared, closing the folder and slamming it down on the coffee table in front of her. "I seriously don't give a fuck if they kill each other at this point. My advice is to give them all the weapons they want and put it on fucking pay-per-view."

"*Ach du lieber Gott*," Gregor Ritter laughed, as he sat down next to her on the couch and wrapped his arm around her shoulder. "I don't think that is how diplomacy is supposed to work, *Mausi*."

"Who are we kidding?" Gen asked, as she sunk down against him and nestled her head against his chest. "No one is solving this shit. They just like fighting each other too much. The best we can hope for is a moratorium, which they will then use to rearm themselves."

Gregor frowned. "Yes, but I don't think you will be able to sell Cook on a 'fuck-em' strategy."

"Look, all I'm saying is that if you have to go back to the 17th century to find a period of reasonable peace and stability, then you're not gonna have much luck."

"You're not wrong," Gregor replied. "Some people enjoy fighting too much to give it up. Sometimes you have to be happy with peace at the moment."

"Then what's the point?" she asked. "Why bother if they are just going to go back to fighting in a few years?"

Gregor pondered the question for a moment.

He understood her frustration. As a member of the GSG-9, Germany's famed counter-terrorism unit, he'd trained for and brought the fight to those who hated his country. When they were called on to intervene, it was often as a dynamic, small unit engagement. He'd often wondered what the long-term ramifications would be or if there would even be any. Then one day he got his answer.

His team had been deployed to Algeria where a terror cell had taken a German medical team hostage. Working with the Algerian *Groupe d'Intervention Spécial,* his team had not only taken down the terrorists and freed the hostages, but they also liberated the village that was being used as a base of operations.

In the aftermath, Gregor had seen the elation on the faces of the locals who had been freed from the abuse by the members of the cell. He realized then that sometimes the bigger wars came down to winning the smallest of battles.

"You must fight for the people you can save today, *Mausi*," he said. "Maybe you are right, maybe there is no point in the long-term, but maybe during the time they are re-arming one person lives. Maybe because of that pause, that person will be able to grow up and become the catalyst that leads to peace. You might not be able to save the world, but you might be able to save the one the world needs."

"You're pretty smart for a knuckle-dragger," she purred.

Gregor reached down and grabbed at her side, making her squeal loudly as she tried to pull away.

"Knock-Knock."

He stopped tickling her, as they turned to see Melody standing in the doorway.

"Gregor was explaining to me how to achieve Middle East peace," Gen laughed.

"Yeah, well if any part of that plan involves me *tickling* world leaders then you might as well tell them to keep shooting each other."

Gen looked over at Gregor and smiled.

"Well, I am all out of suggestions," he laughed, as he stood up. "I will leave the peace talks to you ladies."

"You don't have to leave on my account," Melody said.

"No, it's all good," Gregor replied. "I have a football game I recorded and I need to watch it before someone ruins it by telling me the score."

"We're in America, it's called soccer!" Gen exclaimed, as he walked out.

"*Ja, Ja*," he replied. "Whatever!"

"Don't you *whatever* me, mister," she called.

"If only our adversaries could see the type of ferocious bickering we are capable of," Melody laughed, as she walked over to the wet bar and poured a drink. "It would cause the very pillars of their societies to quake in fear. You want one?"

"No, I'm good," Gen replied. "Gregor is flying up to New York in the morning, so I'll be up bright and early with Wolfie. Hangovers and babies are not a good combination."

"Look at you being a responsible mom. Who would have ever *thunk it*?"

"Certainly not me," Gen laughed, "but I can say that about a lot of other things as well. We've been on a bit of an adventure, haven't we?"

"Yes we have, Chickie," Melody sighed, as she walked over to the balcony and watched the sunset through the ballistic glass.

In the courtyard below, several members of her protection detail walked the perimeter wall. During those fleeting moments of quiet, she couldn't help but reflect on the changes that had occurred in her life that had led her to this place.

She had already been well-acquainted with the perks that came with success in the private sector, but there was something different when it was tied to government service. The first time driving in a motorcade with a police escort; the first time she boarded the Air Force C-32A that bore her official seal on the door and the words United States of America on the fuselage, all served as reminders of who she was now. The understanding that she held the same office that Thomas Jefferson once did was all a bit overwhelming for the bookworm from Richmond Hill.

"Are you okay?"

"Huh?" Melody said as she turned to look back at Gen.

"Are. You. Okay?" Gen repeated slowly.

"I'm fine," Melody laughed as she sat back down on the couch. "I was just thinking that I did not have becoming secretary of state on my bingo card when I was growing up."

"Most people don't, Mel," Gen said. "Hell, we would have acted a lot differently in college if we had known where we'd end up today."

"It always felt like a low bar for me. I measured success in just getting out of Richmond Hill. I have always wondered what would have happened if Professor Thomas had not come into my life."

"You'd probably be some mid-management numbers geek riding the train into work every day just to sit in a fluorescent hell cubicle on Wall Street. All while hoping one of the old geezers upstairs died soon so you could get an office with a view."

"You have quite the imagination," Melody replied.

"I'm just getting ready for when they approach me to do the definitive tell-all book," Gen replied.

"Just remember you were a willing participant with me on this journey, and there may be some statutes of limitations that have not yet expired on some of those highly questionable escapades."

"You raise a good point. I should wait until James becomes director so he can sweep it all under the rug."

Melody smiled, but Gen could sense the subtle change in demeanor.

"What's wrong?"

"Nothing. Why?"

"Bullshit, I saw that," Gen said. "I know you too well, and you haven't been yourself. I figured it was the stress of the trip, but now that we're back home I know it's something else. So are you going to tell me what's got you looking like you're one bad headline away from resigning or do I keep digging?"

Melody sighed, her finger absentmindedly rubbing the rim of the glass. "It's James. I don't know… I feel like we're drifting apart."

Gen's expression softened. "You two have always been fire and steel. This is just distance talking. Hell, I barely see Gregor and we get to live in the same damn house."

"I know, I know," Melody said quickly. "It's not like he has done anything. Not really. But, it feels like every time we talk, it's short, clipped. Either he's distracted or I am."

"Well, it's not like the two of you have important jobs or anything."

"That mid-management accountant thing is starting to sound appealing."

"Yeah, that bubble would burst quickly after one train ride with a drunk trying to use your shoulder as a pillow."

"Ew," Melody shuddered.

"So what happened?"

Melody hesitated for a moment and then said softly, "I'm scared that we are going to end up living parallel lives. It's like we are running alongside each other, but not together. I barely see him anymore. I don't even remember the last time we had dinner or slept in the same bed. How long can a relationship last when the only contact is by phone for a few minutes on the days when we happen to even be awake at the same time?"

"It would be easy to say that you are both at the peak of your careers," Gen said gently, "but the reality is that you are at that peak in two historically noteworthy and stressful careers. It's not supposed to be easy, but that doesn't mean it's not worth fighting for."

A silence stretched between them. Melody stared into her glass as if it held a reflection she didn't want to see.

Gen leaned forward. "Listen. He's got what, maybe six more weeks, two months, in New York before the nomination goes public?"

"Yeah, I think his plan was to make it through the rest of the summer and get through Labor Day."

"Okay, so call it September and add a few weeks onto that for the confirmation process. If everything goes as planned, you guys will be eating dinner together every night before we start hanging the Halloween decorations."

Melody nodded.

"Then this is just the storm before the calm," Gen said. "You'll finally be in the same house, same time zone, same goddamn bed. That changes everything."

"I hope so," Melody murmured.

"You didn't get this far to lose him to time differences and politics," Gen said. "You're Melody Anderson. There is nothing you can't fix when you put your mind to it."

Melody smiled faintly. "You make it sound so easy."

"It's not," Gen said, grabbing Melody's hand and squeezing it tight, "but the good stuff never is."

"Speaking of good stuff, did you ever find out anything on Harel's daughter?"

"Not really," Gen replied, "but I didn't poke too hard. I did find out that she worked for Shin Bet at one time, which would explain how her and James would know each other."

"That makes sense," Melody replied. "And now?"

"Now, not so much," Gen said. "It seems she went off the radar a few years back."

"Mossad?" Mel asked.

"That would be my guess and the reason I backed off. Nothing stays a secret, and I didn't think you wanted word getting back to the General that you were asking about his kid."

"No, you're right. He'll just assume I was curious, but if we dig more, it might set off some alarm bells. I'll just store that information for future reference."

"Just remember it's the past," Gen said.

"Oh, I do, and I intend on keeping it there."

CHAPTER FIFTY-SIX

The White House, Washington, D.C.

Friday, June 12th, 2015 - 6:21 p.m.

Maguire shifted nervously on the pastel-colored couch as his eyes darted around the brightly lit room, taking in the unfamiliar surroundings with an equal dose of awe and discomfort. It felt like he was a young boy who was being asked to behave inside a museum while unseen eyes waited to punish him for any act of misbehavior.

He'd been to the White House on so many occasions that he was no longer affected by the typical astonishment most visitors experienced, but that went out the window when he was met at the West Wing entrance by a member of Cook's security detail and brought up to the private residence. The agent had left him alone, a sign of her respect for him, but he had no doubt that he was still being observed.

As each minute ticked away past his six o'clock appointment, the expansive walls of the Yellow Room seemed to get just a bit smaller. The furnishings of the room gave it the feeling that it had been transported from some grand French château. It was a place that Melody would be at home in, but to Maguire it would be like living in a museum.

His phone buzzed, and he saw he had a new text message from Ang. He opened it and began reading.

I just heard back from a buddy in Intel who works on Flores' detail. Acevedo has been seen several times attending closed-door meetings. It's safe to say that he has come out of retirement.

Maguire frowned.

Theoretically this wasn't his problem anymore, but it still irked him. Whether Barone could win the next election was questionable at best. Flores had political traction because she understood one simple thing: People voted for the promise of free stuff. The threat of a Flores win opened the door to Acevedo returning to the job, and that was not a good thing. Between Rich and him, they had done their best to purge the job of the cancer of political actors, but without vigilance they would quickly return. He didn't care about the politics; he just cared about his people and he would have to make sure protections were in place no matter who won the next election.

The loud metallic click of the door opening propelled him off the seat like a fighter pilot who had just pulled an ejection handle.

"Sit down, James," Cook said pleasantly, as she laid a leather portfolio on the coffee table and sat down on the couch across from him. "I'm sorry to have kept you waiting, but I had a general that needed firing."

"That sounds serious," he replied, taking his seat after she had sat down. "If this isn't a good time, I can always come back."

"Don't be silly," she smiled. "How difficult is it to say, 'Thank you for your service, but you're fired'?"

"Sounds like something that SecDef should be doing," Maguire replied.

Cook rolled her eyes as she reached over and pressed a red button on a small wooden box that sat on the end table next to her. "Let's just say that I had a message to send across the Potomac."

"Well, since you put it that way," Maguire laughed. "I could throw the names of a few admirals your way."

A second later, there was a light rap on the door, and a steward stepped into the room. "Yes, Madame President?"

"Douglas, be a dear and get me an old-fashioned."

"Of course, and for you, sir?" the man asked.

"Coffee, black," Maguire said. "Thank you."

Cook waited for the door to close before continuing. "Don't get me wrong, I love our military, James, but I think a few of my flag officers have forgotten where their allegiance is supposed to lie."

"Anything serious or is that too impertinent of me to ask?"

"It's more like a case of getting too comfy with the military-industrial complex. In many ways, they have forgotten who they work for and instead started focusing on who they were going to work for after they hung up their uniforms."

"I'm sure you are aware that Eisenhower was the first one to raise that alarm over half a century ago," Maguire replied.

"Unfortunately, we were the ones who created that monster and gave it very deep pockets," Cook said. "I remember having a conversation with an aerospace lobbyist once regarding an appropriations bill. It was an absurd amount of money to fund an Air Force project. We were in the minority at the time, and I didn't think it had a snowball's chance in hell of passing, but he just laughed and said the majority whip's PAC had already cashed the re-election campaign check. Good politics rarely survives gray money."

"How do you even begin to fight a system that is symbiotic?" Maguire asked. "As long as there are wars, or even the rumors of war, the military and the manufacturers are going to thrive off of it."

"You don't, and I know that," she replied, "but that doesn't mean we should be the ones picking up the tab. I am all about portraying strength and giving our adversaries something to think about, but there comes a time when being the only kid on the block willing to stand up to the bullies becomes tiresome."

"We've been in that role for a very long time," Maguire laughed. "I saw it in the teams. We'd do training with other countries that treated it as a vacation. The joke was that if anything hit the fan, they would just call the Americans to handle it."

"It's one thing to pick up the tab when your debt to GDP ratio is twenty-five or thirty percent, but entirely different when it's over a hundred percent. Maybe I'm just becoming a grouchy bitch in my old age, but I'm sick of watching everyone else spend their money on luxury items and then begging us to bail them out when the saber rattling starts and don't even get me started on the Middle East bullshit."

"I'm glad I never got into politics," Maguire said.

"Maybe you should," Cook replied. "What the world needs is more shit-kickers and fewer shit-talkers."

"Having one politician in the family is more than enough. I hope she's doing a good job. I really haven't seen all that much of her."

"Sorry about that," Cook smiled. "I needed a little Pitbull to unleash on the world, and I knew she'd be the one who could convey my feelings without causing any permanent injury. Too bad McMasters isn't as effective in dealing with our own people."

"I don't have to tell you this, but the military has its own version of the deep state. A lot of the folks across the river look at new administrations as nothing more than a minor inconvenience to wait out."

"Some of those folks need a reminder that I'm not the one to test," Cook said coldly. "I sent the memo out tonight that if they think they can work against me, or wait me out, they can do it from their homes and not on the government's dime. By the time I'm out of office, their names will have been forgotten."

Maguire nodded.

There was a rap on the door, and the steward returned carrying their drinks and set them on the coffee table. "Is that all, ma'am?"

"Yes, thank you, Douglas."

The man retreated, closing the door behind him.

"Speaking of forgotten," Cook said, taking a sip of her drink. "That's the reason I asked to see you and why we are having this conversation here and not downstairs."

"I was wondering about that," Maguire replied. "I didn't have drinking coffee in the president's residence on my to-do list."

"Sometimes it's good to keep people on their toes," Cook laughed. "Besides, I consider this to be a private matter and avoid any West Wing intrigue."

"You don't think meeting at the residence won't cause more intrigue?"

"Personal intrigue differs from political intrigue," she smiled. "Actually, I wanted to follow up with you on our last conversation and let you know that it has all been resolved."

"I don't understand."

"When you're the president, you have certain latitude in handling matters. McMasters works for me, but so do the rest of the military and the CIA. I ordered a full transfer of the entire record chain and even secondary source material. My people pulled everything from the DEA, CIA and DoD. It's now consolidated on an air-gapped server under DNI control and classified as *Codeword: Eyes Only–Executive Directive*. Even if it could be found, there is only one reader authorized, and that is me."

Maguire frowned.

"You don't seem convinced," she said.

"The records might be gone, but McMasters still knows about it. I can't help but think it might make him even more curious."

"That's my concern, James, not yours," Cook replied, "but I also don't want you worried about what might happen."

She opened the portfolio and slid an envelope toward Maguire.

"What's this?" he asked, picking it up.

"It's a Presidential Memorandum," Cook replied. "Basically it says that for national security reasons nothing happened, but if anything did happen, it was implicitly authorized under a classified compartment of presidential authority and that I have issued you permanent and non-revocable executive immunity from any and all civil or criminal liability."

"You didn't have to do that," Maguire said.

"You gave up a piece of yourself down there, James. The country owes you more than secrecy. It owes you peace."

"I don't know what to say."

"There's nothing to say," Cook replied. "What happened in Mexico was a stain on the CIA, and you shouldn't have to live your life worried about it. I often wonder if Truman realized the potential danger when he created the CIA. I get the concept, at least in theory. The need for a robust intelligence-gathering institution, especially after World War II and the start of the Cold War, but it feels like they went off the rails rather quickly."

"Maybe they should have just stuck to intelligence gathering instead of picking winners and losers," Maguire replied. "Bay of Pigs, September 11th, it feels like they've gotten a lot wrong when it mattered most."

"They are a necessary evil, but I sometimes think we gloss over the evil part."

"Kennedy would have a lot to say on that topic," Maguire said.

"You'll pardon me if I do my best to avoid having that conversation anytime soon," Cook laughed. "That being said, there are changes coming in the not too distant future, ones that won't make me popular with some people, but changes that need to be made, and some of those include you."

"Me? How?"

"I plan on shaking things up significantly in the coming weeks. Everyone in the Executive Branch works for me, but I don't think they necessarily work well together, and in some cases their core mission is being compromised. To start, I'm moving the Secret Service back to the Treasury Department."

"I don't disagree with you on that," Maguire said, "but that's going to go over like a lead-balloon with DHS. No one likes to lose a feather out of their cap."

"They need to be mission-focused, and that means going back to their roots: protection and ensuring that the currency is safe. These two roles should not suffer because they are being used to address other issues within DHS. Besides, I'm going to trade them DEA."

"How will the AG take that?" Maguire asked.

"Judge Mulligan knows my feelings. We spoke about my plans during the vetting process. He knows that the previous administration screwed things up at the border. Having the DEA work with Customs and Border Patrol only makes sense."

"You make this sound like off-season trades," Maguire laughed.

"Oh, but wait, there's more."

"I take it back; this is starting to sound like a midsummer massacre."

"Since you're going to be taking over the Bureau, what's your feeling on the relationship between it and the DOJ?"

"Complicated," Maguire replied.

"That's a word," Cook chuckled.

"You have to remember I'm just a simple city cop," Maguire said a bit uneasily.

"Oh, bullshit, you're anything but simple, James," she said, draining the last of her drink. "Now tell me how you really feel."

"There's a distinct line between enforcement and prosecution, or at least there should be. I don't always agree with what actions attorneys take or don't take, but that's not my job. My position is that I won't tell them how to do their job, and I expect them not to tell me how to do mine."

"I agree," Cook replied. "It was a novel concept a hundred years ago, but now it feels like an unholy alliance, and as a result, they have lost the appearance of impartiality in the eyes of the public. The DOJ needs a healthy dose of sunshine to cleanse it, but I also need to restore trust in the Bureau, and part of that is bringing you in as an outsider and breaking the bond. I want the Bureau to focus on investigating crime without undue pressure from the career lawyers at Justice."

"Are you planning on removing the Bureau from under the DOJ umbrella?" Maguire asked incredulously.

"I am," Cook replied.

"Where are you planning on putting it?"

"I plan on making it subordinate to DNI for now," Cook replied. "Since it is already a member of the intelligence community."

"That will ruffle a lot of feathers," Maguire replied.

"Yours?" Cook asked probingly.

Maguire shook his head. "No, we all work for someone. Plus, I have heard nothing but good things about General Hoyt."

"I've known Wallace for about fifteen years, and I can tell you that he is that rare blend of hands–on, effective manager, but also the type who doesn't get in the way of the people doing their job. That being said, it's just a temporary move. My end goal is to reorganize DHS and remove the redundancy so it can do its job effectively."

"What a novel idea," Maguire laughed.

"It was a good idea, but the execution left a lot to be desired, and I plan on correcting that before I leave office. That being said, moving the bureau to DNI also serves another purpose. This country has become increasingly vulnerable to internal and foreign threats, and I want to give the DNI some teeth."

"Some are going to see that as a threat," Maguire warned.

"Good, they should," Cook shot back. "It would be naïve to think that career Washington would happily do the work of the president, but it would be equally naïve for them to believe I wouldn't remind them of who they work for. Information has always been power in this town, but everything has its limits. I won't have my agenda derailed because someone is leaking it."

"Speaking about information," Maguire said. "I'm sure you have been briefed on the arrests in the City."

"I have," Cook replied, "and it was a brilliant display of police work. Well, at least up to the point of your getting shot."

"It was a calculated risk. Sometimes you just have to roll the dice."

"Roll them like that again and you'll see a side of me you won't like very much. Capeesh?"

"Understood," Maguire replied. "There is one aspect of the case that does have me concerned."

"What is that?"

"There was a level of sophistication that goes beyond what one would have expected. We're working with the Bureau, but without getting too deep into the weeds, the encryption system they were using is rather robust."

"They can't break it?"

"So far they have not been able to," Maguire said. "What troubles me is that it appears their comms were all outbound, which means someone is over them. Maybe they were providing status updates."

"Do you think there are more?"

"I know there are more," Maguire replied. "The question is how deep and far-reaching these tentacles are."

"What did they say?"

"Not much," Maguire replied. "Most of the information we have comes from the conversations my detective had when they pulled him in. They talked about others who were waiting, presumably to see how things played out in New York, but these cells have to be run by someone."

"You think Albright will talk if we offer a deal?"

"No," Maguire said. "I spoke with him briefly before he invoked his right to counsel. He said very little in terms of substantive information, and I get the feeling he isn't the type to take a plea in exchange for snitching. He wasn't gloating; it was more like he was just taking the opportunity to say that the die had already been cast."

"How so?"

"He talked about how nothing could change what was coming," Maguire replied. "That he was just one man who could be replaced, but that others were ready to step into the breach; patriots who would rise up and reclaim the country again."

"More like fanatics," Cook scoffed.

"I wouldn't dismiss them so quickly, Madam President," Maguire replied, as he pulled an envelope out of his jacket pocket and handed it to her.

"What's this?"

"The full transcript of his interview," Maguire replied. "Like I said, it's short on substance, but he says a lot of nuanced stuff. My sense is that this is something you need to take seriously. We think it's stopped in New York, but what happens when it pops up in Los Angeles, or Chicago, or D.C. for that matter? What happens if the next chapter in the plan has it kicking off simultaneously in those cities or others? What if those arrests spur them on to martyr status in a greater cause?"

"You're that concerned?" Cook asked.

"I am. When you have conducted as many interviews as I have, both the polite ones and the not so polite, you start to develop an intuition. I've seen them all: the nut-jobs, the hardcore fanatics, the true believers. This just feels different. Let me ask you a question. You're Catholic, correct?"

"I am a non-practicing one, according to Cardinal Dwyer, but yes, why?"

"You believe Jesus is coming back one day?"

"Yes, but what does this have to do with Albright?"

"That's the impression I got from him regarding his level of faith in this," Maguire replied. "He believes that nothing can stop what is coming, and he is going to have a ringside seat."

"Well, you stopped him, so there is that, but if you feel this strongly about it, then maybe I should have Judge Mulligan look into this," Cook said. "If this threat goes beyond New York, like you believe it does, then he can have the U.S. Attorney's Office investigate it under interstate grounds."

"I think that would be the most prudent thing to do at this point."

"Then I think it's time for you to head back to New York and start getting your affairs in order," Cook said. "I already made it clear to Whitehead that I expect his resignation letter on my desk by September 1st or he can expect my termination letter on his September 2nd. He doesn't have much backbone, and his ego won't let him get fired, so I expect him to commence an extended vacation in the coming weeks."

"And you're confident that I can get confirmed?" Maguire asked.

"I already know you will," Cook smiled. "Once Whitehead signals his intention to step down, I will announce you as my choice. The Office of Legislative Affairs will assign someone to guide you through the interview process."

"Sounds like fun," Maguire laughed.

"It'll be many things, James, but fun it won't be," Cook replied, before being interrupted by a knock at the door.

"Come in," she called out.

The door opened, and a young male aide poked his head in. "Madame President, the Speaker is on line two. He needs to talk to you about the Safe Streets Bill coming up for a vote on Monday and that it is important."

"Someone please shoot me," Cook muttered.

"I'll let you get to work," Maguire said as he stood up. "Thank you for everything."

"If you need any resources for your investigation, just let me know," Cook said, hugging him.

"Thank you, I will."

CHAPTER FIFTY-SEVEN

The White House, Washington, D.C.

Friday, June 12th, 2015 - 7:53 p.m.

"They'll let anyone in the White House these days."

Maguire pivoted to see retired Senior Chief Petty Officer (SEAL) Roy Gentry, affectionately known as *Mother* to his misguided frogmen, standing off to the side of the West Wing entrance door.

"I thought they posted a Marine here to keep people like you away," Maguire laughed.

"I sent him to get me a fresh cup of coffee since you were taking so goddamn long," Gentry laughed. "You need a ride?"

"Nah, Melody wasn't really thrilled with my little stunt back in New York, so she was kind enough to assign some of her DSS babysitters," Maguire replied as the two men began walking toward the Old Executive Office Building. "They have orders to bring me directly to her place after I'm done here."

"Smart woman," Gentry replied. "She doesn't need you to cause an international incident that she would have to fix."

"I hear those Brazilian churrascaria places can be brutal," Maguire said as they made their way over to the parking area on West Executive Avenue.

"So how'd your meeting go?" Gentry asked when they were far enough away.

"Mexico is no longer an issue," Maguire replied as he motioned for the agents in the nearby Suburban to follow them.

"I know."

"I figured you did," Maguire said.

"That woman missed her calling. She would have made a brilliant detective."

"Cook is tenacious."

"She took a deep dive and called me in for a chat," Gentry replied. "We had a heart to heart chat over some good Navy coffee."

"Did you get one of those fancy letters too?" Maguire asked.

Gentry nodded. "I've got to admit, that woman has balls of steel."

"She's moving ahead with my nomination," Maguire said. "It'll go public in September."

"I guess the lady has got things under control."

"I have a question for you," Maguire said. "Are those geriatric fingers still good on a keyboard?"

"No," Gentry replied, holding up his middle finger at Maguire, "but I stole a kid from DARPA who graduated at the top of his class from Carnegie Mellon, and he loves breaking things. He makes Fort Meade look like a middle school computer lab. Why?"

Maguire reached into his pocket and removed a USB drive and handed it to Gentry. "I need to know what's on this thing."

"This related to the shit that went down recently?" Gentry asked, sliding it into his pocket.

"Yeah."

"Your people couldn't handle it?"

"It's encrypted," Maguire replied. "Even the Bureau folks are stumped."

"Allegedly stumped."

"That thought had crossed my mind," Maguire replied. "Sometimes it is hard to know who is playing for the team and who is betting against it, but either way I am still in the dark. Think your boy can help shed some light?"

"Encryption is only a suggestion to him," Gentry replied.

"If my gut is right, whatever is on that drive is going to show that New York was just the test run for a much bigger op."

"I'll put my little gremlin on it right away."

"How long do you think it'll take? Maguire asked.

Gentry shrugged. “Depends. If it is off-the-shelf stuff, 256-bit AES or some homemade junk, he’ll slice through it in a couple of hours, tops, but if it’s got layers, custom keys, maybe even quantum shielding, then it could take days. Weeks, if someone knew what they were doing.”

“So you’re saying it’s a coin toss?”

“No, I’m saying that if anyone can open it, he can,” Gentry replied. “The clock just depends on how paranoid your vigilante friends were.”

“This is close-hold.”

Gentry nodded. “He works in a bubble. It won’t go anywhere.”

“Maybe I’m the one who is paranoid.”

“Like the man said, ‘Just because you’re paranoid doesn’t mean they aren’t after you.’”

“I can always count on you to be inspirational,” Maguire laughed.

“That’s because I had to read inspirational quotes just to motivate myself to deal with you and those other misfits,” Gentry replied. “Now what are you going to do?”

“I was told to head back home and start getting my affairs in order.”

Gentry grabbed his arm and stopped him. “You sure about this, Paddy? You’re a good man, hell, you’re one of the finest SEALs I’ve ever had the pleasure of knowing, but this place…”

Gentry paused and looked around cautiously. “D.C. is hostile territory, and it’s a target-rich environment.”

“I’m too old to reenlist and make an honest living, Chief.”

“You and me both,” Gentry scoffed.

“Besides, the writing is on the wall back in New York,” Maguire replied. “I’ve pissed off too many people to feel comfortable. It’s not a question of if, but when.”

“You always did have questionable social skills.”

“Truth hurts.”

"Especially when you're dealing with weak-minded individuals," Gentry said. "Just remember that if you piss off the wrong person here, you will wish you were back in Mexico."

"Some days I do, Mother," Maguire said softly. "Even in that chaos, things felt a lot simpler."

Gentry nodded knowingly. "Did the boss say anything about McMasters?"

"Just that she would handle it," Maguire replied, "but I'd feel better knowing you were monitoring things. I'd like to avoid any gotcha moments when they haul my ass through the Capitol."

"You go back to New York and do what you need to do," Gentry replied. "I'll keep my nose to the grindstone down here."

"I appreciate that," Maguire said, shaking Gentry's hand.

"Watch your six, Paddy, and I'll let you know what I come up with."

"Thanks, and you do the same. If I'm right about what could be on that drive, and I pray to God I'm not, this won't be a pleasant voyage."

"All we can do is plan accordingly and keep our heads on a swivel."

"Hooyah, Chief," Maguire said, as one of the DSS agents opened the door.

"Fair winds and following seas," Gentry replied. "I'll be in touch."

CHAPTER FIFTY-EIGHT

Georgetown, Washington, D.C.

Saturday, June 13th, 2015 - 12:11 p.m.

"You're late," Colonel Richard Chambliss groused.

"Fashionably so," Dean Oliver said dismissively, as he took the seat across from the man.

Chambliss was dressed in civilian clothes for this meeting, but if he was trying to blend in, he had failed miserably. He might have swapped out the pressed and starched military uniform for casual attire, but he couldn't change the look or demeanor of a career soldier.

"Besides," Oliver continued, "I wanted to ensure that this conversation was private."

It was a backhanded jab at the man, but it landed.

"You don't think I checked beforehand?" Chambliss snapped.

"Two is one, one is none," Oliver replied. "I'm sure you heard that at least once in your career, Colonel. Caution is something that you can never have enough of in this business."

Chambliss frowned, but let it go.

He didn't want to admit it, but Oliver was right. To the other people walking past the outdoor café on Wisconsin Avenue NW, they were nothing more than two men enjoying a midday respite, when in reality they were co-conspirators in a plan they believed would forever change the history of the United States.

A waitress emerged from inside carrying a carafe and a mug. "Would you like some coffee?"

"Thank you," Oliver said with a smile.

The young woman smiled back warmly as she laid the mug on the table and filled it up. "Can I get you anything else?"

"Maybe in a bit," Chambliss said tersely.

Oliver watched the street behind the anonymity of a pair of dark gray Ray-Bans, looking for any tells, as he sipped his coffee.

Chambliss annoyed him, and sometimes it was hard to bite his tongue. The man had the habit of treating everyone beneath his rank as a peon, while simultaneously prostrating himself before anyone whom he believed could help him achieve a star on his shoulder. What was truly perplexing was the fact that Chambliss was, by all accounts, a very effective administrator. He recalled a conversation with Lieutenant General Joe Dwyer, who confessed that people put up with the brown-nosing because they knew he would accomplish any assignment given to him. If Chambliss had just been a straight-shooter, he would most likely have already gotten his first star.

Oliver assumed that Chambliss had joined the cause, not because he necessarily believed in all of it, but simply to propel his career when the dust settled.

"They caught the cell in New York," Chambliss said, taking a sip of his coffee.

"So I heard," Oliver replied, his eyes continuing to scan the street.

"Any idea how?"

Oliver turned his gaze back to Chambliss and gave him a quizzical look. "I assumed that the purpose of this meeting was to provide me with that information."

"We had flagged the private phone numbers for the group back when it first started," Chambliss explained.

"I thought they were supposed to be using burners," Oliver asked.

"They were, but you know how things are. People get lazy. Anyway, this was at the starting stage, before they had even done anything. We had put up quiet markers, no alerts unless someone probed them."

"I guess it is safe to say that someone probed them."

"A few weeks back, the system tripped," Chambliss explained. "Albright's number popped."

"You didn't think that was an important thing to let us know?"

"It was just one number. Whoever did it ran a bulk list, just dumped it into a wide-net trace system. No filters, no metadata prioritization. If it weren't for Albright's number popping, we might've missed it entirely."

"Just his number?" Oliver pressed.

"At first," Chambliss said. "Then two more numbers flagged in a secondary hop. Not on the initial list, but linked to Albright's activity."

"Jesus Christ," Oliver whispered. "Why didn't you shut it down?"

"Because it just looked like noise," Chambliss said. "We get this crap all the time; private actors, foreign intel, sometimes just AI-predictive net sweeps gone rogue. Ninety-nine percent of it is garbage. Nothing you could call actionable, just enough to give you a case of mild heartburn."

"And what about the one percent?" Oliver asked.

"We immediately went in and checked all the numbers, including the burners, and there was zero activity," Chambliss countered.

"What was the scope of the number search?"

"All New York City numbers," Chambliss said. "Local area codes: 212, 718, 646, 917."

"Do we have any idea who might have been behind this? Could Maguire's people have done a search?"

"Maybe, but doubtful," Chambliss said. "The packets bounced through five nodes: Reykjavík, Bucharest, São Paulo, Frankfurt, and ended in Jakarta. Each hop was masked by rotating spoof servers, military-grade obfuscation. Then the trail just... evaporated."

"Evaporated?"

"Yeah, no residual. No callback trail. No signature. It was like it had never been there."

"That's not amateur work," Oliver conceded. "Who has the capability to do that?"

"Outside of Fort Meade?" Chambliss asked. "Maybe half a dozen agencies, but the signature didn't match anything domestic like NSA or Langley. My money's on a foreign snooping op."

"Seems like a lot of work went in to try to hide this. Any thoughts on who we might be dealing with?"

"Could have been one of our friends," Chambliss replied. "Five Eyes or Mossad. Maybe someone was trying out a new program and didn't want to get caught. Hell, for all we know, they got a new Ivan in Centre 16 to train."

"And all the burners were clean?" Oliver asked.

"Zero activity," Chambliss said confidently.

"What about the other cells? Any searches run on them?"

"No, this seems to have been limited to that one search."

"Make sure the others are being monitored in real time. If any of them pings I want to know about it immediately."

"I've already had my people begin scrubbing the data from the provider servers." Chambliss replied. "You don't think this will put the op in jeopardy, do you?"

Oliver shook his head. "No. We anticipated cell loss; built it into the model. This just happened quicker than expected, but it's of no consequence. The media will run with it for a few days before moving onto the next topic, and the rest of the country will go back to sleep thinking justice won."

"What about Maguire? What if he pulled in a favor and he was behind this?"

"Then it's just a New York issue after all," Oliver replied. "Regardless, he'll be dealt with."

Chambliss leaned in, his voice low. "Do you think we can pull this off?"

"It's kind of late in the game to be asking that kind of question," Oliver laughed, "but yes, I do. These groups are the spark, but the real work comes after. It used to be easy — backroom handshakes, quiet funding, politicians with just enough brains to know when to shut up and cash the check. Now we've got freak shows masquerading as legislators on the Hill who are more interested in who's screwing whom, what bathrooms people can use, and shaving a half-degree off the ice caps in Antarctica. And at the center of this debacle is the woman who would be queen trying to win a Nobel Prize for getting everyone to sing campfire songs."

"And here I always had you pegged for a fanboy," Chambliss laughed.

"I was," Oliver replied, "at least until she started believing her own press. Don't get me wrong, I respect her. You don't get to move into the White House without being at the top of your game, but you should never try to reinvent yourself in front of the people who know where the bodies are buried.

"Hypothetically speaking, of course."

"Everything said in this town is hypothetical," Oliver laughed.

"You think the civvies are ready for what's coming?" Chambliss asked.

Oliver studied the people passing by on the sidewalk. They were young, distracted; glued to their phones and wrapped up in their own little worlds. Society as a whole had changed. Aside from the permanent class of paid malcontents, who were always willing to protest for a paycheck, the majority of Americans seemed to have checked out. People weren't angry anymore; they were just tired. Like frogs in a pot, they hadn't noticed the water heating up. Now it was boiling, and nobody was jumping out. Somewhere along the way, outrage turned into apathy, not because they stopped caring, but because caring didn't change anything.

"No, but they'll adapt," Oliver replied.

"Where do you think we are with the timeline before things start moving forward?"

"Now that we know it works," Oliver said, "the other cells will be activated soon. They'll start ramping things up by July. The media will report that they are copycats. By August, the counter protestors will kick in."

"Who doesn't love riots during the dog days of summer?" Chambliss laughed.

"Once the local systems start to buckle, when the police and fire assets are stressed to the breaking point, Cook will be pressured into sending in the guard to restore order, which will backfire once they get attacked and are forced to take action."

"I'm not happy about our people being sacrificed to the mob."

"We've been sacrificing soldiers since the first armies were raised," Oliver replied. "Do you think the average infantryman gives a rat's ass whose cock the queen fucks or how liberated foreign oil will drive down the price in Pasadena by fifteen cents? Fuck, we've been waging wars for BS since the beginning of recorded time. The Italians once fought a war over a goddamn wooden bucket in the fourteenth century. At least this time they'll be sacrificed for a noble cause."

"When the locals start protesting the inevitable martial law orders, then their politicians will point their fingers and condemn D.C. That is when the fuse gets real short."

"And if it fails?" Chambliss asked. "It sounds good until you start realizing most of us won't fare very well in prison."

Oliver looked at the man and broke out in laughter.

"I don't see what's so funny about prison," Chambliss said with annoyance.

"Is that what you're worried about? Prison?" Oliver asked. "My dear colonel, if this operation fails, prison will be the least of our worries. Knowing Cook, we will all be hanging from lampposts on Constitution Avenue."

"That's a hell of a picture."

"No different from what the Founders faced."

"The Founders wouldn't have approved of this kind of radical change," Chambliss said.

"The Founders would've been stacking bodies years ago. Hell, they would have opened fire on the citizenry for electing half these lunatics into office."

Chambliss motioned for the waitress, holding up his mug. She returned a moment later with the carafe and refilled both.

"There is something else," he said after the woman had left.

Oliver's eyes narrowed. "That sounds ominous."

"Maybe," Chambliss replied. "It's Mannion. He's unhappy."

"About what?" Oliver asked.

"He doesn't like the seat he's been promised. He thinks he deserves a higher place at the table."

Oliver's expression shifted. Just slightly, but it was enough to telegraph that he wasn't pleased.

"Don't shoot the messenger."

"How did you hear?" Oliver asked.

"We had dinner," Chambliss explained. "He was just venting, but I figured you would want to know before it becomes a bigger issue."

Oliver nodded.

Rear Admiral Walter Mannion was the newly minted military advisor for the director of national intelligence. It sounded like a prestigious title, but effectively he'd been shipped off, and he knew his career was at a standstill. In fact, he was quite bitter at what he perceived to be a professional slight and one that would mostly end with a forced retirement unless something changed. The writing was clearly on the wall, but Mannion's ego wouldn't allow him to go quietly. At least Chambliss had the good manners not to be demanding and to play nice.

"I just figured you'd want to know."

Oliver nodded.

"Walt's not a bad guy," Chambliss said. "He just had the bad luck to cross paths with the Vice CNO back when they were both commanders in the fleet. Maybe you can smooth things over."

"I'll see what I can do."

"Thanks," Chambliss said. "Hey, I've got to get going. I'm taking my grandson to his first ball game tonight. Hoping he brings the Nationals some luck and they make it back to the playoffs."

"Have fun," Oliver smiled. "I've got this."

"Thanks."

Oliver watched the man walk away, slightly amused at the idea that the playoffs might actually be held.

I guess they could be playing, he thought. *They went back to playing baseball a week after September 11th. People are content when they have distractions.*

Fifteen minutes later he had paid the bill, gotten the waitresses' phone number and made his way back to his car.

He started the car and placed a call.

"Yeah, everything is fine," Oliver said when the person on the other end answered. "It looks like this was entirely centered on New York, but it is a potential issue. We might want to stress to the others that any past comms could be problematic."

Oliver listened.

"No, they have supposedly buttoned everything down and are removing any problematic data from the providers. If someone looks there won't be any information to find, although that might also be suspicious if someone got nosy."

Matters like this weren't part of his normal operational portfolio, but the person he worked for was in charge of everything, so it became his issue to deal with, but he considered this a self-inflicted wound.

He didn't have to tell his boss that he had told him so, the man already knew he had argued against starting the op in New York City, but had been overruled by the others who believed that it was the best place to gauge reaction. To him, it was poking the bear unnecessarily. He had pushed for starting in Los Angeles or Chicago; where natural community tensions could be exploited. His position was that New Yorkers were simply too apathetic to be an accurate measure. He also considered Maguire to be a wildcard that they didn't need to deal with so early in the op.

His background in Special Forces had taught him that SEALs weren't gods, but they were highly motivated and extremely resourceful. They met every challenge head-on. If they couldn't solve the problem with what they had in their toolbox, they had no problem improvising. If Maguire was behind this, then he had found the weak link and exploited it. That meant he could potentially share that information with others. He would have to make the argument that Maguire needed to be included in the list of persons that needed to be removed.

"There is another potential issue we need to consider," he said. "Mannion's not happy."

Oliver listened to the man on the other end vent. He understood his frustration. This was all supposed to be for the greater good, but personal ambition among the group's members often overshadowed that.

"If you're asking my opinion, I think he has the potential makings of another Fromm," Oliver replied, referencing General Friedrich Fromm, who was the commander of the German reserve army during World War II. Fromm, who initially supported Operation Valkyrie, the 1944 plot to kill Adolf Hitler, subsequently ordered the arrest and execution of several key members, after learning Hitler had survived, so that he could distance himself from the coup, "but, unlike Fromm, I don't believe that he brings enough to the table to warrant the risk."

Oliver listened.

"Yes, I agree, and when the time comes, I will take care of it personally."

Oliver waited until the man hung up and then pulled away from the curb. He had made a point of creating a personal file for each of the people involved, at least the major players, so he had immediate access to all the information necessary to act, should the need arise.

Unlike the others, Mannion would be easy to deal with. He was divorced, lived alone, and considered himself to be an ornithologist. He even taught a class on the subject at the local community college. Most of his free time was spent viewing and photographing birds at the different wildlife preserves in Northern

Virginia. When the time was right, Mannion would walk into the forest one last time and then become part of the circle of life.

To say this operation was once in a lifetime would be a gross understatement. It was a once in a thousand lifetimes and perhaps the last chance to right the ship and redefine America's future.

The Founding Father's dream was being destroyed by an enemy that had been graciously invited to sit at the table of American exceptionalism only to stab the host in the back. Hack politicians, some of whom had escaped from third-world shit-holes, were actively attempting to undermine it to prove we were not better than anyone else; embracing the tenets of communism because, this time, they knew how to do it properly.

"Assholes," Oliver fumed.

We were abandoning friends for political capital and leaving them to fend for themselves. Europe was falling at a rapid pace, victims of a collective death cult mentality that eschewed national pride for diversity, and if nothing changed, the cancer would spread here.

It already has, he grudgingly admitted.

The time had come to put an end to the political insanity that was gripping the nation. D.C. had turned a deaf ear to the electorate, and now they would pay the price. They had tried to bring about the necessary change through the ballot box, but that had failed, so now it was up to them to bring about the change through the cartridge box.

America would finally regain its place as the world's preeminent superpower and be led by military leaders who understood the sacrifices that were necessary to preside over a great and prosperous nation.

As noted anti-socialist writer John Basil Barnhill once famously said, "*Where the people fear the government, you have tyranny. Where the government fears the people, you have liberty.*"

And the government was about to learn a very bloody lesson.

CHAPTER FIFTY-NINE

Kalorama Triangle, Washington, D.C.

Sunday, June 14th, 2015 - 10:21 a.m.

Melody sat in her home office, reading the briefing concerning Turkey's latest incursion into northern Syria, and listening to the hum of the encrypted line as her call was connected to Polish Prime Minister Lukasz Wojcik.

Turkish military units had attacked the Syrian Democratic Forces, a Kurdish-led military alliance in Syria, killing dozens of Kurdish fighters allied with the U.S.

"Melody, I am so sorry to keep you waiting. I was on the phone with the Chief of the General Staff," Wojcik said.

"Trust me, I completely understand, Luka. The phones have been burning up on my end as well."

"It's good to hear your voice, although I wish it were under better circumstances. This business with Drogan in Syria is completely unwarranted and a damn mess."

"I agree one hundred percent," Melody replied. "My expectations of him were pretty low to begin with, but I guess they weren't low enough. All the promises he made when he was elected president evaporated quickly, and now that he has the reins of power, it's back to business as usual."

"Elected!" Wojcik laughed. "More like selected. Drogan is nothing more than a mouthpiece for the regime, but at least he no longer controls the parliament."

"Provided they don't fracture over time," Melody cautioned.

"True, it is a cautionary alliance. How did Cook take the news?"

"Once she stopped screaming? Not good. She has always been a staunch supporter of the SDF, especially after all the blood they spilled helping us fight ISIS, and she sees this as a cheap shot from a supposed ally."

"Turkey has always been a problem child, and its allegiance to NATO has been questionable."

"The Cold War made for some strange relationships, and now we have to deal with it," Melody replied. "Syria's a clusterfuck, but what isn't in the Middle East these days? That being said, Cook's done playing nice. It was bad enough that they had been cozying up with Moscow and Beijing, all while waving the alliance flag when it suited them, but this attack on the Kurds, so early in his presidency..."

"Drogan's betting we'll just sit on our hands because that's what we have always done."

Melody looked up and saw Maguire standing in the doorway holding two drinks.

Thank you, she mouthed, as she waved him in.

He set the drink down on her desk and took a seat on the couch.

"He grossly miscalculated," Melody replied. "Cook has had it with Turkey playing both sides. You don't get to kiss up to Russia, buy their S-400s, and then pretend you're a loyal NATO partner. This Syria stunt was the last straw. She's ready to send a message he won't forget."

"Good. It's about time someone put him in his place. What's the plan? I assume you're not just going to issue another strongly worded statement."

"Oh, that ship has sailed, figuratively and literally," Melody laughed. "Cook has ordered the USS Theodore Roosevelt to park off Cyprus by next week. Full carrier strike group. F/A-18s, Hawkeyes, the works. We're also locking down northern Syria with combat air patrols. If he thinks he can use Syria's chaos to screw with the SDF, he's in for a rude awakening. One wrong move and he'll have more than a downed drone to cry about over his boza."

"Bold move. Drogan won't like that carrier sitting in his backyard. Cyprus is close enough to make him sweat. But what if he escalates? Turkey has a habit of doubling down when cornered."

"Let him try. If he wants a pissing match, he'll regret it. Cook's already got Treasury drawing up sanctions that'll hit him where it hurts. His economy's already on shaky ground, and he's facing a hostile parliament. Forget getting back in the F-35 program; we're talking measures that'll make his lira look like Monopoly money. And if he pushes further, well, those air patrols have rules of engagement that'll make any Turkish incursion have a terrible day."

Wojcik let out a low whistle. "That's a hammer. I like it. We've got your back here in Warsaw, but you know he'll scream about sovereignty and NATO betrayal. He might even cozy up to Moscow even more."

"He can scream all he wants. If he runs to Putin, he's burning his last bridges with us. NATO's not perfect, Luka, but it's our line in the sand. Drogan needs to decide if he's in or out. President Cook's betting the ground is too shaky right now and he'll blink first."

"For our sake, I hope you're right. Poland's got enough to worry about with Russia on our doorstep. We can't afford a fractured alliance. Keep us posted on those patrols, and if you need us to lean on the EU to tighten the screws, just say the word. The president loves to make the bureaucrats in Brussels cry."

"Much appreciated, Luka. I will definitely keep you in the loop, and we will talk again soon."

Melody ended the call and slumped back in her seat.

"Look at you," Maguire smiled, "kicking ass all around the world."

"Not sure about the kicking ass, but I've got a solid handle on the dragging ass," she said, grabbing her drink and joining him on the couch.

"That ass still looks amazing," he said, pulling her close.

"You just want to get lucky," she laughed, taking a sip of her drink.

"The thought had crossed my mind."

"After that little stunt you pulled with Angelo, I should cut you off and teach you a lesson."

"Life is already doing a good enough job with that," he replied.

"I've missed this… Missed us. When you called me to say you were coming down to talk to Cook and spending the weekend, I almost had a panic attack waiting for something to come up and torpedo it."

Maguire held her tight, feeling her bury her head into his chest.

"How do we get us back?" she asked.

"Sleeping under the same roof would be a good start, but if that doesn't work I still have some Navy connections. Maybe we can schedule a nice romantic getaway and watch the war unfold from the flight deck of the Roosevelt."

"I'm scared."

"About?" Maguire asked.

"That it won't be enough."

"Gen and Gregor seem to be doing okay, and they have a baby to take care of."

"Gen's job really hasn't changed; she's still my right hand, but now I'm the right hand to the president, and my office comes with twenty-four time zones. I'm worried the job is going to come between us and we won't recover."

"Angel, you and I are not the first couple to have high-profile jobs, and, yeah, it can definitely be stressful, but only if we allow it."

"Now you sound like Gen."

"There's a reason the two of you work so well together," he replied. "For all her idiosyncrasies, she's one of the most grounded people I know and has an uncanny knack for compartmentalization."

"She does thrive in chaos."

"We're making excuses," Maguire replied. "Yes, the work might be exponentially harder, more demanding, but there are ways for us to connect that can lower the pressure."

"I just want this again. You, here with me, because I feel lost without you. Every waking moment I'm surrounded by people, except the one person that matters most."

Maguire leaned down and kissed her head. "If everything goes according to Cook's plan, I'll be here permanently before the holidays, and things will get easier."

"And if they don't?"

"I'll resign and be a stay-at-home boy-toy," he replied.

That elicited a deep, unguarded laugh that erupted with a sincerity she hadn't felt in ages.

"I think you might be a little past the boy-toy stage, cowboy."

"Oh yeah," he said, taking the drink out of her hand and setting it on the table, before lifting her up in his arms. "We'll see about that."

"Help! Help!" she laughed as he wrapped her up in his arms and carried her toward the door.

"Is everything okay?" Special Agent Jeremy Hicks asked, appearing in the doorway, with a mix of concern and confusion on his face.

"Oh my God, no, we're fine," Melody laughed. "We were just—"

"Engaged in diplomatic negotiations," Maguire interjected. "Long overdue negotiations."

"Very long overdue," Melody smiled.

"Goodnight, Madam Secretary," Hicks grinned, as he turned and walked away. "And good luck," he called out before disappearing around the corner.

"You're forgiven," Melody said, her breath warm against his neck as she kissed him. "Now take me to bed and let's renegotiate the terms of our alliance."

About the Author

Andrew Nelson is a former law enforcement professional with twenty-two years of service, including two decades with the New York City Police Department. During his NYPD career, he served as a detective in the Intelligence Division, conducting sensitive investigations and providing dignitary protection to world leaders. He rose to the rank of sergeant before retiring in 2005.

Drawing on real-world experience from the streets, interrogation rooms, and command-level decision-making, Nelson writes crime fiction that explores power, loyalty, corruption, and the human cost of justice. He is the author of the *James Maguire* and *Alex Taylor* mystery series, as well as several non-fiction works examining the NYPD's Emergency Service Unit and the lasting aftermath of the September 11, 2001, terrorist attack.

For more information please visit:

www.andrewgnelson.org

www.ingramcontent.com/pod-product-compliance
Lightning Source LLC
La Vergne TN
LVHW020532100826
845148LV00010B/1431